ASCENDER

VOLUME ONE: THE HAUNTED GALAXY

JEFF LEMIRE • DUSTIN NGUYEN
STORYTELLERS

STEVE WANDS
LETTERING & DESIGN

DUSTIN NGUYEN
COVER

WILL DENNIS
EDITOR

IMAGE COMICS, INC. • **Robert Kirkman**: Chief Operating Officer • **Erik Larsen**: Chief Financial Officer • **Todd McFarlane**: President • **Marc Silvestri**: Chief Executive Officer • **Jim Valentino**: Vice President • **Eric Stephenson**: Publisher / Chief Creative Officer • **Jeff Boison**: Director of Publishing Planning & Book Trade Sales • **Chris Ross**: Director of Digital Sales • **Jeff Stang**: Director of Direct Market Sales • **Kat Salazar**: Director of PR & Marketing • **Drew Gill**: Cover Editor • **Heather Doornink**: Production Director • **Nicole Lapalme**: Controller • **IMAGECOMICS.COM**

Ryan Brewer: Production Artist

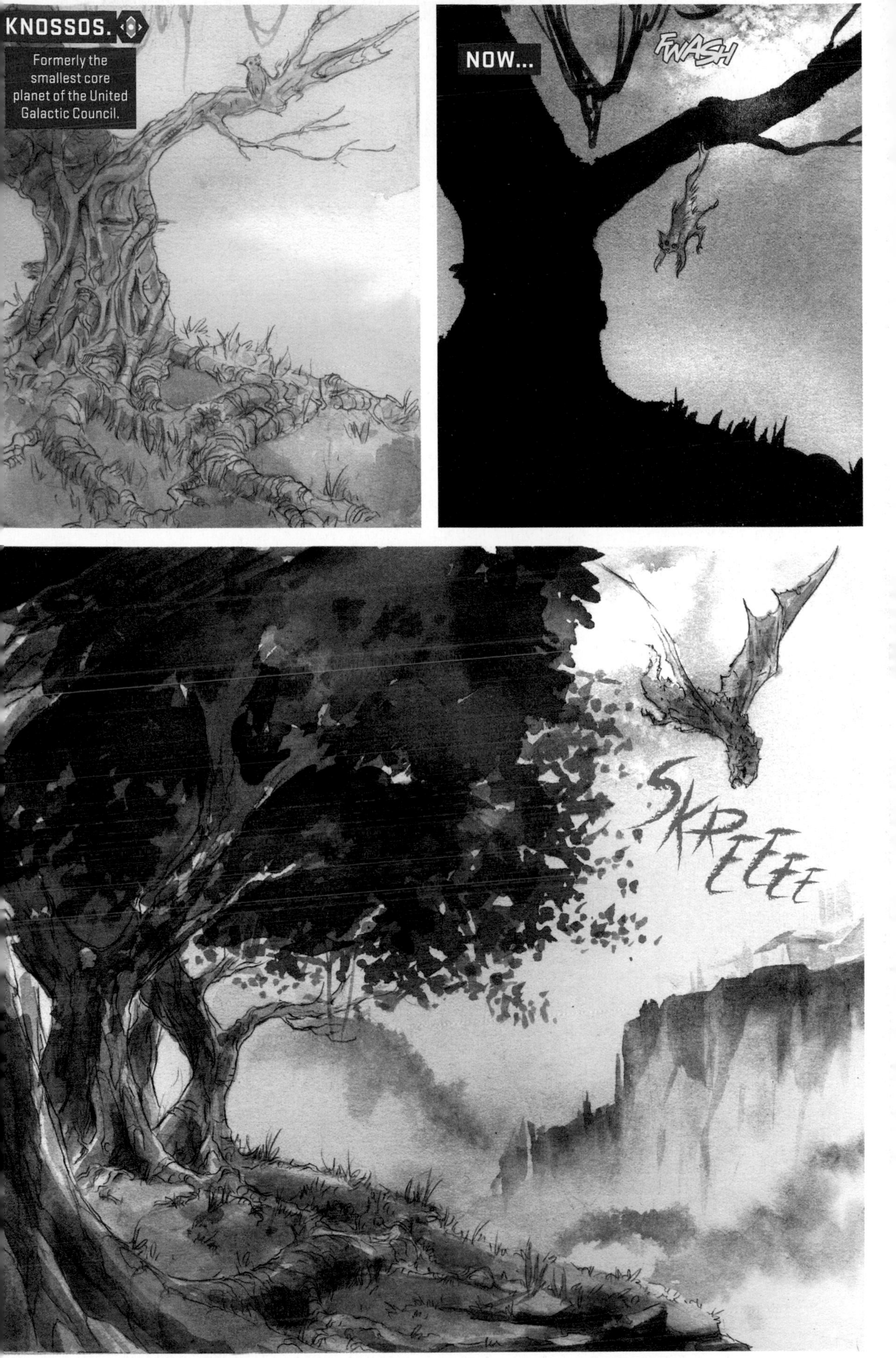
KNOSSOS.
Formerly the smallest core planet of the United Galactic Council.
NOW...
FWASH
SKREEEE

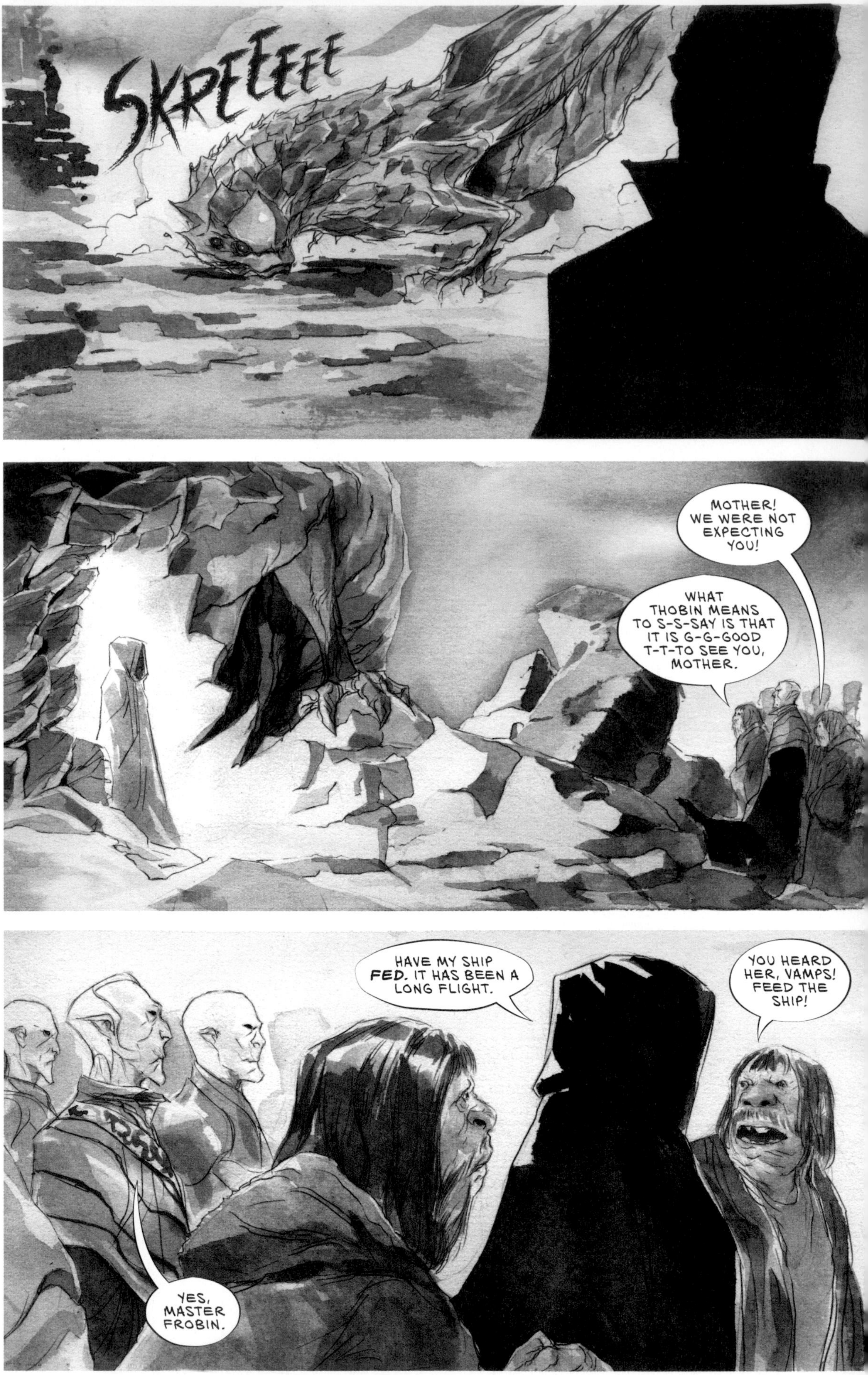
SKREEEEE
MOTHER! WE WERE NOT EXPECTING YOU!
WHAT THOBIN MEANS TO S-S-SAY IS THAT IT IS G-G-GOOD T-T-TO SEE YOU, MOTHER.
HAVE MY SHIP **FED.** IT HAS BEEN A LONG FLIGHT.
YOU HEARD HER, VAMPS! FEED THE SHIP!
YES, MASTER FROBIN.

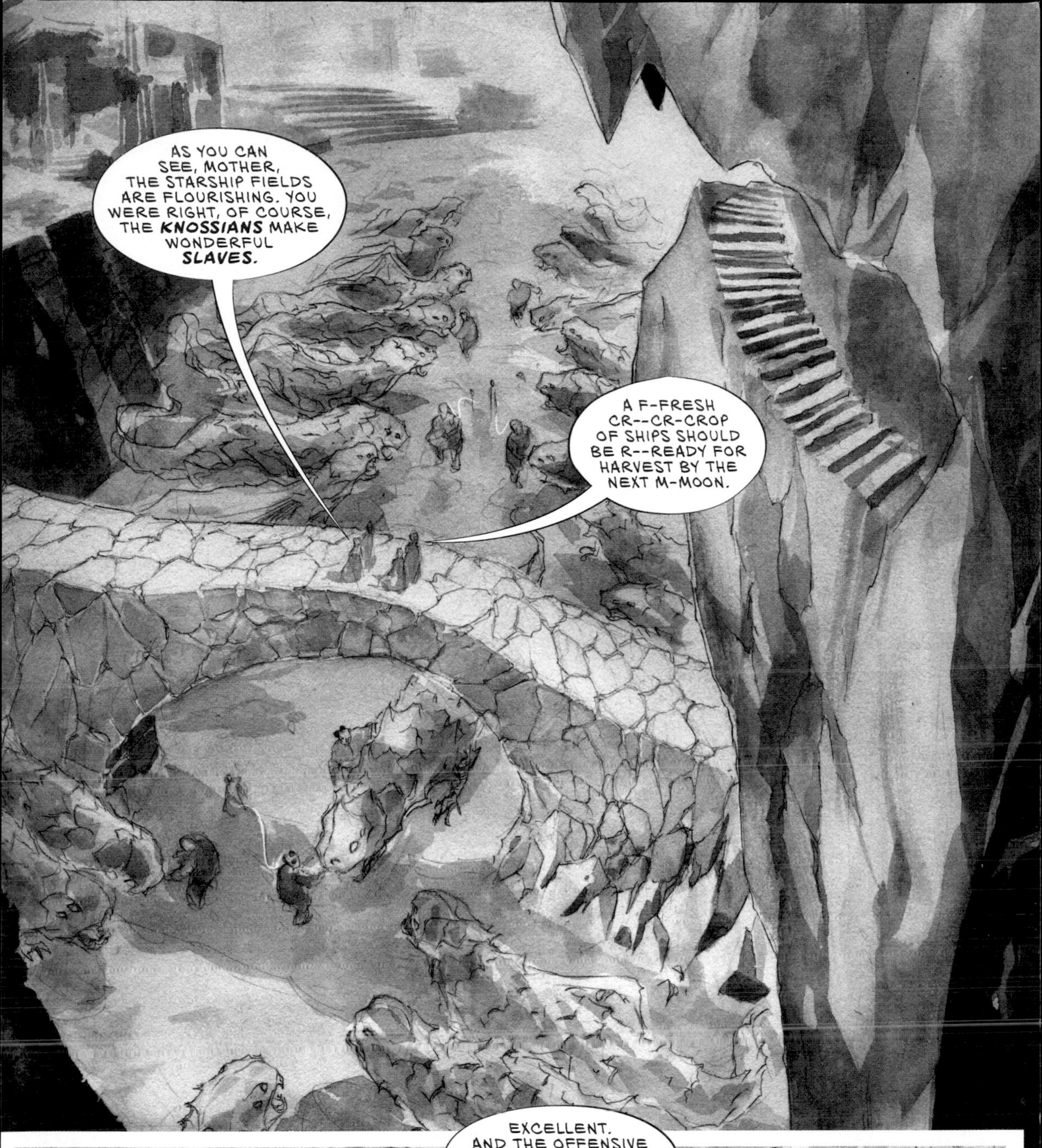
AS YOU CAN SEE, MOTHER, THE STARSHIP FIELDS ARE FLOURISHING. YOU WERE RIGHT, OF COURSE, THE **KNOSSIANS** MAKE WONDERFUL ***SLAVES.***
A F-FRESH CR--CR-CROP OF SHIPS SHOULD BE R--READY FOR HARVEST BY THE NEXT M-MOON.

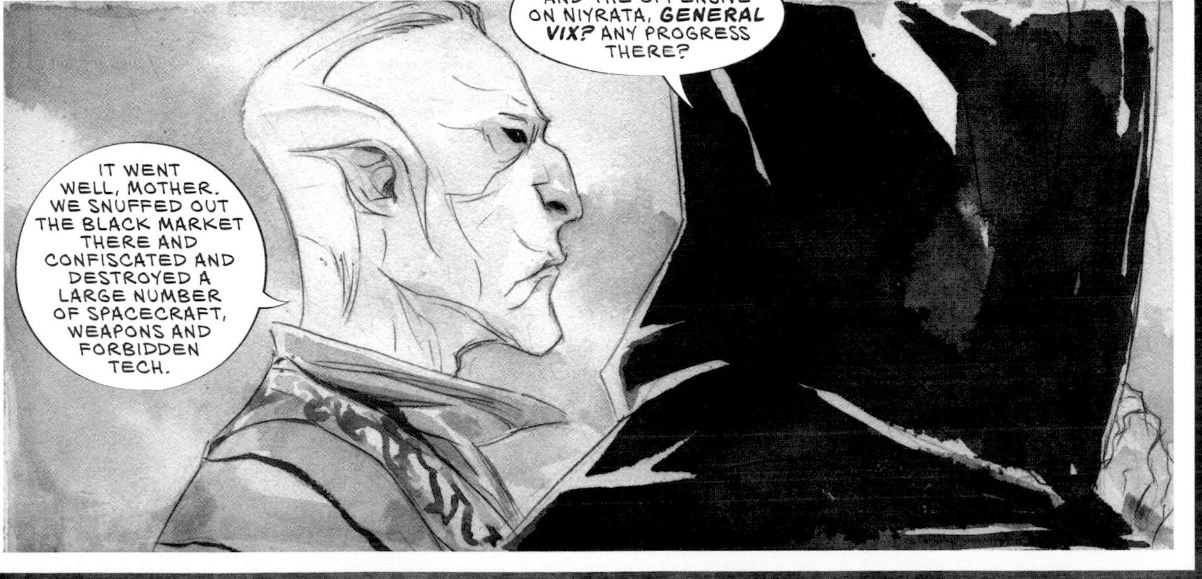
EXCELLENT. AND THE OFFENSIVE ON NIYRATA, ***GENERAL VIX?*** ANY PROGRESS THERE?
IT WENT WELL, MOTHER. WE SNUFFED OUT THE BLACK MARKET THERE AND CONFISCATED AND DESTROYED A LARGE NUMBER OF SPACECRAFT, WEAPONS AND FORBIDDEN TECH.

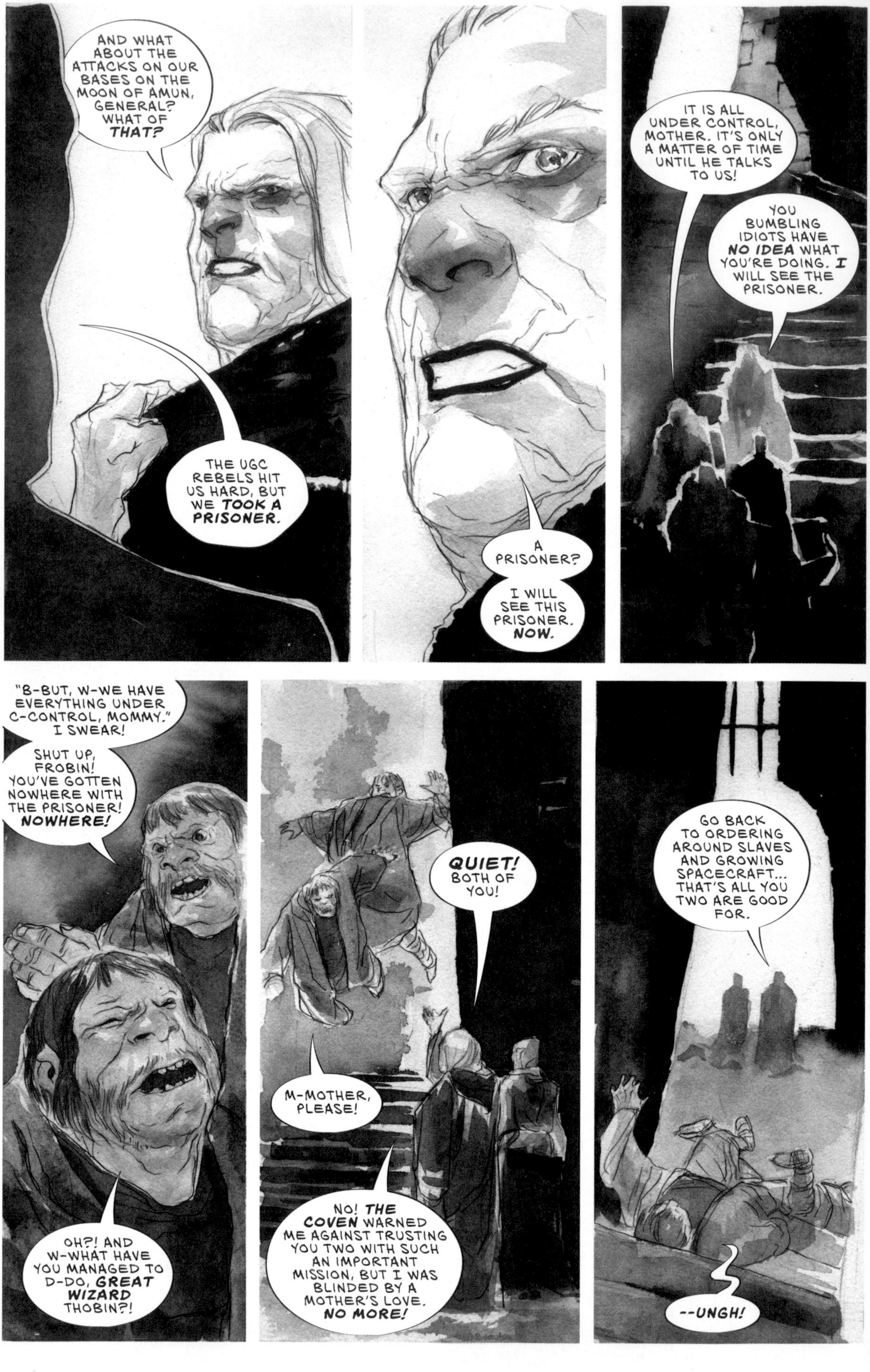
AND WHAT ABOUT THE ATTACKS ON OUR BASES ON THE MOON OF AMUN, GENERAL? WHAT OF THAT?
THE UGC REBELS HIT US HARD, BUT WE TOOK A PRISONER.
A PRISONER?
I WILL SEE THIS PRISONER. NOW.
IT IS ALL UNDER CONTROL, MOTHER. IT'S ONLY A MATTER OF TIME UNTIL HE TALKS TO US!
YOU BUMBLING IDIOTS HAVE NO IDEA WHAT YOU'RE DOING. I WILL SEE THE PRISONER.
"B-BUT, W-WE HAVE EVERYTHING UNDER C-CONTROL, MOMMY." I SWEAR!
SHUT UP, FROBIN! YOU'VE GOTTEN NOWHERE WITH THE PRISONER! NOWHERE!
OH?! AND W-WHAT HAVE YOU MANAGED TO D-DO, GREAT WIZARD THOBIN?!
QUIET! BOTH OF YOU!
M-MOTHER, PLEASE!
NO! THE COVEN WARNED ME AGAINST TRUSTING YOU TWO WITH SUCH AN IMPORTANT MISSION, BUT I WAS BLINDED BY A MOTHER'S LOVE. NO MORE!
GO BACK TO ORDERING AROUND SLAVES AND GROWING SPACECRAFT... THAT'S ALL YOU TWO ARE GOOD FOR.
--UNGH!

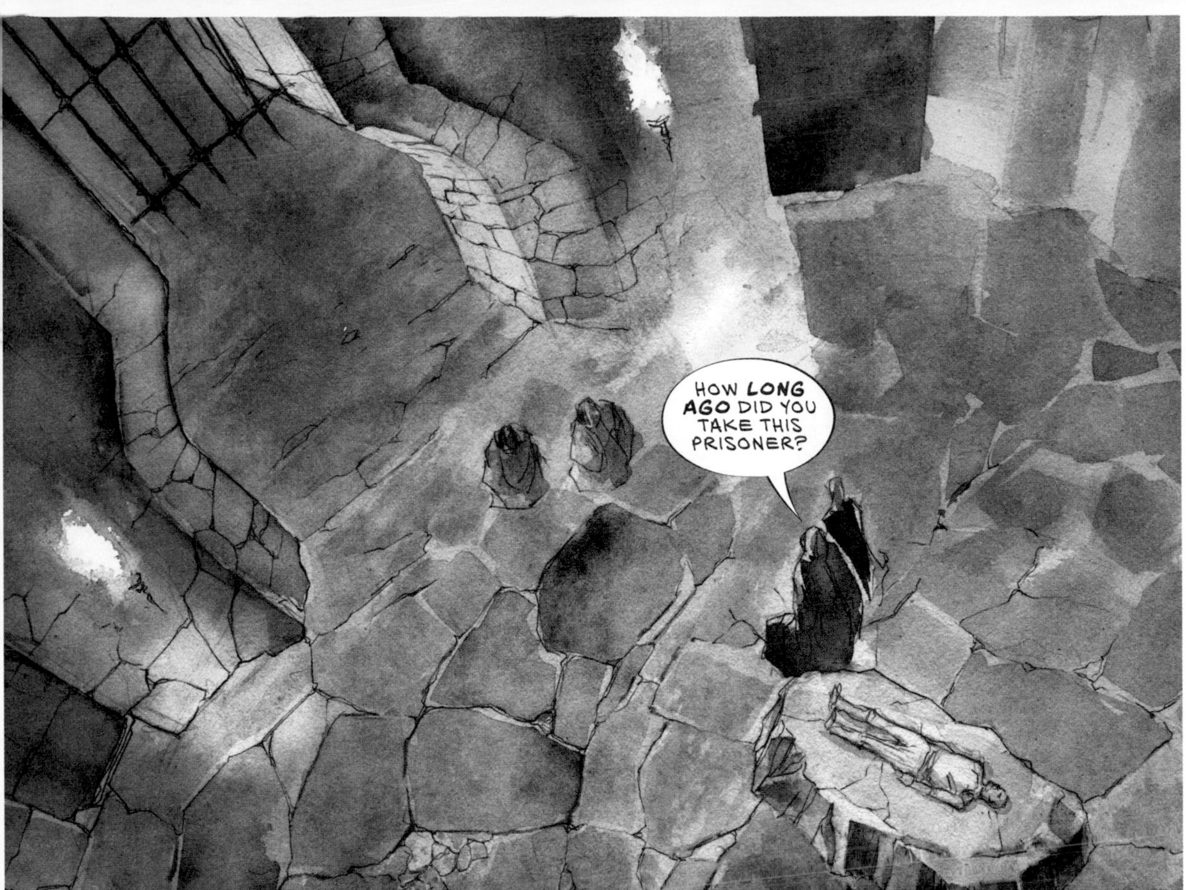
HOW **LONG AGO** DID YOU TAKE THIS PRISONER?

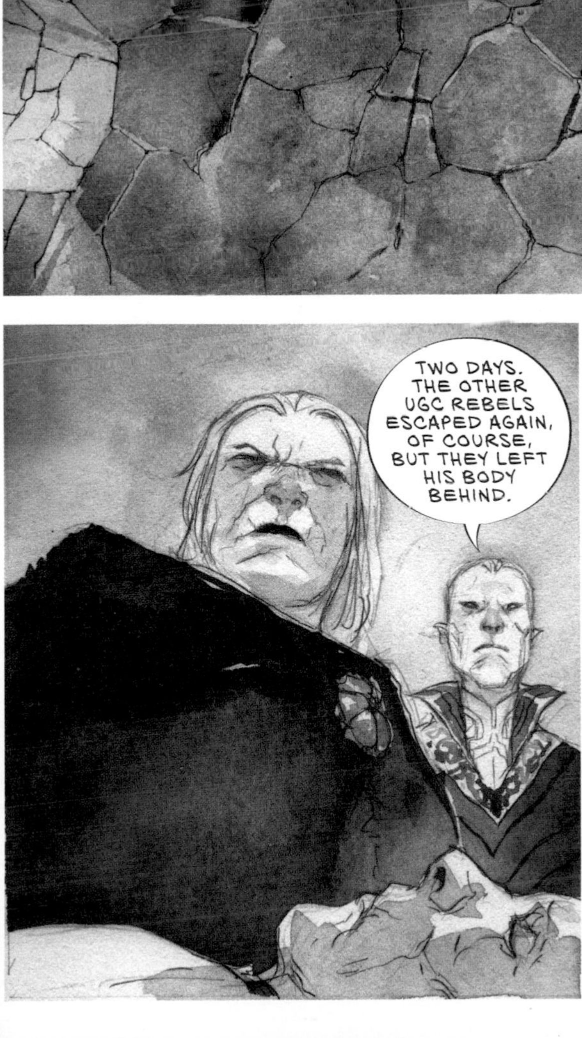
TWO DAYS. THE OTHER UGC REBELS ESCAPED AGAIN, OF COURSE, BUT THEY LEFT HIS BODY BEHIND.

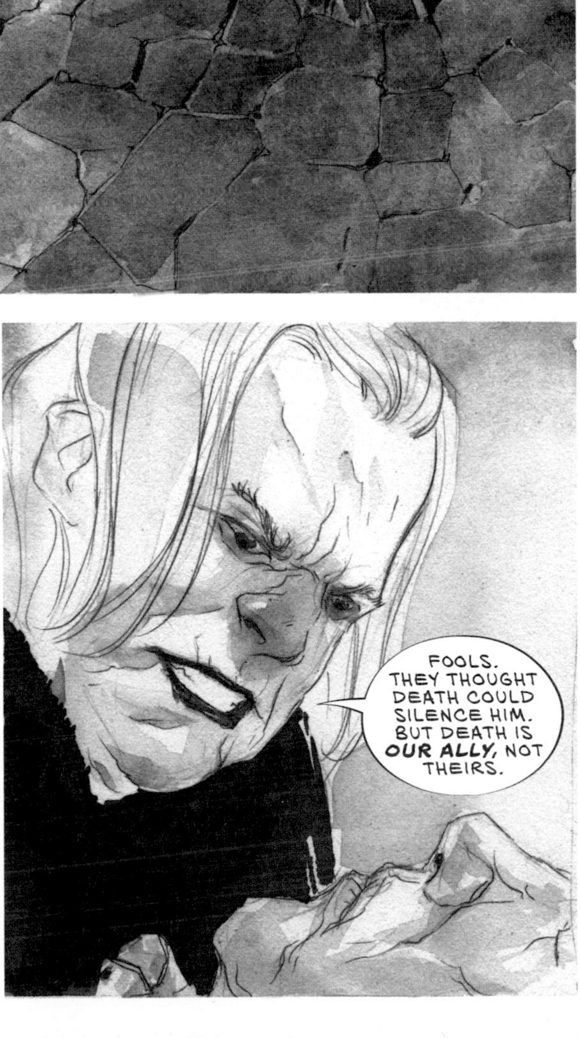
FOOLS. THEY THOUGHT DEATH COULD SILENCE HIM. BUT DEATH IS ***OUR ALLY,*** NOT THEIRS.

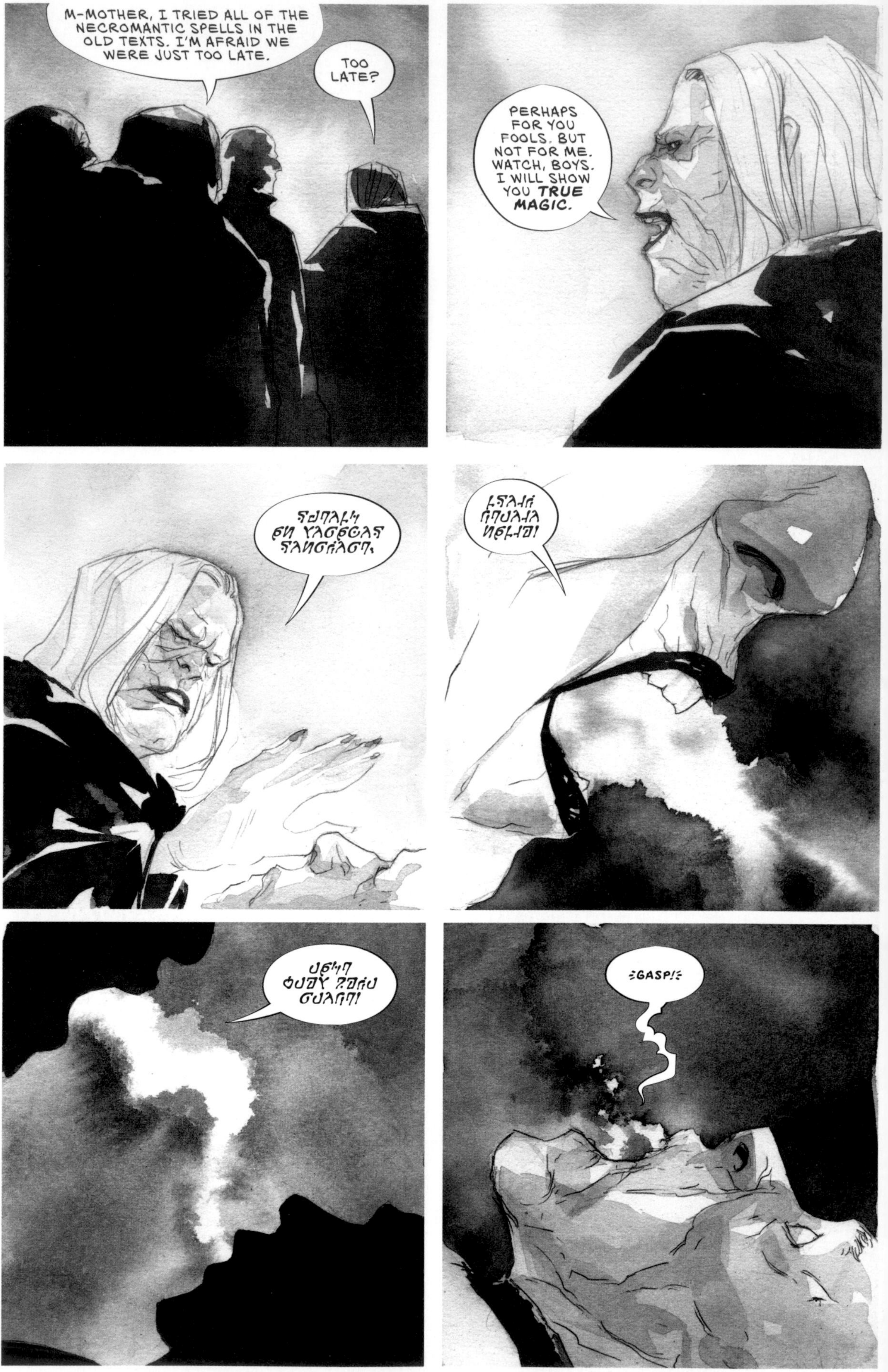
M-MOTHER, I TRIED ALL OF THE NECROMANTIC SPELLS IN THE OLD TEXTS. I'M AFRAID WE WERE JUST TOO LATE.
TOO LATE?
PERHAPS FOR YOU FOOLS. BUT NOT FOR ME. WATCH, BOYS. I WILL SHOW YOU TRUE MAGIC.
GASP!

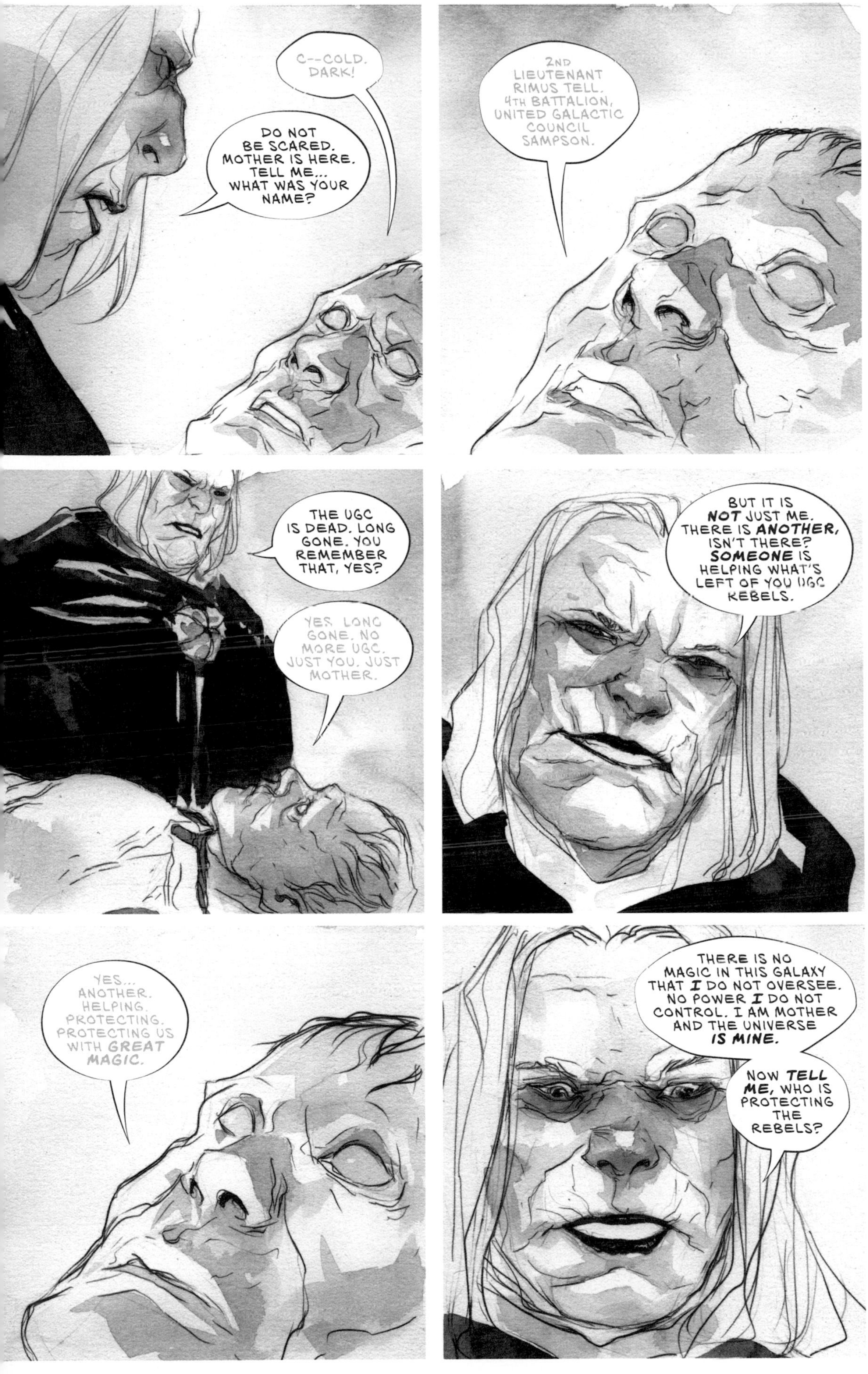
C--COLD. DARK!
DO NOT BE SCARED. MOTHER IS HERE. TELL ME... WHAT WAS YOUR NAME?
2ND LIEUTENANT RIMUS TELL. 4TH BATTALION, UNITED GALACTIC COUNCIL SAMPSON.
THE UGC IS DEAD. LONG GONE. YOU REMEMBER THAT, YES?
YES. LONG GONE. NO MORE UGC. JUST YOU. JUST MOTHER.
BUT IT IS **NOT** JUST ME. THERE IS **ANOTHER,** ISN'T THERE? **SOMEONE** IS HELPING WHAT'S LEFT OF YOU UGC REBELS.
YES... ANOTHER. HELPING. PROTECTING. PROTECTING US WITH **GREAT MAGIC.**
THERE IS NO MAGIC IN THIS GALAXY THAT ***I*** DO NOT OVERSEE. NO POWER ***I*** DO NOT CONTROL. I AM MOTHER AND THE UNIVERSE **IS MINE.**
NOW ***TELL ME,*** WHO IS PROTECTING THE REBELS?

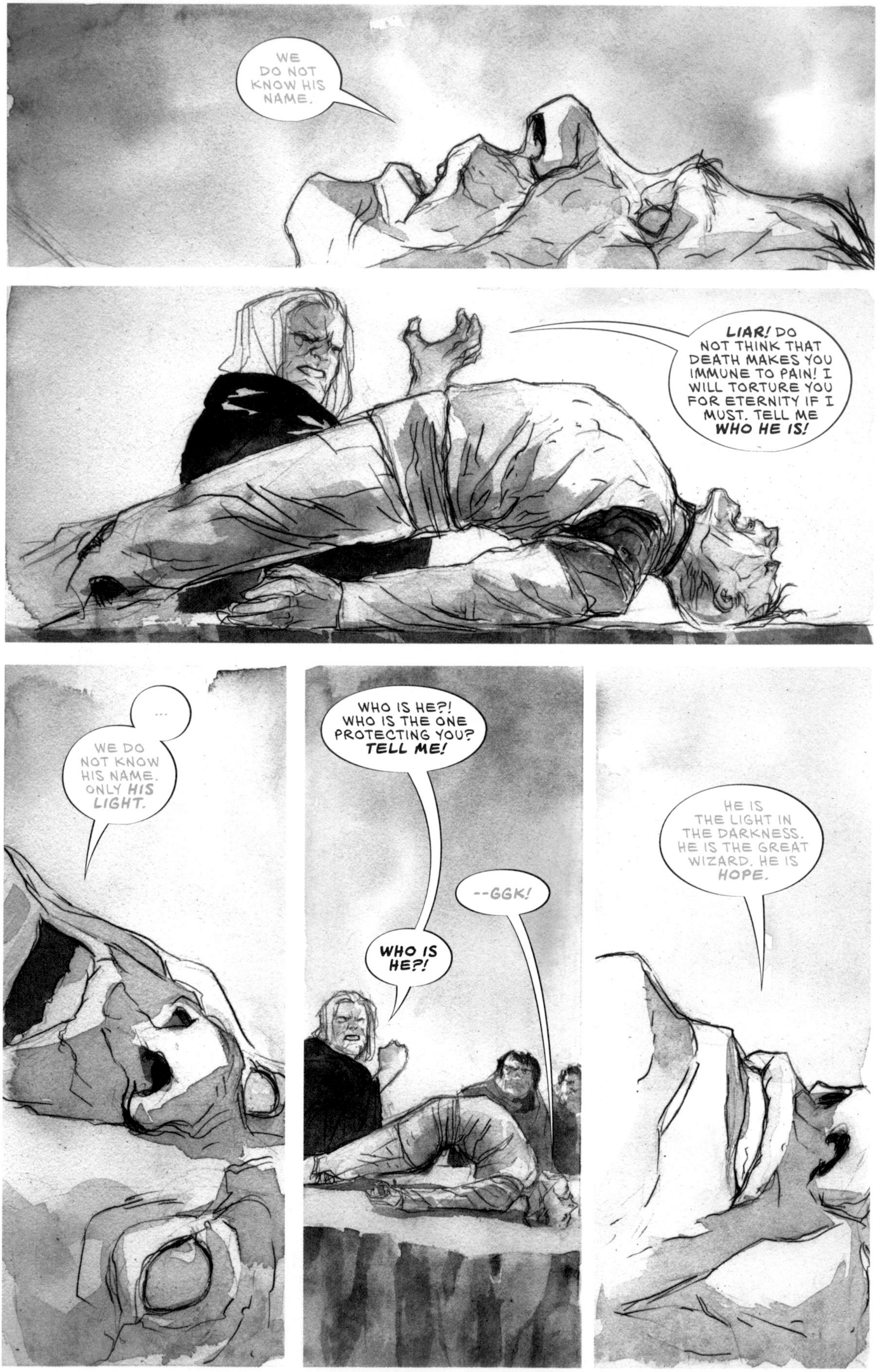
WE DO NOT KNOW HIS NAME.
LIAR! DO NOT THINK THAT DEATH MAKES YOU IMMUNE TO PAIN! I WILL TORTURE YOU FOR ETERNITY IF I MUST. TELL ME WHO HE IS!
...
WE DO NOT KNOW HIS NAME. ONLY HIS LIGHT.
WHO IS HE?! WHO IS THE ONE PROTECTING YOU? TELL ME!
WHO IS HE?!
--GGK!
HE IS THE LIGHT IN THE DARKNESS. HE IS THE GREAT WIZARD. HE IS HOPE.

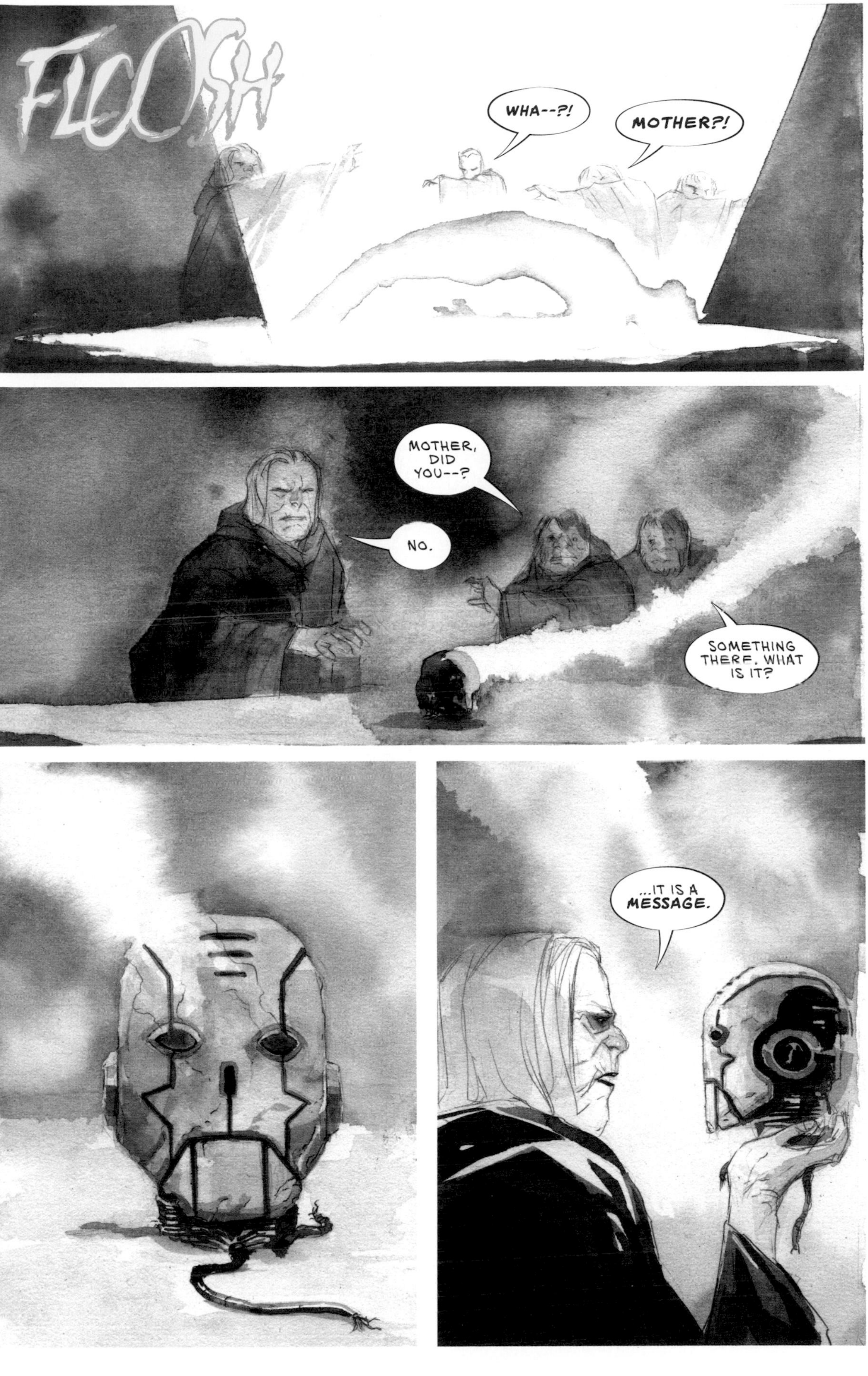
FLOOSH
WHA--?!
MOTHER?!
MOTHER, DID YOU--?
NO.
SOMETHING THERE. WHAT IS IT?
...IT IS A MESSAGE.

ASCE

NDER

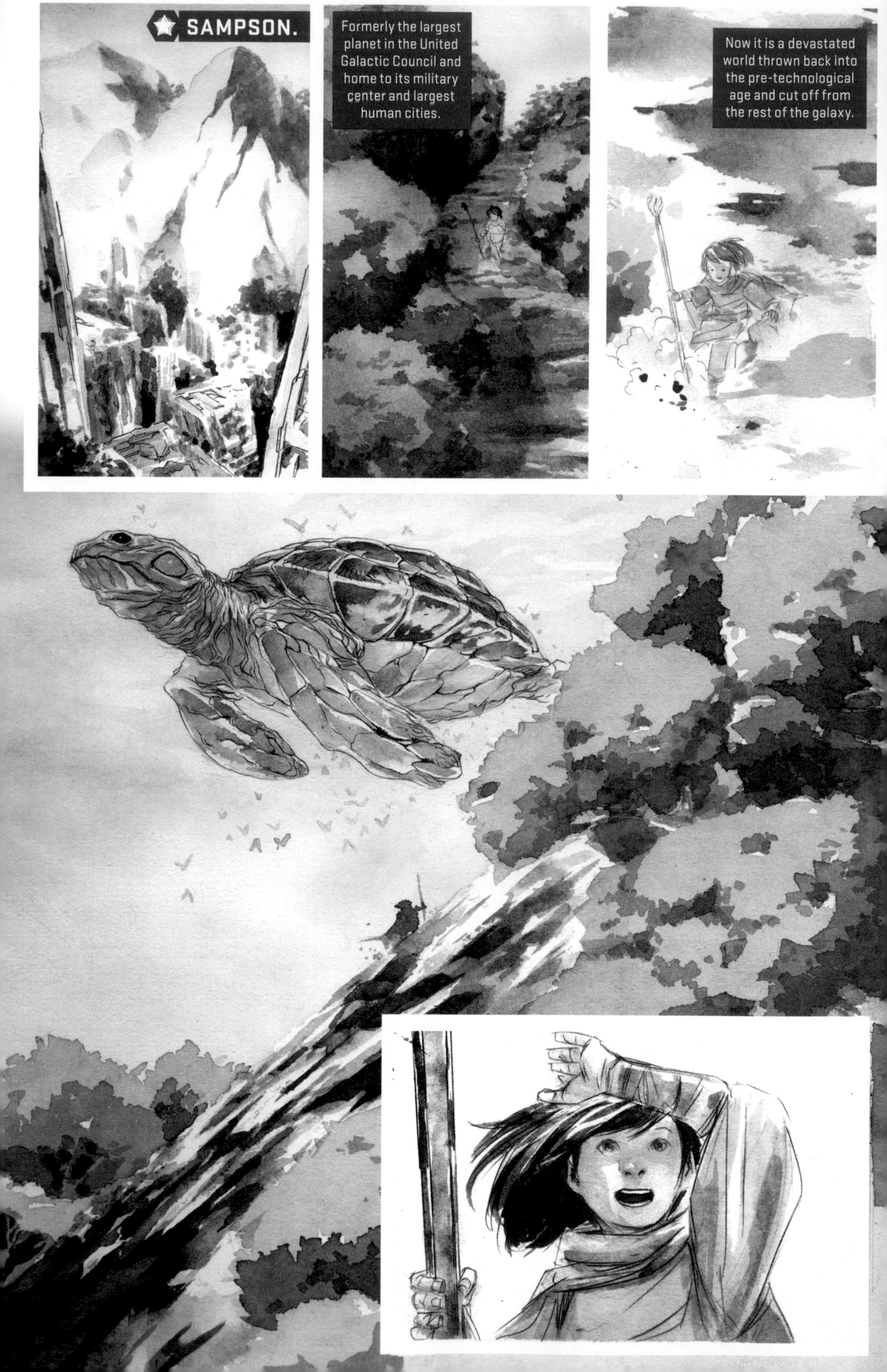
SAMPSON.
Formerly the largest planet in the United Galactic Council and home to its military center and largest human cities.
Now it is a devastated world thrown back into the pre-technological age and cut off from the rest of the galaxy.

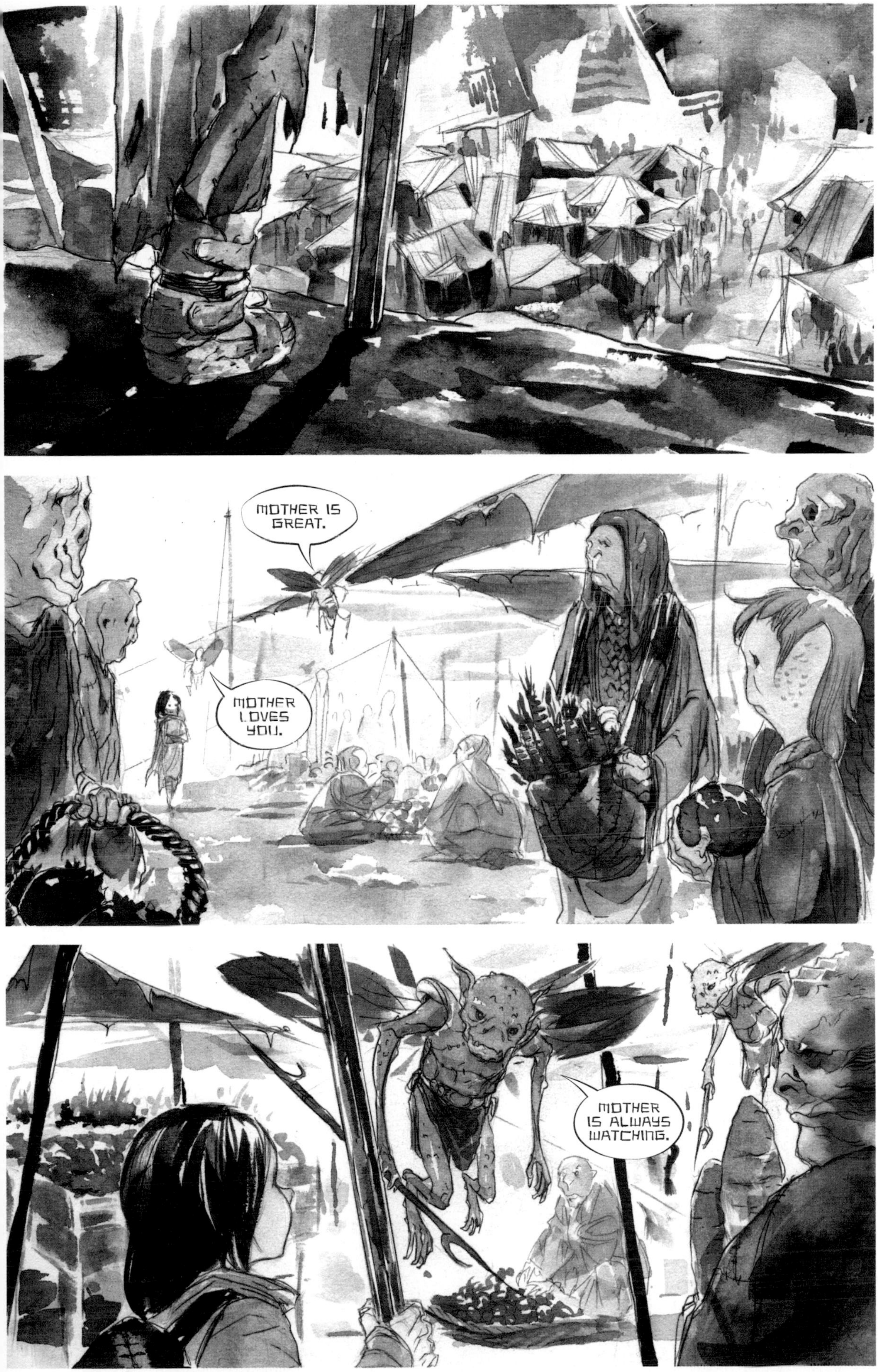
MOTHER IS GREAT.
MOTHER LOVES YOU.
MOTHER IS ALWAYS WATCHING.

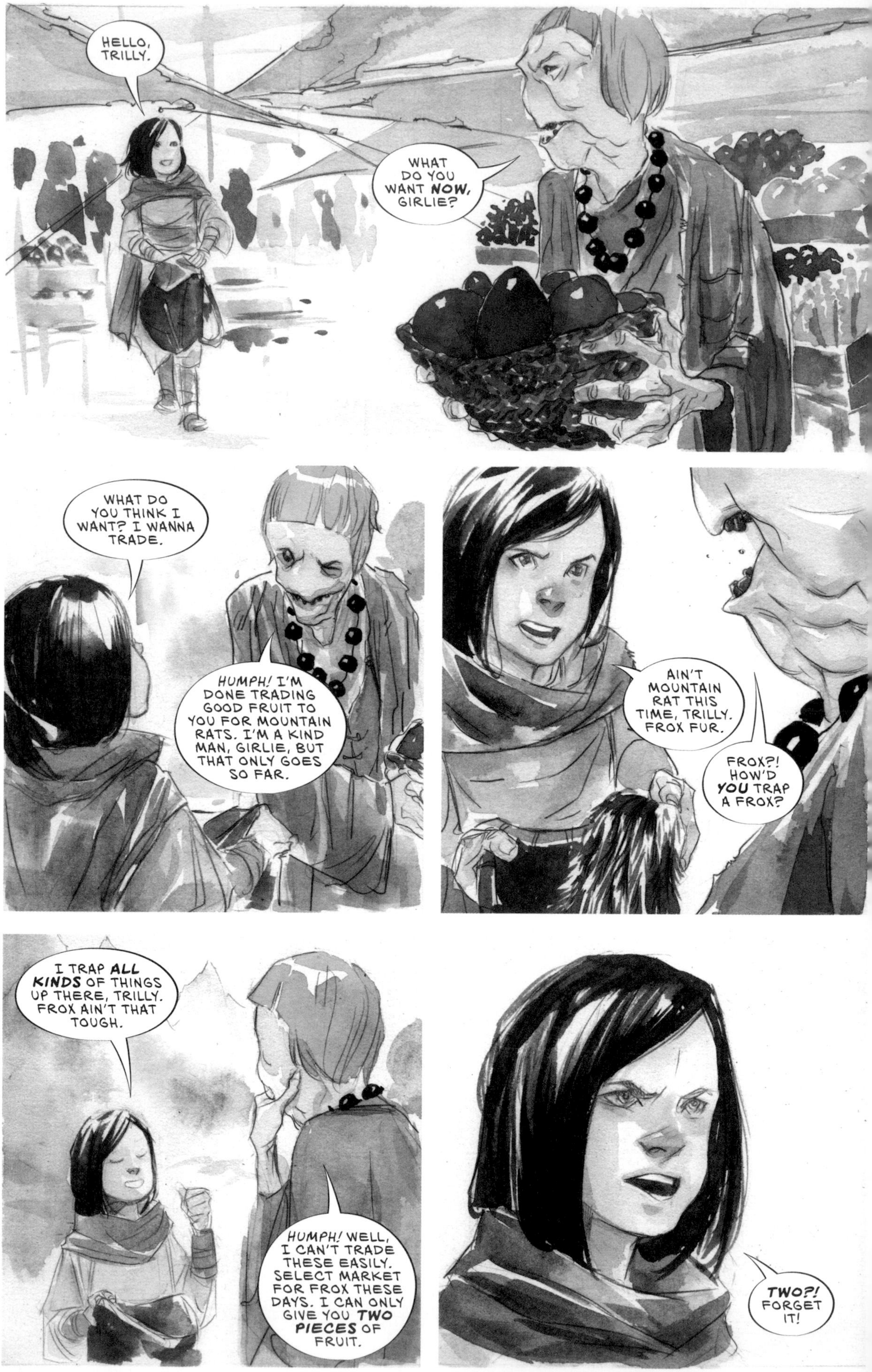
HELLO, TRILLY.
WHAT DO YOU WANT **NOW,** GIRLIE?
WHAT DO YOU THINK I WANT? I WANNA TRADE.
HUMPH! I'M DONE TRADING GOOD FRUIT TO YOU FOR MOUNTAIN RATS. I'M A KIND MAN, GIRLIE, BUT THAT ONLY GOES SO FAR.
AIN'T MOUNTAIN RAT THIS TIME, TRILLY. FROX FUR.
FROX?! HOW'D **YOU** TRAP A FROX?
I TRAP **ALL KINDS** OF THINGS UP THERE, TRILLY. FROX AIN'T THAT TOUGH.
HUMPH! WELL, I CAN'T TRADE THESE EASILY. SELECT MARKET FOR FROX THESE DAYS. I CAN ONLY GIVE YOU **TWO PIECES** OF FRUIT.
TWO?! FORGET IT!

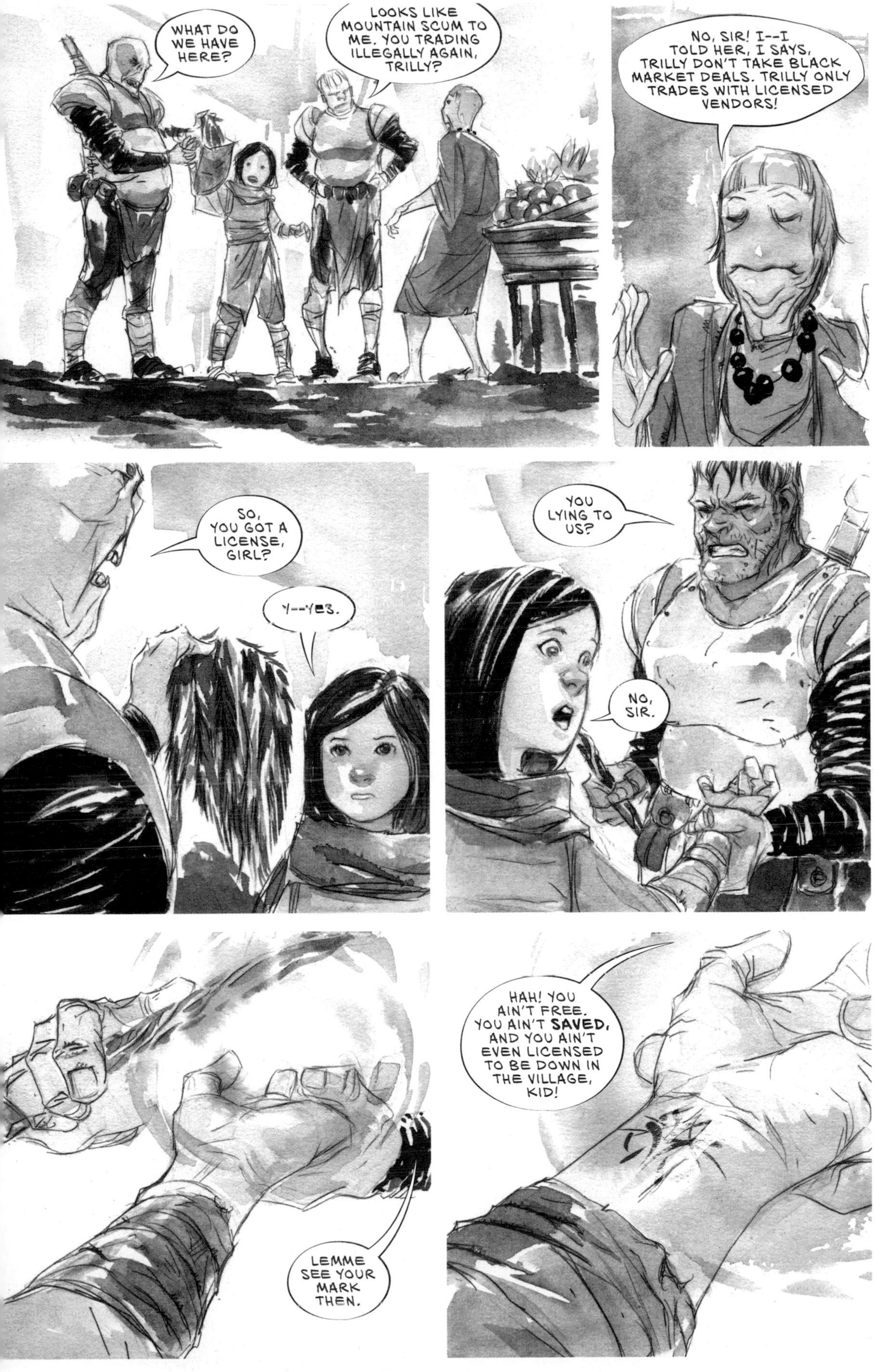
WHAT DO WE HAVE HERE?
LOOKS LIKE MOUNTAIN SCUM TO ME. YOU TRADING ILLEGALLY AGAIN, TRILLY?
NO, SIR! I--I TOLD HER, I SAYS, TRILLY DON'T TAKE BLACK MARKET DEALS. TRILLY ONLY TRADES WITH LICENSED VENDORS!
SO, YOU GOT A LICENSE, GIRL?
Y--YES.
YOU LYING TO US?
NO, SIR.
LEMME SEE YOUR MARK THEN.
HAH! YOU AIN'T FREE. YOU AIN'T **SAVED**, AND YOU AIN'T EVEN LICENSED TO BE DOWN IN THE VILLAGE, KID!

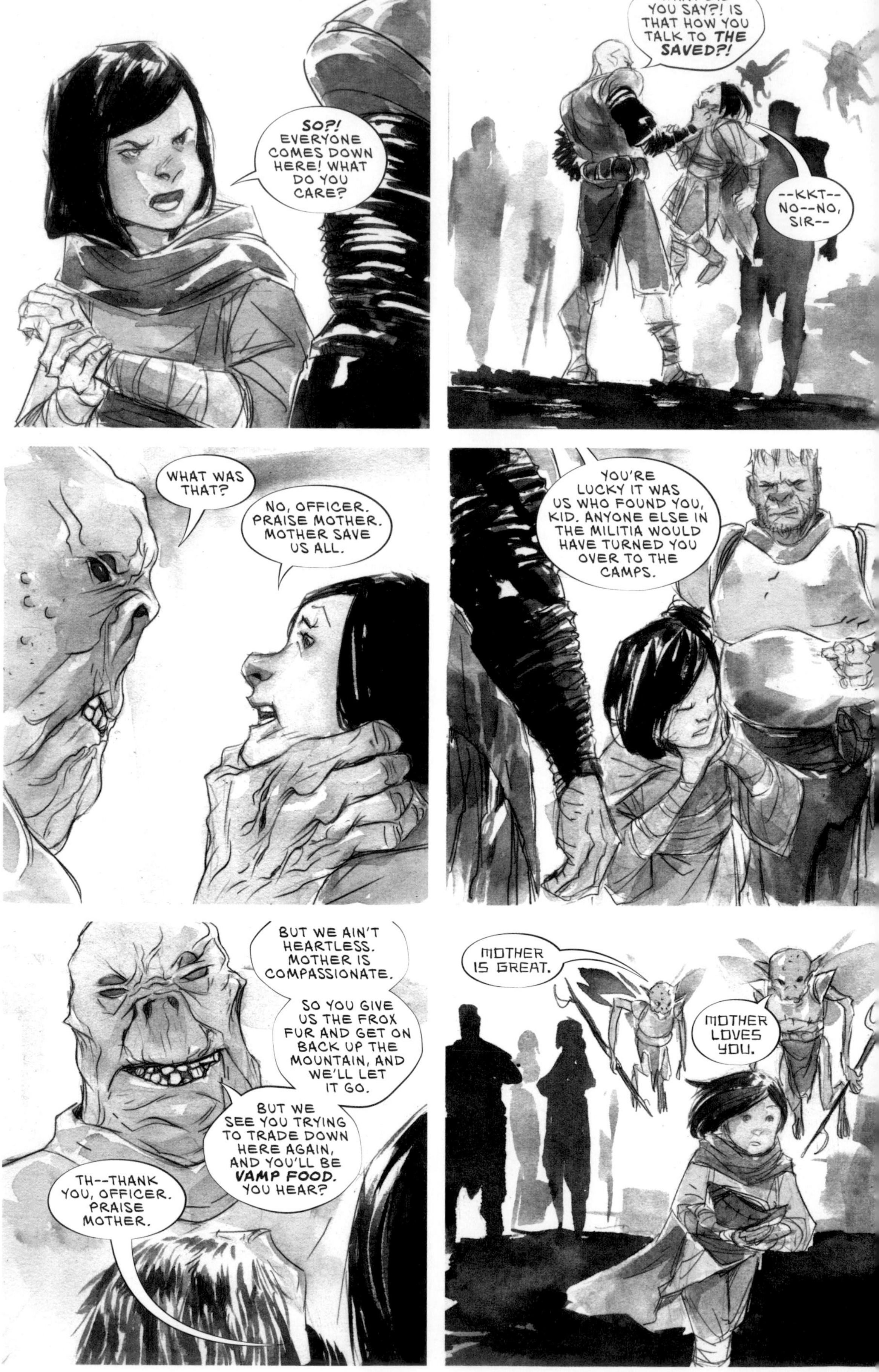
SO?! EVERYONE COMES DOWN HERE! WHAT DO YOU CARE?
WHAT DID YOU SAY?! IS THAT HOW YOU TALK TO THE SAVED?!
--KKT-- NO--NO, SIR--
WHAT WAS THAT?
NO, OFFICER. PRAISE MOTHER. MOTHER SAVE US ALL.
YOU'RE LUCKY IT WAS US WHO FOUND YOU, KID. ANYONE ELSE IN THE MILITIA WOULD HAVE TURNED YOU OVER TO THE CAMPS.
BUT WE AIN'T HEARTLESS. MOTHER IS COMPASSIONATE.
SO YOU GIVE US THE FROX FUR AND GET ON BACK UP THE MOUNTAIN, AND WE'LL LET IT GO.
BUT WE SEE YOU TRYING TO TRADE DOWN HERE AGAIN, AND YOU'LL BE VAMP FOOD. YOU HEAR?
TH--THANK YOU, OFFICER. PRAISE MOTHER.
MOTHER IS GREAT.
MOTHER LOVES YOU.

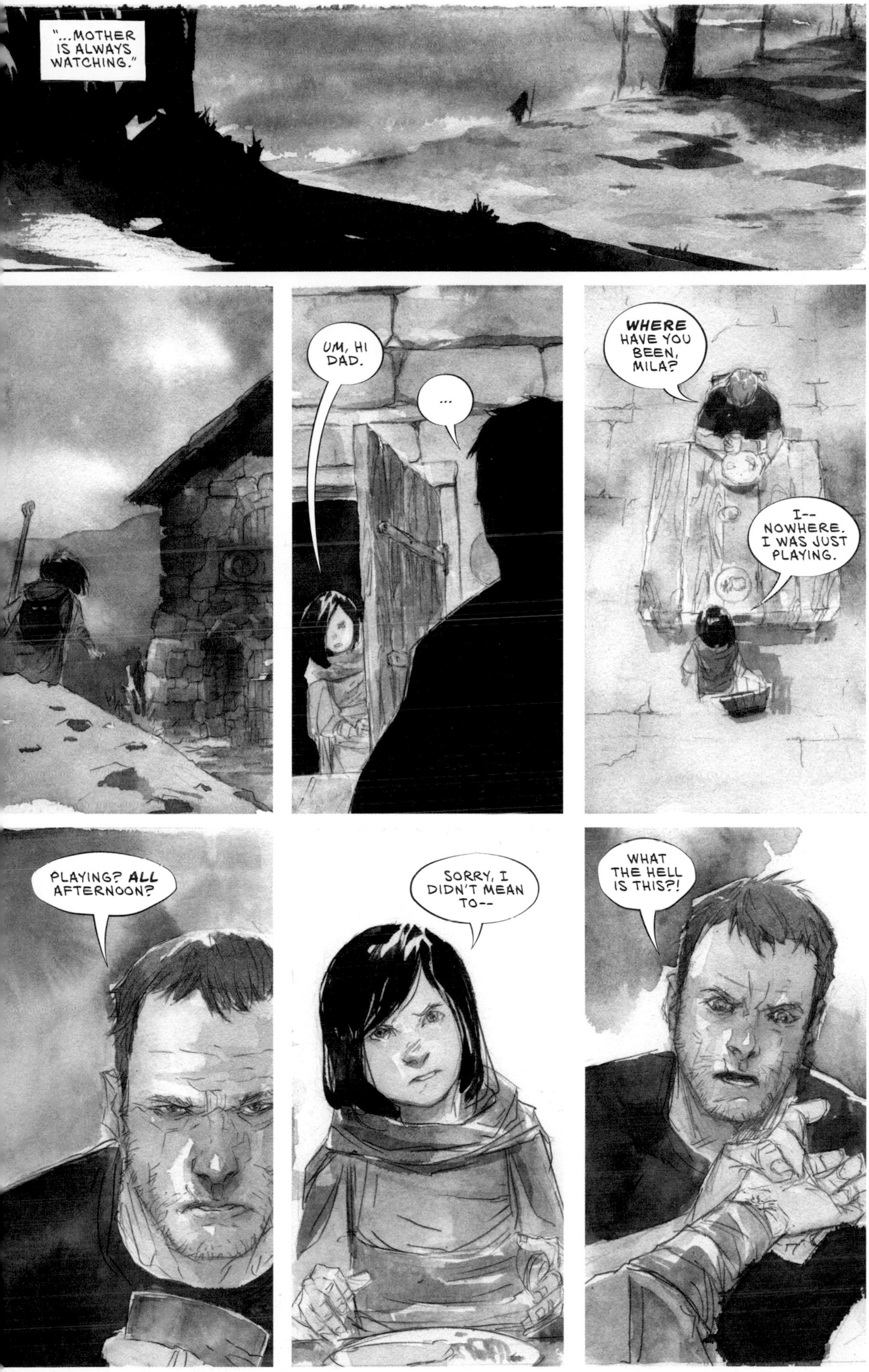
"...MOTHER IS ALWAYS WATCHING."
UM, HI DAD.
...
WHERE HAVE YOU BEEN, MILA?
I-- NOWHERE. I WAS JUST PLAYING.
PLAYING? ALL AFTERNOON?
SORRY, I DIDN'T MEAN TO--
WHAT THE HELL IS THIS?!

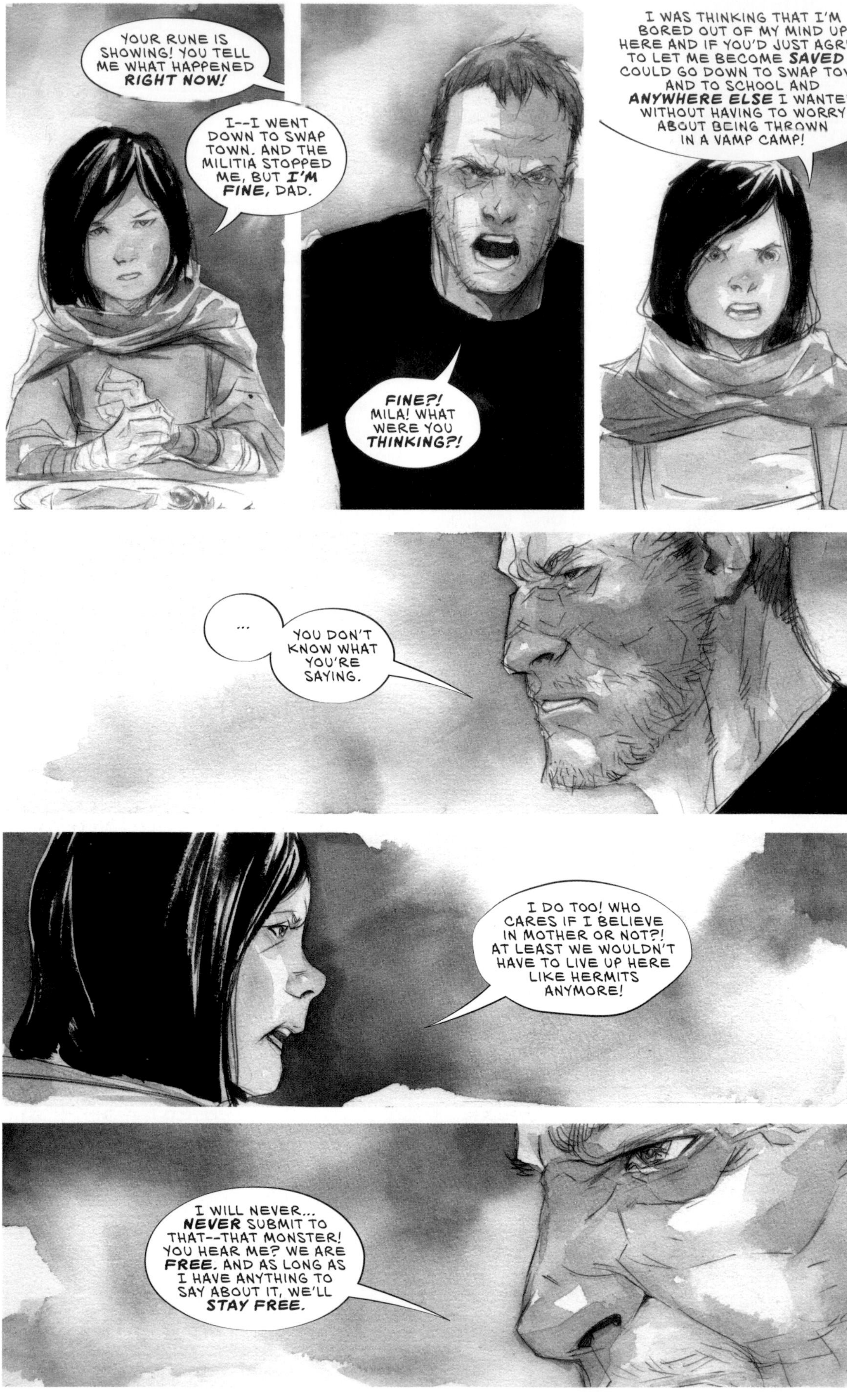
YOUR RUNE IS SHOWING! YOU TELL ME WHAT HAPPENED **RIGHT NOW!**
I--I WENT DOWN TO SWAP TOWN. AND THE MILITIA STOPPED ME, BUT **I'M FINE,** DAD.
FINE?! MILA! WHAT WERE YOU ***THINKING?!***
I WAS THINKING THAT I'M BORED OUT OF MY MIND UP HERE AND IF YOU'D JUST AGREE TO LET ME BECOME **SAVED** I COULD GO DOWN TO SWAP TOWN AND TO SCHOOL AND **ANYWHERE ELSE** I WANTED WITHOUT HAVING TO WORRY ABOUT BEING THROWN IN A VAMP CAMP!
...
YOU DON'T KNOW WHAT YOU'RE SAYING.
I DO TOO! WHO CARES IF I BELIEVE IN MOTHER OR NOT?! AT LEAST WE WOULDN'T HAVE TO LIVE UP HERE LIKE HERMITS ANYMORE!
I WILL NEVER... **NEVER** SUBMIT TO THAT--THAT MONSTER! YOU HEAR ME? WE ARE **FREE.** AND AS LONG AS I HAVE ANYTHING TO SAY ABOUT IT, WE'LL ***STAY FREE.***

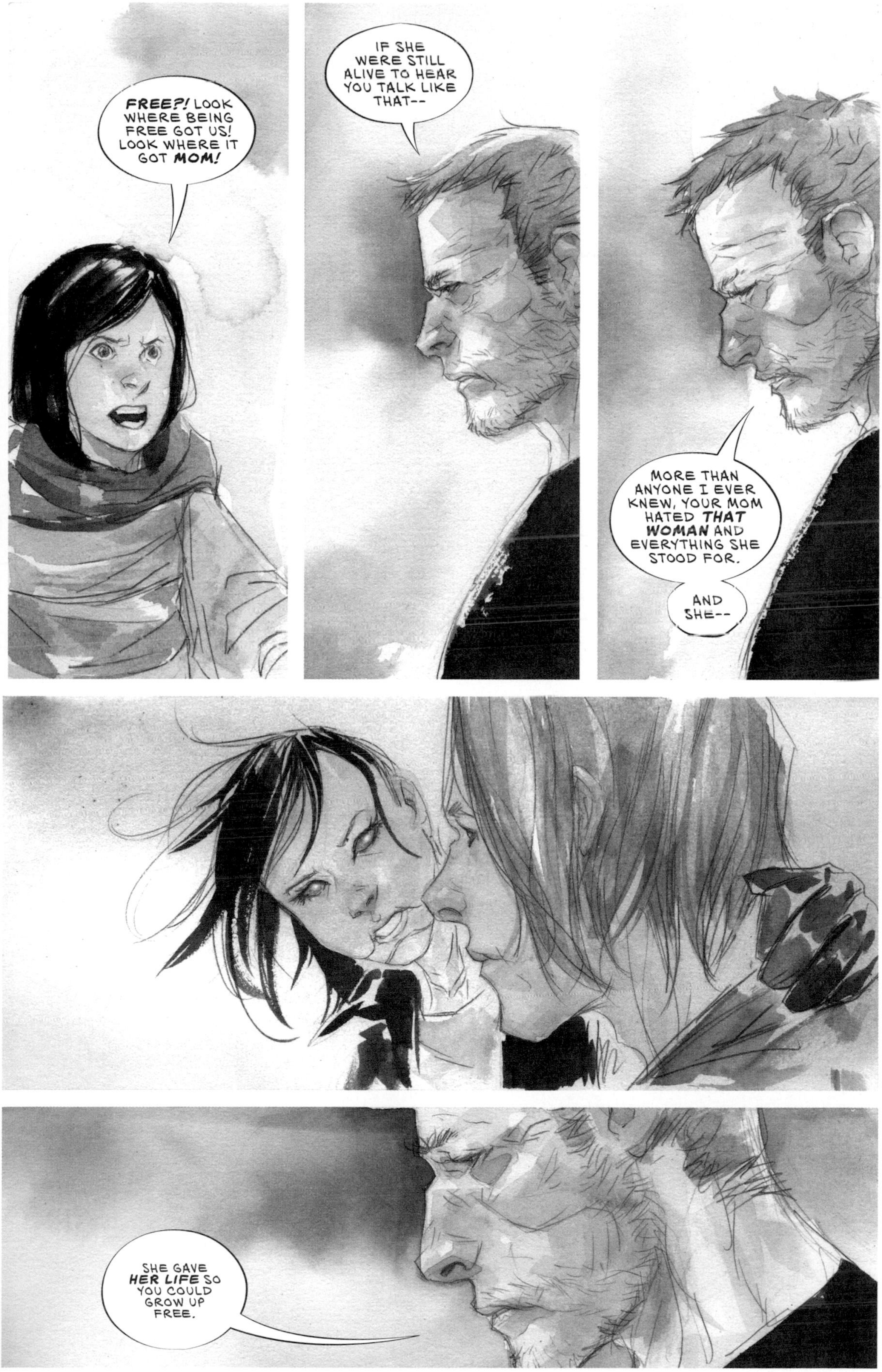

FREE?! LOOK WHERE BEING FREE GOT US! LOOK WHERE IT GOT ***MOM!***
IF SHE WERE STILL ALIVE TO HEAR YOU TALK LIKE THAT--
MORE THAN ANYONE I EVER KNEW, YOUR MOM HATED ***THAT WOMAN*** AND EVERYTHING SHE STOOD FOR.
AND SHE--
SHE GAVE ***HER LIFE*** SO YOU COULD GROW UP FREE.

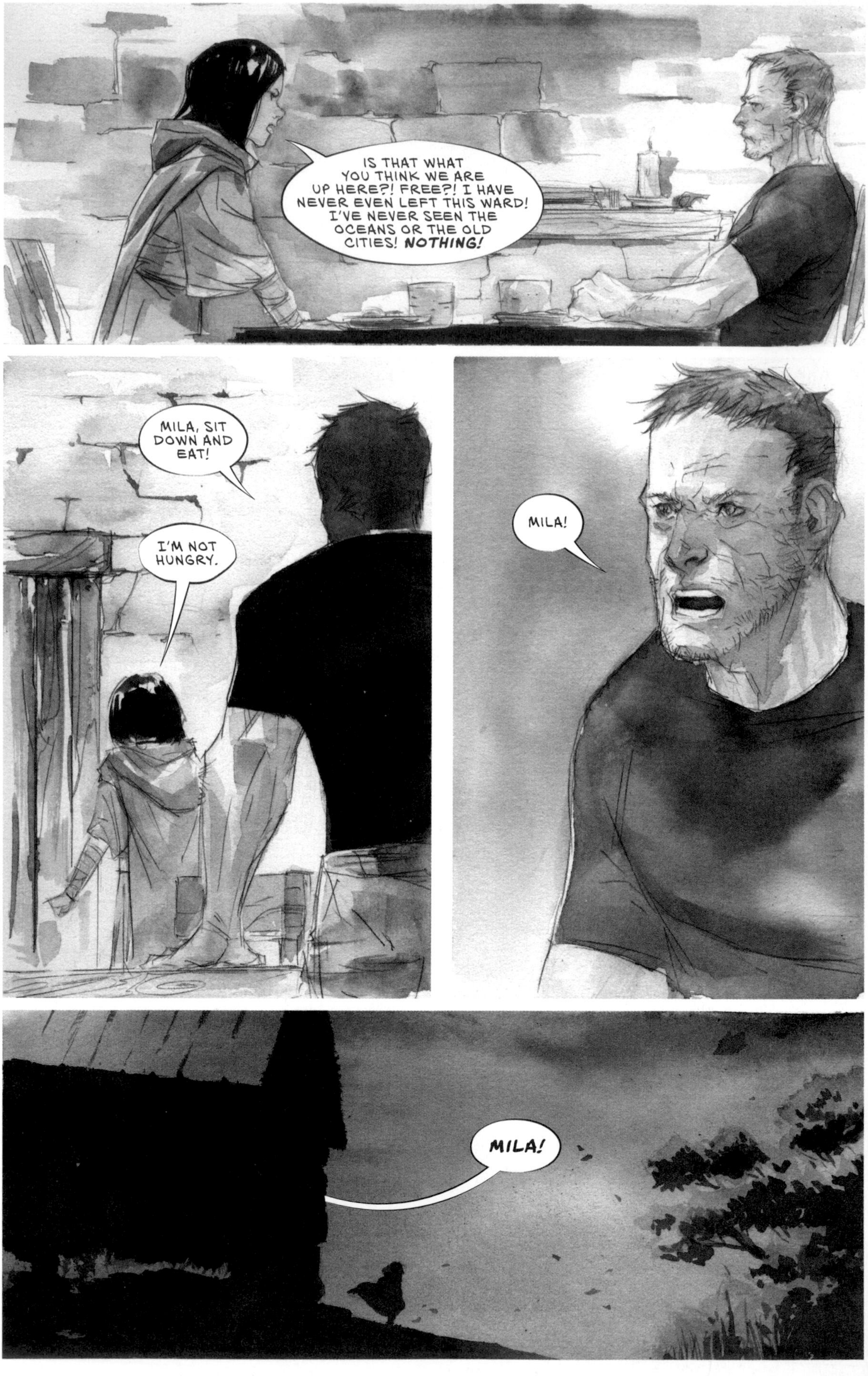
IS THAT WHAT YOU THINK WE ARE UP HERE?! FREE?! I HAVE NEVER EVEN LEFT THIS WARD! I'VE NEVER SEEN THE OCEANS OR THE OLD CITIES! **NOTHING!**
MILA, SIT DOWN AND EAT!
I'M NOT HUNGRY.
MILA!
MILA!

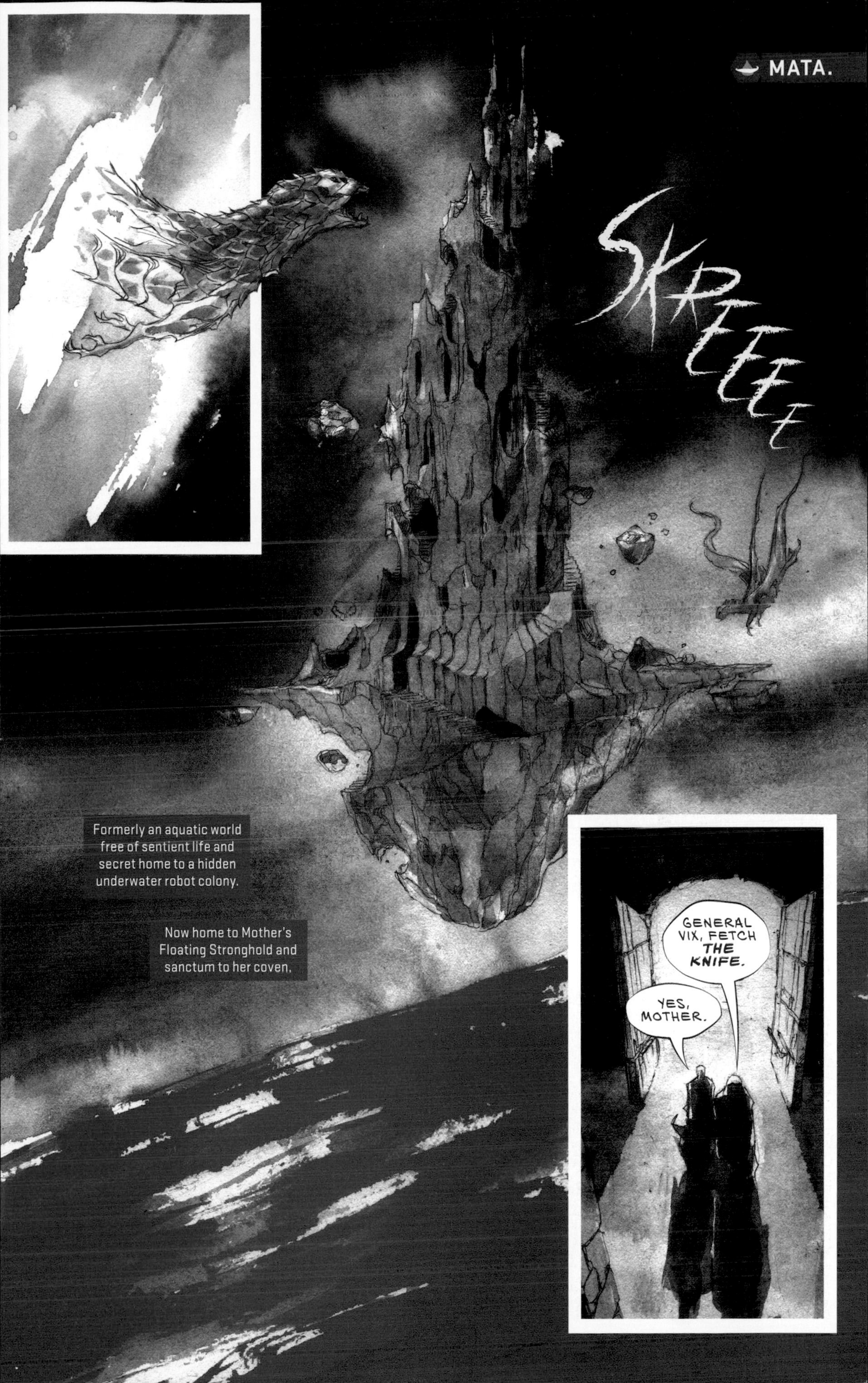
MATA.
SKREEEEE
Formerly an aquatic world free of sentient life and secret home to a hidden underwater robot colony.
Now home to Mother's Floating Stronghold and sanctum to her coven.
GENERAL VIX, FETCH THE KNIFE.
YES, MOTHER.

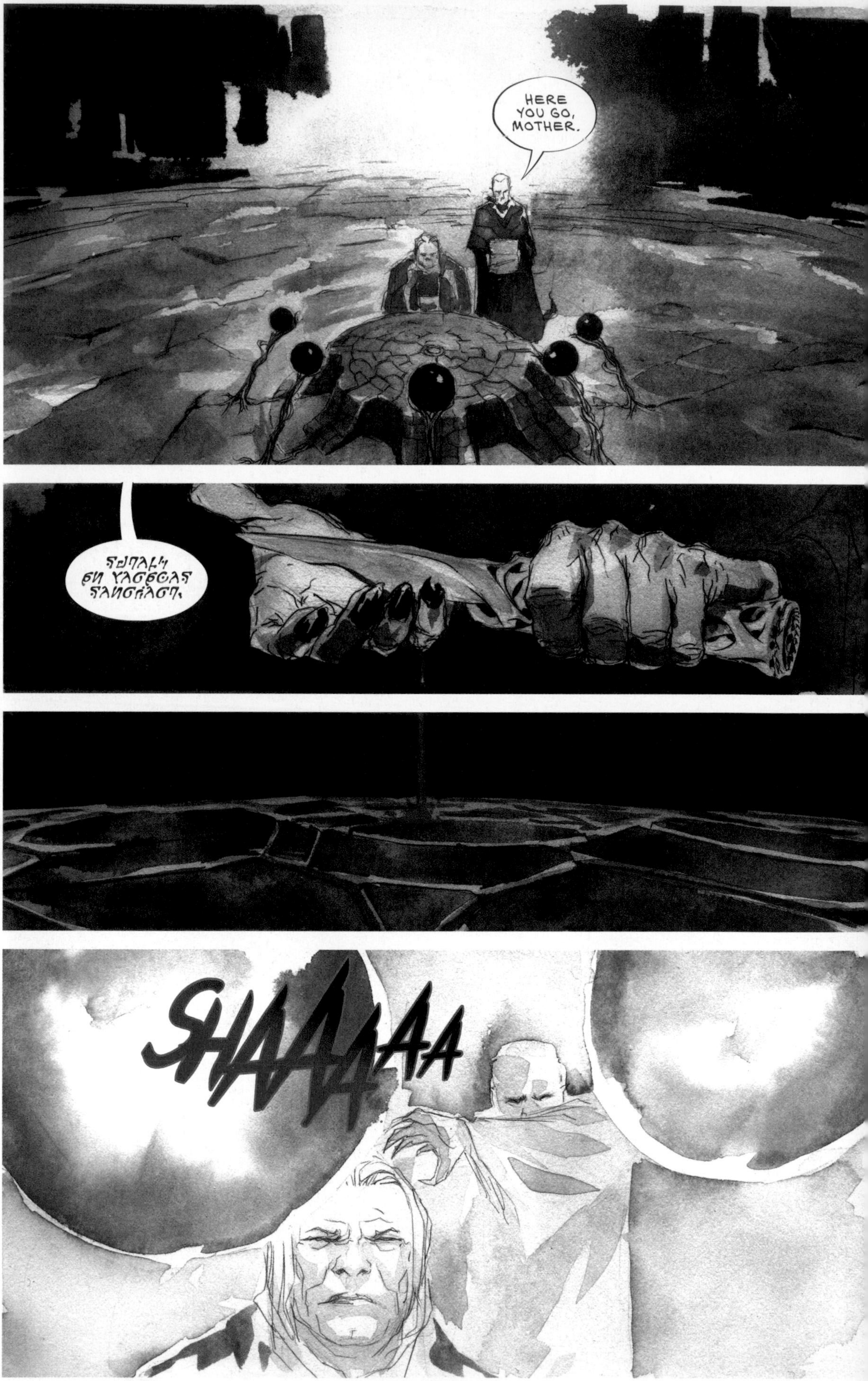
HERE YOU GO, MOTHER.
SHAAAAAA

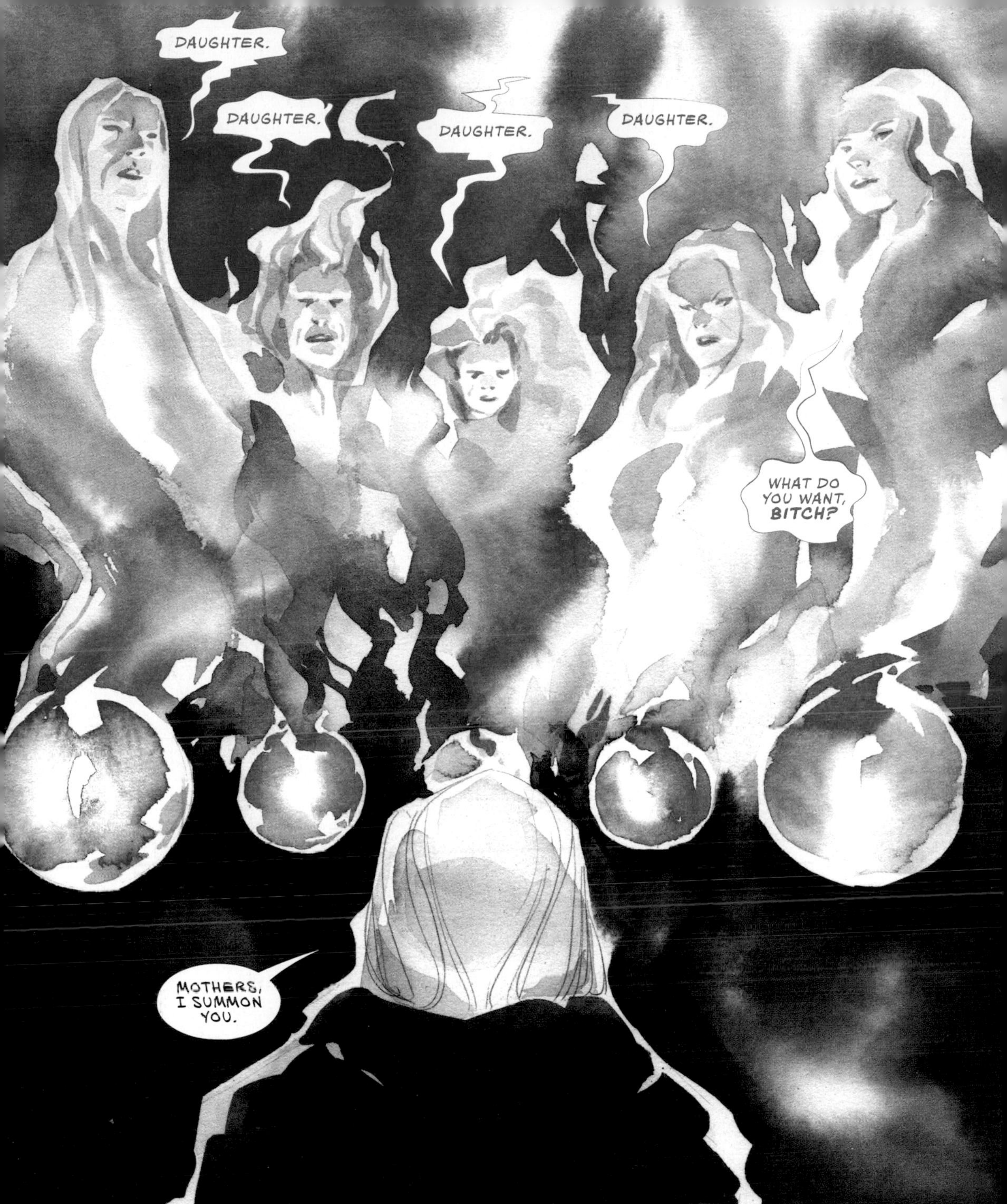
DAUGHTER.
DAUGHTER.
DAUGHTER.
DAUGHTER.
WHAT DO YOU WANT, **BITCH?**
MOTHERS, I SUMMON YOU.
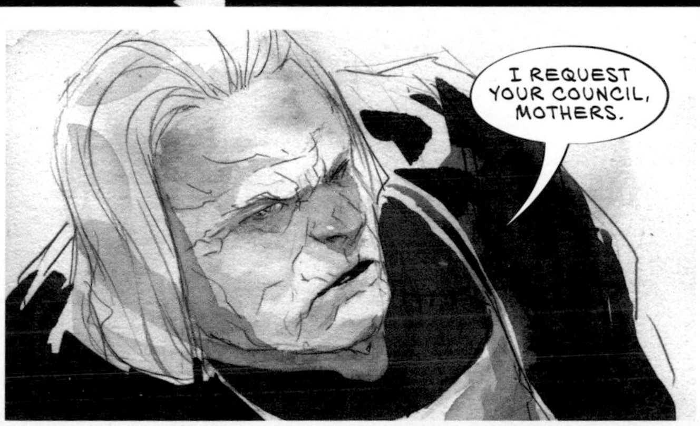
I REQUEST YOUR COUNCIL, MOTHERS.
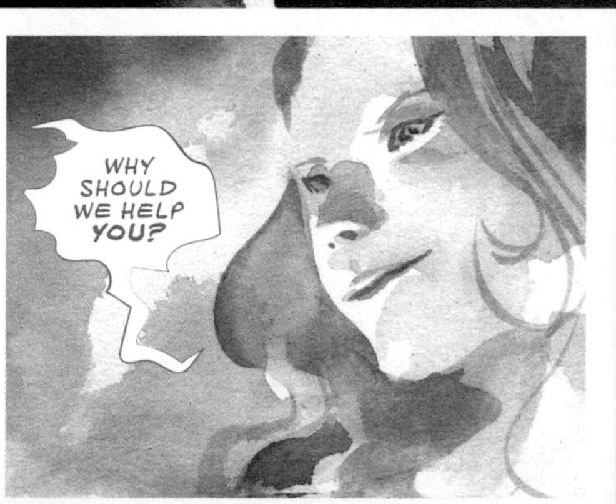
WHY SHOULD WE HELP **YOU?**

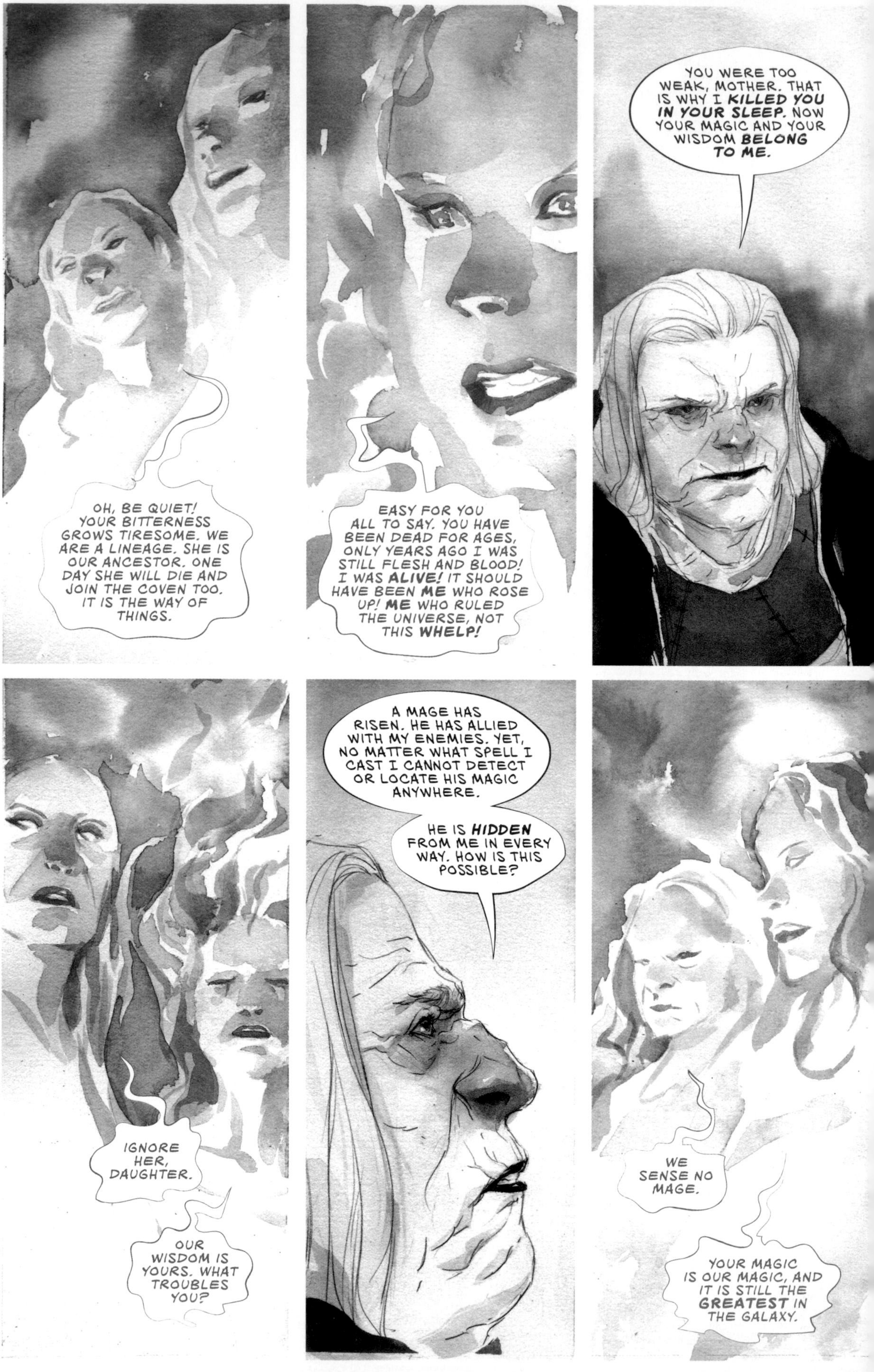
OH, BE QUIET! YOUR BITTERNESS GROWS TIRESOME. WE ARE A LINEAGE. SHE IS OUR ANCESTOR. ONE DAY SHE WILL DIE AND JOIN THE COVEN TOO. IT IS THE WAY OF THINGS.
EASY FOR YOU ALL TO SAY. YOU HAVE BEEN DEAD FOR AGES, ONLY YEARS AGO I WAS STILL FLESH AND BLOOD! I WAS ALIVE! IT SHOULD HAVE BEEN ME WHO ROSE UP! ME WHO RULED THE UNIVERSE, NOT THIS WHELP!
YOU WERE TOO WEAK, MOTHER. THAT IS WHY I KILLED YOU IN YOUR SLEEP. NOW YOUR MAGIC AND YOUR WISDOM BELONG TO ME.
IGNORE HER, DAUGHTER.
OUR WISDOM IS YOURS. WHAT TROUBLES YOU?
A MAGE HAS RISEN. HE HAS ALLIED WITH MY ENEMIES. YET, NO MATTER WHAT SPELL I CAST I CANNOT DETECT OR LOCATE HIS MAGIC ANYWHERE.
HE IS HIDDEN FROM ME IN EVERY WAY. HOW IS THIS POSSIBLE?
WE SENSE NO MAGE.
YOUR MAGIC IS OUR MAGIC, AND IT IS STILL THE GREATEST IN THE GALAXY.

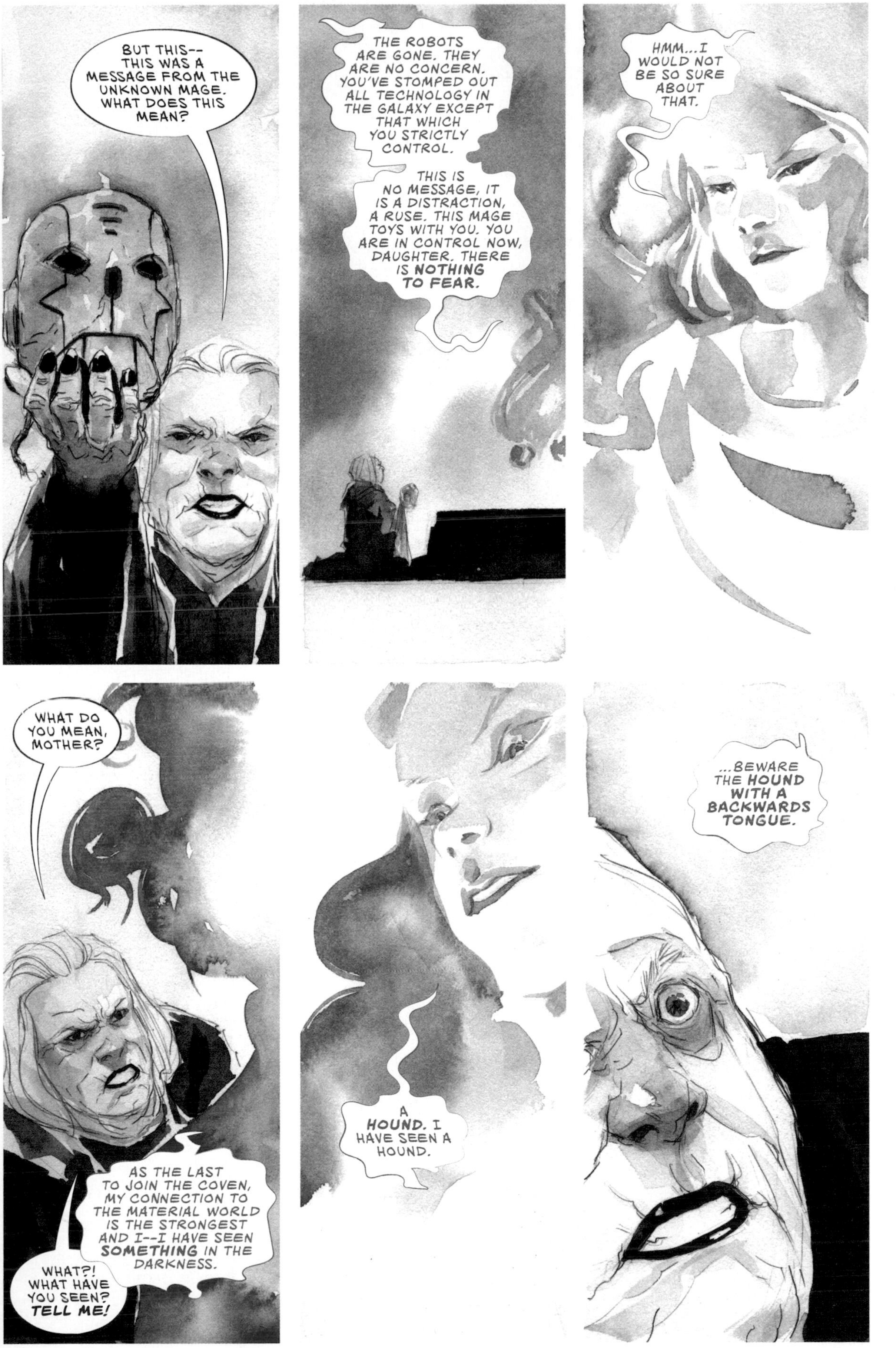
BUT THIS-- THIS WAS A MESSAGE FROM THE UNKNOWN MAGE. WHAT DOES THIS MEAN?
THE ROBOTS ARE GONE. THEY ARE NO CONCERN. YOU'VE STOMPED OUT ALL TECHNOLOGY IN THE GALAXY EXCEPT THAT WHICH YOU STRICTLY CONTROL.
THIS IS NO MESSAGE, IT IS A DISTRACTION, A RUSE. THIS MAGE TOYS WITH YOU. YOU ARE IN CONTROL NOW, DAUGHTER. THERE IS **NOTHING TO FEAR.**
HMM...I WOULD NOT BE SO SURE ABOUT THAT.
WHAT DO YOU MEAN, MOTHER?
AS THE LAST TO JOIN THE COVEN, MY CONNECTION TO THE MATERIAL WORLD IS THE STRONGEST AND I--I HAVE SEEN **SOMETHING** IN THE DARKNESS.
WHAT?! WHAT HAVE YOU SEEN? ***TELL ME!***
A **HOUND.** I HAVE SEEN A HOUND.
...BEWARE THE **HOUND WITH A BACKWARDS TONGUE.**

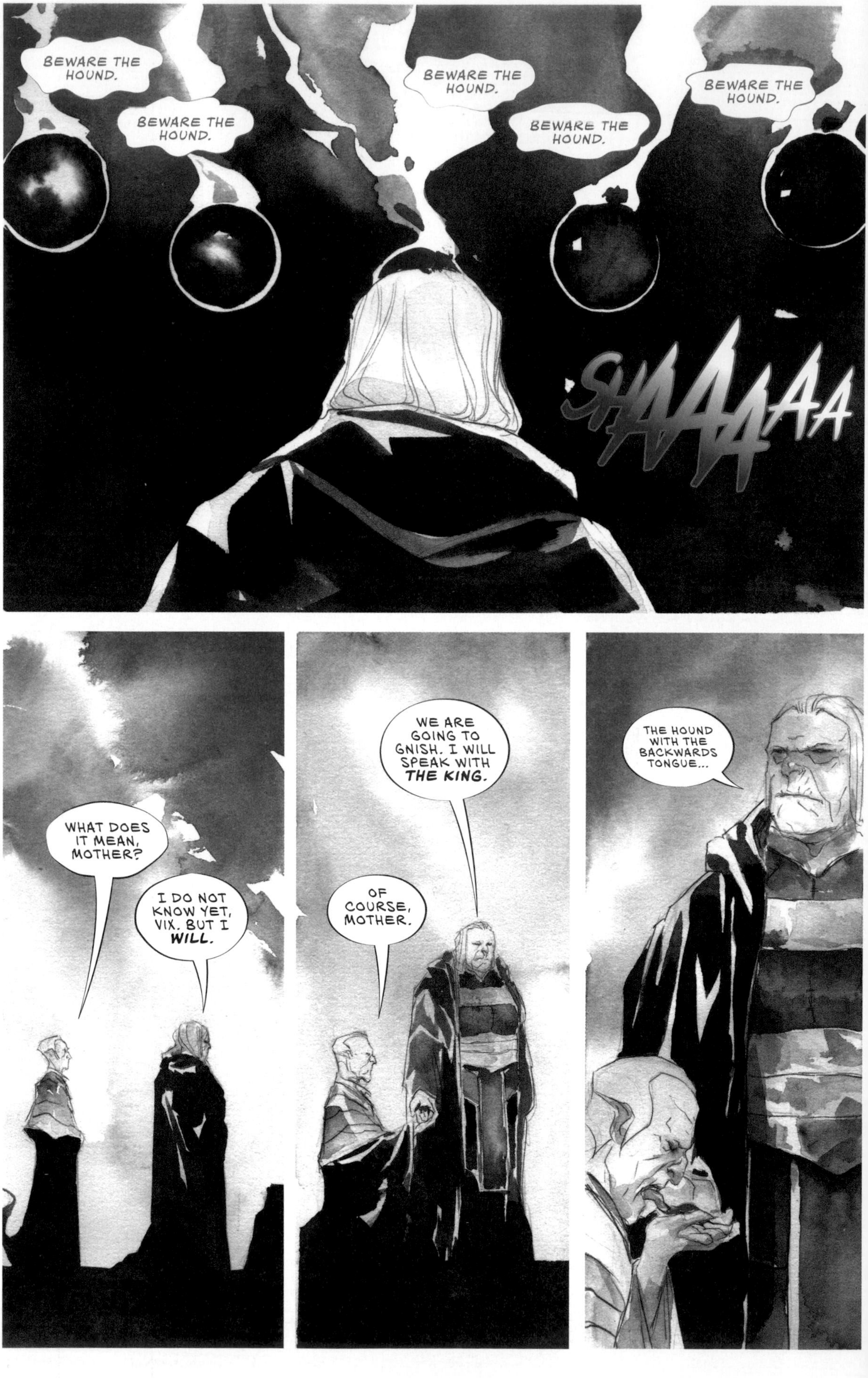
BEWARE THE HOUND.
BEWARE THE HOUND.
BEWARE THE HOUND.
BEWARE THE HOUND.
BEWARE THE HOUND.
SHAAAAAA
WHAT DOES IT MEAN, MOTHER?
I DO NOT KNOW YET, VIX. BUT I **WILL.**
WE ARE GOING TO GNISH. I WILL SPEAK WITH **THE KING.**
OF COURSE, MOTHER.
THE HOUND WITH THE BACKWARDS TONGUE...

There has to be more than this.

There just has to be.

Why couldn't I have been born when we still had spaceships and shiftdrives?

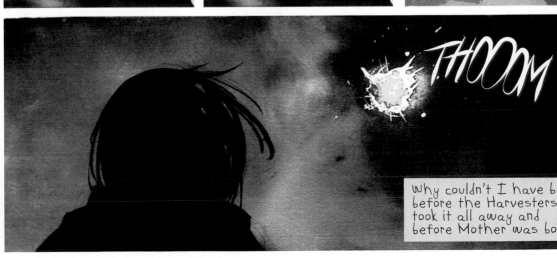

THOOOM

Why couldn't I have been before the Harvesters took it all away and before Mother was born?

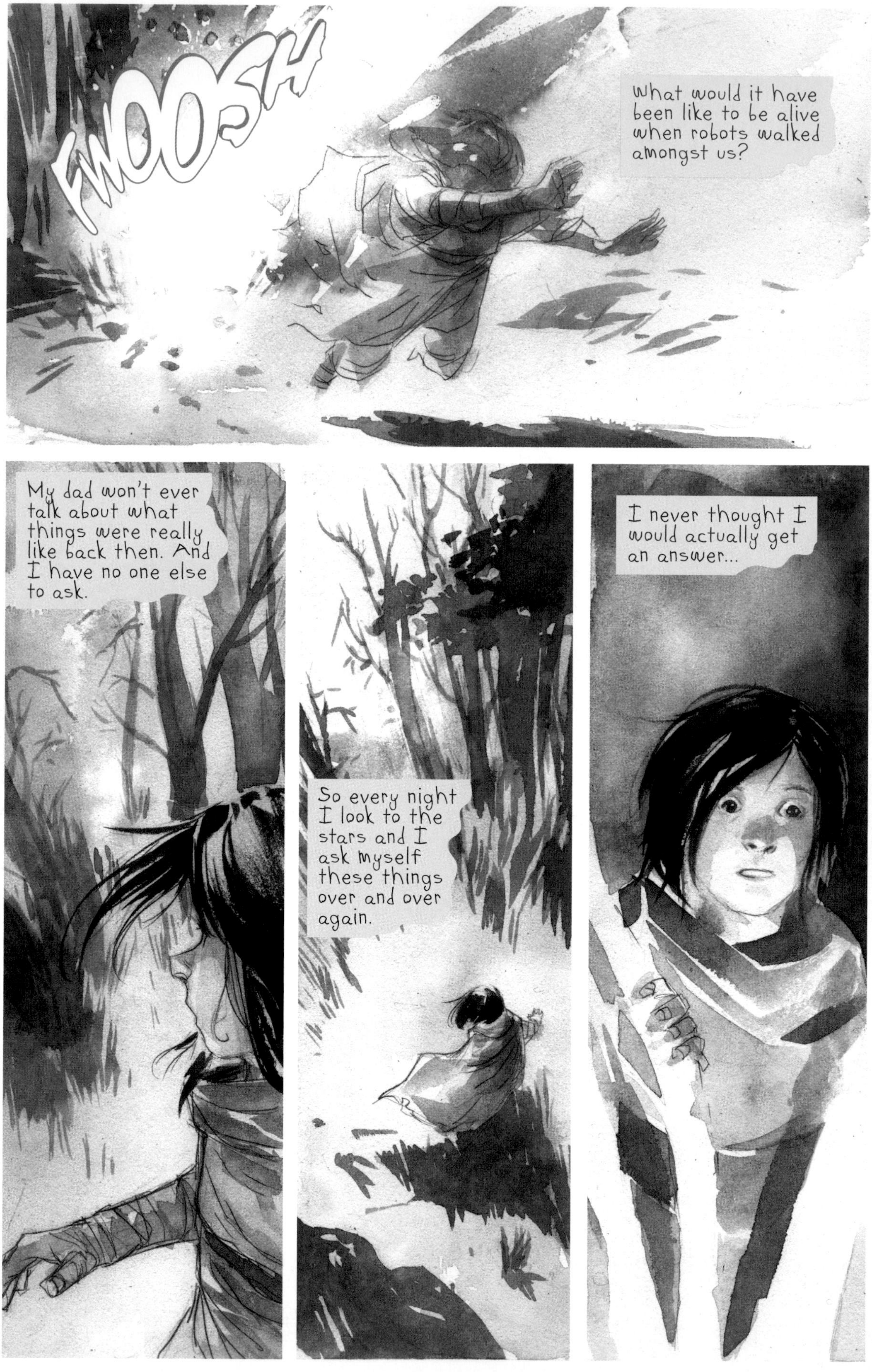
FWOOSH
What would it have been like to be alive when robots walked amongst us?
My dad won't ever talk about what things were really like back then. And I have no one else to ask.
So every night I look to the stars and I ask myself these things over and over again.
I never thought I would actually get an answer...

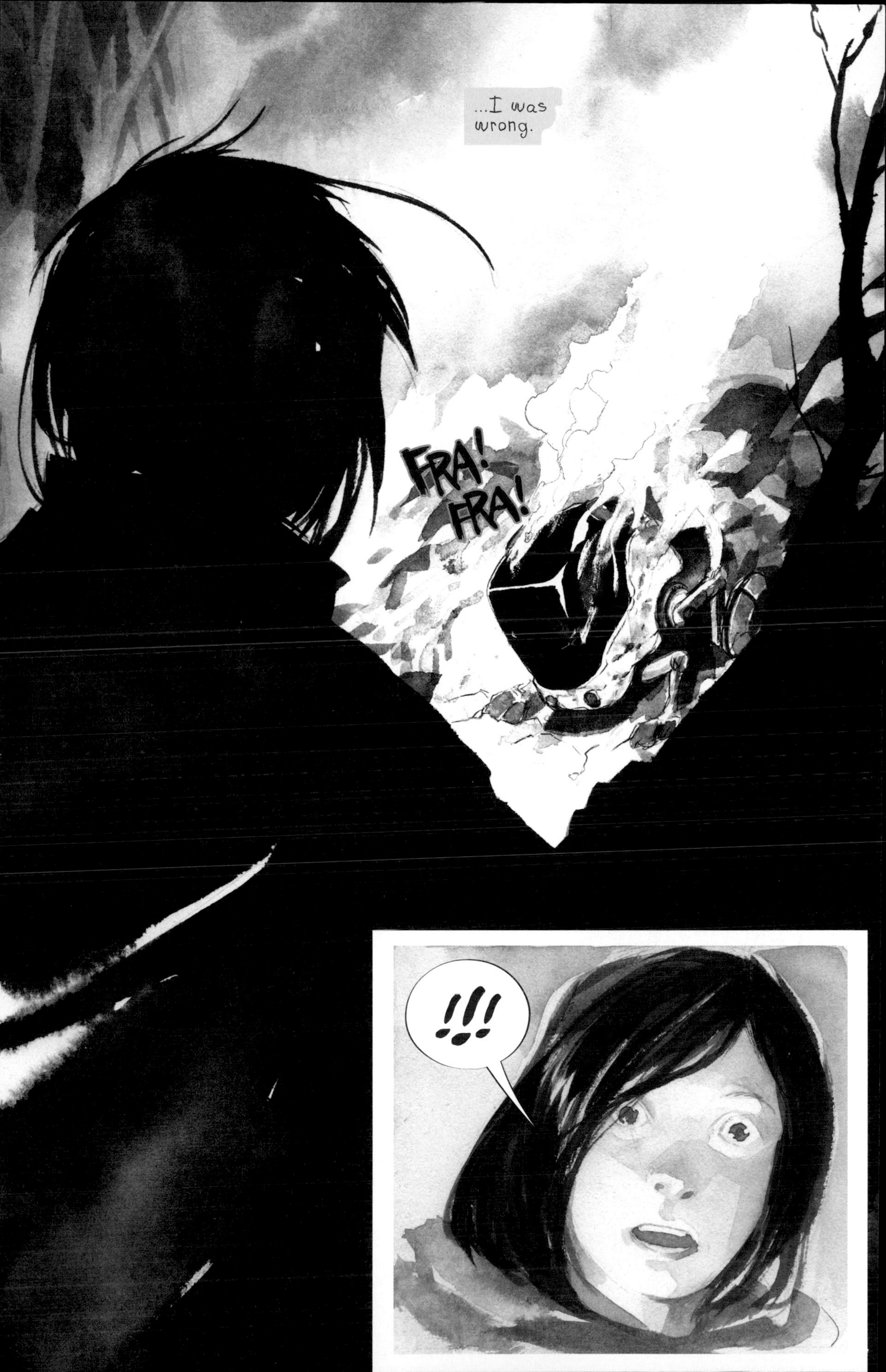
...I was wrong.
FRA! FRA!
!!!

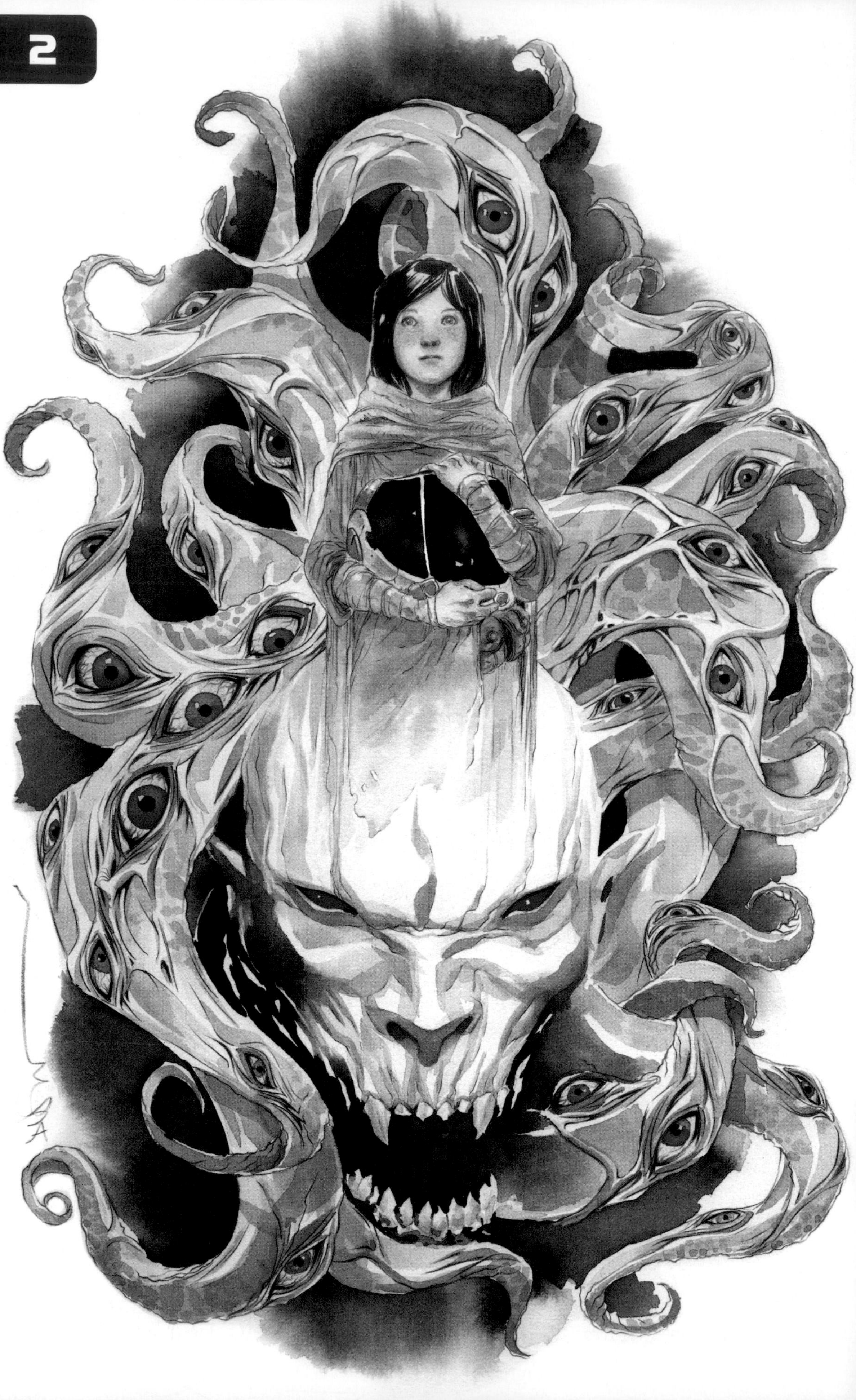

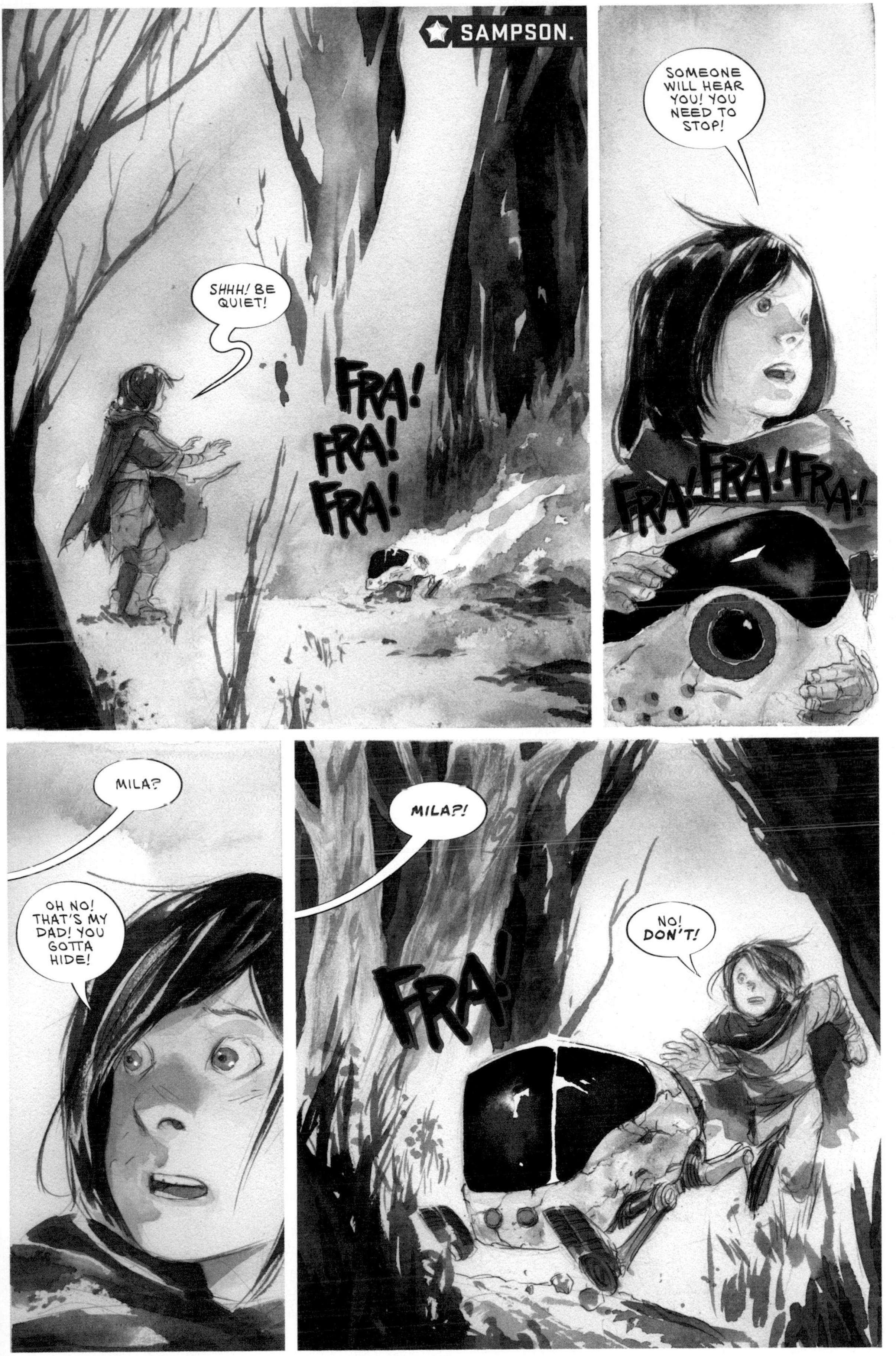
SAMPSON.
SHHH! BE QUIET!
FRA! FRA! FRA!
SOMEONE WILL HEAR YOU! YOU NEED TO STOP!
FRA! FRA! FRA!
MILA?
OH NO! THAT'S MY DAD! YOU GOTTA HIDE!
MILA?!
FRA!
NO! DON'T!

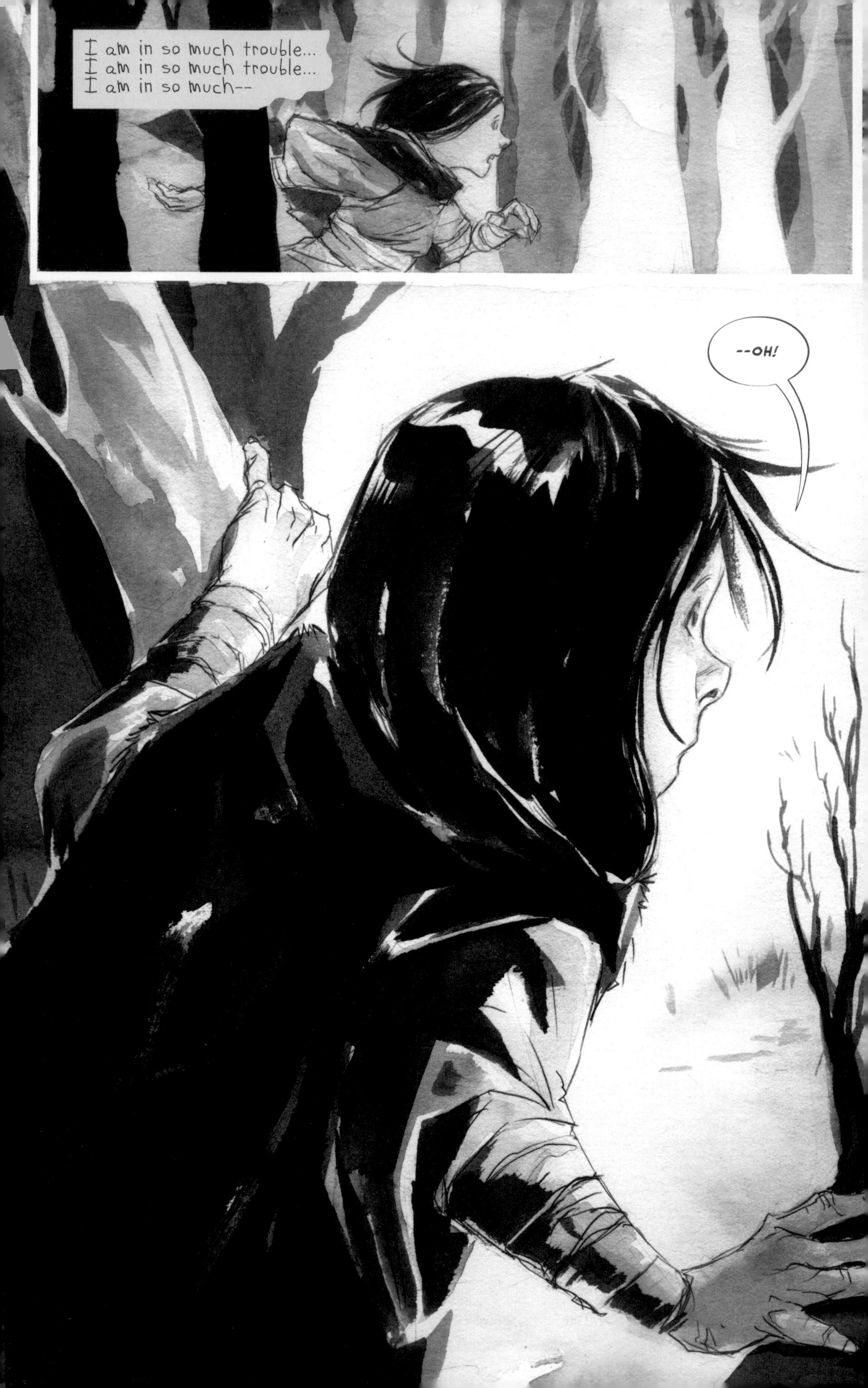
I am in so much trouble...
I am in so much trouble...
I am in so much--
--OH!

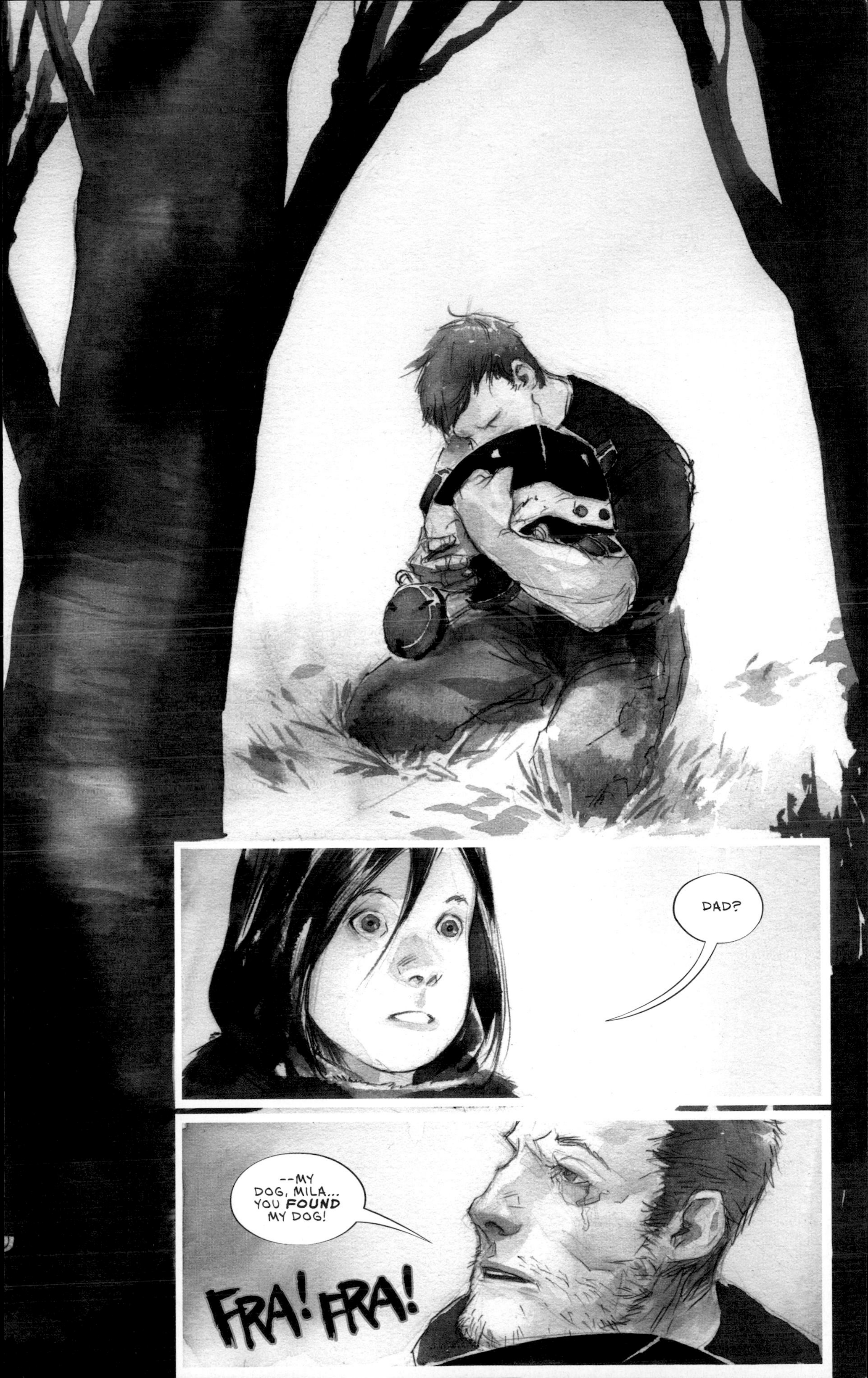
DAD?
--MY DOG, MILA... YOU **FOUND** MY DOG!
FRA! FRA!

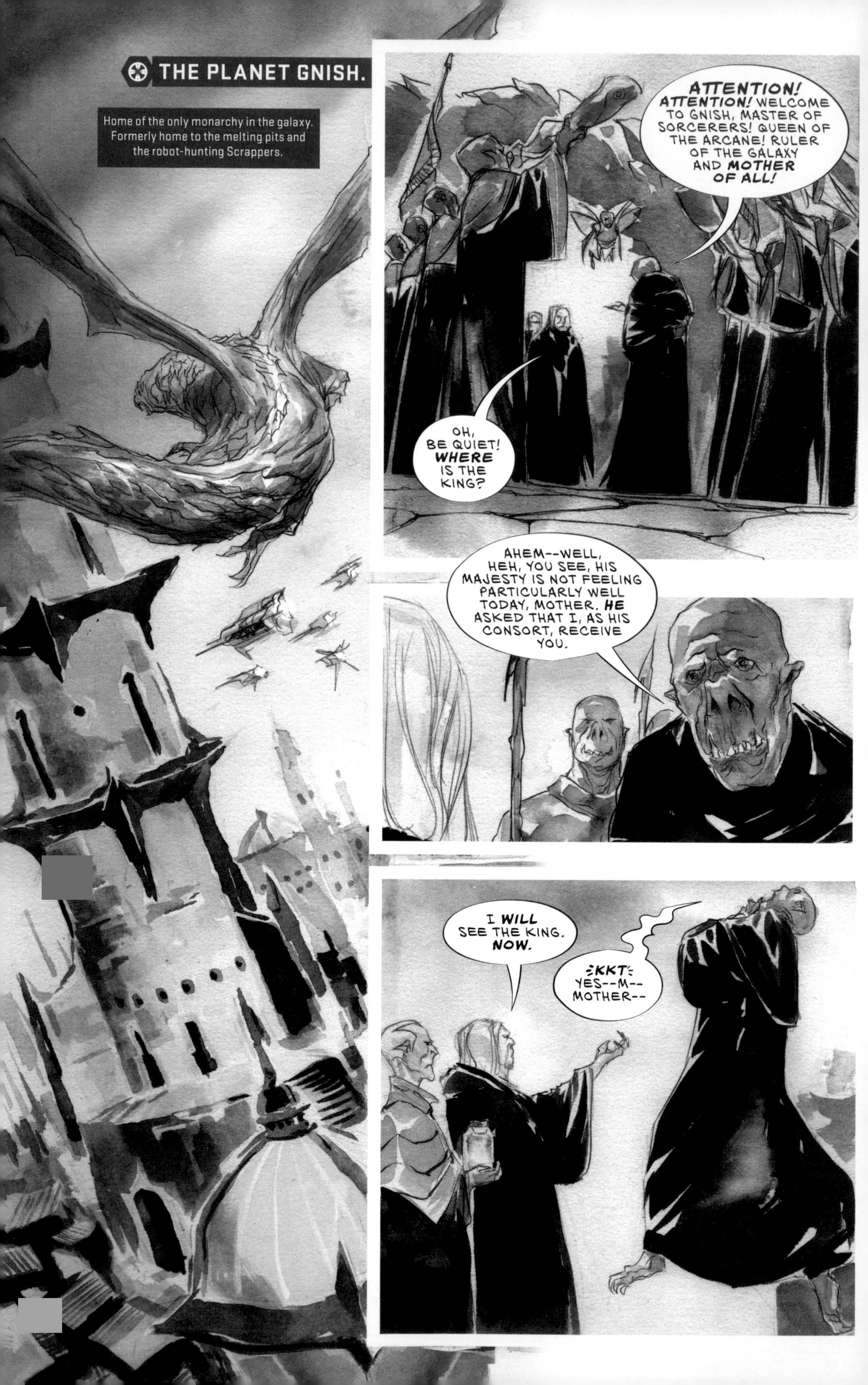
THE PLANET GNISH.
Home of the only monarchy in the galaxy. Formerly home to the melting pits and the robot-hunting Scrappers.
ATTENTION! ATTENTION! WELCOME TO GNISH, MASTER OF SORCERERS! QUEEN OF THE ARCANE! RULER OF THE GALAXY AND MOTHER OF ALL!
OH, BE QUIET! WHERE IS THE KING?
AHEM--WELL, HEH, YOU SEE, HIS MAJESTY IS NOT FEELING PARTICULARLY WELL TODAY, MOTHER. HE ASKED THAT I, AS HIS CONSORT, RECEIVE YOU.
I WILL SEE THE KING. NOW.
KKT YES--M--MOTHER--

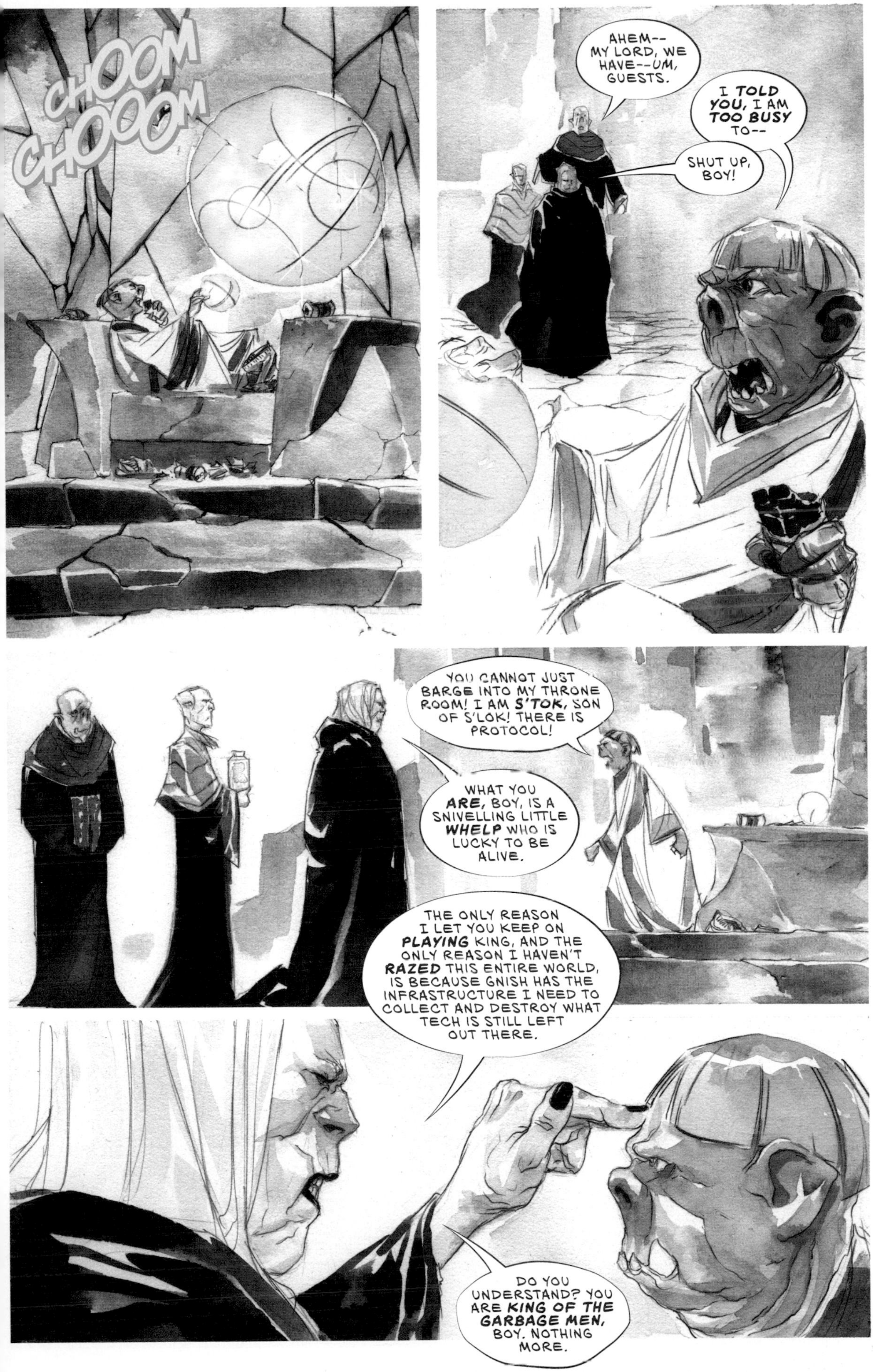
CHOOM CHOOOM
AHEM-- MY LORD, WE HAVE--UM, GUESTS.
I TOLD YOU, I AM TOO BUSY TO--
SHUT UP, BOY!
YOU CANNOT JUST BARGE INTO MY THRONE ROOM! I AM S'TOK, SON OF S'LOK! THERE IS PROTOCOL!
WHAT YOU ARE, BOY, IS A SNIVELLING LITTLE WHELP WHO IS LUCKY TO BE ALIVE.
THE ONLY REASON I LET YOU KEEP ON PLAYING KING, AND THE ONLY REASON I HAVEN'T RAZED THIS ENTIRE WORLD, IS BECAUSE GNISH HAS THE INFRASTRUCTURE I NEED TO COLLECT AND DESTROY WHAT TECH IS STILL LEFT OUT THERE.
DO YOU UNDERSTAND? YOU ARE KING OF THE GARBAGE MEN, BOY. NOTHING MORE.

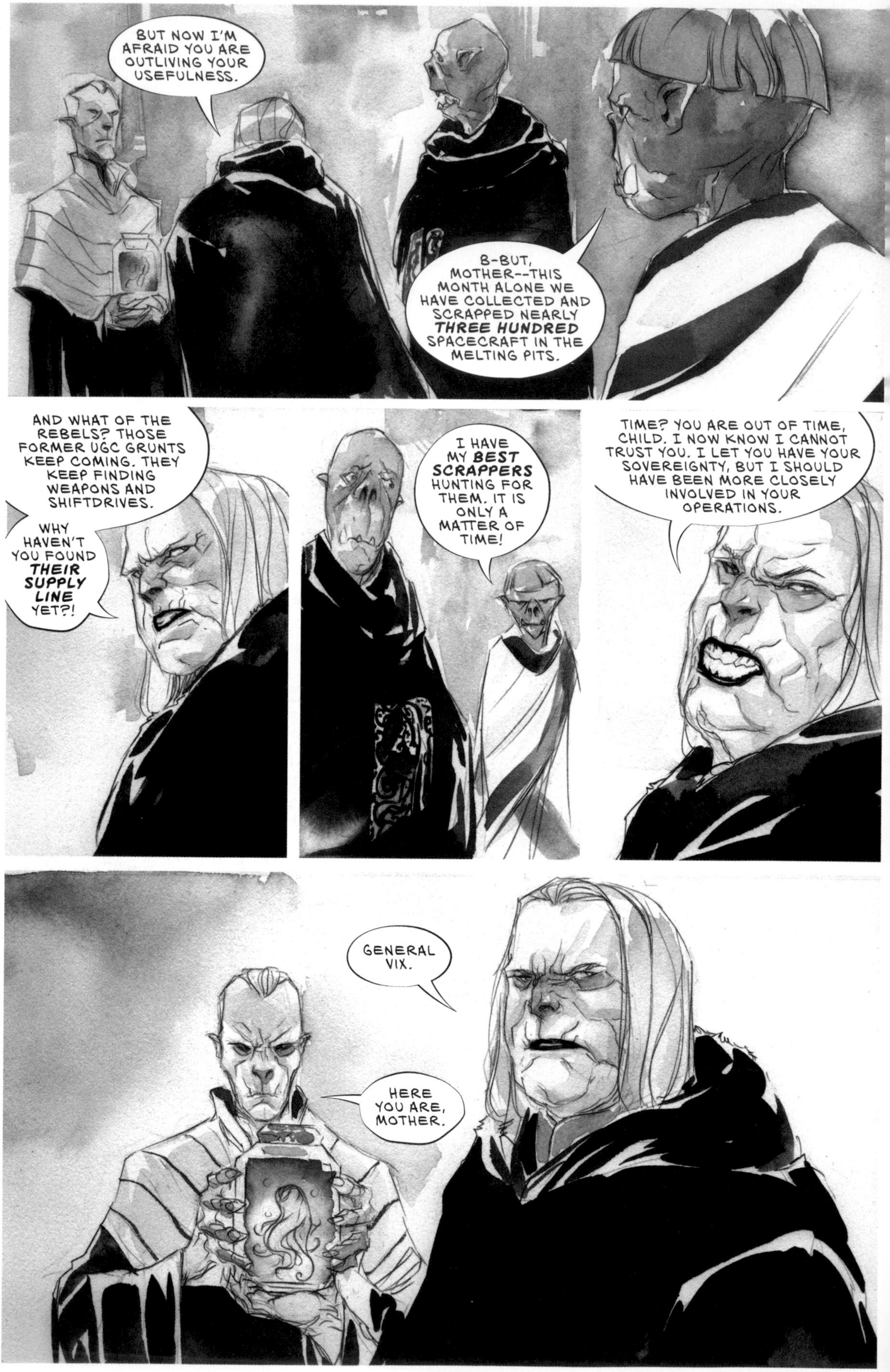
BUT NOW I'M AFRAID YOU ARE OUTLIVING YOUR USEFULNESS.
B-BUT, MOTHER--THIS MONTH ALONE WE HAVE COLLECTED AND SCRAPPED NEARLY **THREE HUNDRED** SPACECRAFT IN THE MELTING PITS.
AND WHAT OF THE REBELS? THOSE FORMER UGC GRUNTS KEEP COMING. THEY KEEP FINDING WEAPONS AND SHIFTDRIVES.
WHY HAVEN'T YOU FOUND **THEIR SUPPLY LINE** YET?!
I HAVE MY **BEST SCRAPPERS** HUNTING FOR THEM. IT IS ONLY A MATTER OF TIME!
TIME? YOU ARE OUT OF TIME, CHILD. I NOW KNOW I CANNOT TRUST YOU. I LET YOU HAVE YOUR SOVEREIGNTY, BUT I SHOULD HAVE BEEN MORE CLOSELY INVOLVED IN YOUR OPERATIONS.
GENERAL VIX.
HERE YOU ARE, MOTHER.

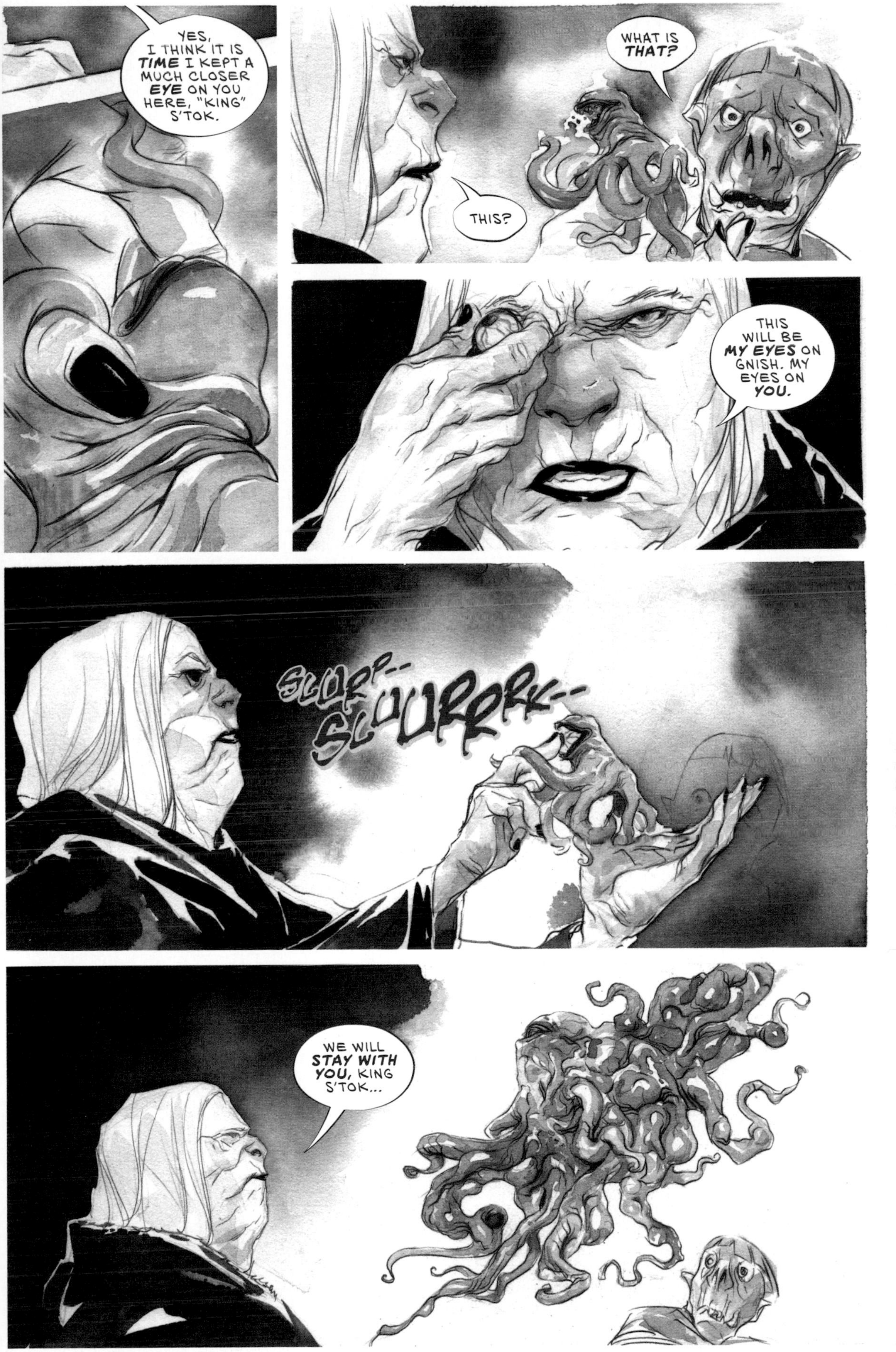
YES, I THINK IT IS TIME I KEPT A MUCH CLOSER EYE ON YOU HERE, "KING" S'TOK.
WHAT IS THAT?
THIS?
THIS WILL BE MY EYES ON GNISH. MY EYES ON YOU.
SLURP-- SLUURRRK--
WE WILL STAY WITH YOU, KING S'TOK...

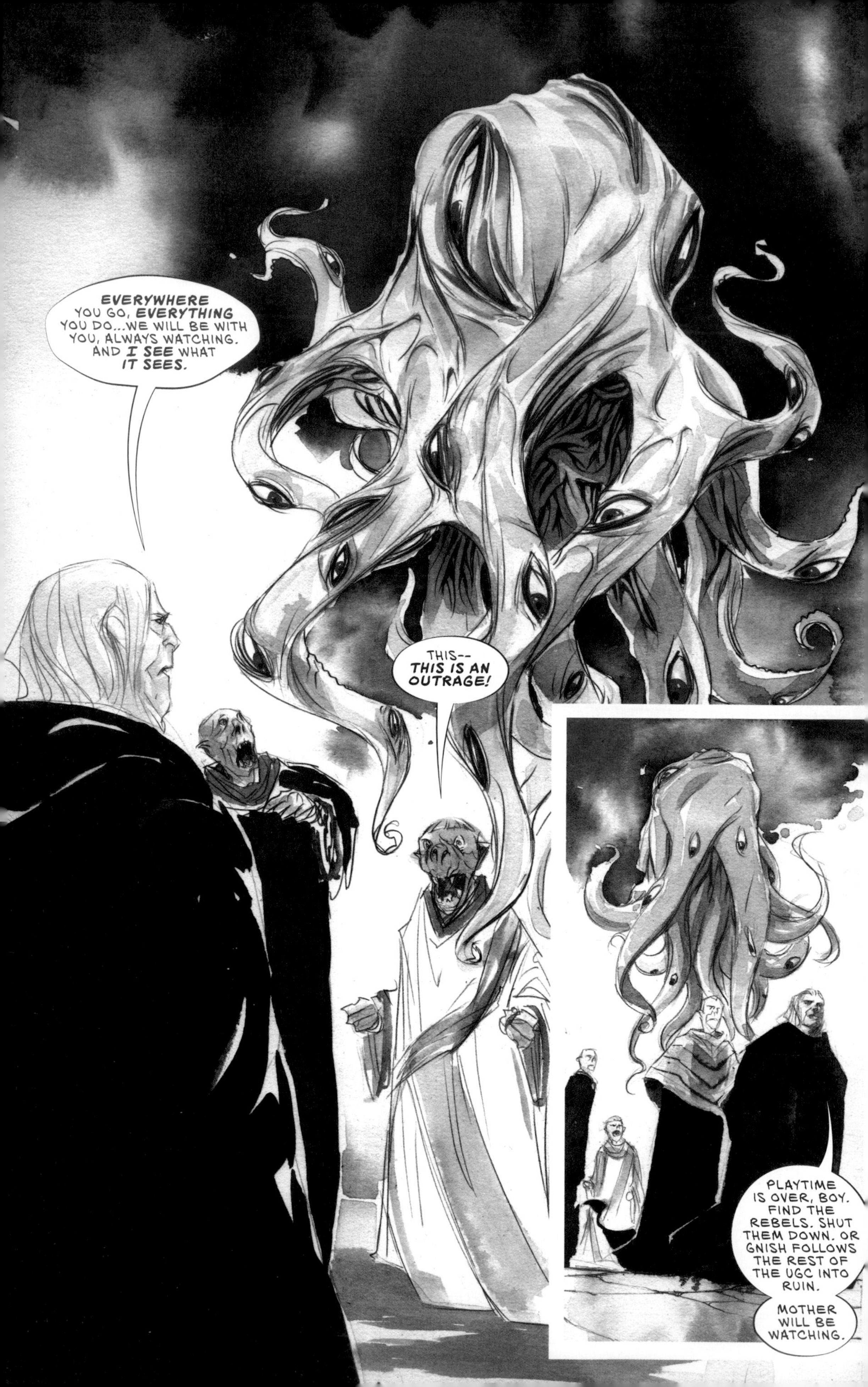
EVERYWHERE YOU GO, EVERYTHING YOU DO...WE WILL BE WITH YOU, ALWAYS WATCHING. AND I SEE WHAT IT SEES.
THIS-- THIS IS AN OUTRAGE!
PLAYTIME IS OVER, BOY. FIND THE REBELS. SHUT THEM DOWN. OR GNISH FOLLOWS THE REST OF THE UGC INTO RUIN.
MOTHER WILL BE WATCHING.

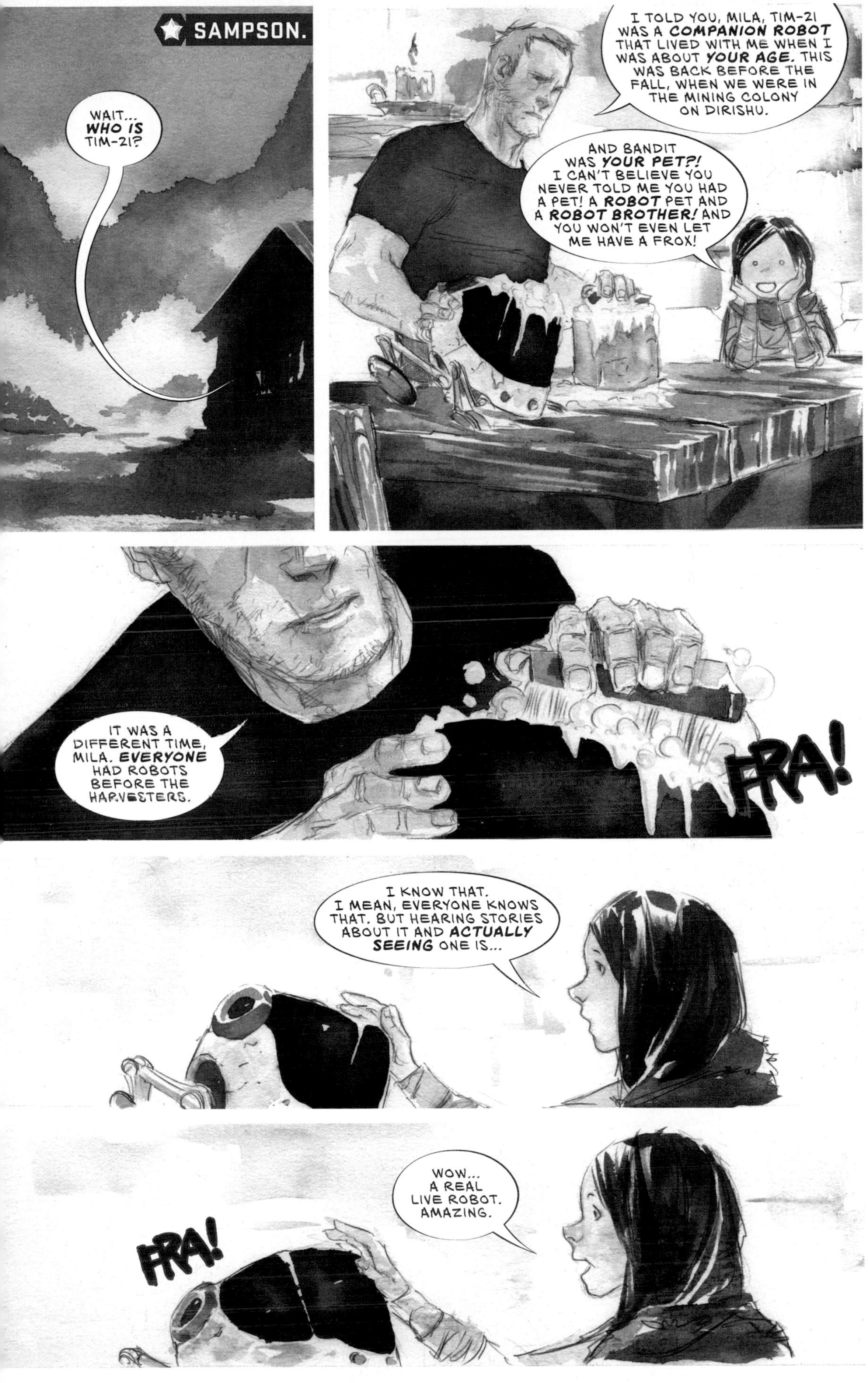
SAMPSON.
WAIT... WHO IS TIM-21?
I TOLD YOU, MILA, TIM-21 WAS A COMPANION ROBOT THAT LIVED WITH ME WHEN I WAS ABOUT YOUR AGE. THIS WAS BACK BEFORE THE FALL, WHEN WE WERE IN THE MINING COLONY ON DIRISHU.
AND BANDIT WAS YOUR PET?! I CAN'T BELIEVE YOU NEVER TOLD ME YOU HAD A PET! A ROBOT PET AND A ROBOT BROTHER! AND YOU WON'T EVEN LET ME HAVE A FROX!
IT WAS A DIFFERENT TIME, MILA. EVERYONE HAD ROBOTS BEFORE THE HARVESTERS.
FRA!
I KNOW THAT. I MEAN, EVERYONE KNOWS THAT. BUT HEARING STORIES ABOUT IT AND ACTUALLY SEEING ONE IS...
FRA!
WOW... A REAL LIVE ROBOT. AMAZING.

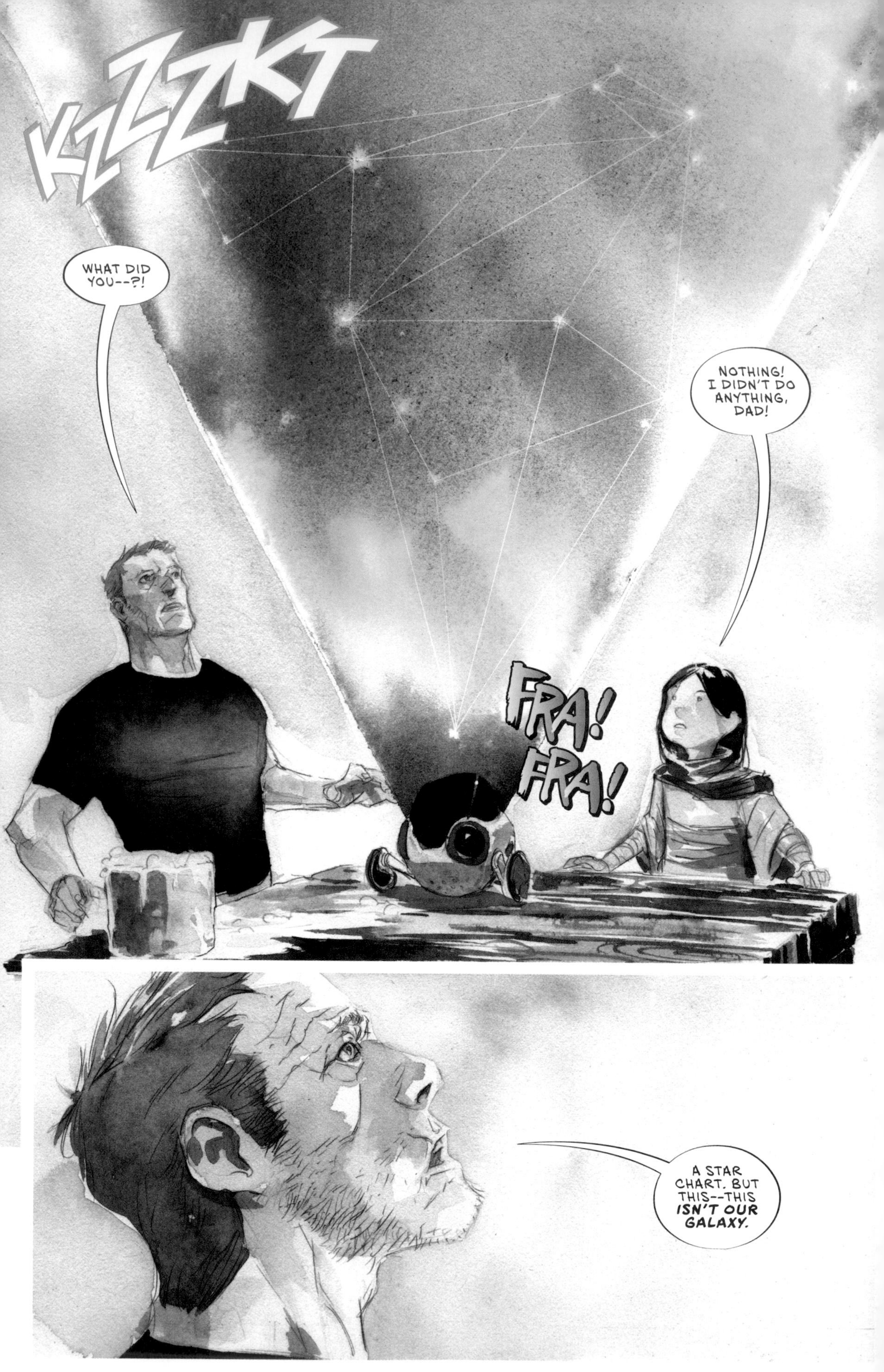
KZZZKT
WHAT DID YOU--?!
NOTHING! I DIDN'T DO ANYTHING, DAD!
FRA! FRA!
A STAR CHART. BUT THIS--THIS ISN'T OUR GALAXY.

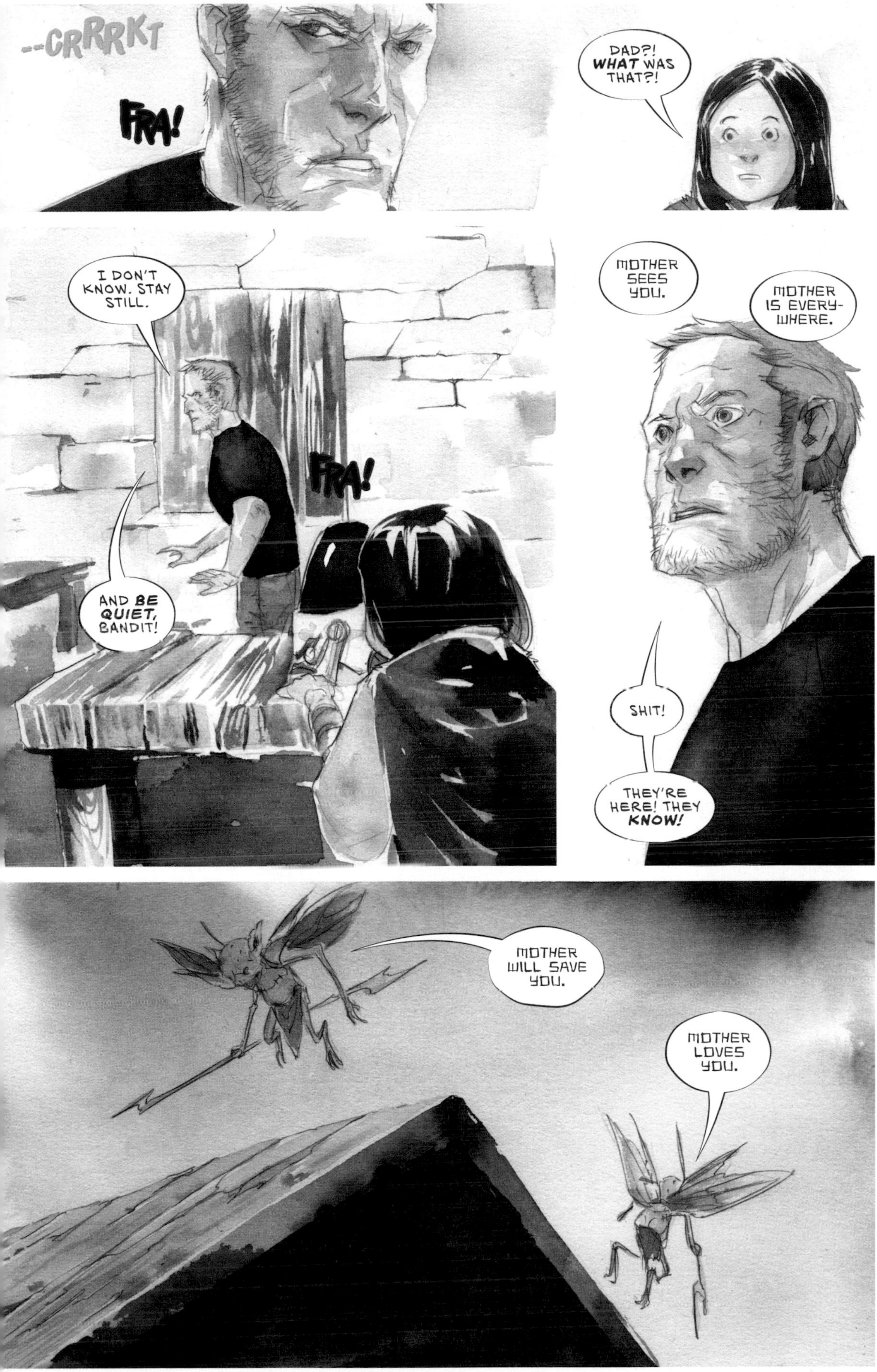
--CRRRKT
FRA!
DAD?! WHAT WAS THAT?!
I DON'T KNOW. STAY STILL.
AND BE QUIET, BANDIT!
FRA!
MOTHER SEES YOU.
MOTHER IS EVERY-WHERE.
SHIT!
THEY'RE HERE! THEY KNOW!
MOTHER WILL SAVE YOU.
MOTHER LOVES YOU.

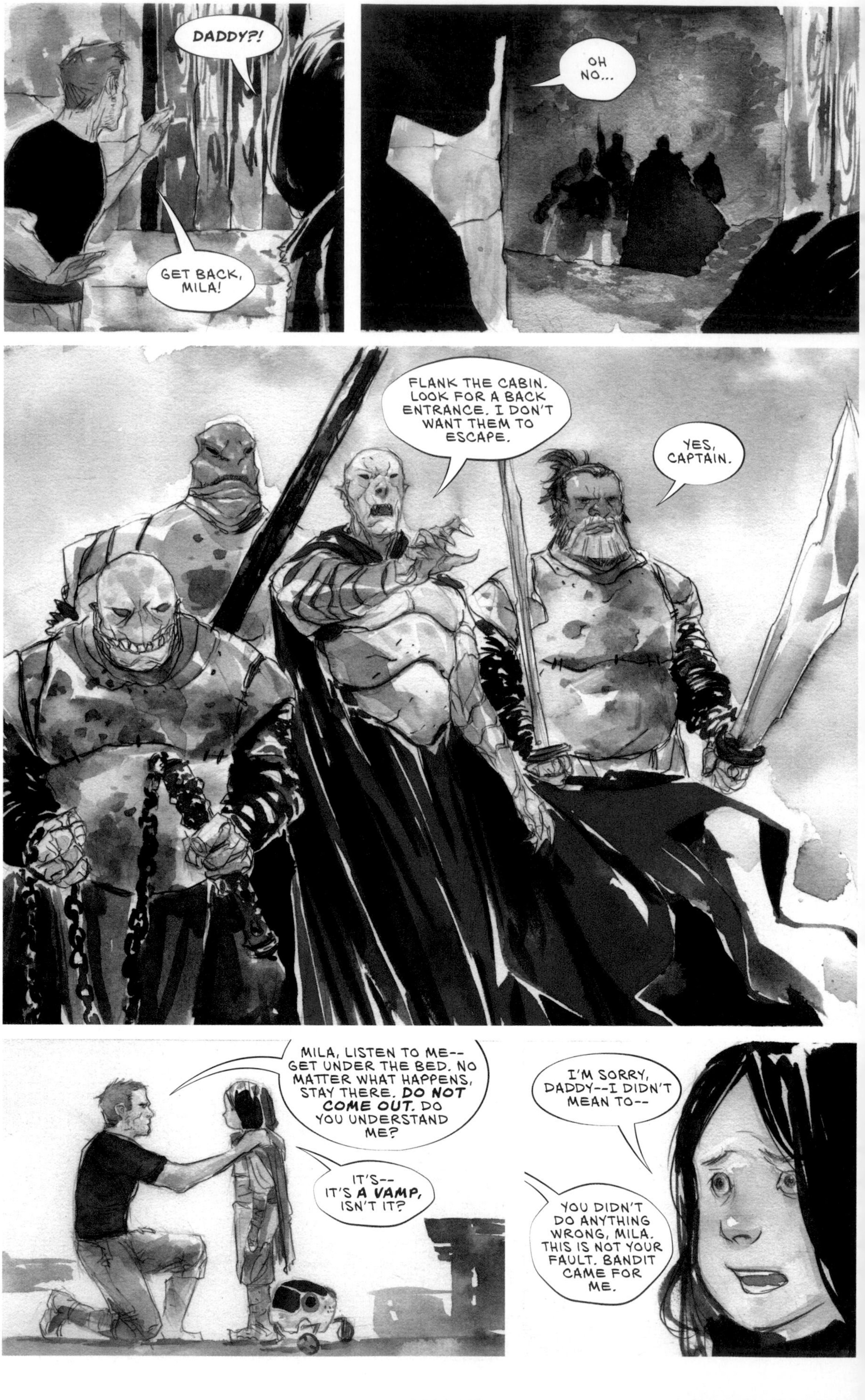
DADDY?!
GET BACK, MILA!
OH NO...
FLANK THE CABIN. LOOK FOR A BACK ENTRANCE. I DON'T WANT THEM TO ESCAPE.
YES, CAPTAIN.
MILA, LISTEN TO ME-- GET UNDER THE BED. NO MATTER WHAT HAPPENS, STAY THERE. **DO NOT COME OUT.** DO YOU UNDERSTAND ME?
IT'S-- IT'S **A VAMP,** ISN'T IT?
I'M SORRY, DADDY--I DIDN'T MEAN TO--
YOU DIDN'T DO ANYTHING WRONG, MILA. THIS IS NOT YOUR FAULT. BANDIT CAME FOR ME.

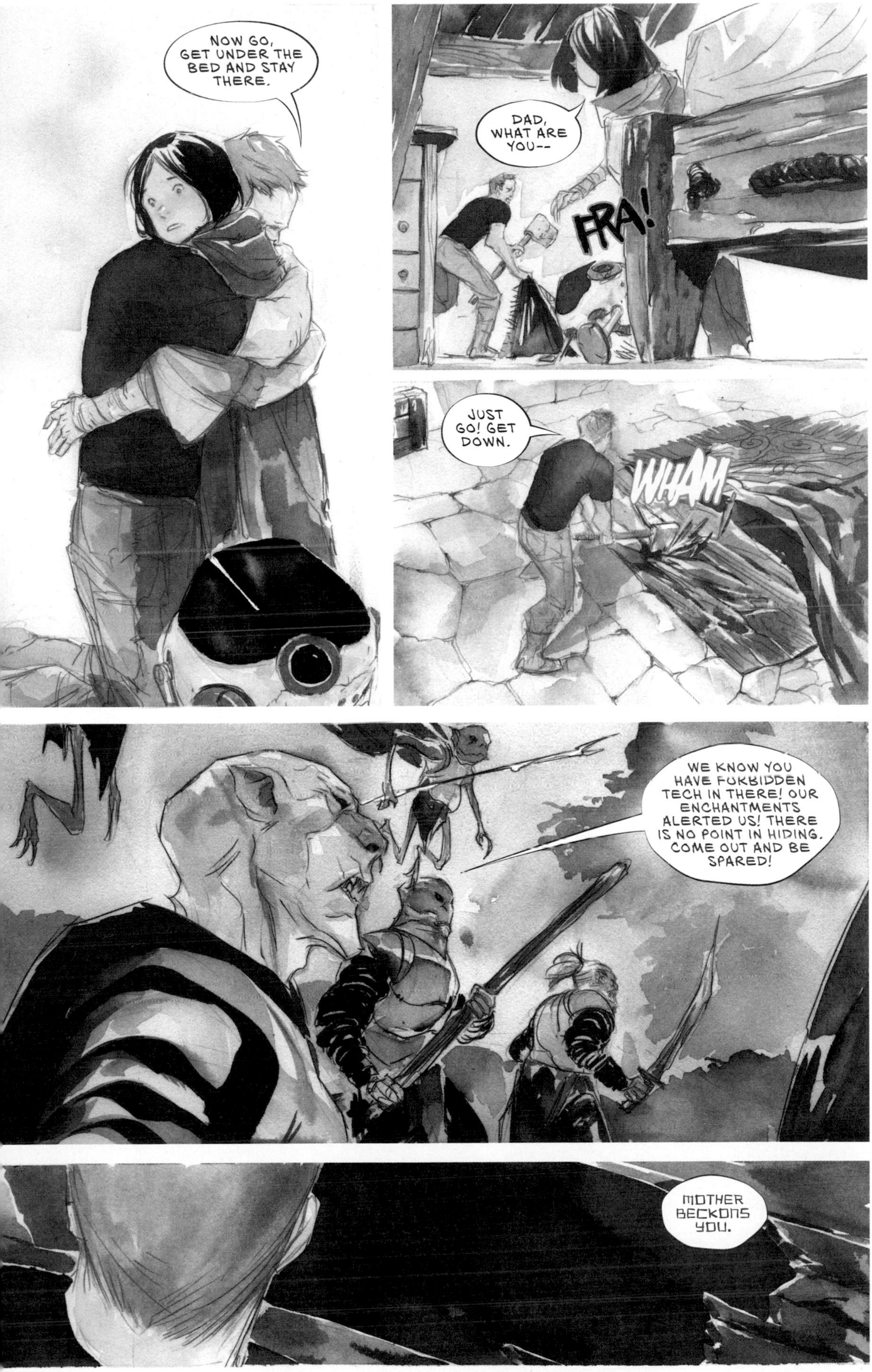
NOW GO, GET UNDER THE BED AND STAY THERE.
DAD, WHAT ARE YOU--
FRA!
JUST GO! GET DOWN.
WHAM
WE KNOW YOU HAVE FORBIDDEN TECH IN THERE! OUR ENCHANTMENTS ALERTED US! THERE IS NO POINT IN HIDING. COME OUT AND BE SPARED!
MOTHER BECKONS YOU.

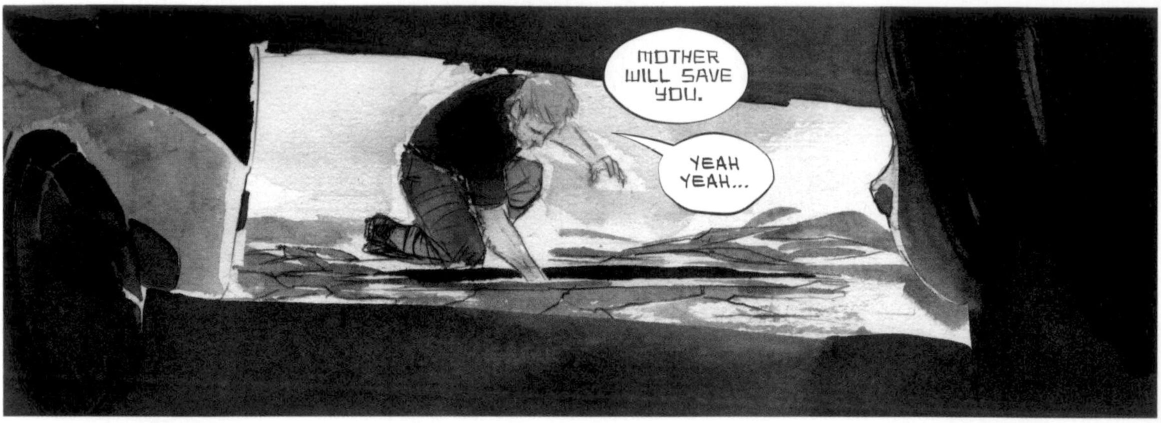
MOTHER WILL SAVE YOU.
YEAH YEAH...

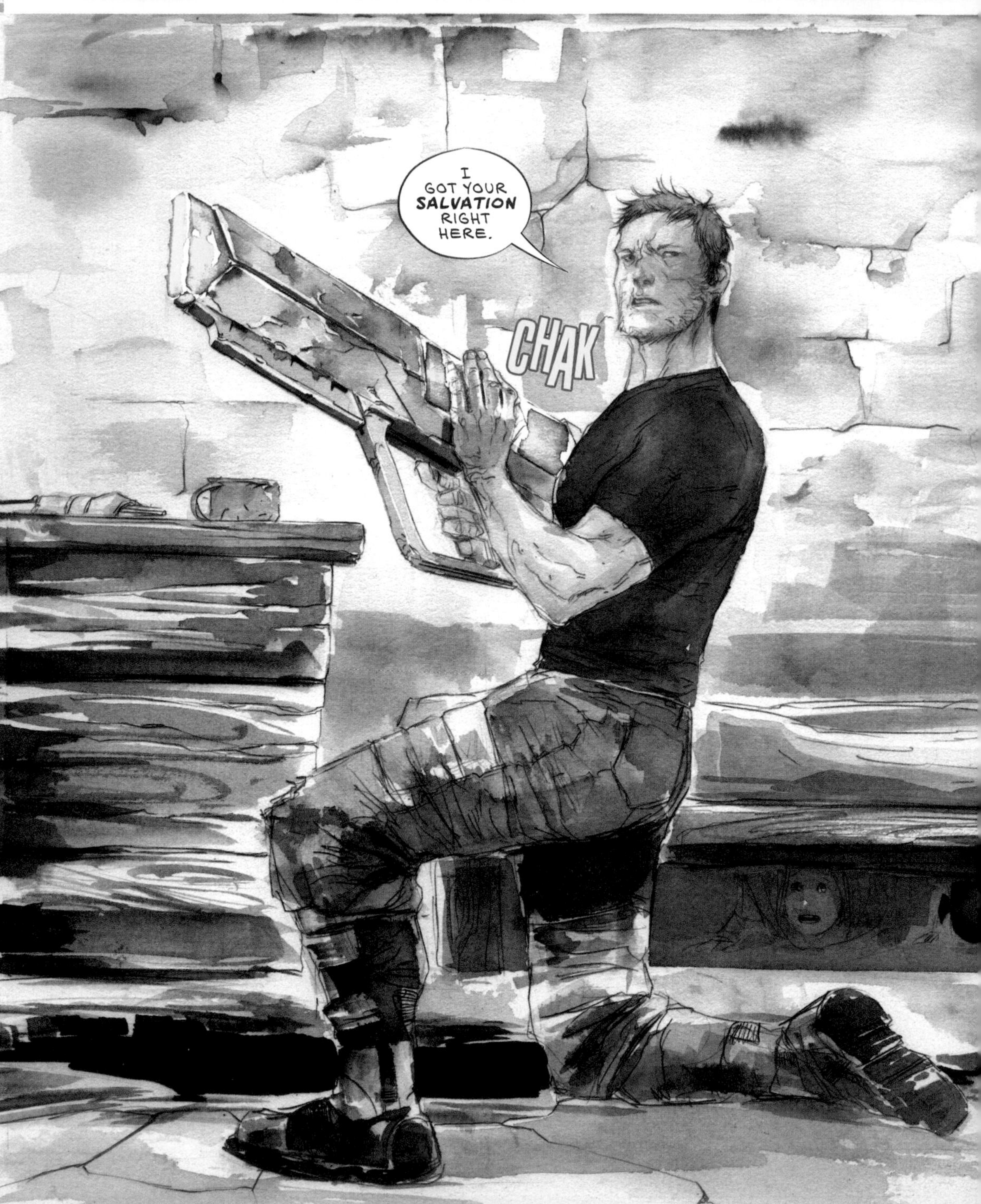
I GOT YOUR **SALVATION** RIGHT HERE.
CHAK

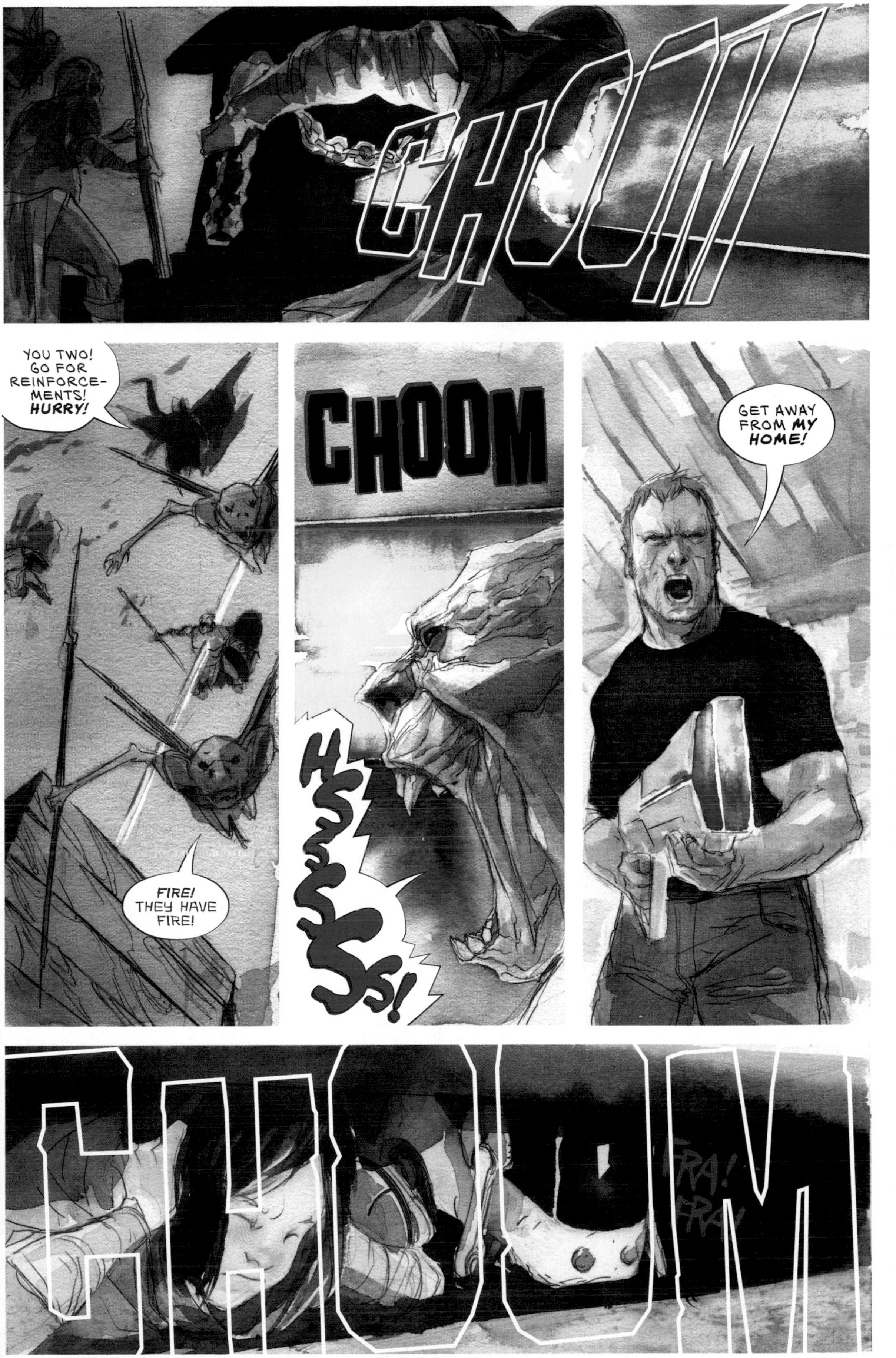
CHOOM
YOU TWO! GO FOR REINFORCE-MENTS! HURRY!
FIRE! THEY HAVE FIRE!
CHOOM
HSSSSSS!
GET AWAY FROM MY HOME!
CHOOM
FRA!

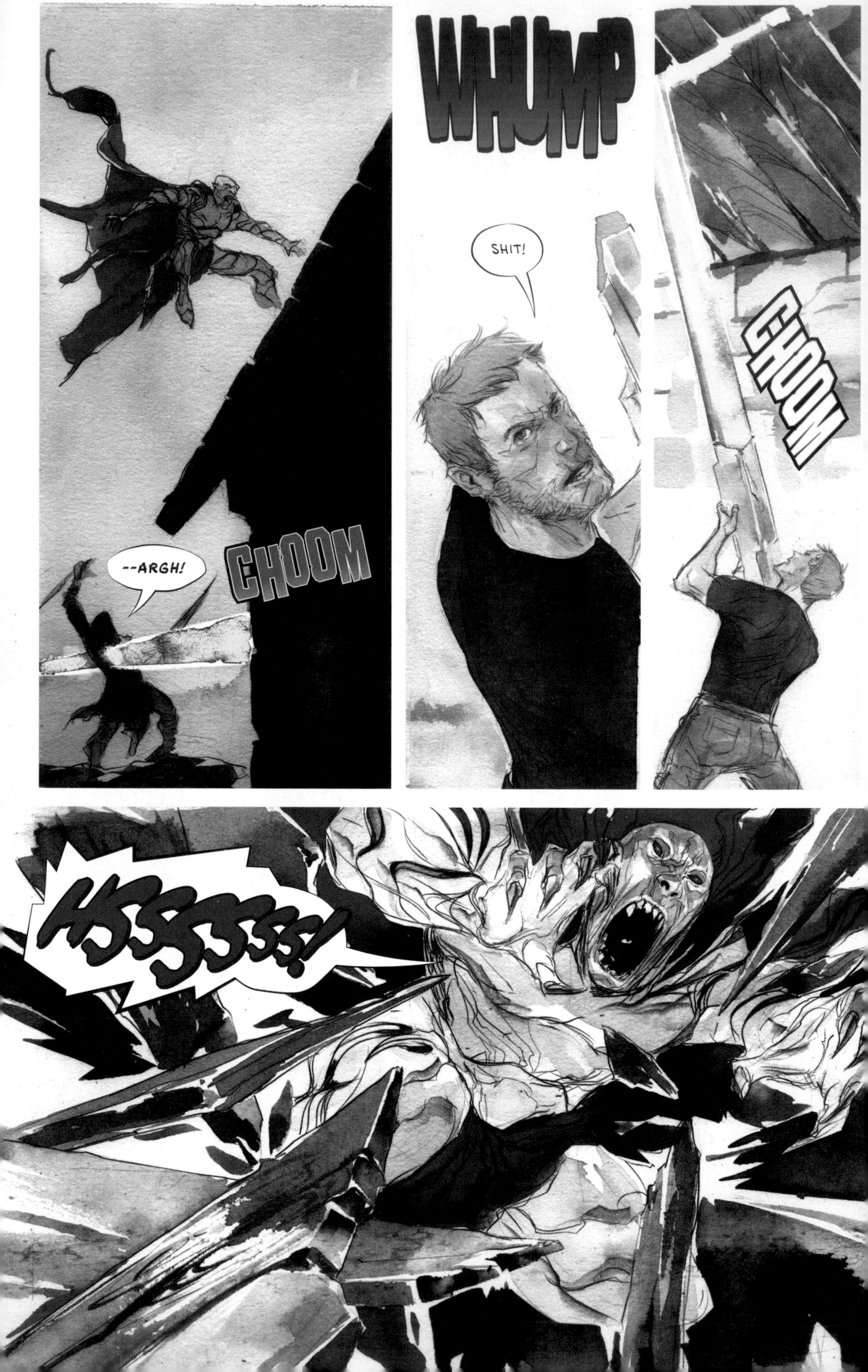
--ARGH!
CHOOM
WHUMP
SHIT!
CHOOM
HSSSSSS!

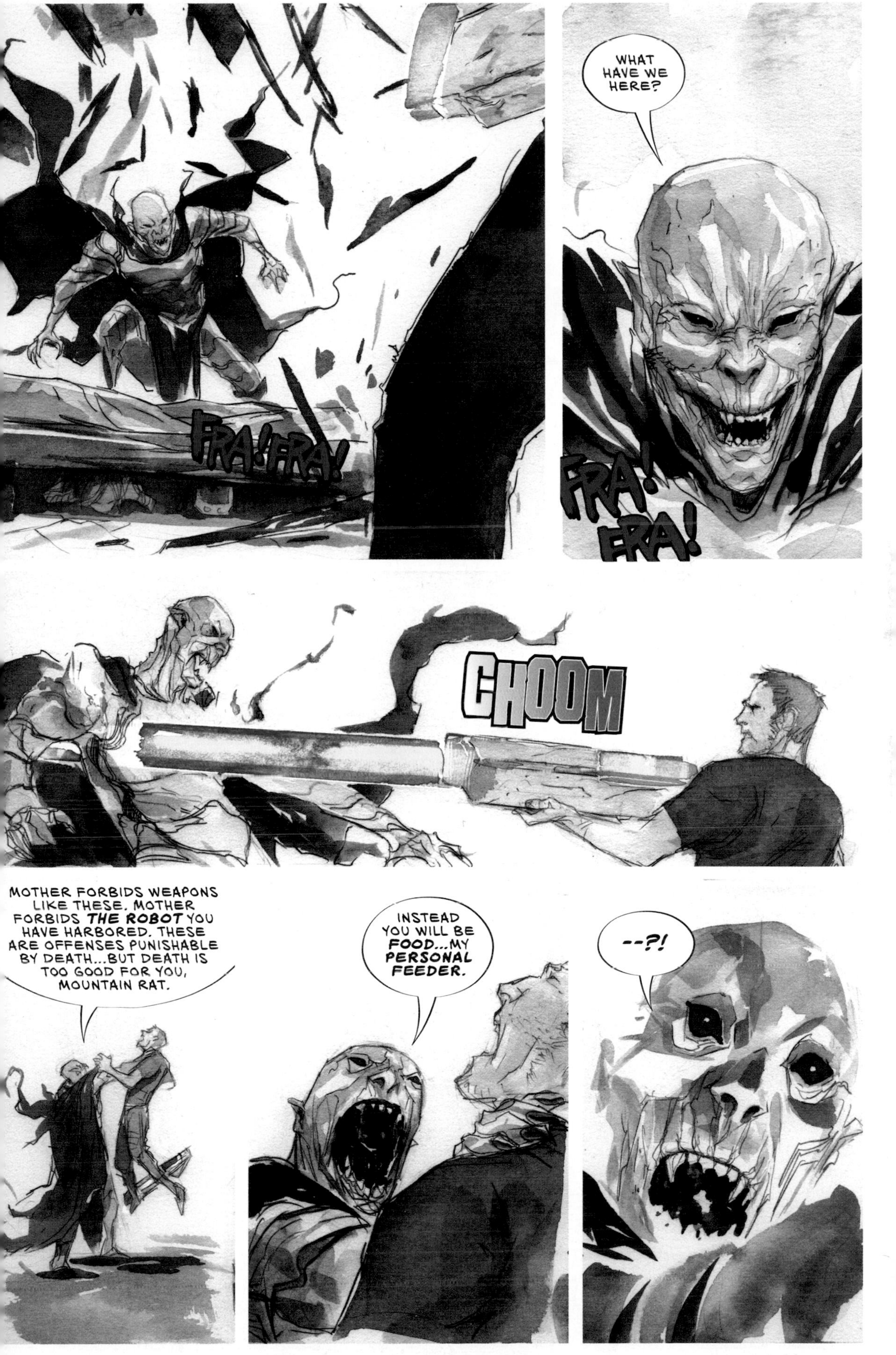
FRA! FRA!
WHAT HAVE WE HERE?
FRA! FRA!
CHOOM
MOTHER FORBIDS WEAPONS LIKE THESE. MOTHER FORBIDS THE ROBOT YOU HAVE HARBORED. THESE ARE OFFENSES PUNISHABLE BY DEATH...BUT DEATH IS TOO GOOD FOR YOU, MOUNTAIN RAT.
INSTEAD YOU WILL BE FOOD...MY PERSONAL FEEDER.
--?!

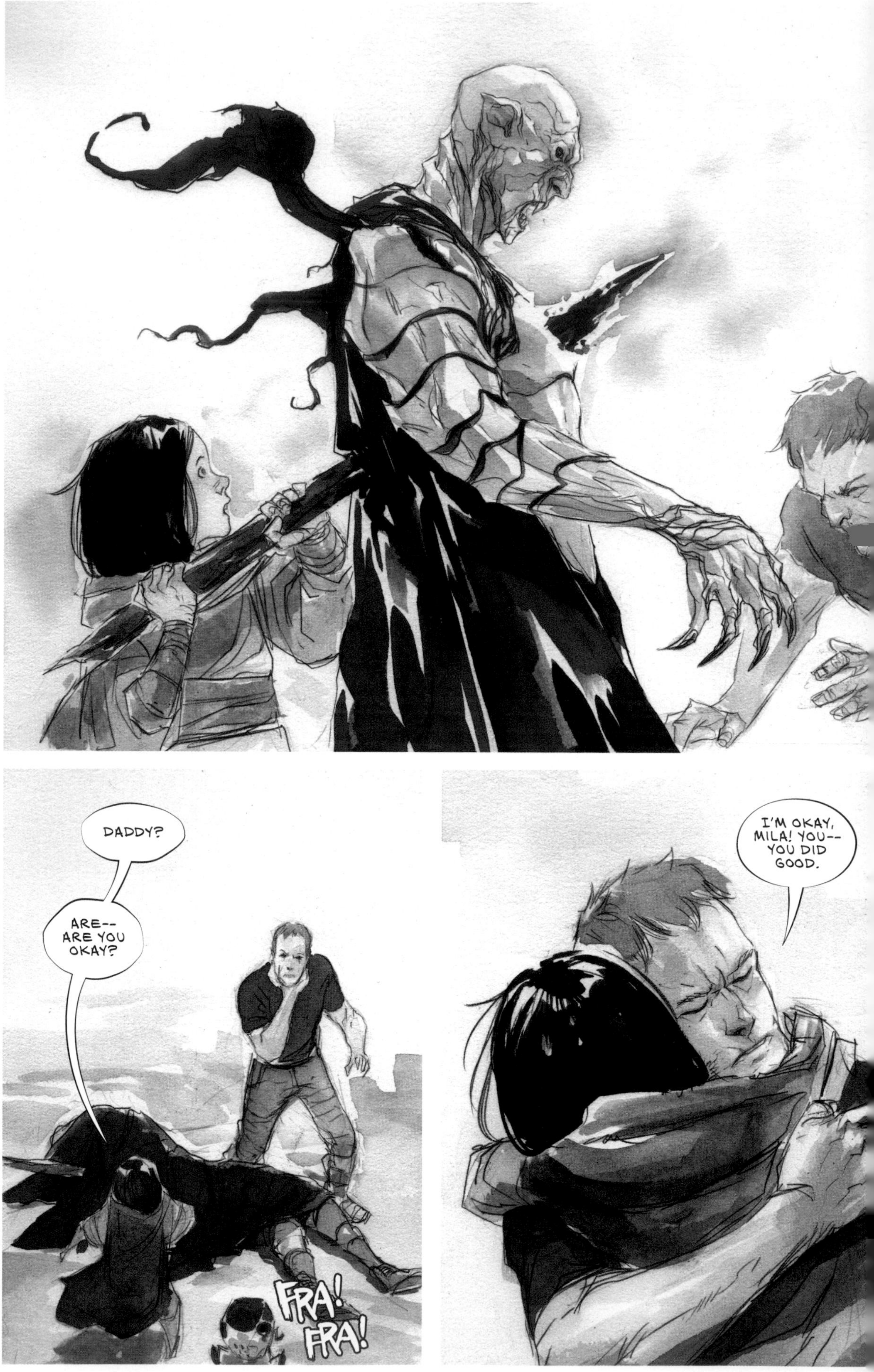
DADDY?
ARE-- ARE YOU OKAY?
FRA! FRA!
I'M OKAY, MILA! YOU-- YOU DID GOOD.

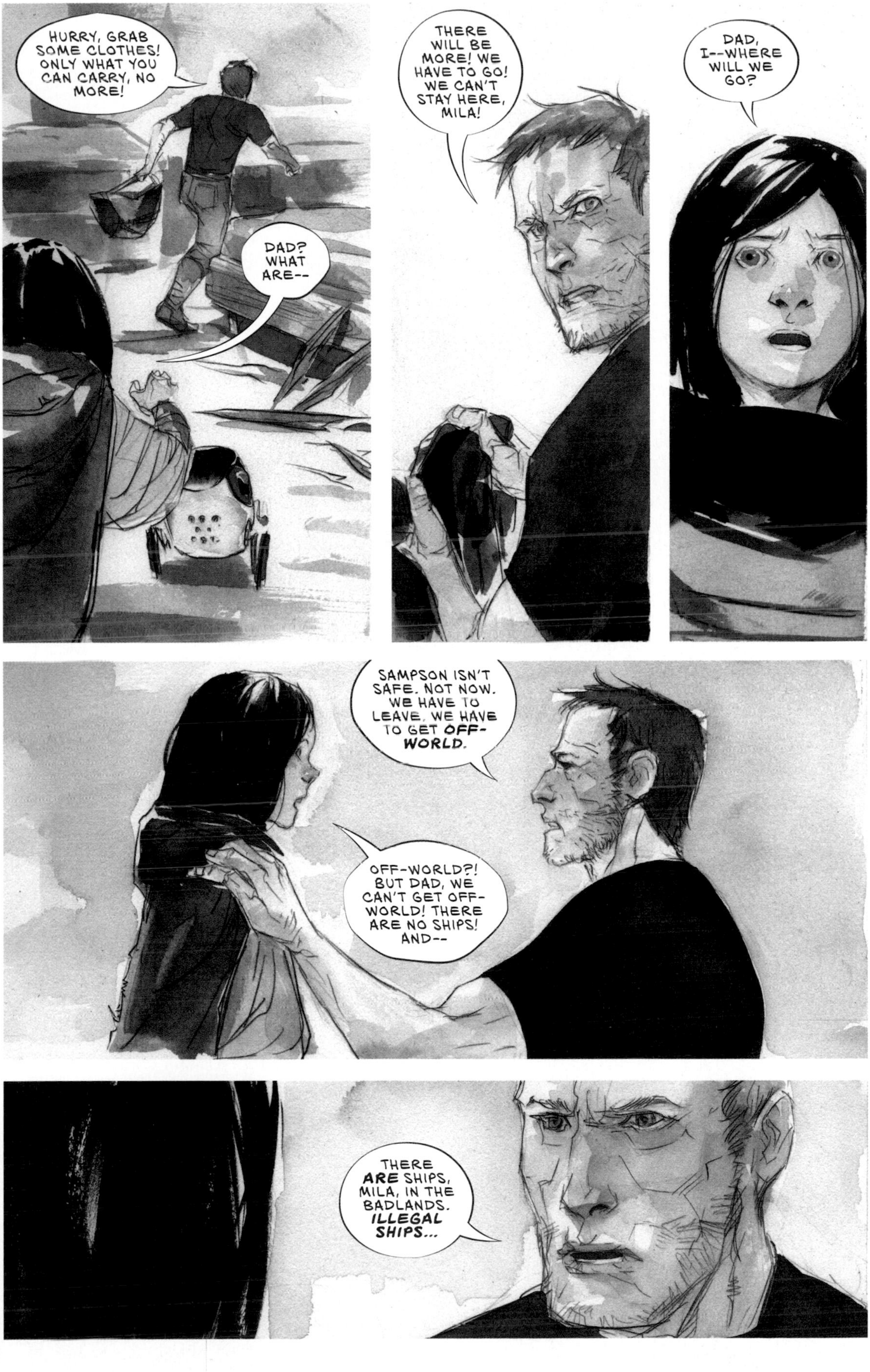
HURRY, GRAB SOME CLOTHES! ONLY WHAT YOU CAN CARRY, NO MORE!
DAD? WHAT ARE--
THERE WILL BE MORE! WE HAVE TO GO! WE CAN'T STAY HERE, MILA!
DAD, I--WHERE WILL WE GO?
SAMPSON ISN'T SAFE. NOT NOW. WE HAVE TO LEAVE. WE HAVE TO GET **OFF-WORLD**.
OFF-WORLD?! BUT DAD, WE CAN'T GET OFF-WORLD! THERE ARE NO SHIPS! AND--
THERE **ARE** SHIPS, MILA, IN THE BADLANDS. **ILLEGAL SHIPS...**

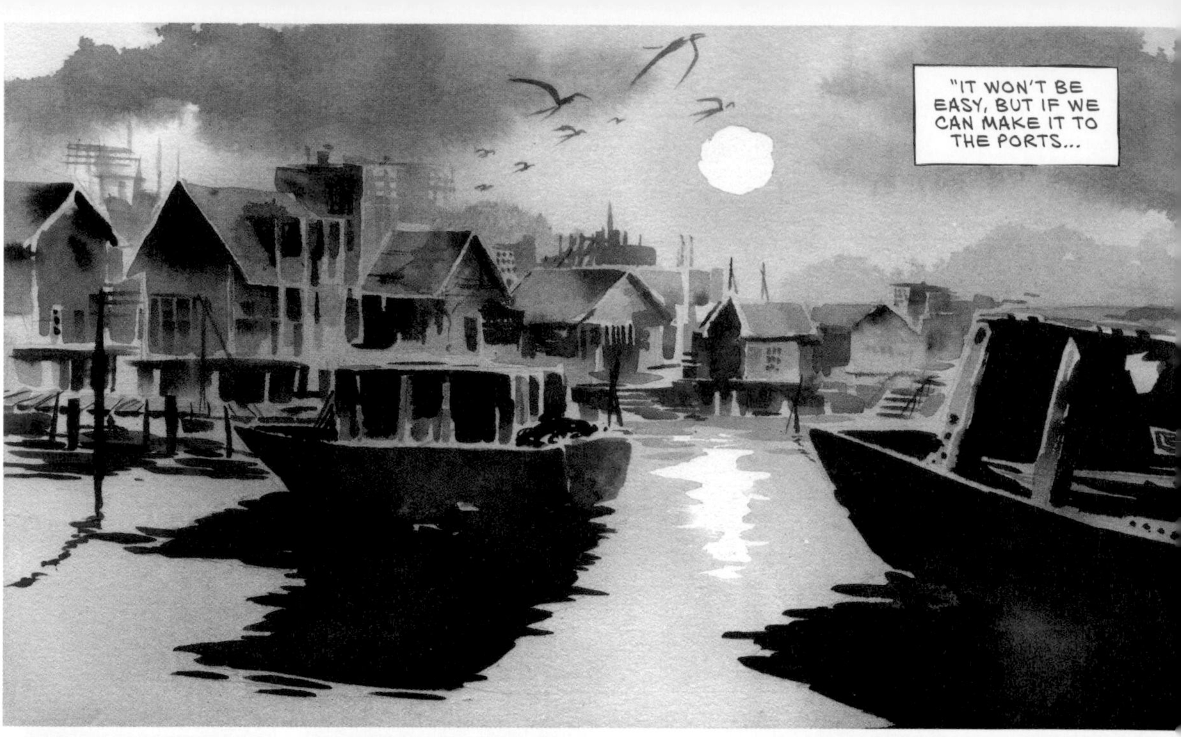
"IT WON'T BE EASY, BUT IF WE CAN MAKE IT TO THE PORTS...

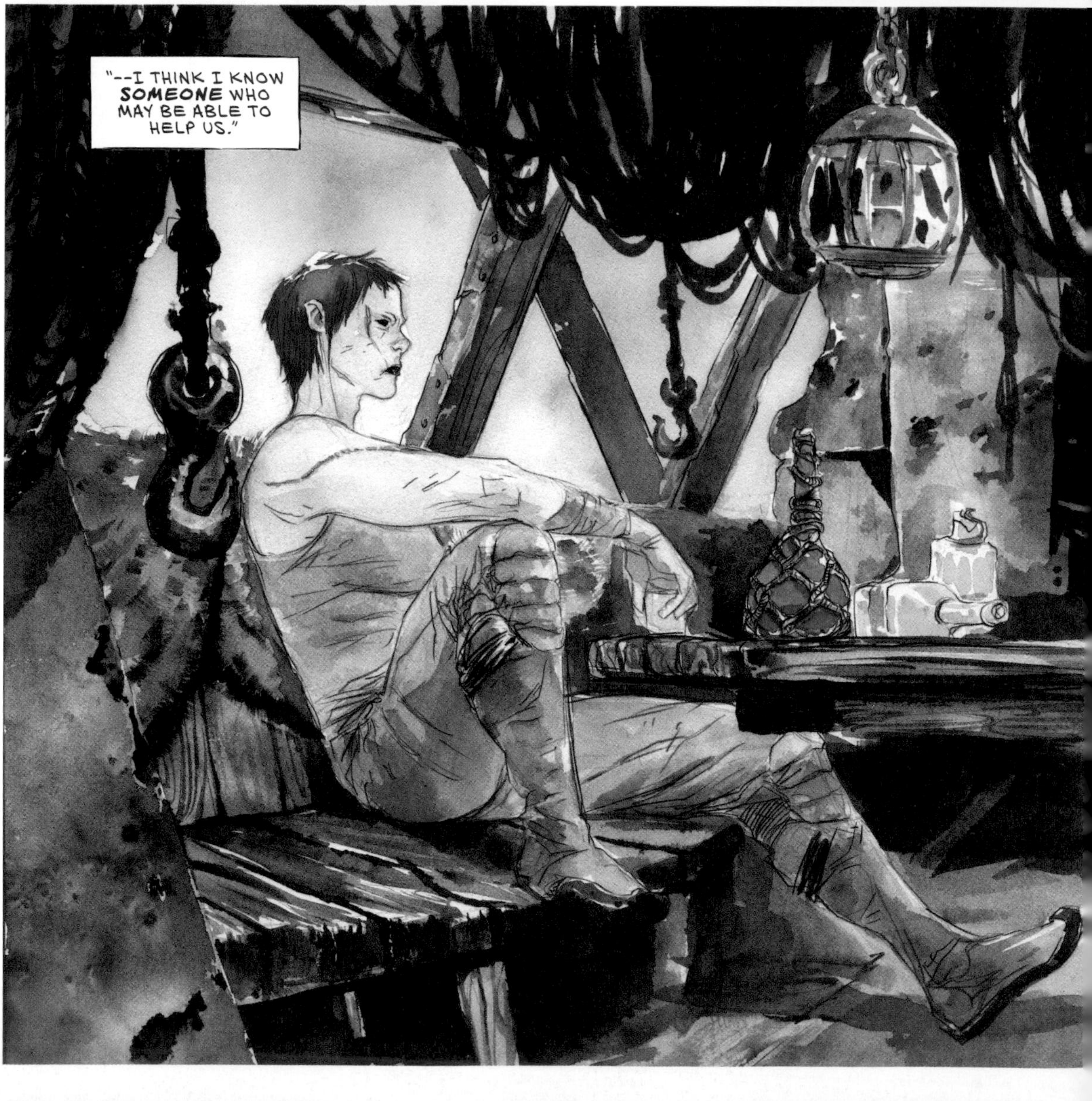
"--I THINK I KNOW SOMEONE WHO MAY BE ABLE TO HELP US."

3

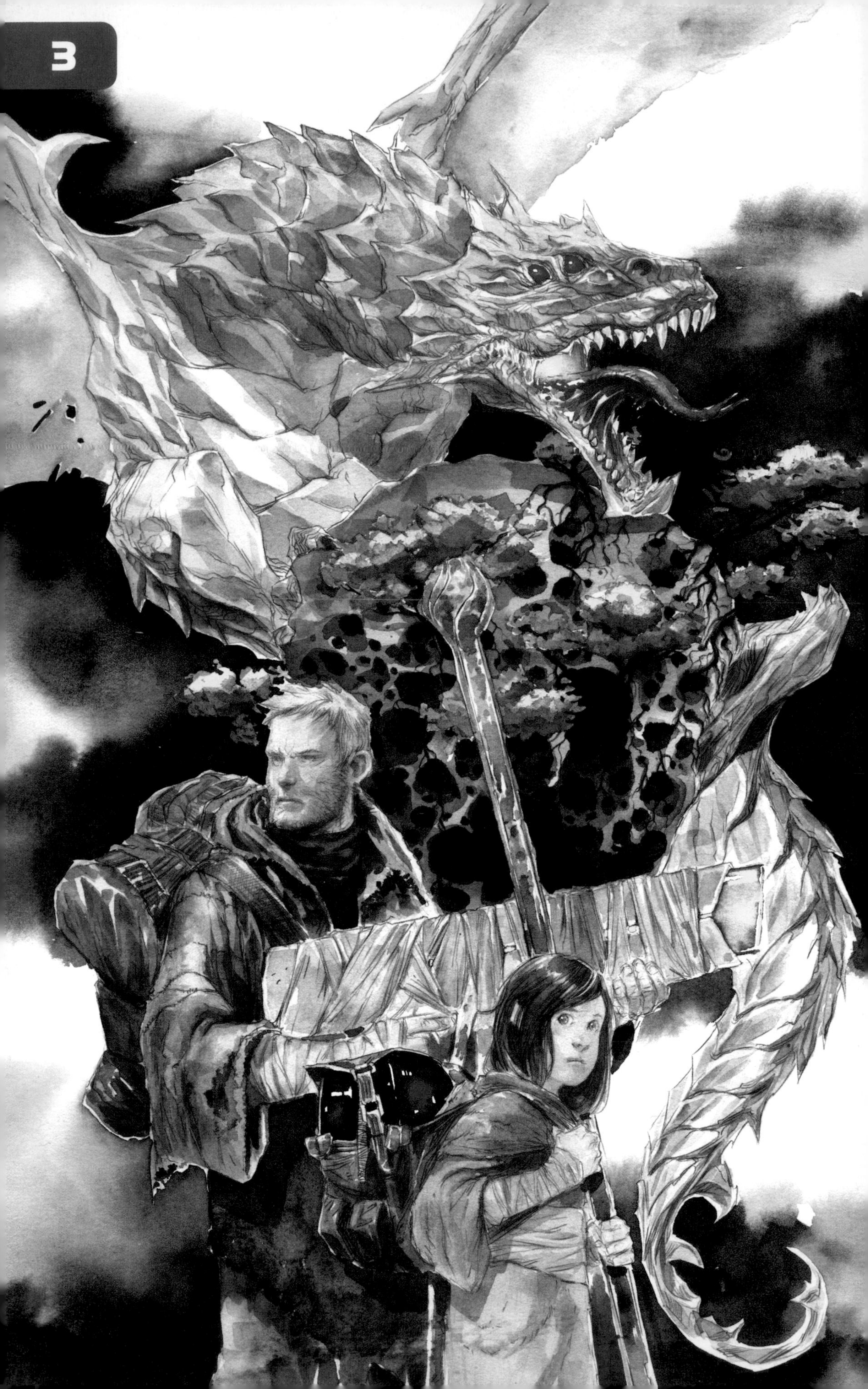

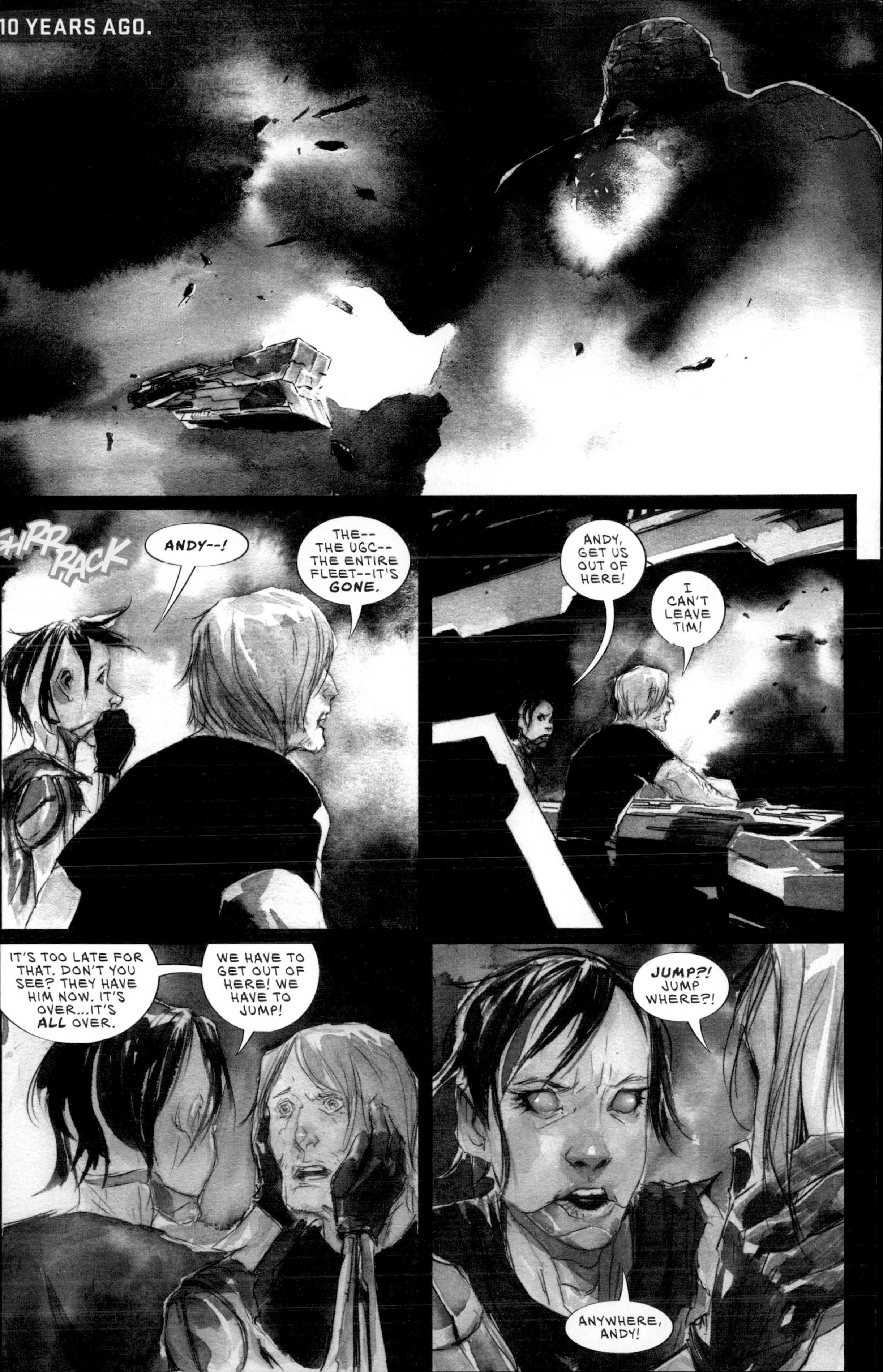
10 YEARS AGO.
SHRRRACK
ANDY--!
THE-- THE UGC-- THE ENTIRE FLEET--IT'S GONE.
ANDY, GET US OUT OF HERE!
I CAN'T LEAVE TIM!
IT'S TOO LATE FOR THAT. DON'T YOU SEE? THEY HAVE HIM NOW. IT'S OVER...IT'S ALL OVER.
WE HAVE TO GET OUT OF HERE! WE HAVE TO JUMP!
JUMP?! JUMP WHERE?!
ANYWHERE, ANDY!

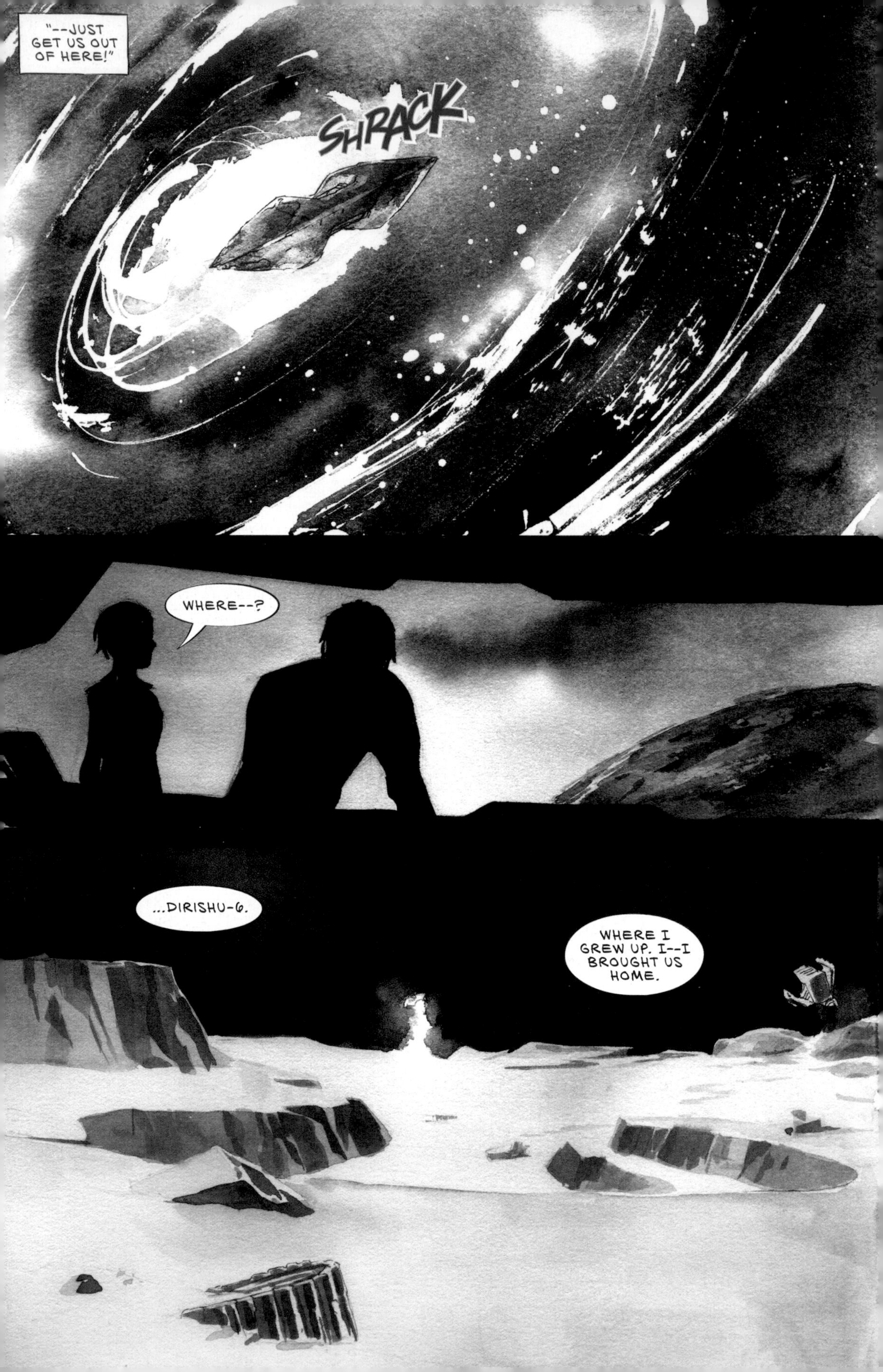
"--JUST GET US OUT OF HERE!"
SHRACK
WHERE--?
...DIRISHU-6.
WHERE I GREW UP. I--I BROUGHT US HOME.

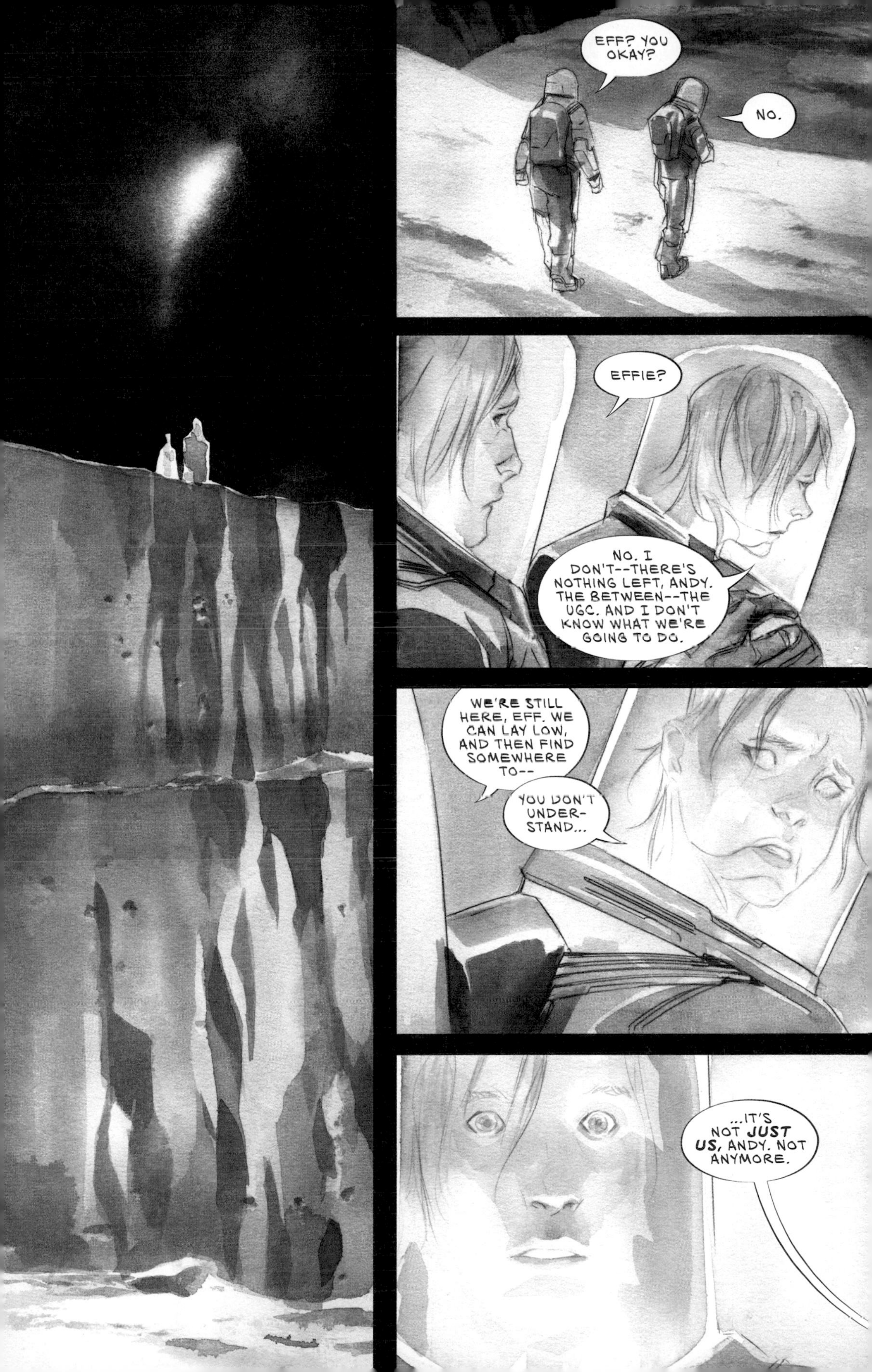
EFF? YOU OKAY?
NO.
EFFIE?
NO. I DON'T--THERE'S NOTHING LEFT, ANDY. THE BETWEEN--THE UGC. AND I DON'T KNOW WHAT WE'RE GOING TO DO.
WE'RE STILL HERE, EFF. WE CAN LAY LOW, AND THEN FIND SOMEWHERE TO--
YOU DON'T UNDER-STAND...
...IT'S NOT **JUST US**, ANDY. NOT ANYMORE.

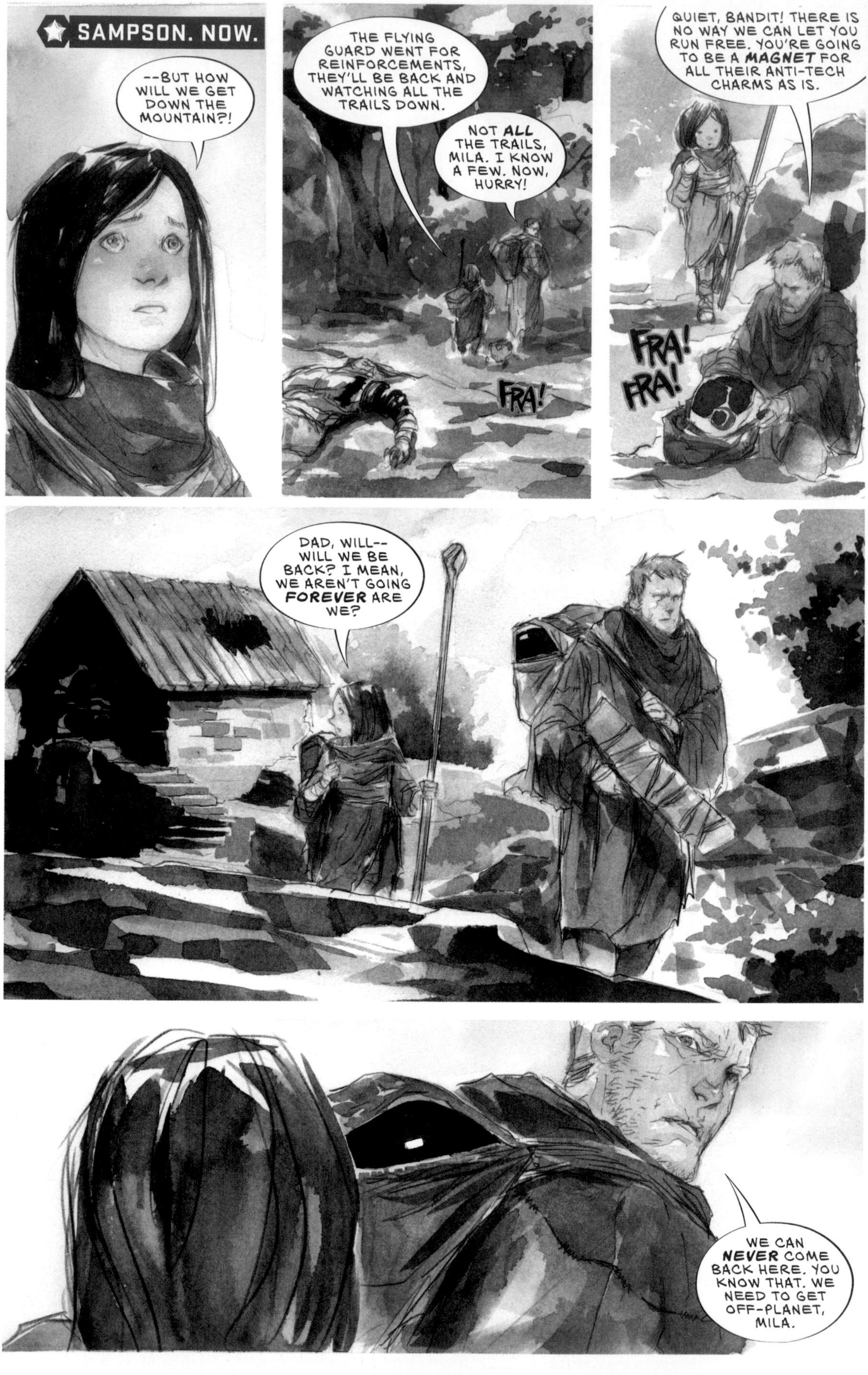
SAMPSON. NOW.
--BUT HOW WILL WE GET DOWN THE MOUNTAIN?!
THE FLYING GUARD WENT FOR REINFORCEMENTS, THEY'LL BE BACK AND WATCHING ALL THE TRAILS DOWN.
NOT ALL THE TRAILS, MILA. I KNOW A FEW. NOW, HURRY!
FRA!
QUIET, BANDIT! THERE IS NO WAY WE CAN LET YOU RUN FREE. YOU'RE GOING TO BE A MAGNET FOR ALL THEIR ANTI-TECH CHARMS AS IS.
FRA! FRA!
DAD, WILL-- WILL WE BE BACK? I MEAN, WE AREN'T GOING FOREVER ARE WE?
WE CAN NEVER COME BACK HERE. YOU KNOW THAT. WE NEED TO GET OFF-PLANET, MILA.

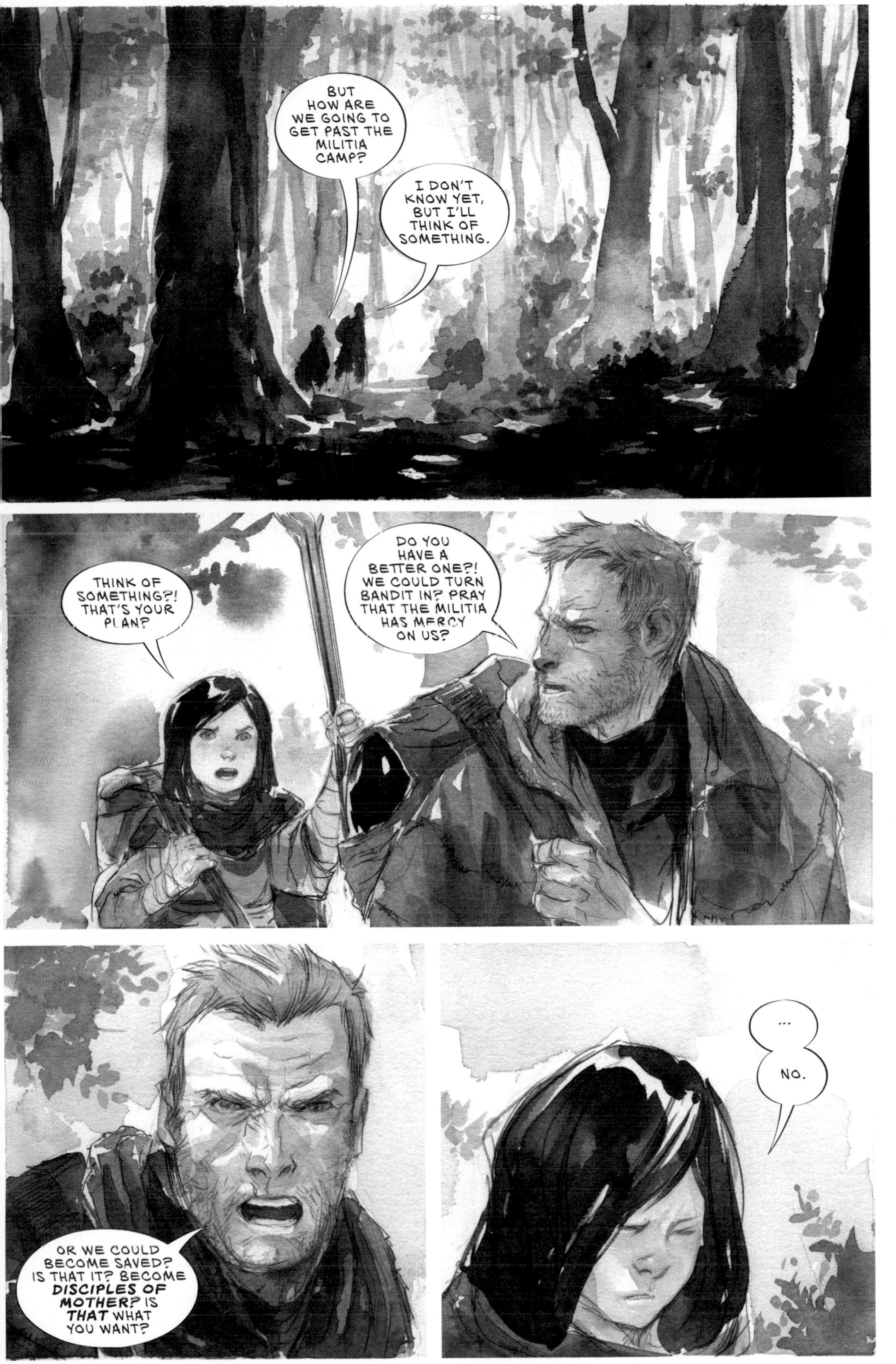
BUT HOW ARE WE GOING TO GET PAST THE MILITIA CAMP?
I DON'T KNOW YET, BUT I'LL THINK OF SOMETHING.
THINK OF SOMETHING?! THAT'S YOUR PLAN?
DO YOU HAVE A BETTER ONE?! WE COULD TURN BANDIT IN? PRAY THAT THE MILITIA HAS MERCY ON US?
OR WE COULD BECOME SAVED? IS THAT IT? BECOME DISCIPLES OF MOTHER? IS THAT WHAT YOU WANT?
...
NO.

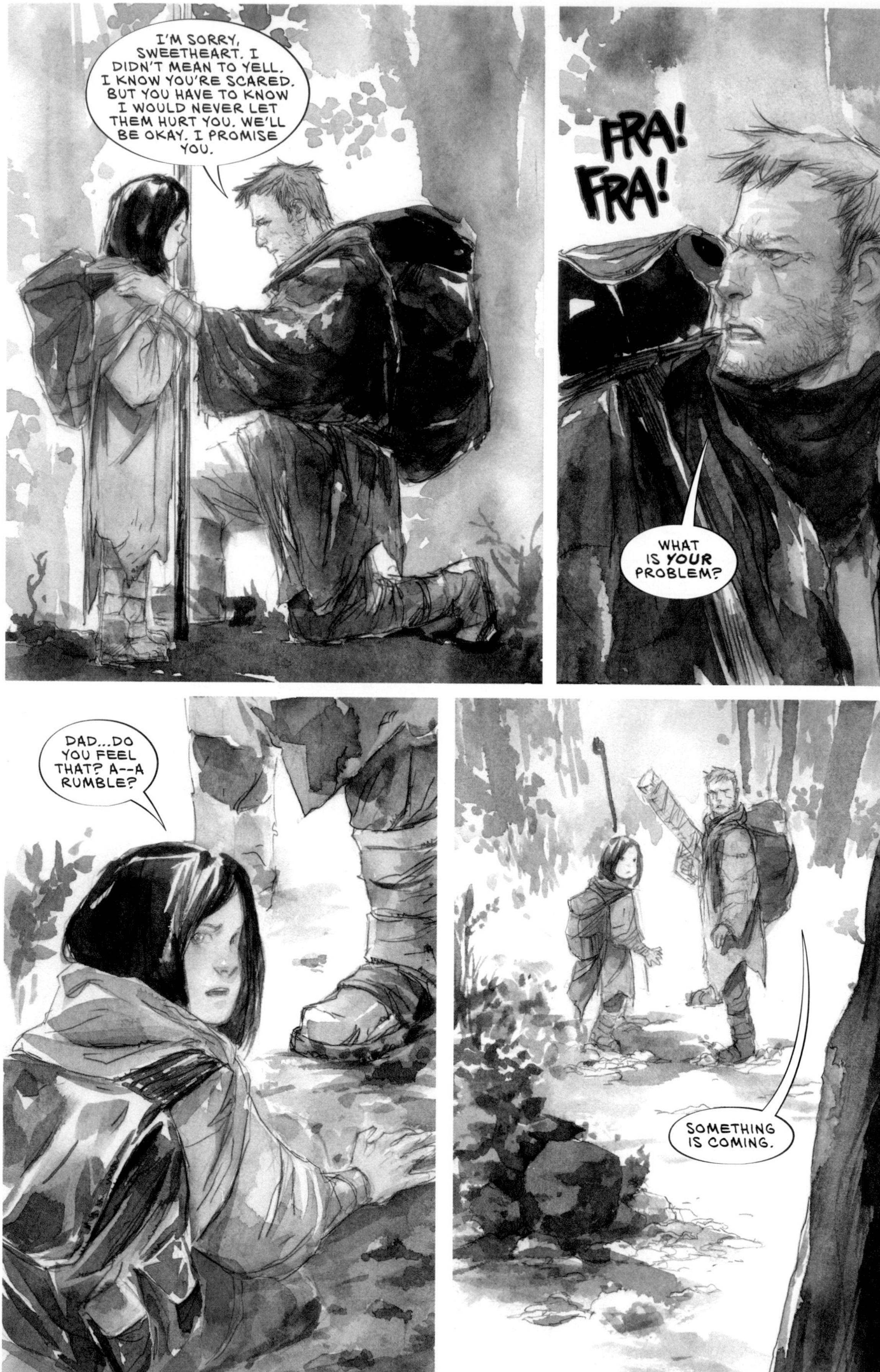
I'M SORRY, SWEETHEART. I DIDN'T MEAN TO YELL. I KNOW YOU'RE SCARED. BUT YOU HAVE TO KNOW I WOULD NEVER LET THEM HURT YOU. WE'LL BE OKAY. I PROMISE YOU.
FRA! FRA!
WHAT IS **YOUR** PROBLEM?
DAD...DO YOU FEEL THAT? A--A RUMBLE?
SOMETHING IS COMING.

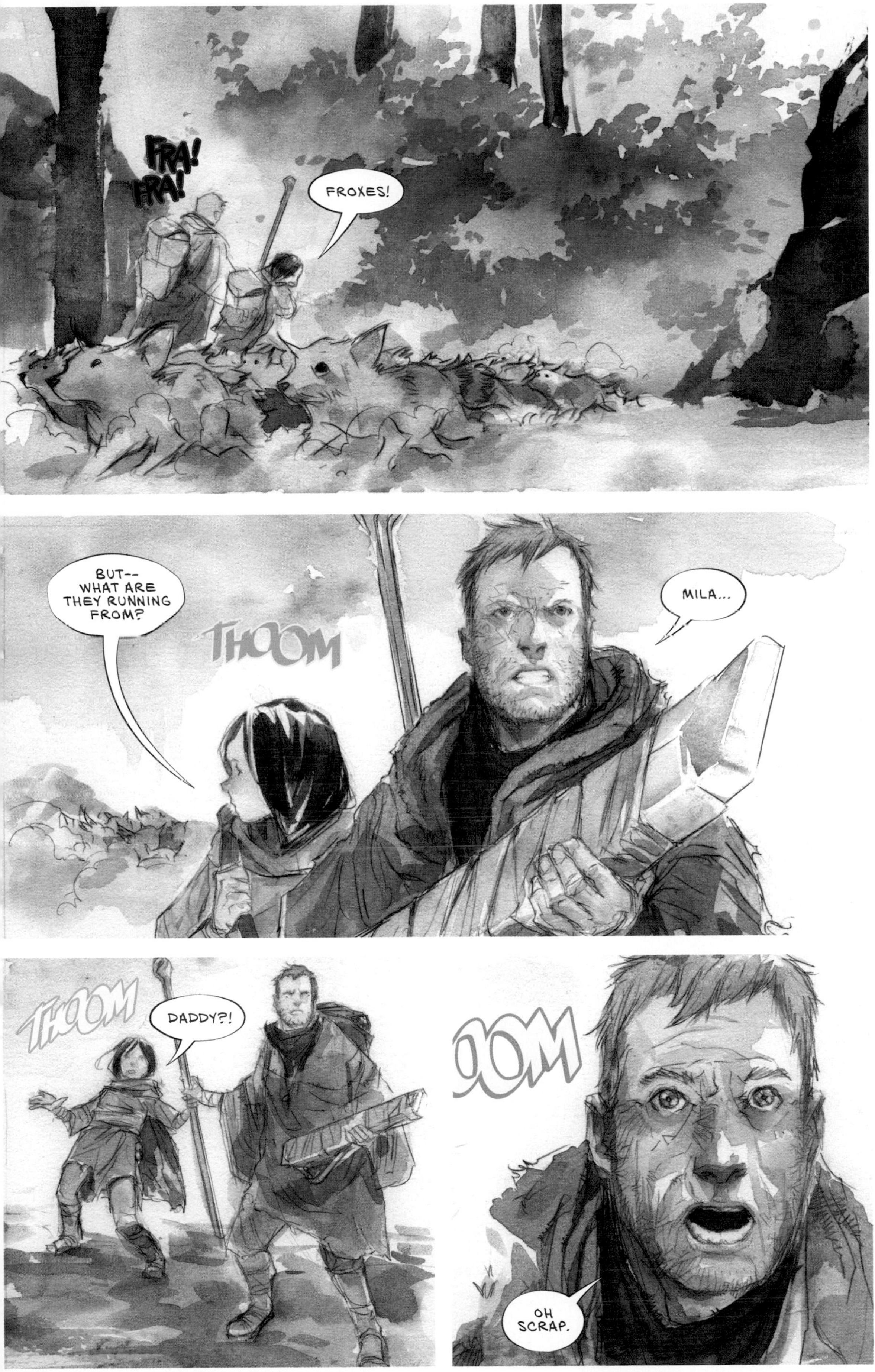
FRA!
FRA!
FROXES!
BUT-- WHAT ARE THEY RUNNING FROM?
THOOM
MILA...
THOOM
DADDY?!
OOM
OH SCRAP.

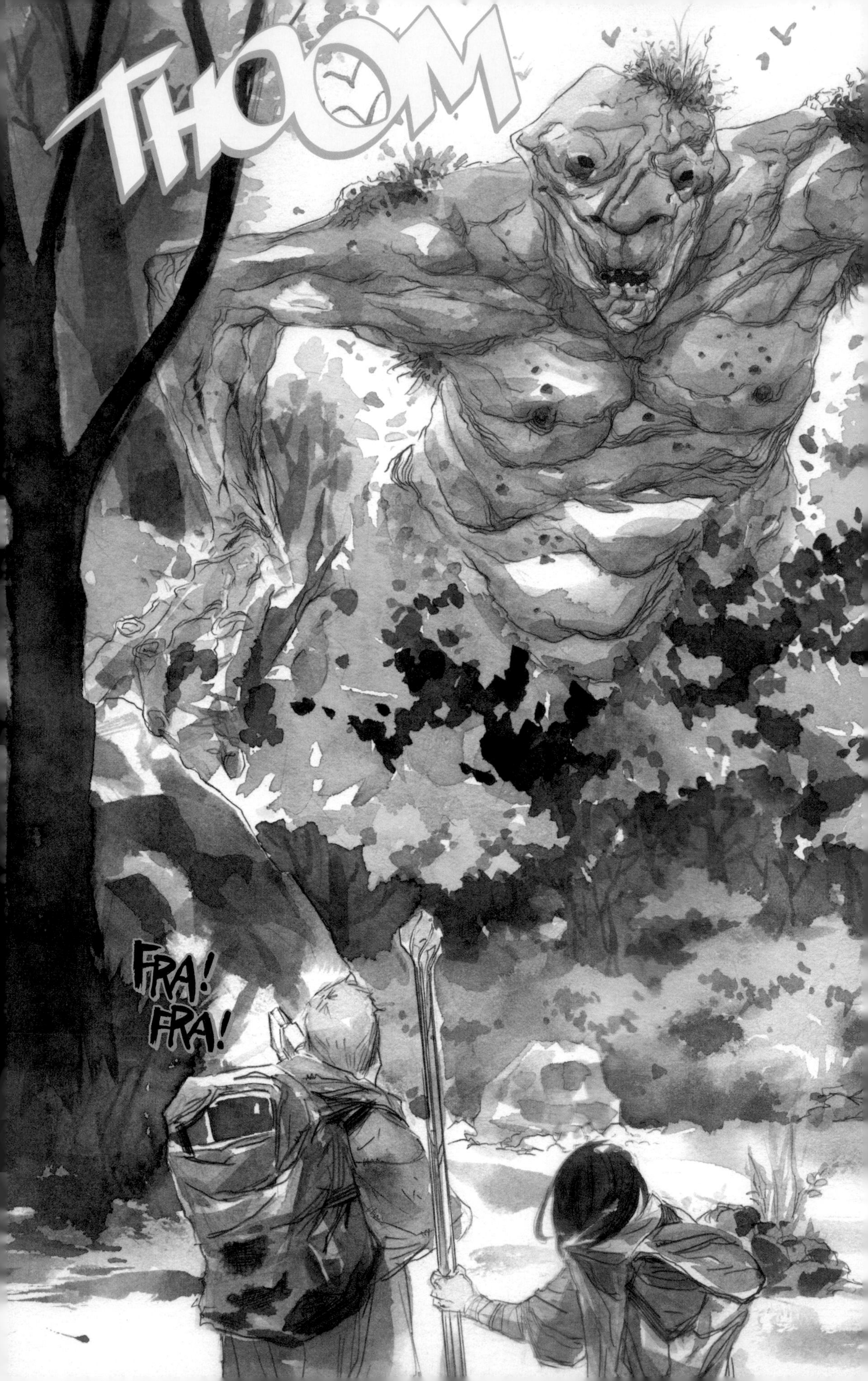
THOOM
FRA!
FRA!

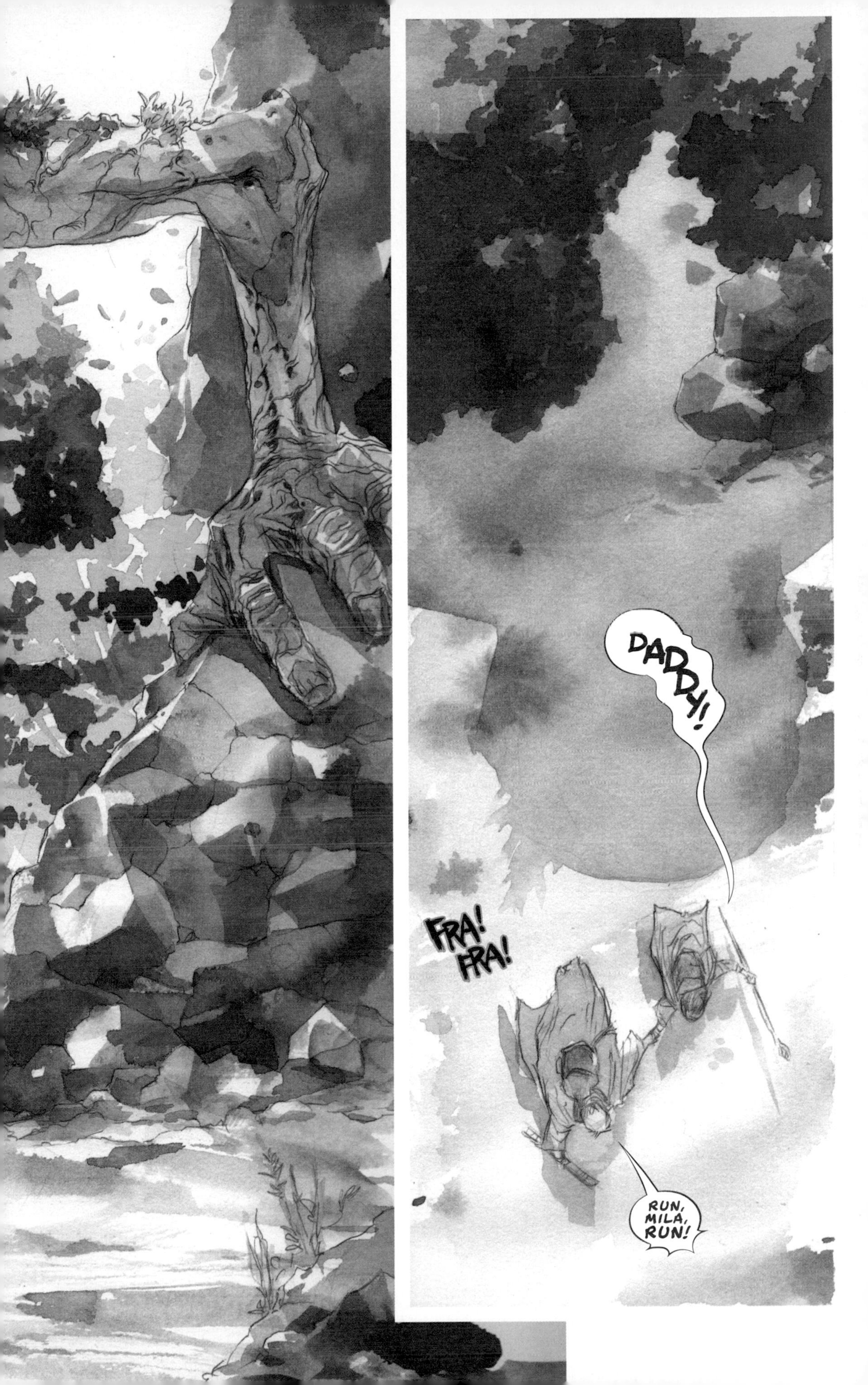
DADDY!
FRA! FRA!
RUN, MILA, RUN!

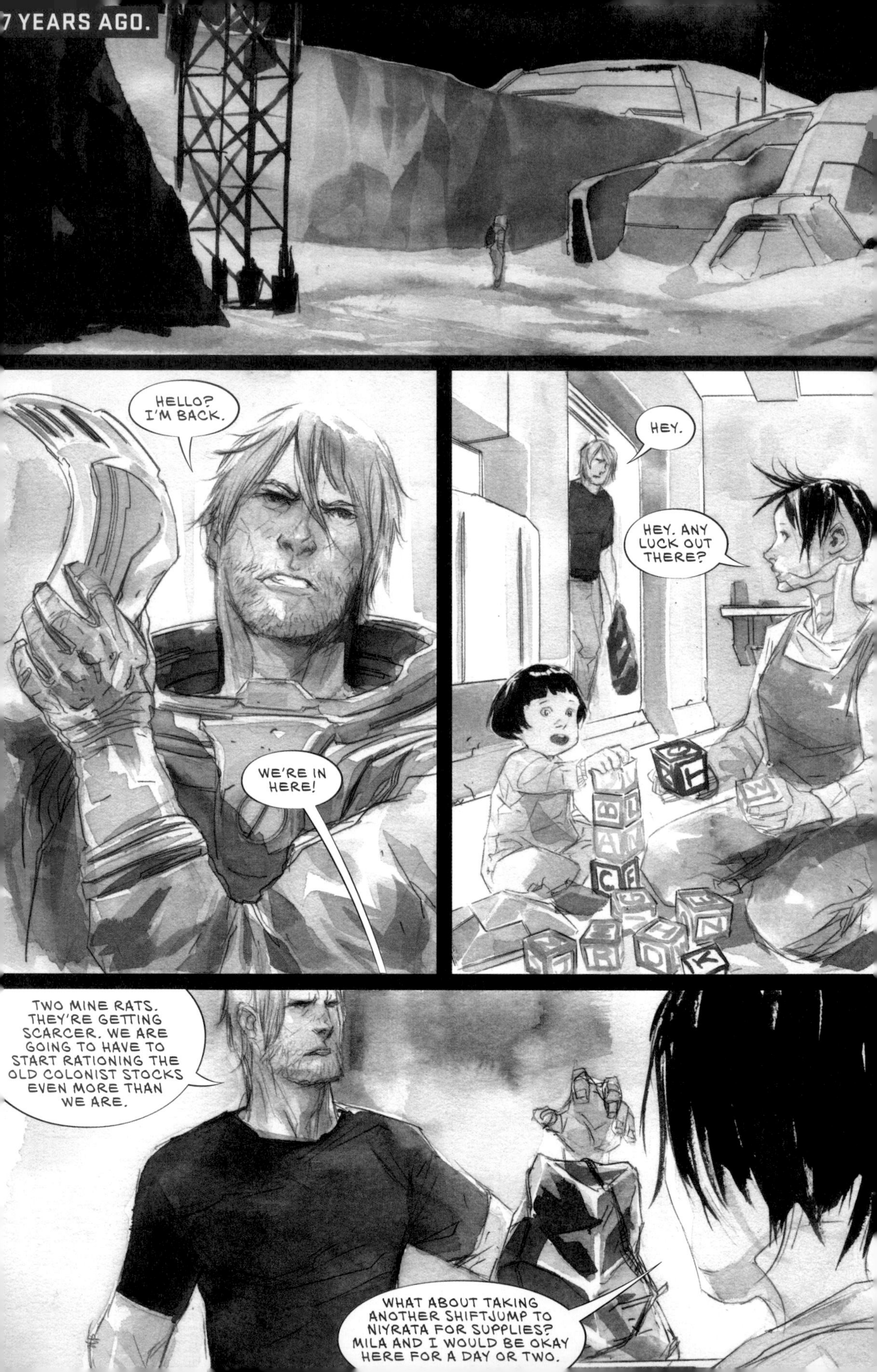
7 YEARS AGO.
HELLO? I'M BACK.
WE'RE IN HERE!
HEY.
HEY. ANY LUCK OUT THERE?
TWO MINE RATS. THEY'RE GETTING SCARCER. WE ARE GOING TO HAVE TO START RATIONING THE OLD COLONIST STOCKS EVEN MORE THAN WE ARE.
WHAT ABOUT TAKING ANOTHER SHIFTJUMP TO NIYRATA FOR SUPPLIES? MILA AND I WOULD BE OKAY HERE FOR A DAY OR TWO.

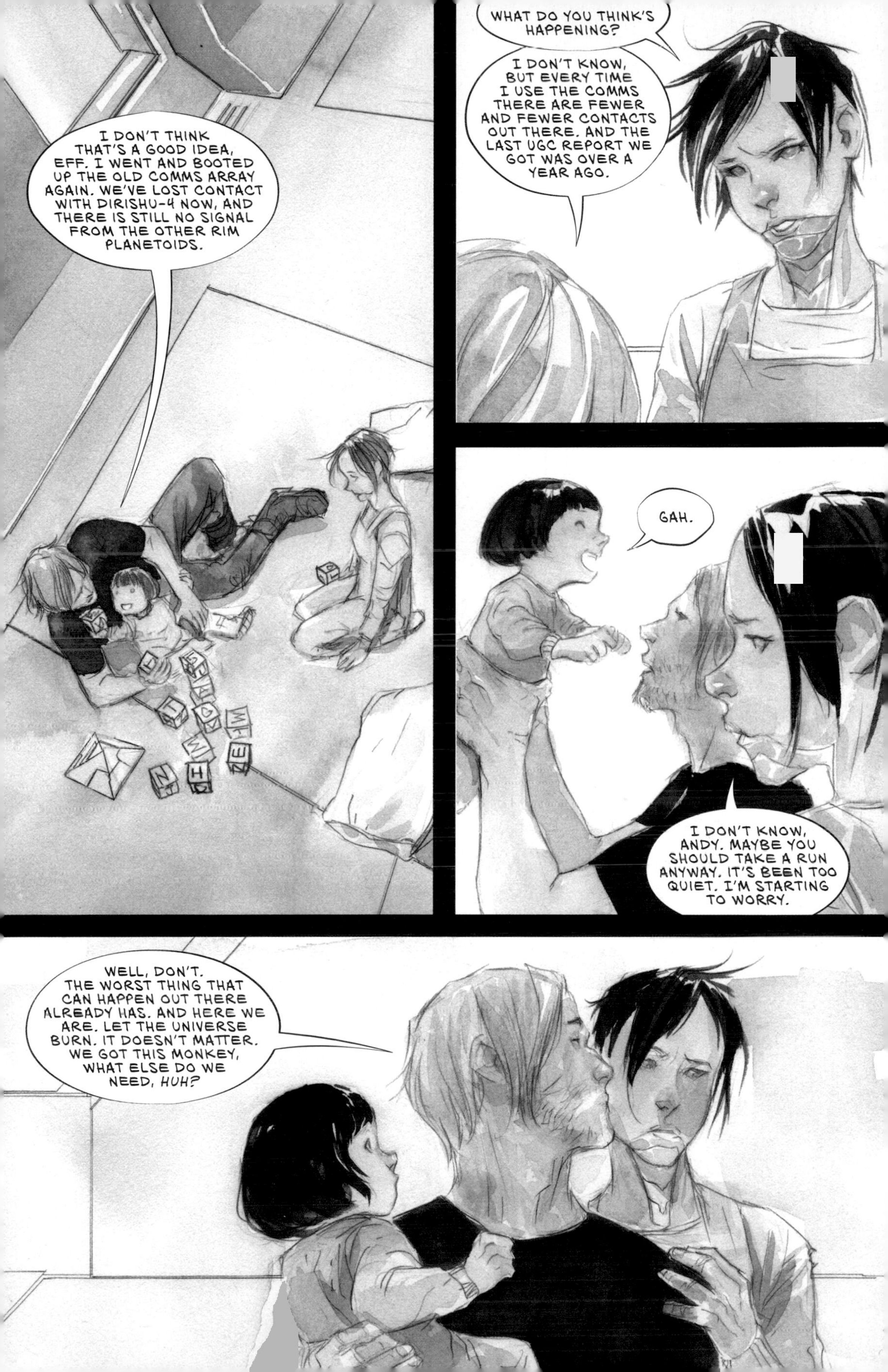
I DON'T THINK THAT'S A GOOD IDEA, EFF. I WENT AND BOOTED UP THE OLD COMMS ARRAY AGAIN. WE'VE LOST CONTACT WITH DIRISHU-4 NOW, AND THERE IS STILL NO SIGNAL FROM THE OTHER RIM PLANETOIDS.
WHAT DO YOU THINK'S HAPPENING?
I DON'T KNOW, BUT EVERY TIME I USE THE COMMS THERE ARE FEWER AND FEWER CONTACTS OUT THERE. AND THE LAST UGC REPORT WE GOT WAS OVER A YEAR AGO.
GAH.
I DON'T KNOW, ANDY. MAYBE YOU SHOULD TAKE A RUN ANYWAY. IT'S BEEN TOO QUIET. I'M STARTING TO WORRY.
WELL, DON'T. THE WORST THING THAT CAN HAPPEN OUT THERE ALREADY HAS. AND HERE WE ARE. LET THE UNIVERSE BURN. IT DOESN'T MATTER. WE GOT THIS MONKEY, WHAT ELSE DO WE NEED, *HUH*?

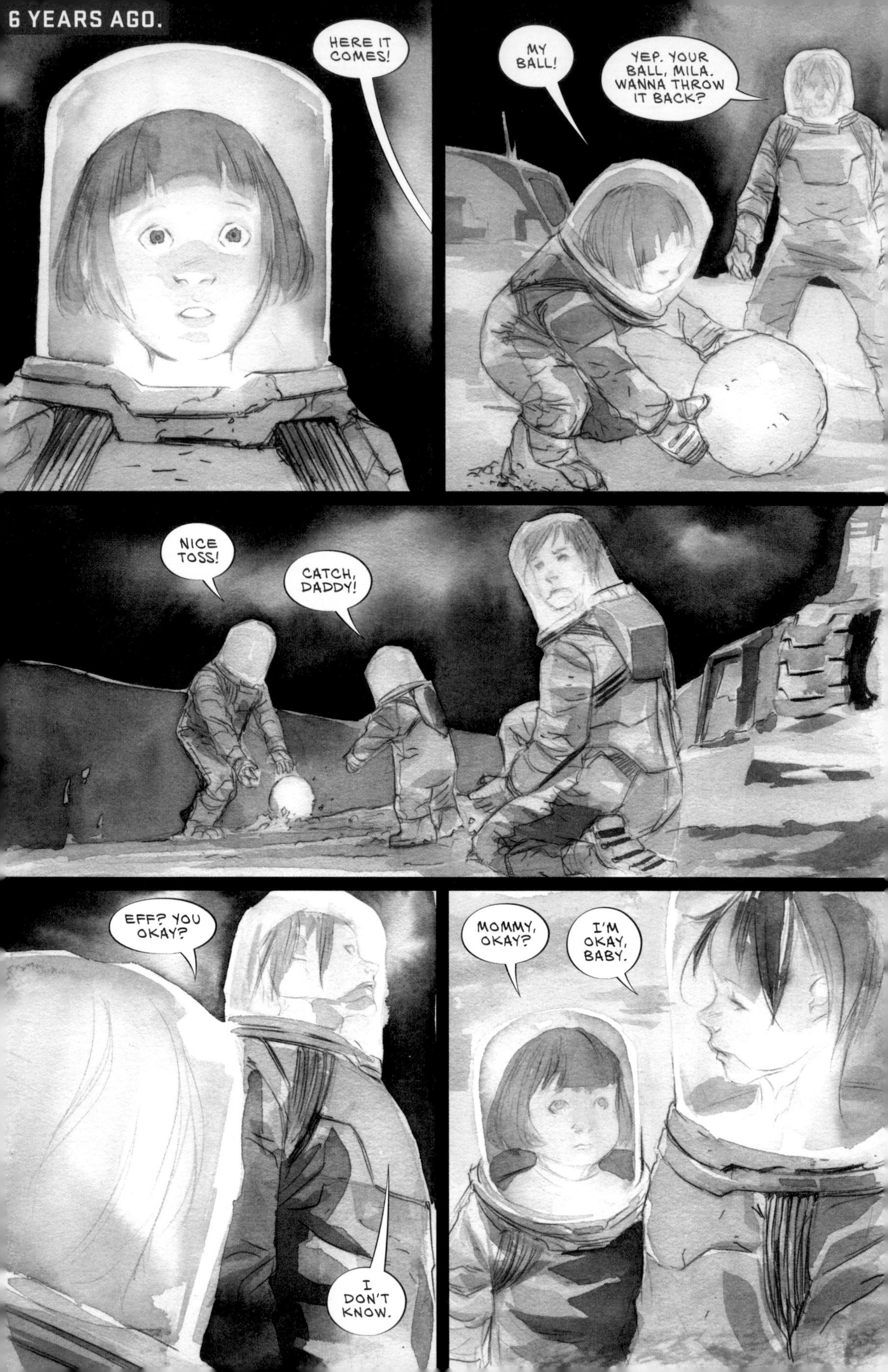
6 YEARS AGO.
HERE IT COMES!
MY BALL!
YEP. YOUR BALL, MILA. WANNA THROW IT BACK?
NICE TOSS!
CATCH, DADDY!
EFF? YOU OKAY?
I DON'T KNOW.
MOMMY, OKAY?
I'M OKAY, BABY.

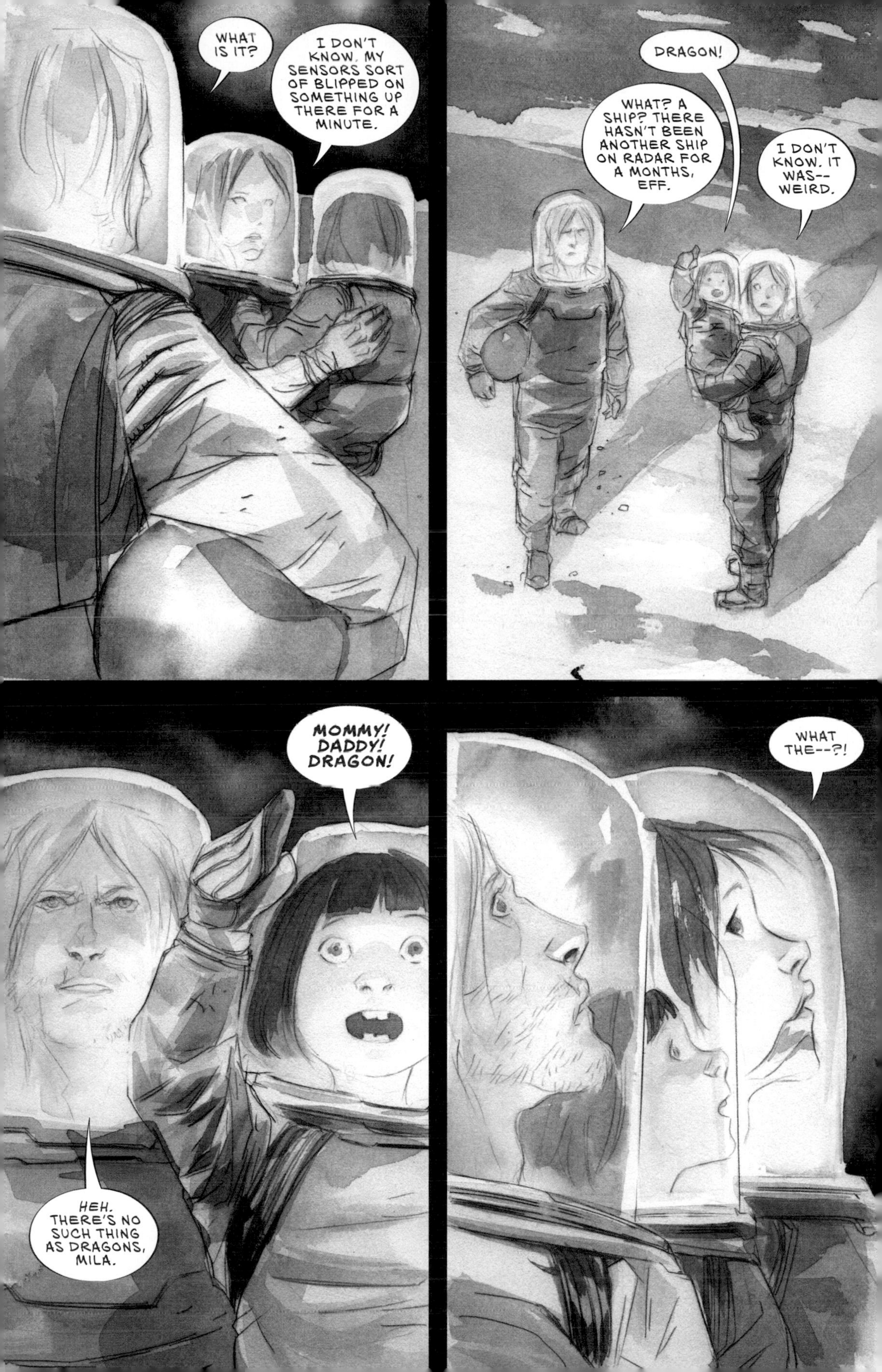
WHAT IS IT?
I DON'T KNOW. MY SENSORS SORT OF BLIPPED ON SOMETHING UP THERE FOR A MINUTE.
DRAGON!
WHAT? A SHIP? THERE HASN'T BEEN ANOTHER SHIP ON RADAR FOR A MONTHS, EFF.
I DON'T KNOW. IT WAS--WEIRD.
MOMMY! DADDY! DRAGON!
HEH. THERE'S NO SUCH THING AS DRAGONS, MILA.
WHAT THE--?!

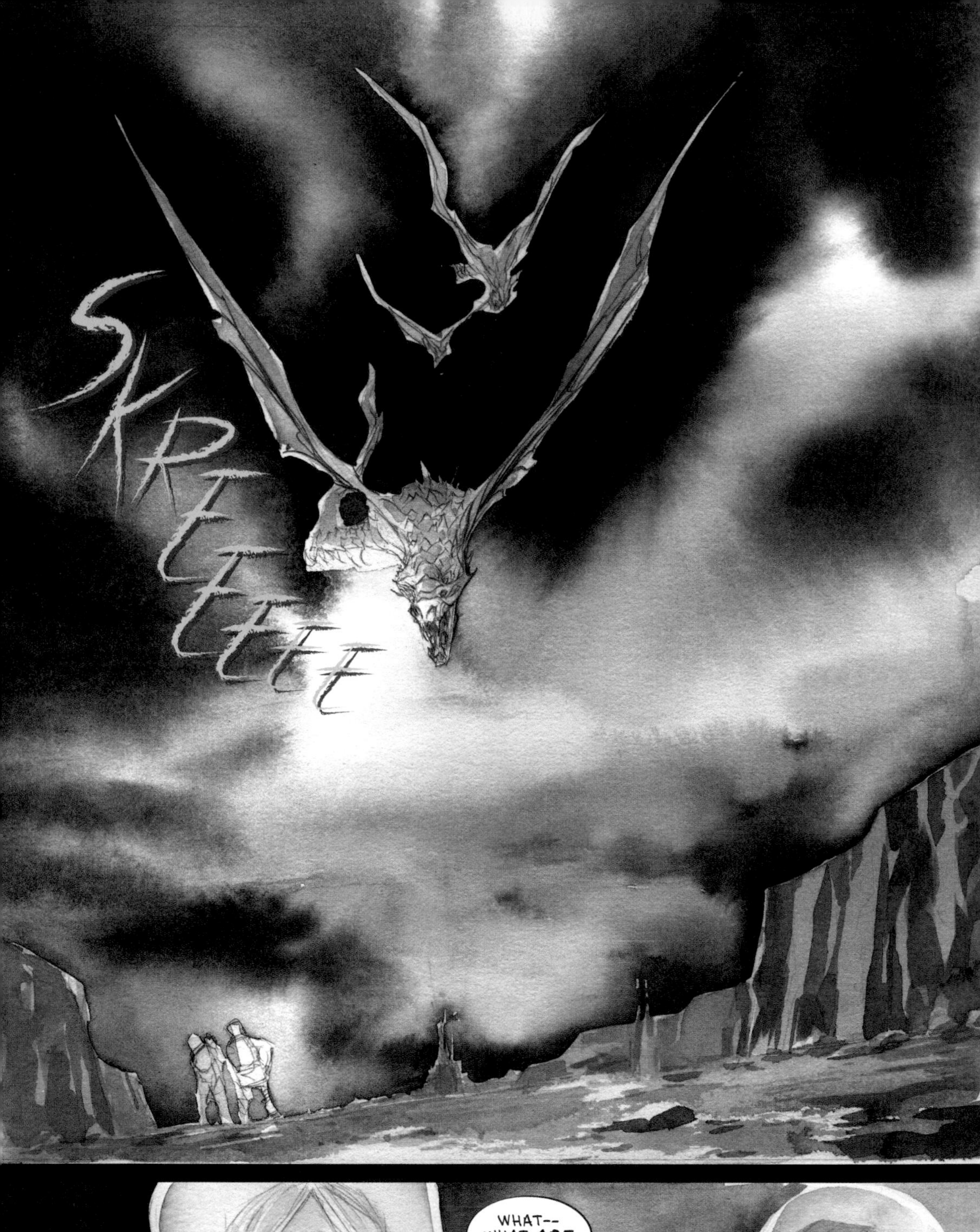
SKREEEEEE

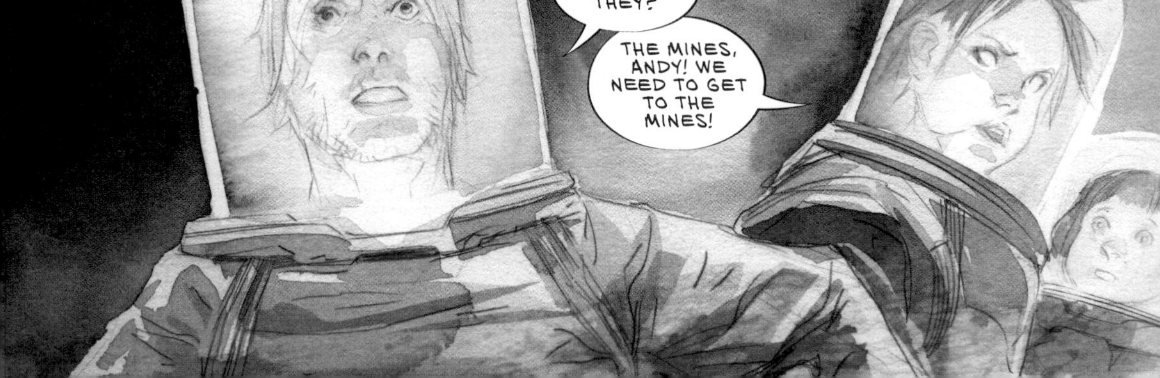
WHAT-- WHAT **ARE** THEY?
THE MINES, ANDY! WE NEED TO GET TO THE MINES!

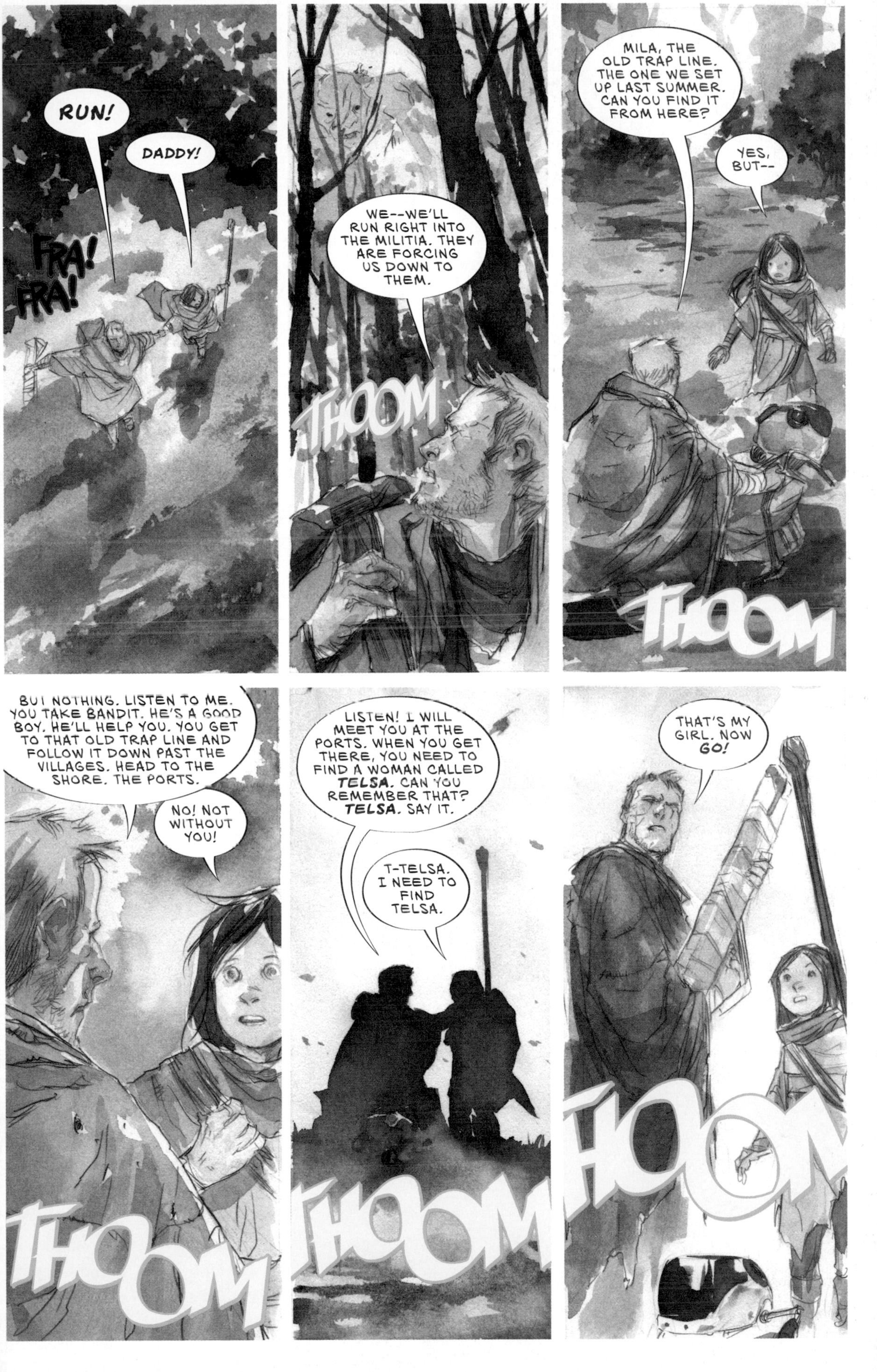
RUN!
DADDY!
FRA! FRA!
WE--WE'LL RUN RIGHT INTO THE MILITIA. THEY ARE FORCING US DOWN TO THEM.
THOOM
MILA, THE OLD TRAP LINE. THE ONE WE SET UP LAST SUMMER. CAN YOU FIND IT FROM HERE?
YES, BUT--
THOOM
BUT NOTHING. LISTEN TO ME. YOU TAKE BANDIT. HE'S A GOOD BOY. HE'LL HELP YOU. YOU GET TO THAT OLD TRAP LINE AND FOLLOW IT DOWN PAST THE VILLAGES. HEAD TO THE SHORE. THE PORTS.
NO! NOT WITHOUT YOU!
THOOM
LISTEN! I WILL MEET YOU AT THE PORTS. WHEN YOU GET THERE, YOU NEED TO FIND A WOMAN CALLED TELSA. CAN YOU REMEMBER THAT? TELSA. SAY IT.
T-TELSA. I NEED TO FIND TELSA.
THOOM
THAT'S MY GIRL. NOW GO!
THOOM

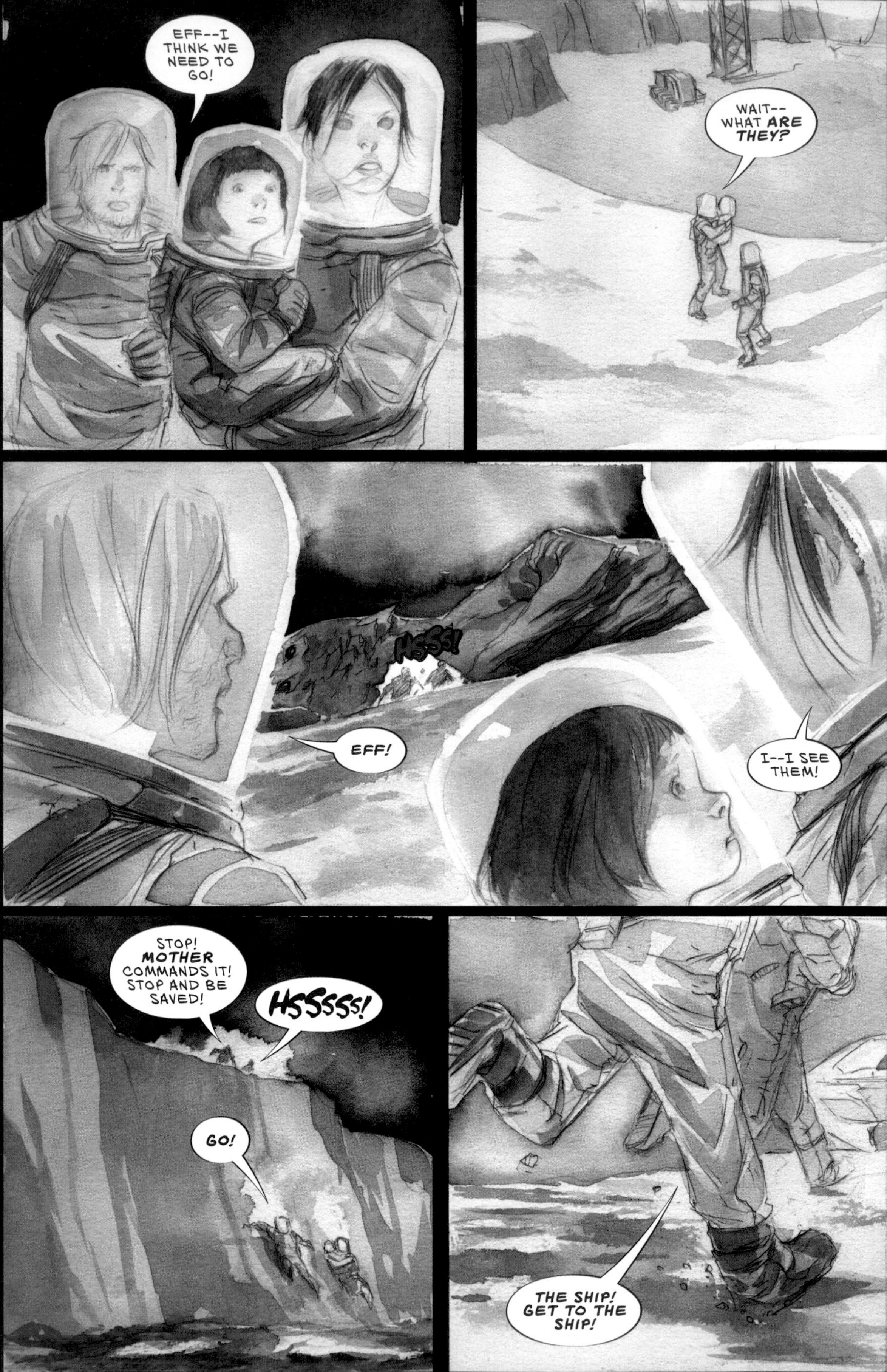
EFF--I THINK WE NEED TO GO!
WAIT-- WHAT ARE THEY?
HSSS!
EFF!
I--I SEE THEM!
STOP! MOTHER COMMANDS IT! STOP AND BE SAVED!
HSSSSS!
GO!
THE SHIP! GET TO THE SHIP!

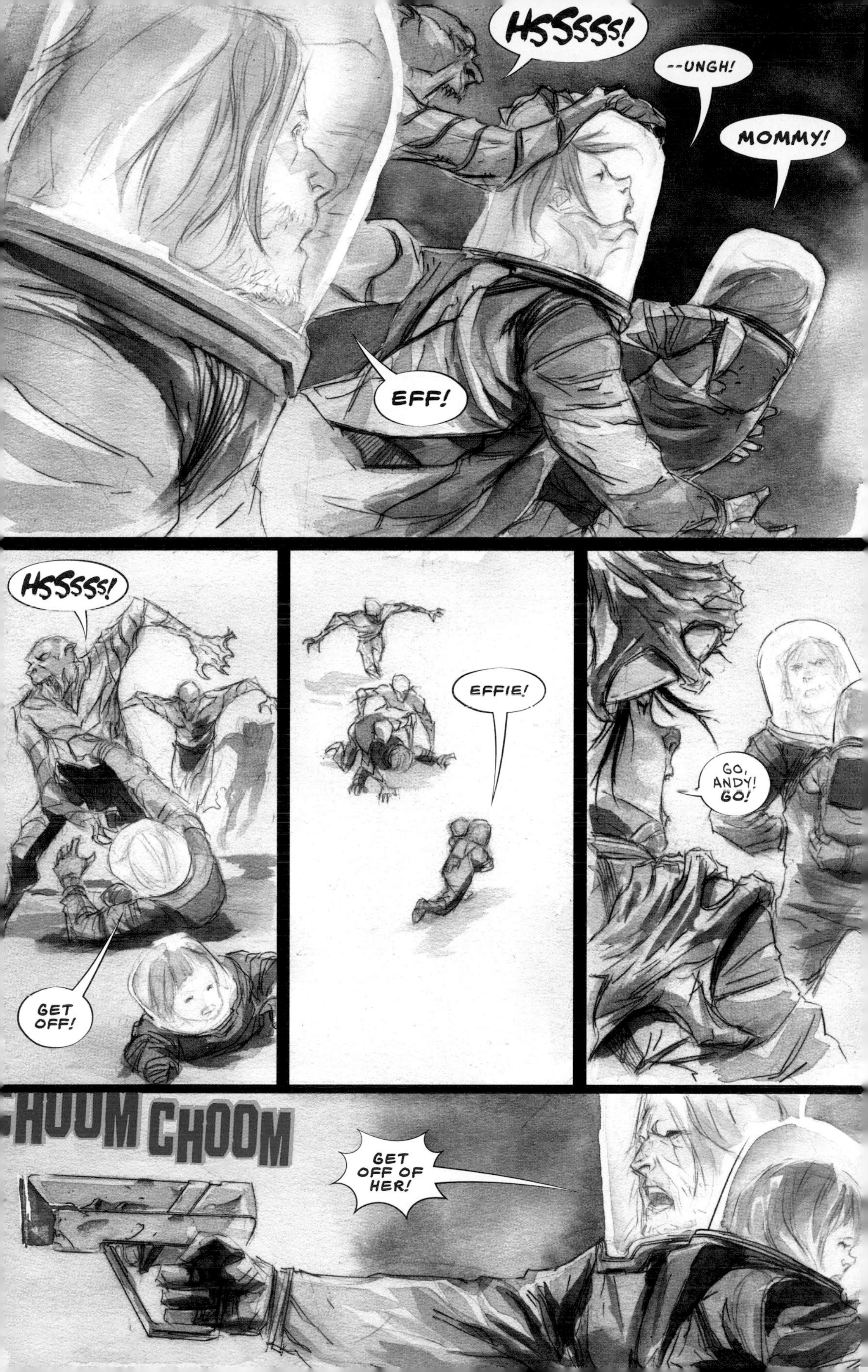
HSSSSS!
--UNGH!
MOMMY!
EFF!
HSSSSS!
GET OFF!
EFFIE!
GO, ANDY! GO!
CHOOM CHOOM
GET OFF OF HER!

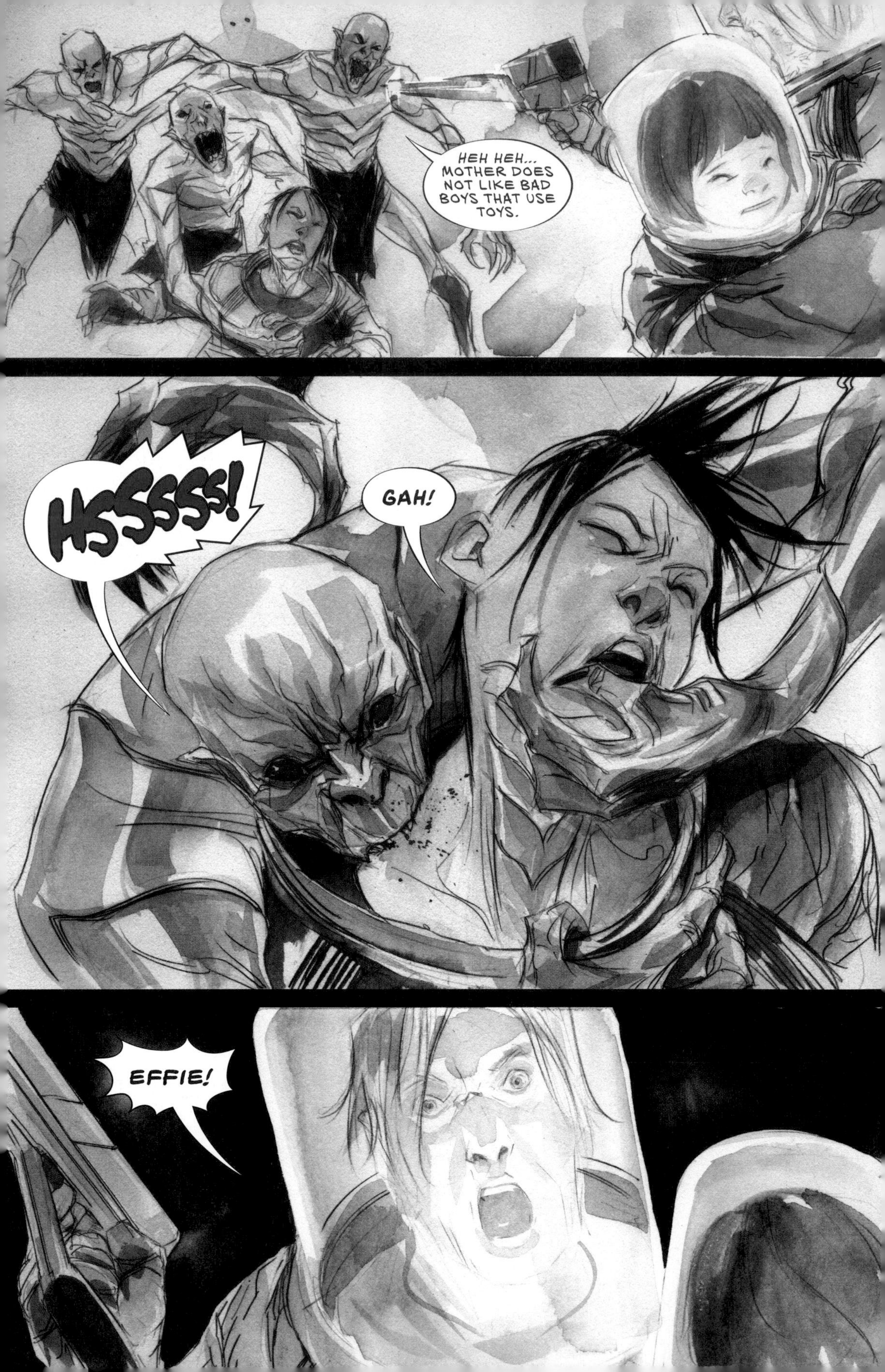
HEH HEH... MOTHER DOES NOT LIKE BAD BOYS THAT USE TOYS.
HSSSSS!
GAH!
EFFIE!

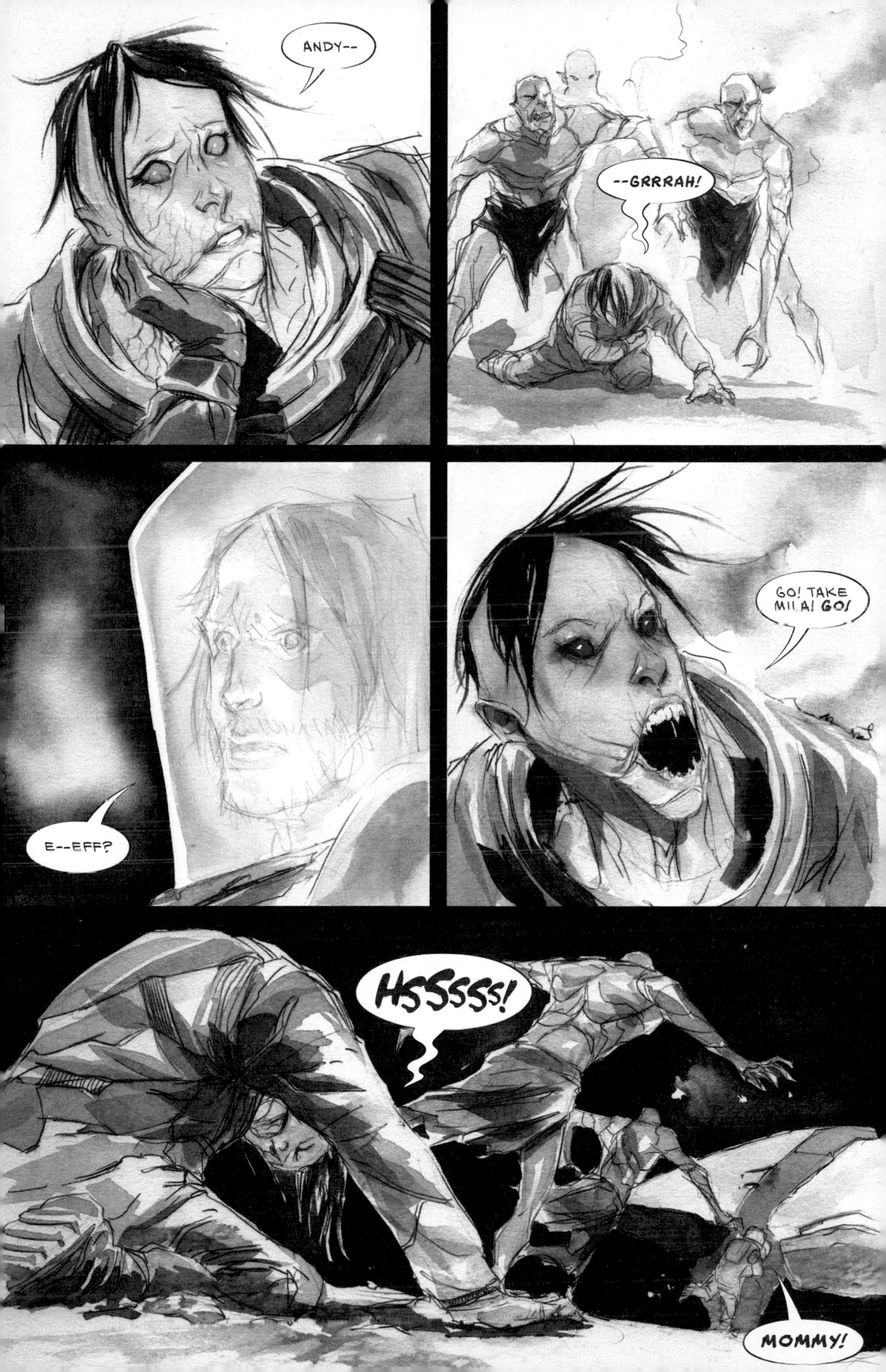
ANDY--
--GRRRAH!
E--EFF?
GO! TAKE MILA! GO!
HSSSSS!
MOMMY!

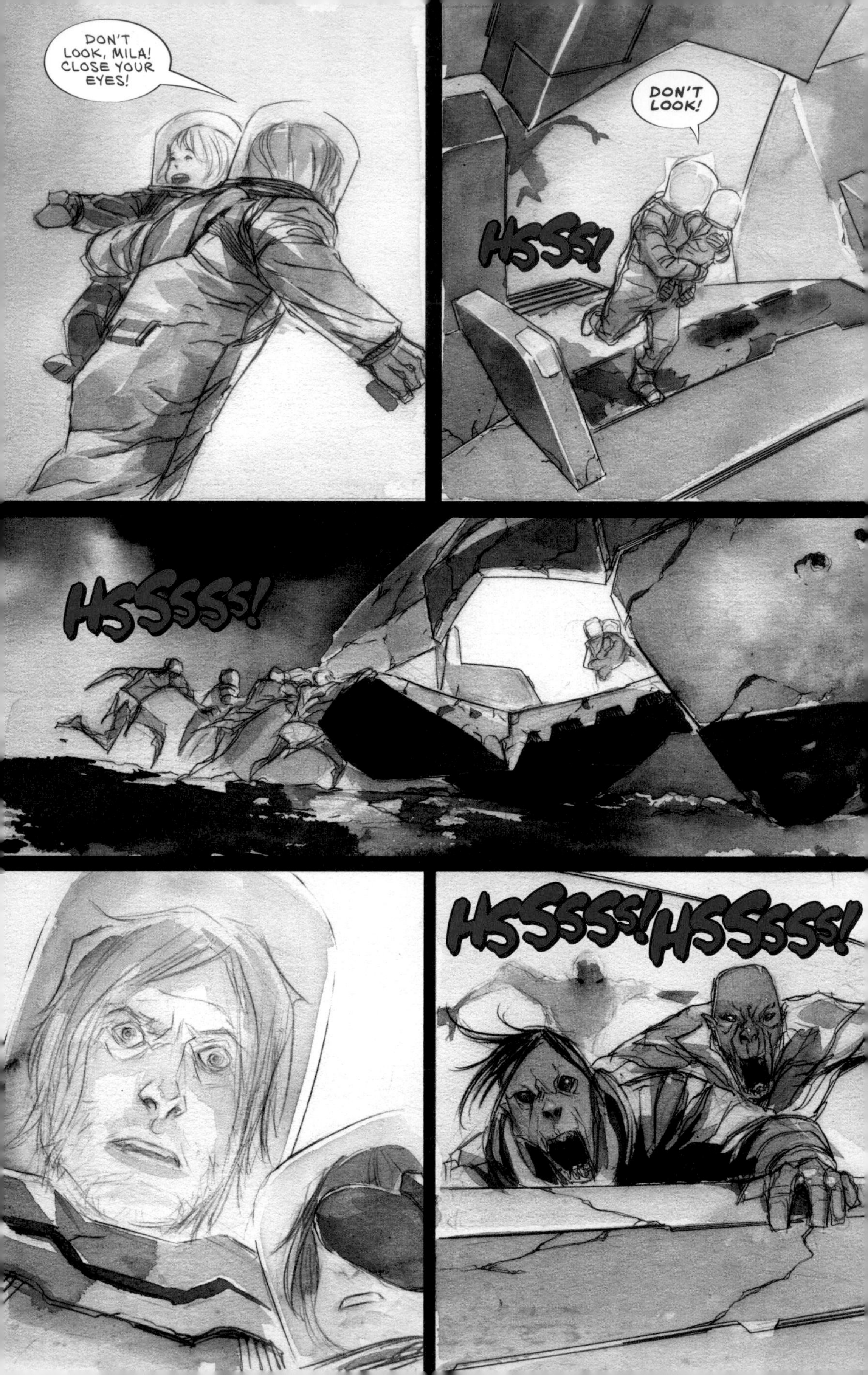
DON'T LOOK, MILA! CLOSE YOUR EYES!
DON'T LOOK!
HSSS!
HSSSSS!
HSSSSS! HSSSSS!

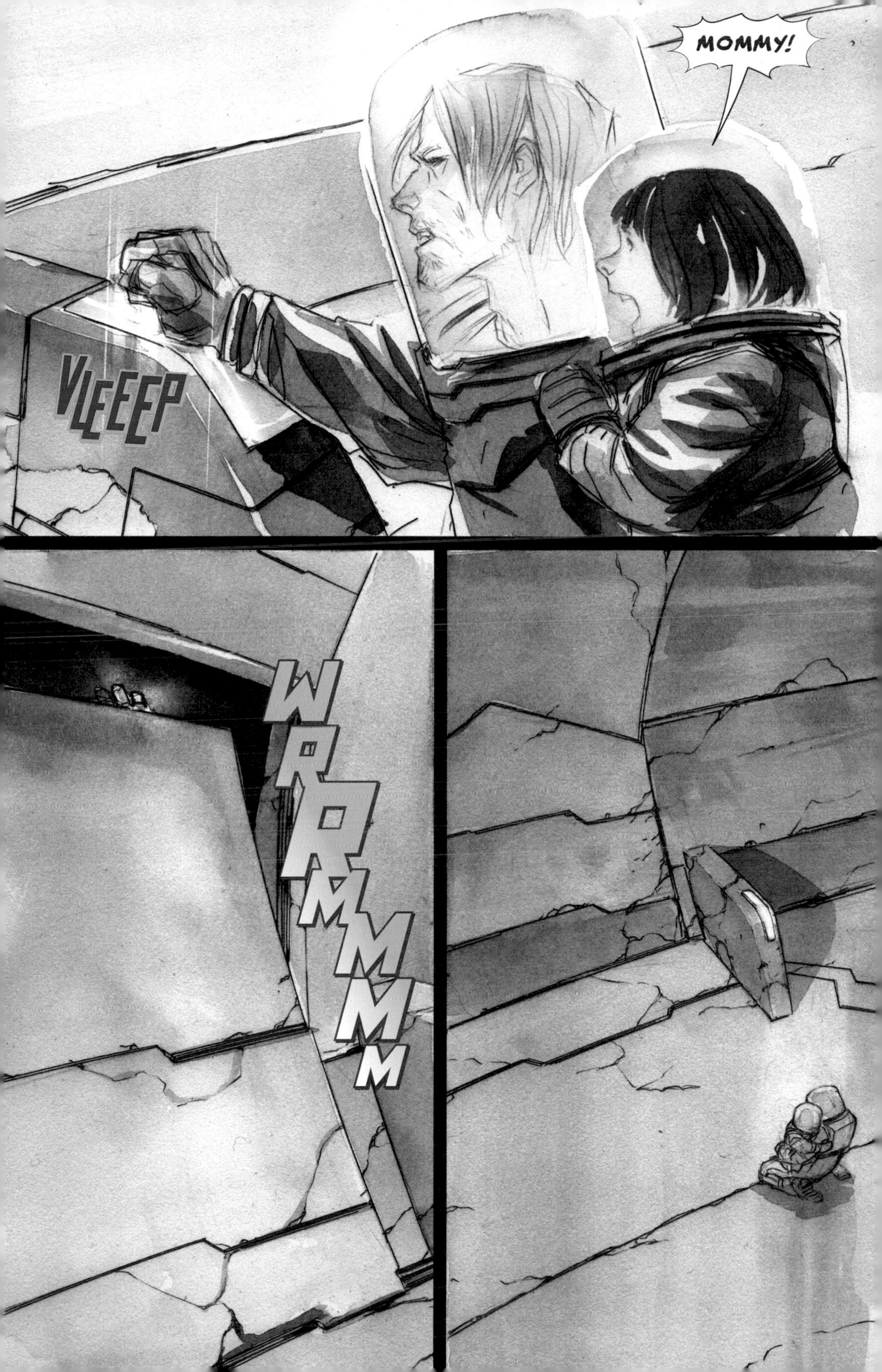
MOMMY!
VLEEEP
WRRMMMMM

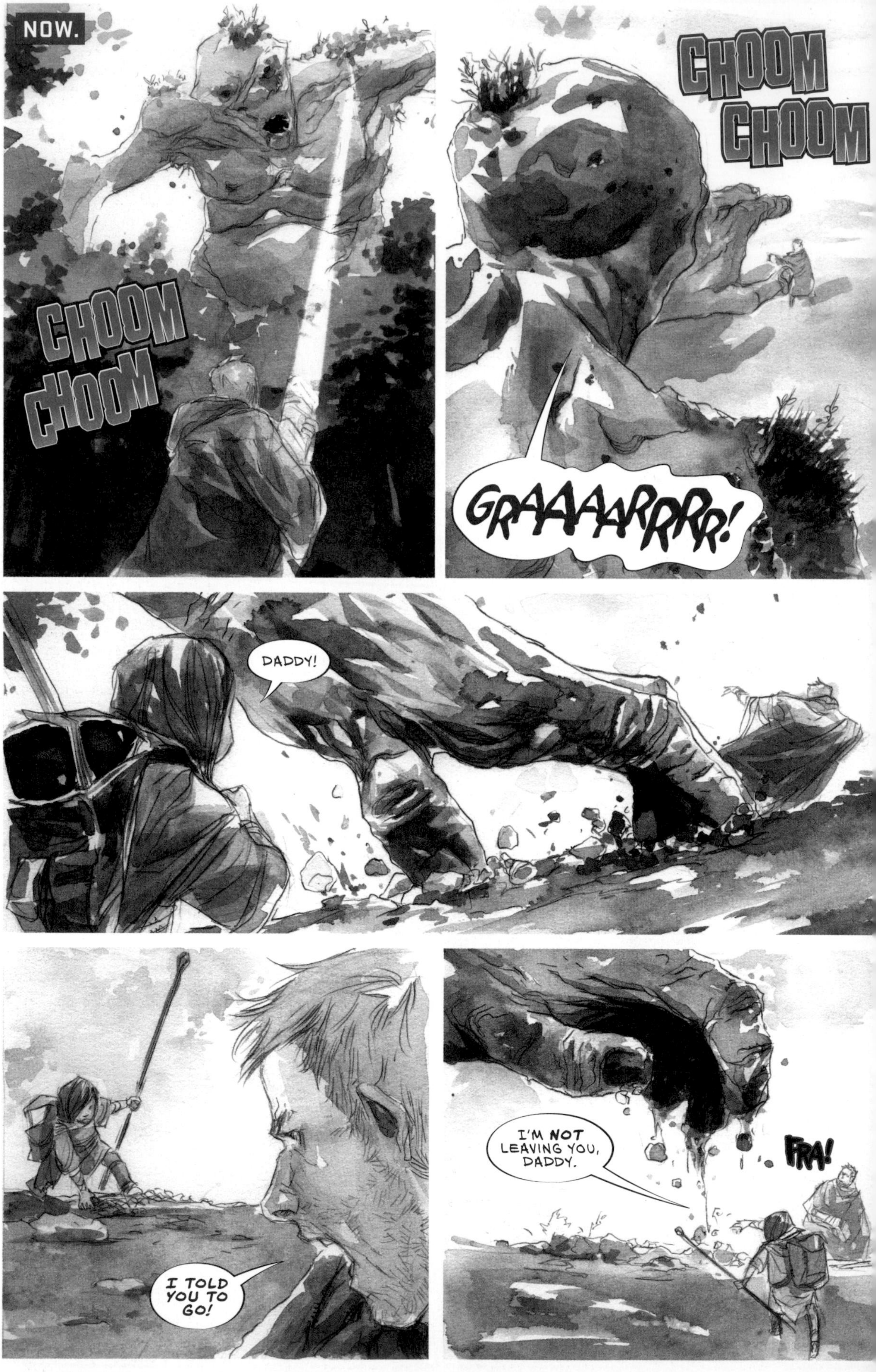
NOW.
CHOOM CHOOM
CHOOM CHOOM
GRAAAARRRR!
DADDY!
I TOLD YOU TO GO!
I'M **NOT** LEAVING YOU, DADDY.
FRA!

BANDIT, NO! COME BACK!
FRA!
BANDIT! GET OUT OF HERE!
FRA!
FRA!
EEP! DANGER DETECTED--ACTIVATE GUARD DOG MODE.
FRA!
BANDIT?
CHAK
FRA!
FRA!

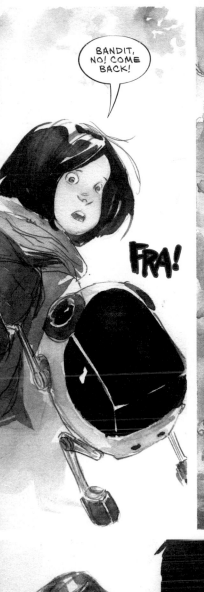

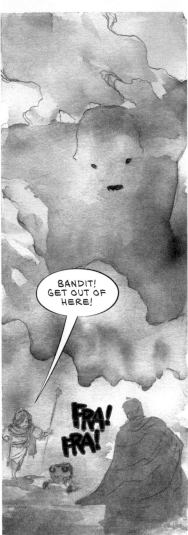

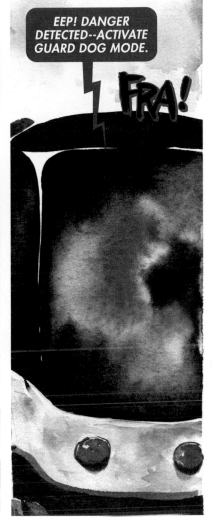

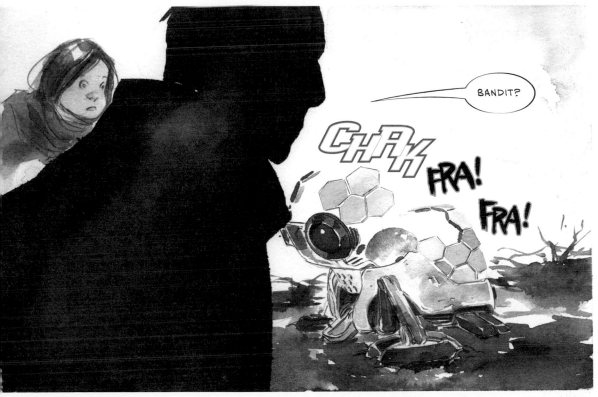

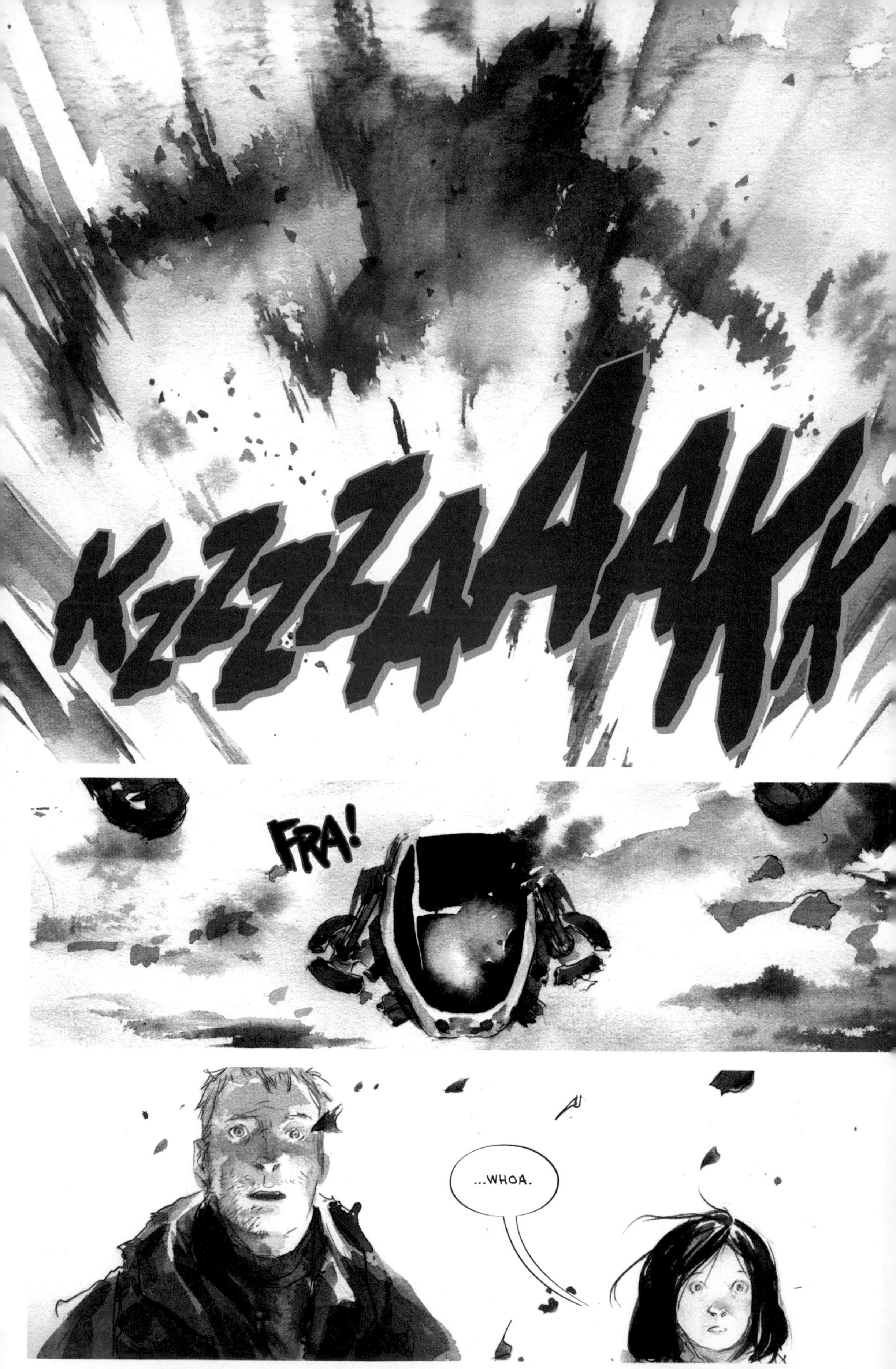
KZZZZAAAKK
FRA!
...WHOA.

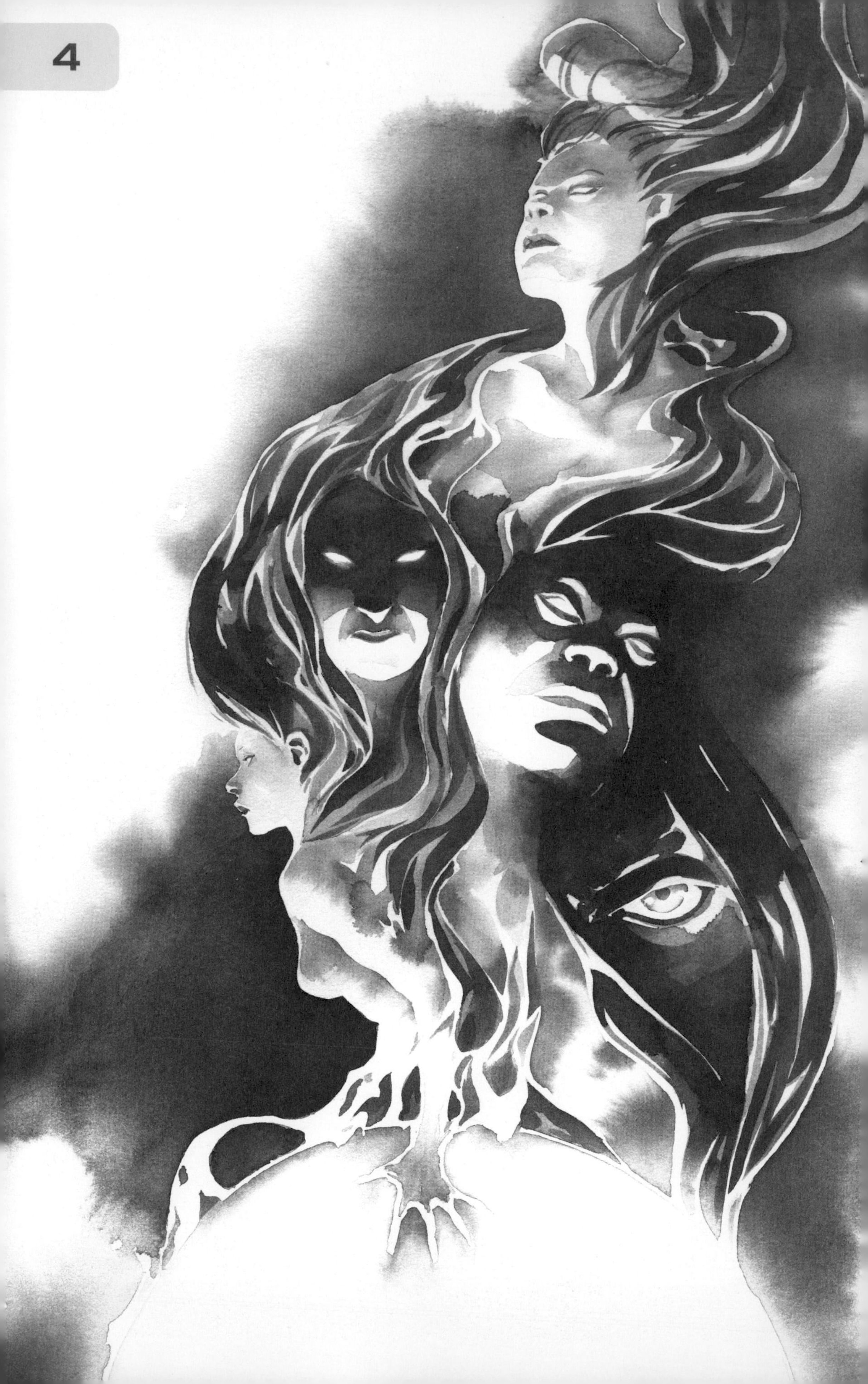

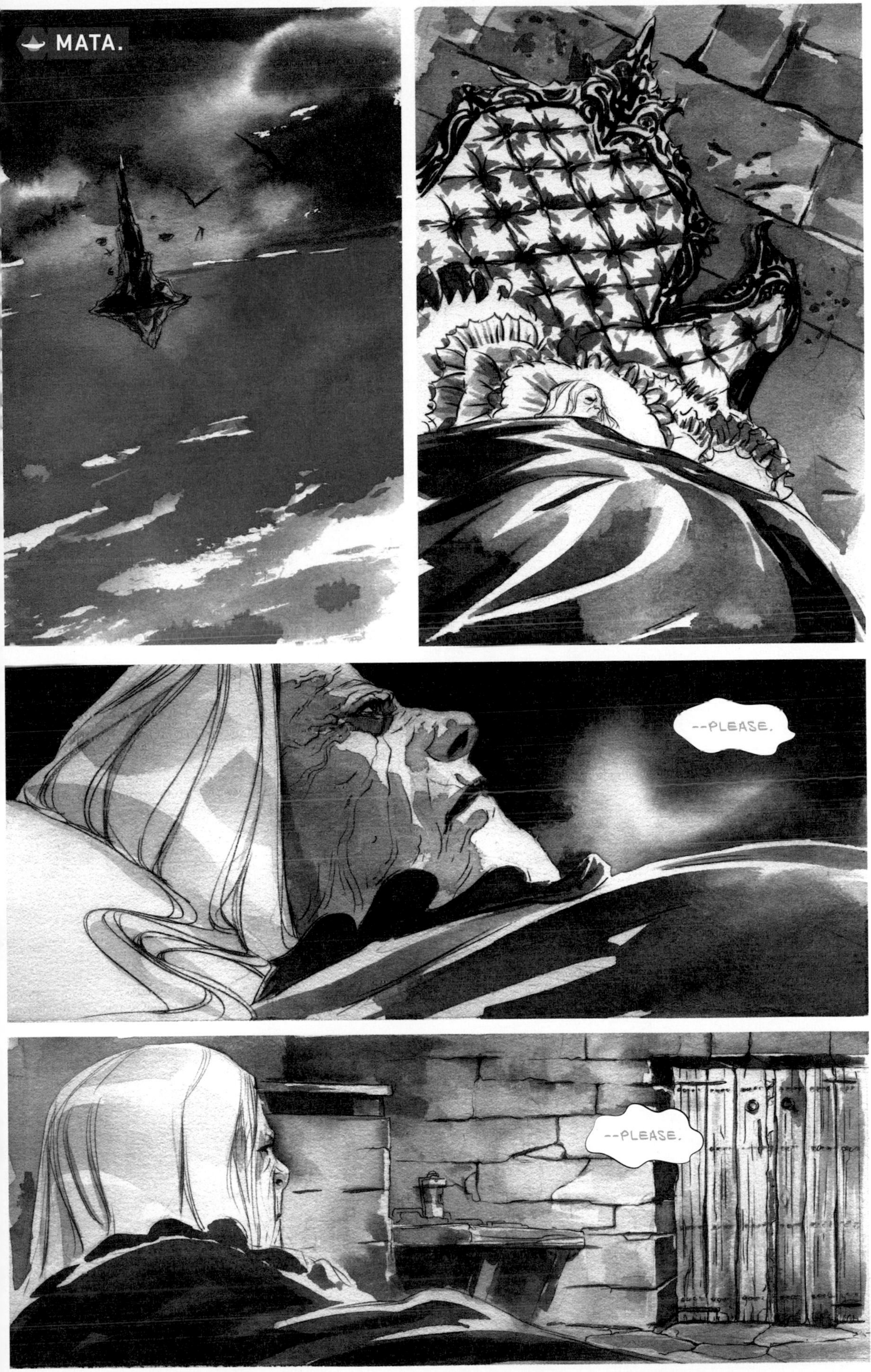
MATA.
--PLEASE.
--PLEASE.

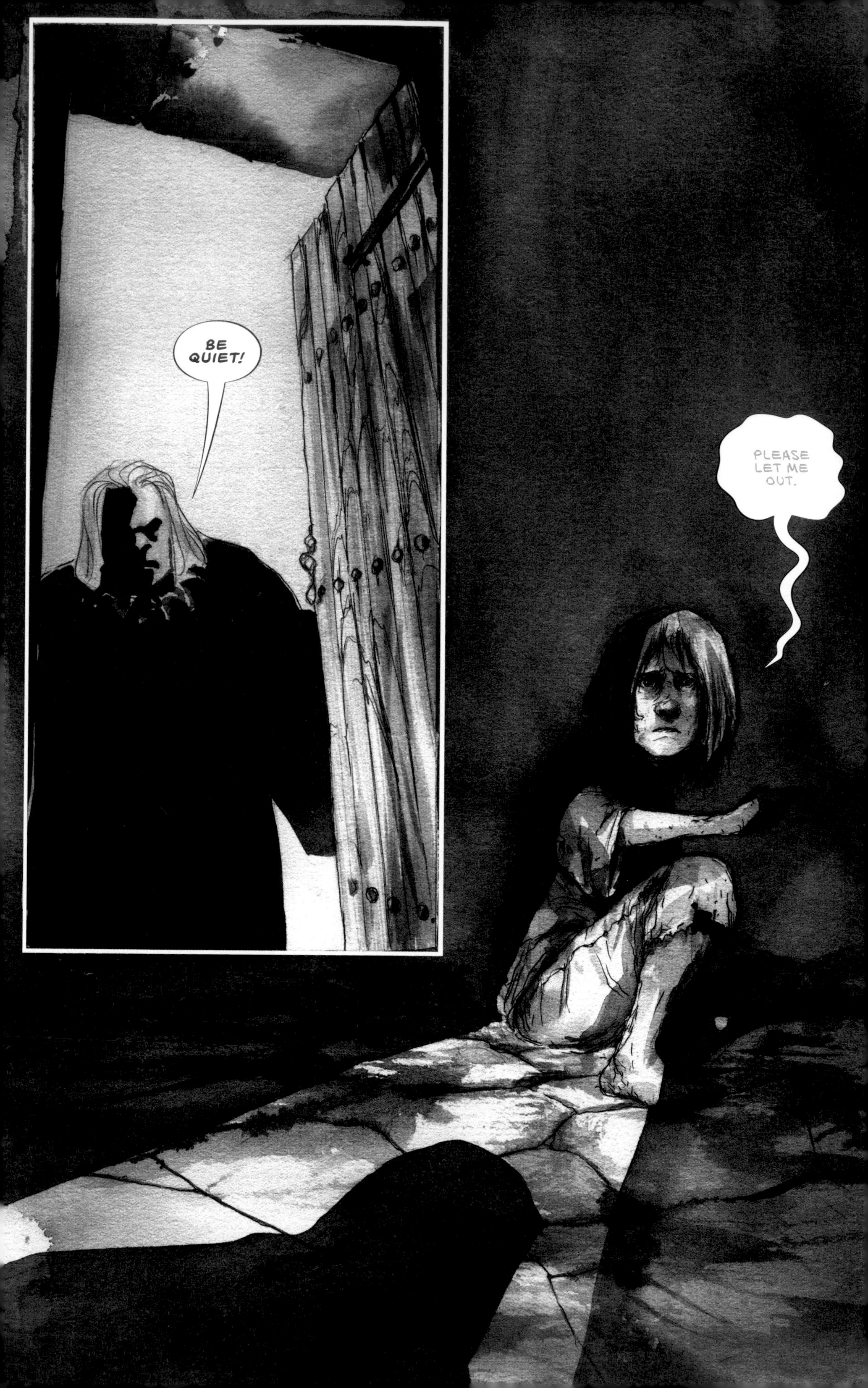
BE QUIET!
PLEASE LET ME OUT.

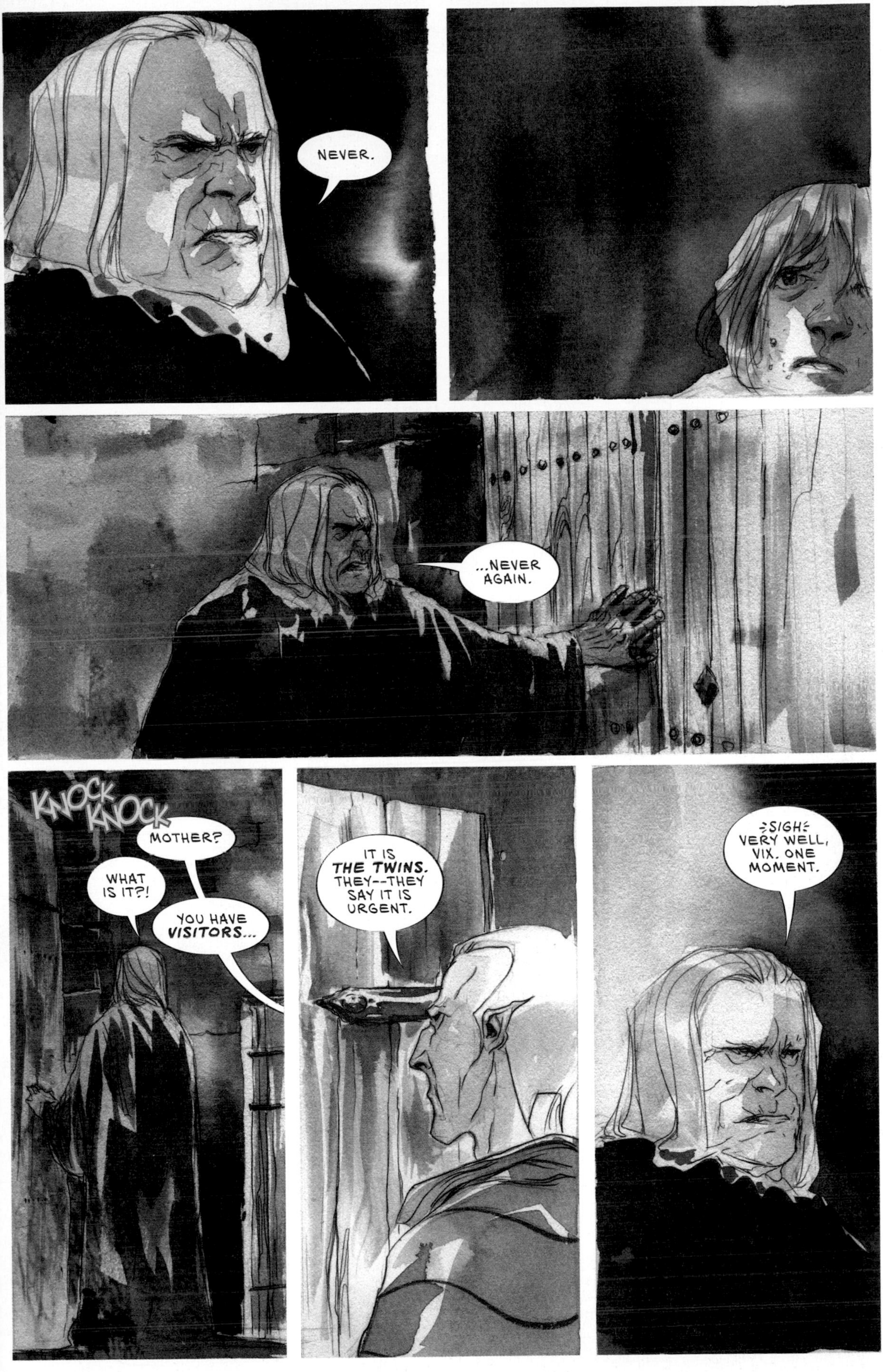
NEVER.
...NEVER AGAIN.
KNOCK KNOCK
MOTHER?
WHAT IS IT?!
YOU HAVE VISITORS...
IT IS THE TWINS. THEY--THEY SAY IT IS URGENT.
=SIGH= VERY WELL, VIX. ONE MOMENT.

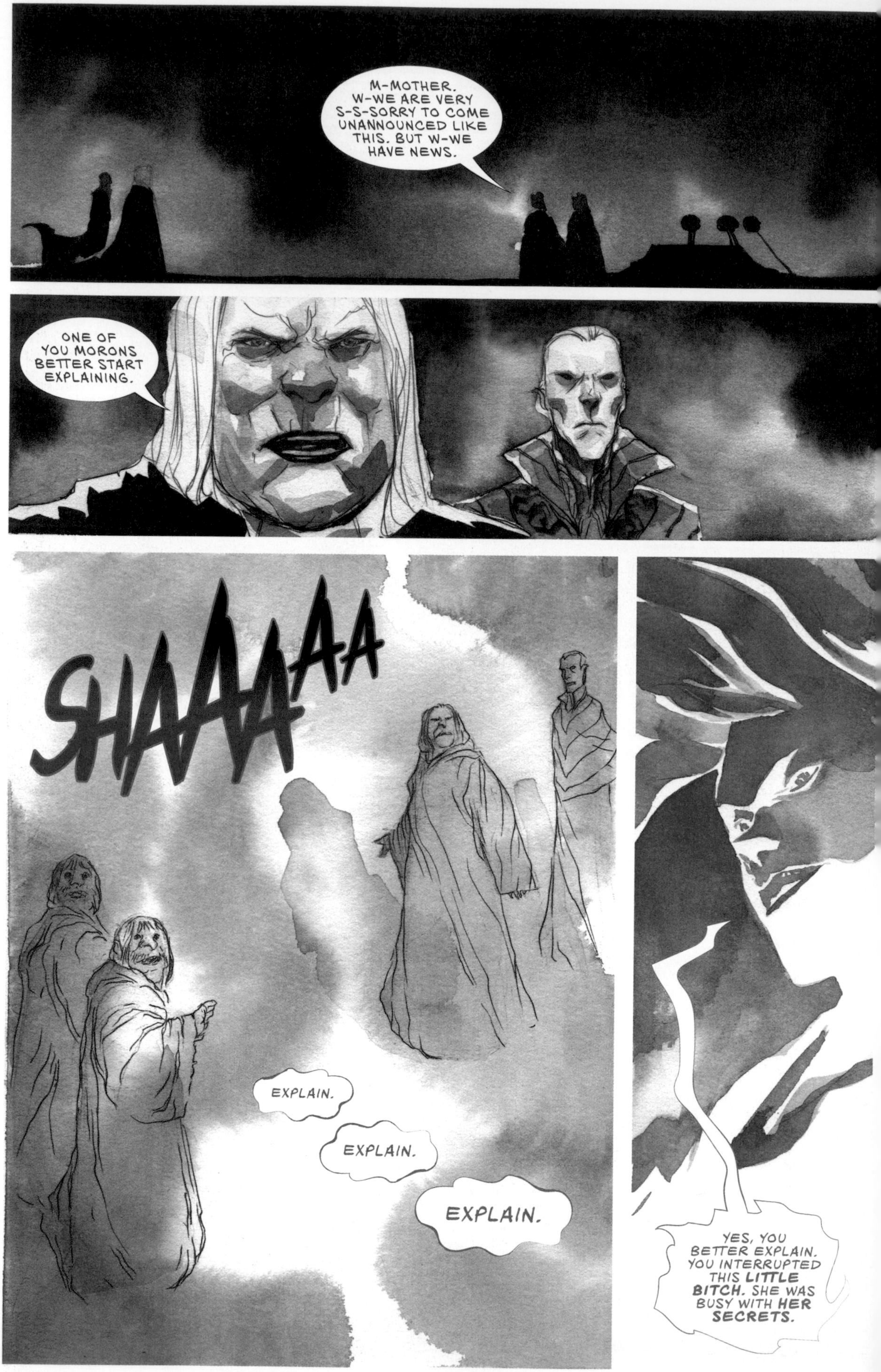
M-MOTHER. W-WE ARE VERY S-S-SORRY TO COME UNANNOUNCED LIKE THIS. BUT W-WE HAVE NEWS.
ONE OF YOU MORONS BETTER START EXPLAINING.
SHAAAAAA
EXPLAIN.
EXPLAIN.
EXPLAIN.
YES, YOU BETTER EXPLAIN. YOU INTERRUPTED THIS **LITTLE BITCH.** SHE WAS BUSY WITH **HER SECRETS.**

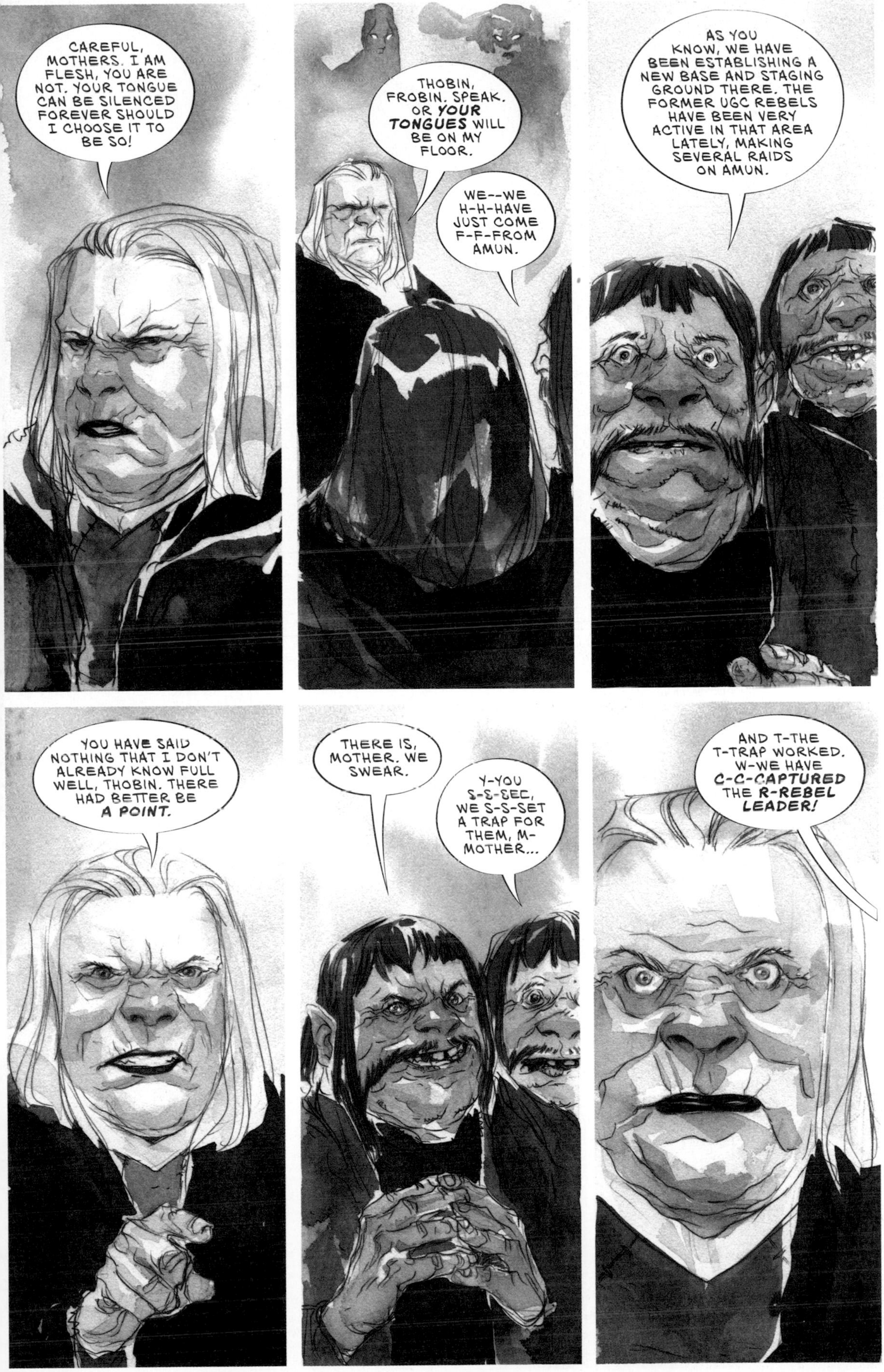
CAREFUL, MOTHERS. I AM FLESH, YOU ARE NOT. YOUR TONGUE CAN BE SILENCED FOREVER SHOULD I CHOOSE IT TO BE SO!
THOBIN, FROBIN. SPEAK. OR **YOUR TONGUES** WILL BE ON MY FLOOR.
WE--WE H-H-HAVE JUST COME F-F-FROM AMUN.
AS YOU KNOW, WE HAVE BEEN ESTABLISHING A NEW BASE AND STAGING GROUND THERE. THE FORMER UGC REBELS HAVE BEEN VERY ACTIVE IN THAT AREA LATELY, MAKING SEVERAL RAIDS ON AMUN.
YOU HAVE SAID NOTHING THAT I DON'T ALREADY KNOW FULL WELL, THOBIN. THERE HAD BETTER BE ***A POINT.***
THERE IS, MOTHER. WE SWEAR.
Y-YOU S-S-SEC, WE S-S-SET A TRAP FOR THEM, M-MOTHER...
AND T-THE T-TRAP WORKED. W-WE HAVE ***C-C-CAPTURED*** THE ***R-REBEL LEADER!***

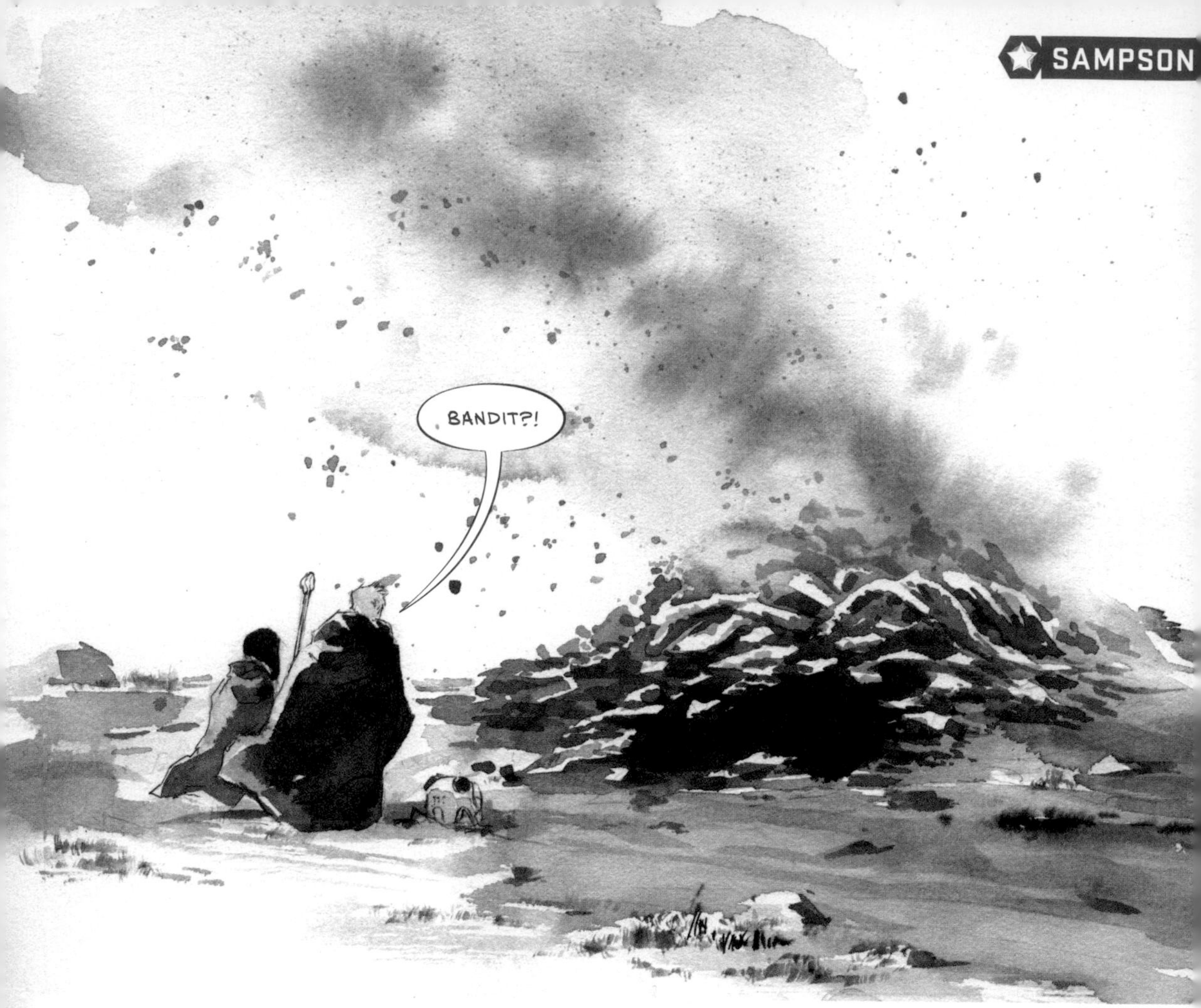
BANDIT?!

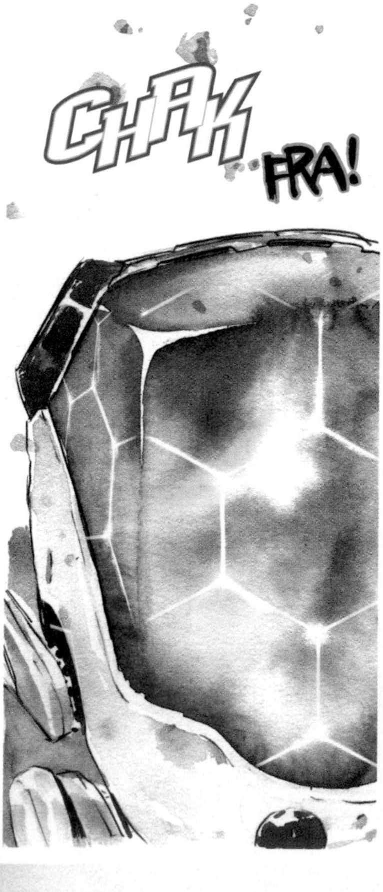
CHAK
FRA!

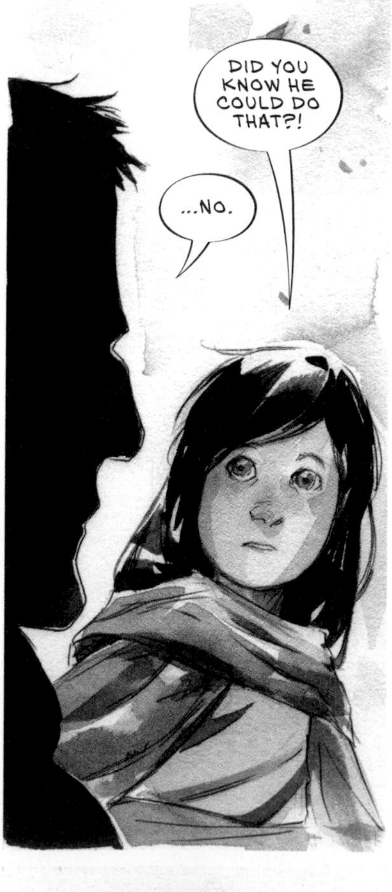
DID YOU KNOW HE COULD DO THAT?!
...NO.

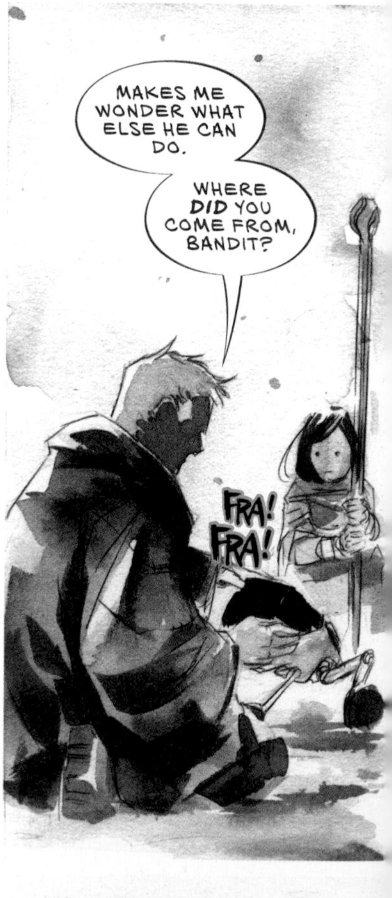
MAKES ME WONDER WHAT ELSE HE CAN DO.
WHERE DID YOU COME FROM, BANDIT?
FRA! FRA!

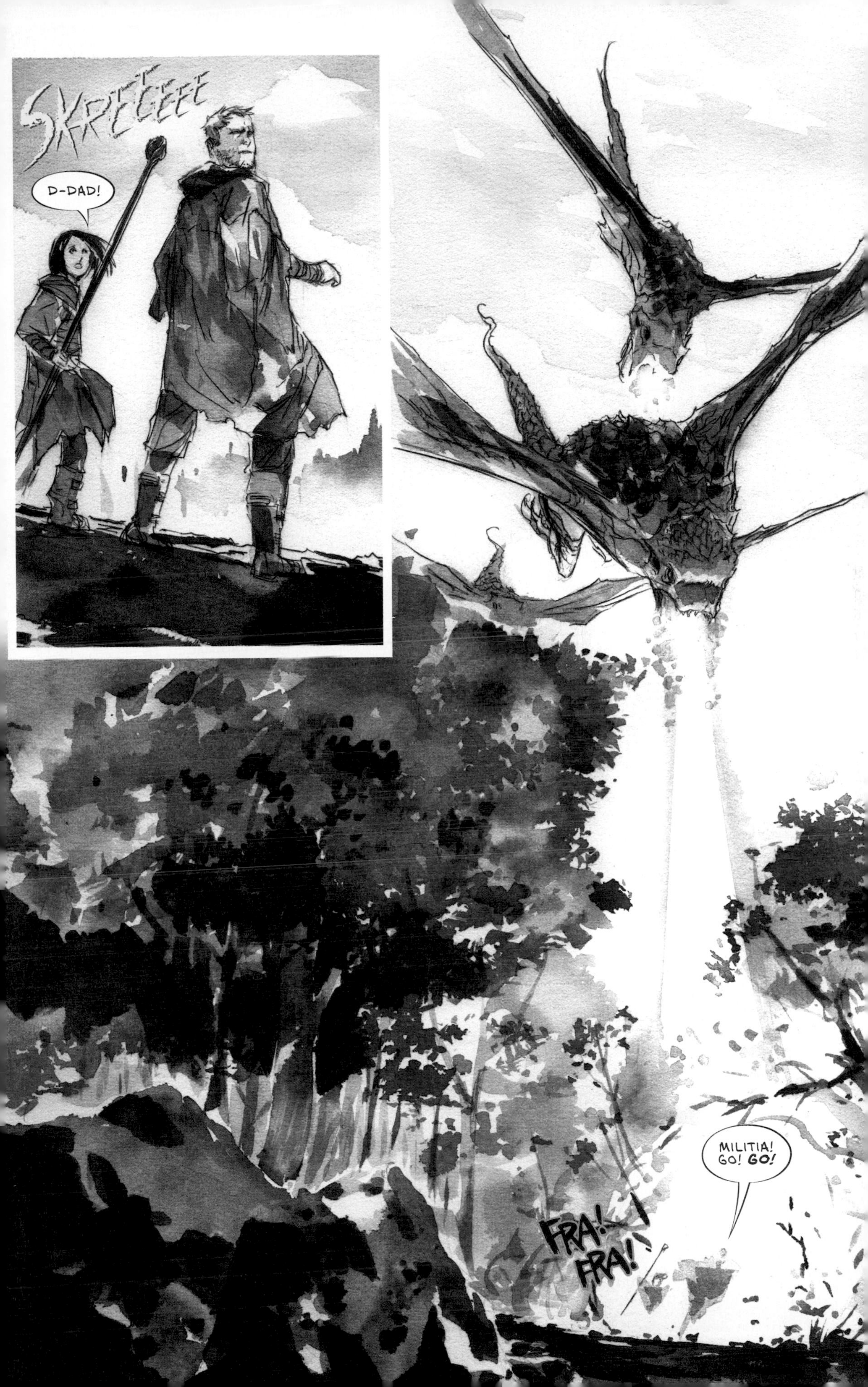
SKREEEEE
D-DAD!
MILITIA! GO! GO!
FRA! FRA!

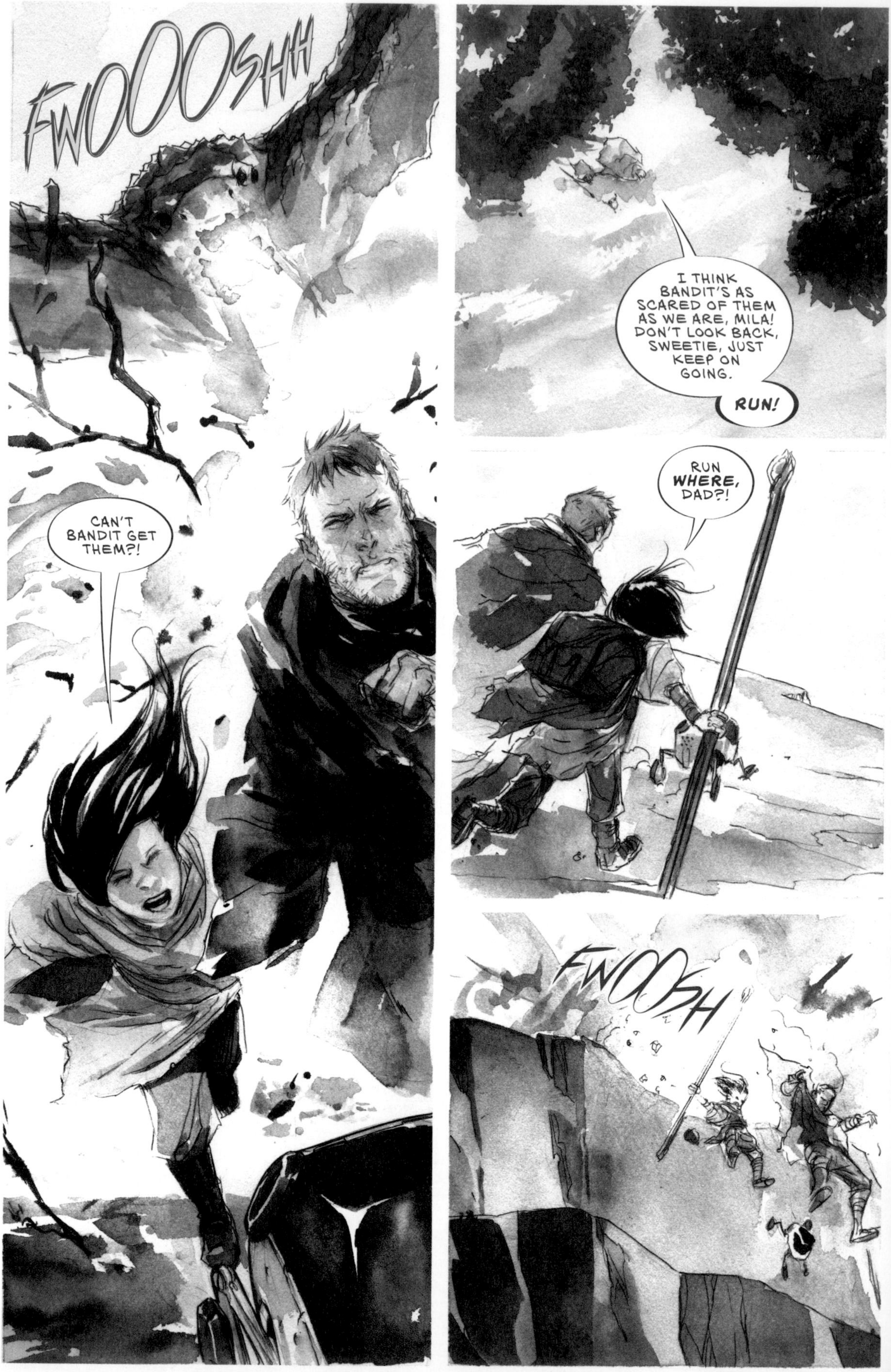
FWOOOSHH
CAN'T BANDIT GET THEM?!
I THINK BANDIT'S AS SCARED OF THEM AS WE ARE, MILA! DON'T LOOK BACK, SWEETIE, JUST KEEP ON GOING.
RUN!
RUN WHERE, DAD?!
FWOOSH

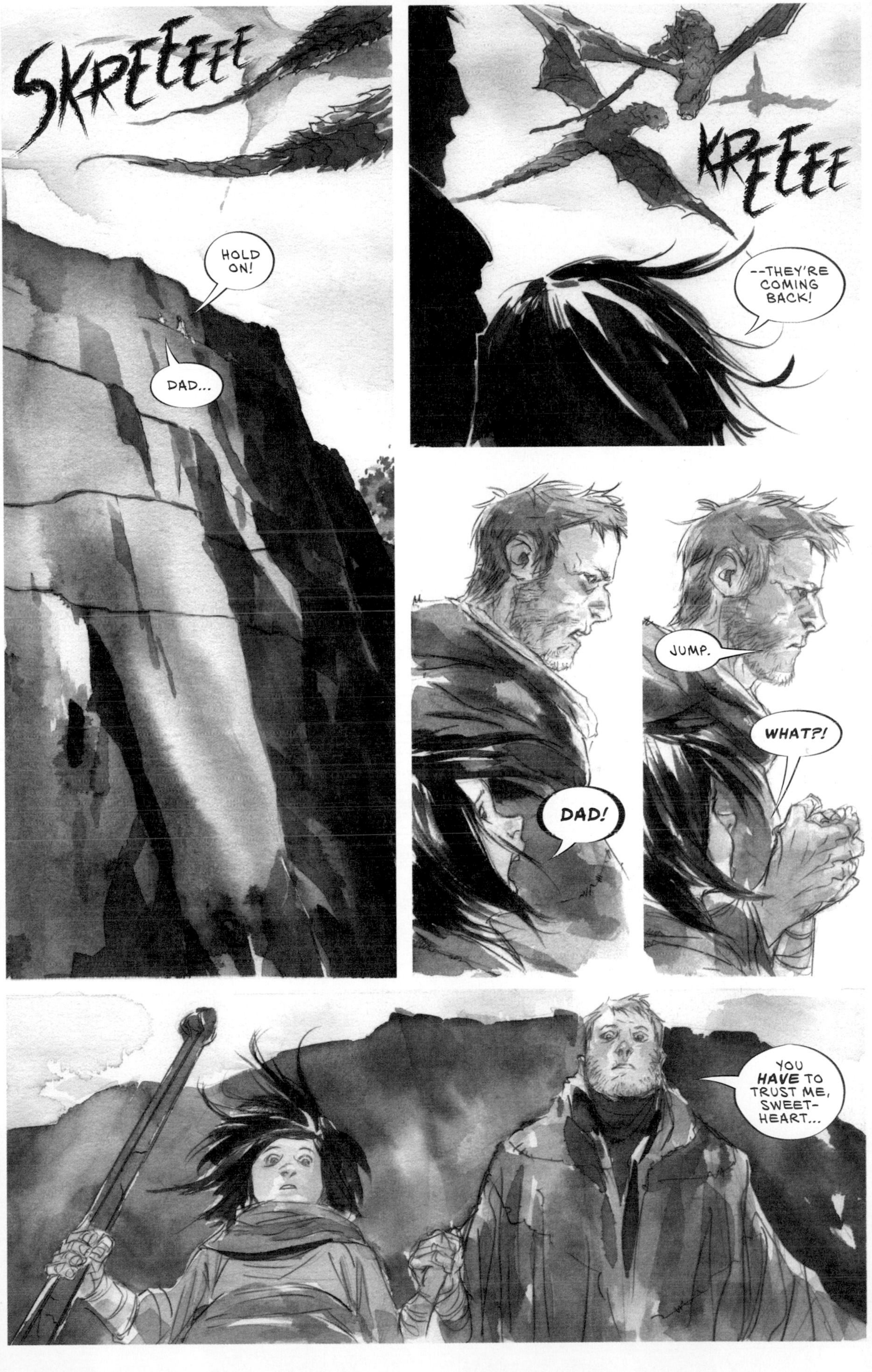
SKREEEEE
HOLD ON!
DAD...
KREEEE
--THEY'RE COMING BACK!
DAD!
JUMP.
WHAT?!
YOU **HAVE** TO TRUST ME, SWEET-HEART...

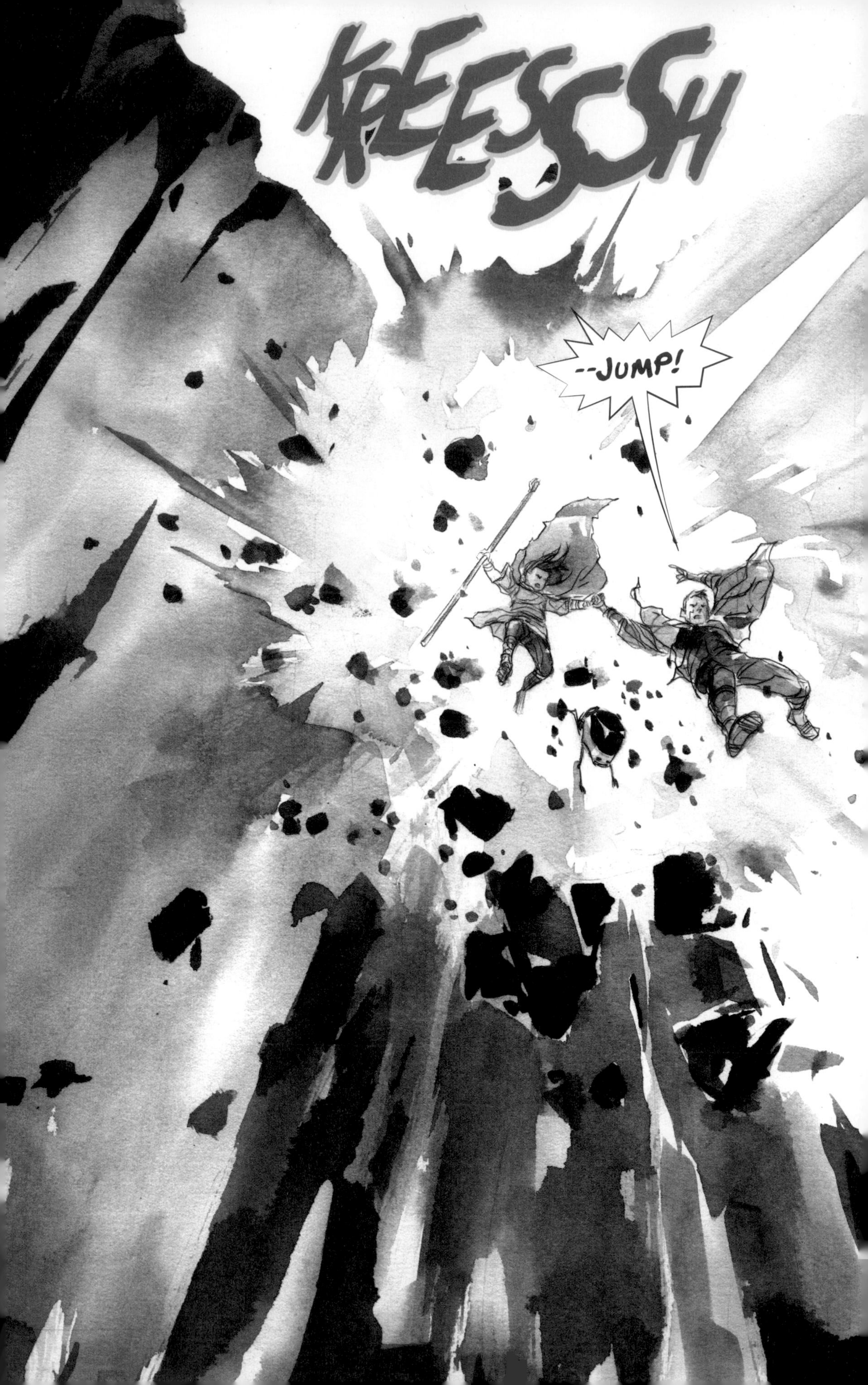
KREESSH
--JUMP!

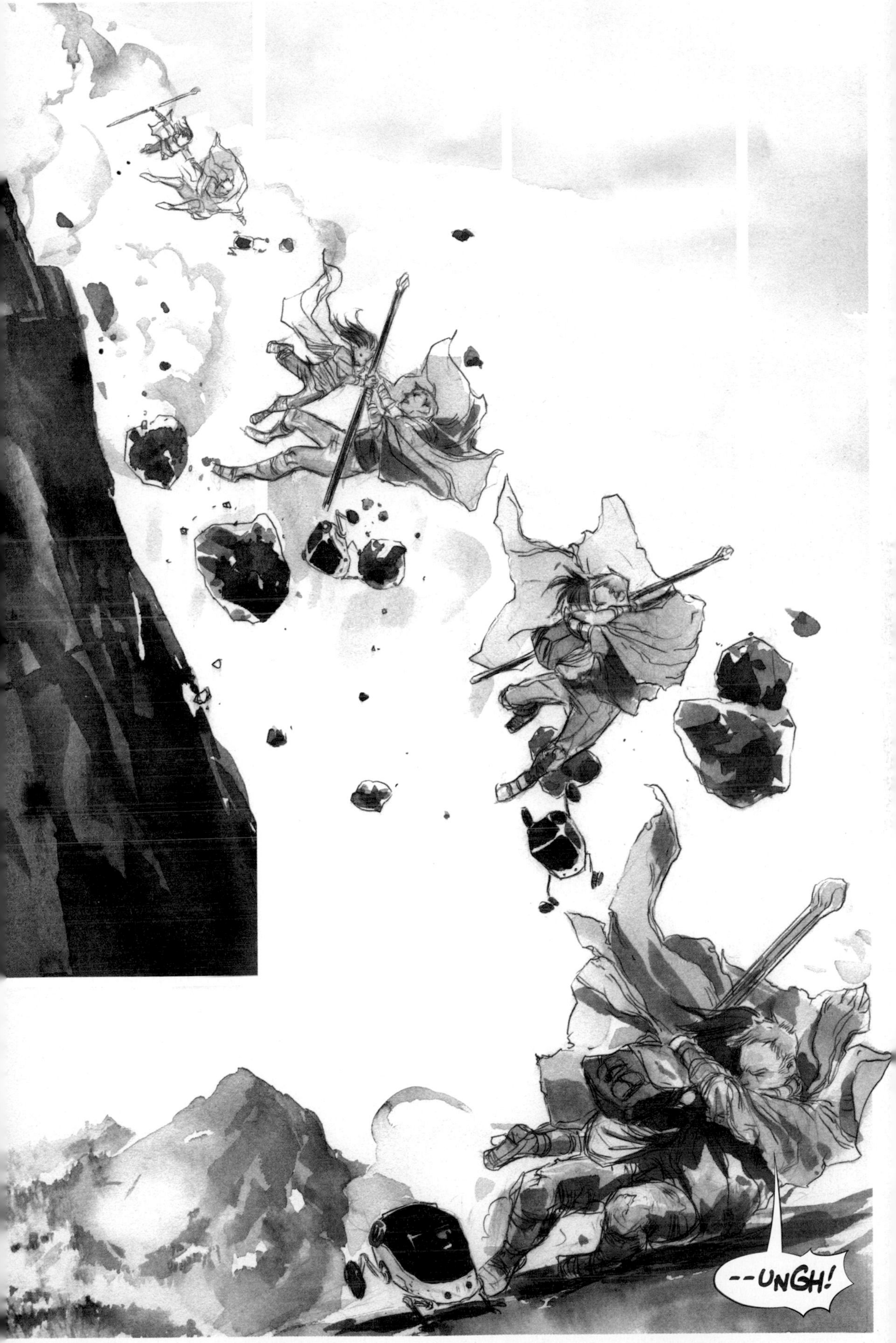
--UNGH!

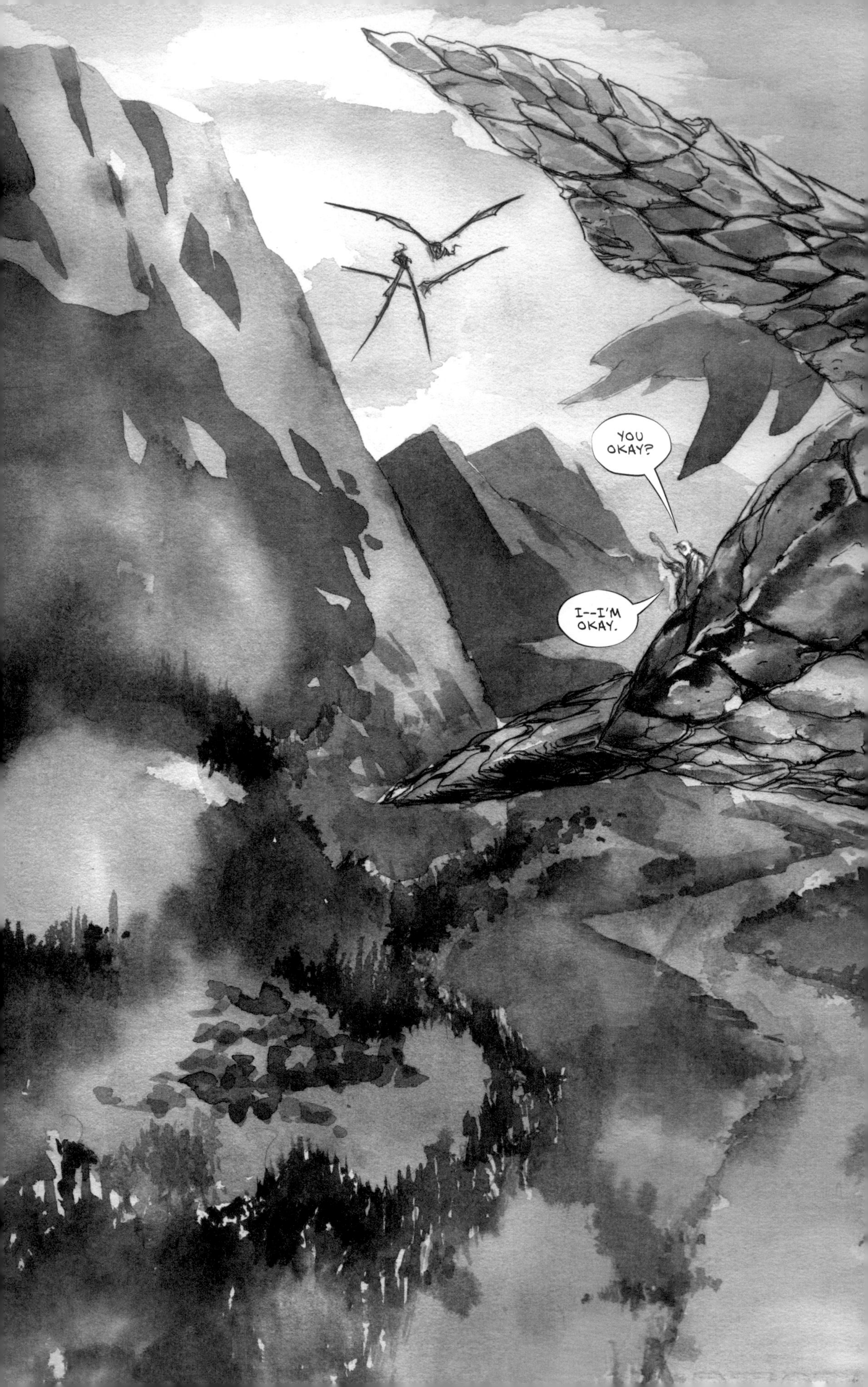
YOU OKAY?
I--I'M OKAY.

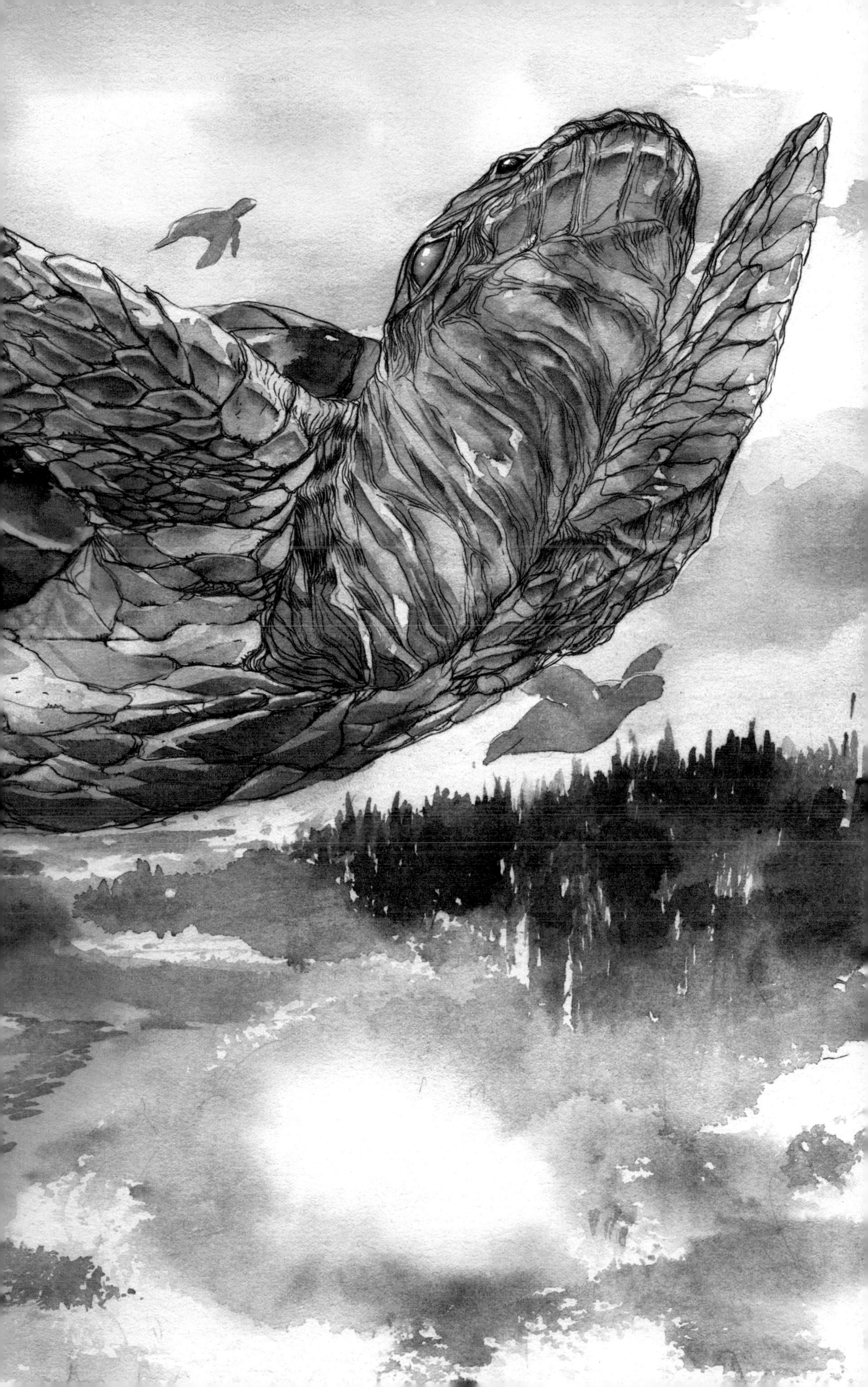

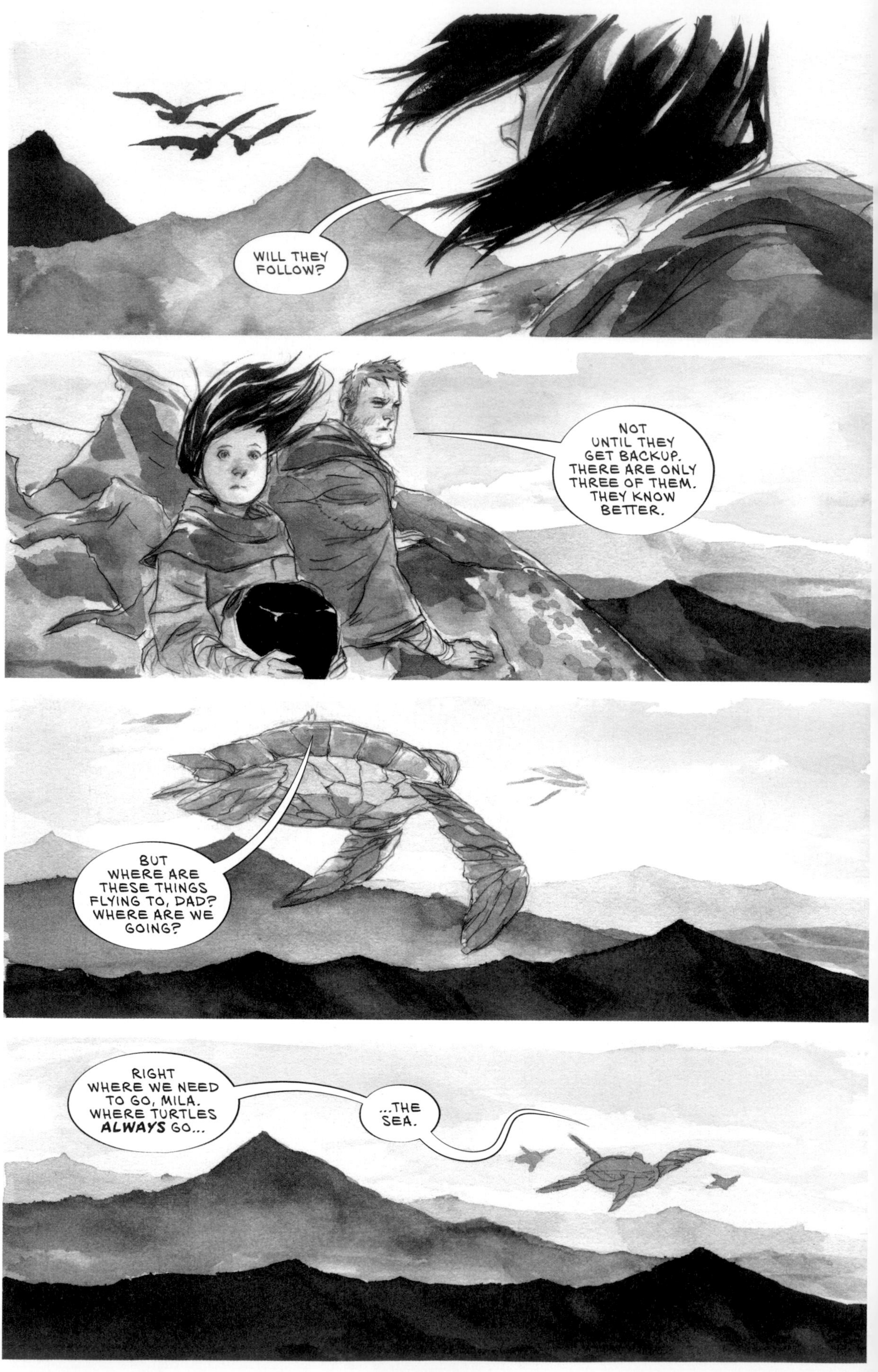
WILL THEY FOLLOW?
NOT UNTIL THEY GET BACKUP. THERE ARE ONLY THREE OF THEM. THEY KNOW BETTER.
BUT WHERE ARE THESE THINGS FLYING TO, DAD? WHERE ARE WE GOING?
RIGHT WHERE WE NEED TO GO, MILA. WHERE TURTLES **ALWAYS** GO...
...THE SEA.

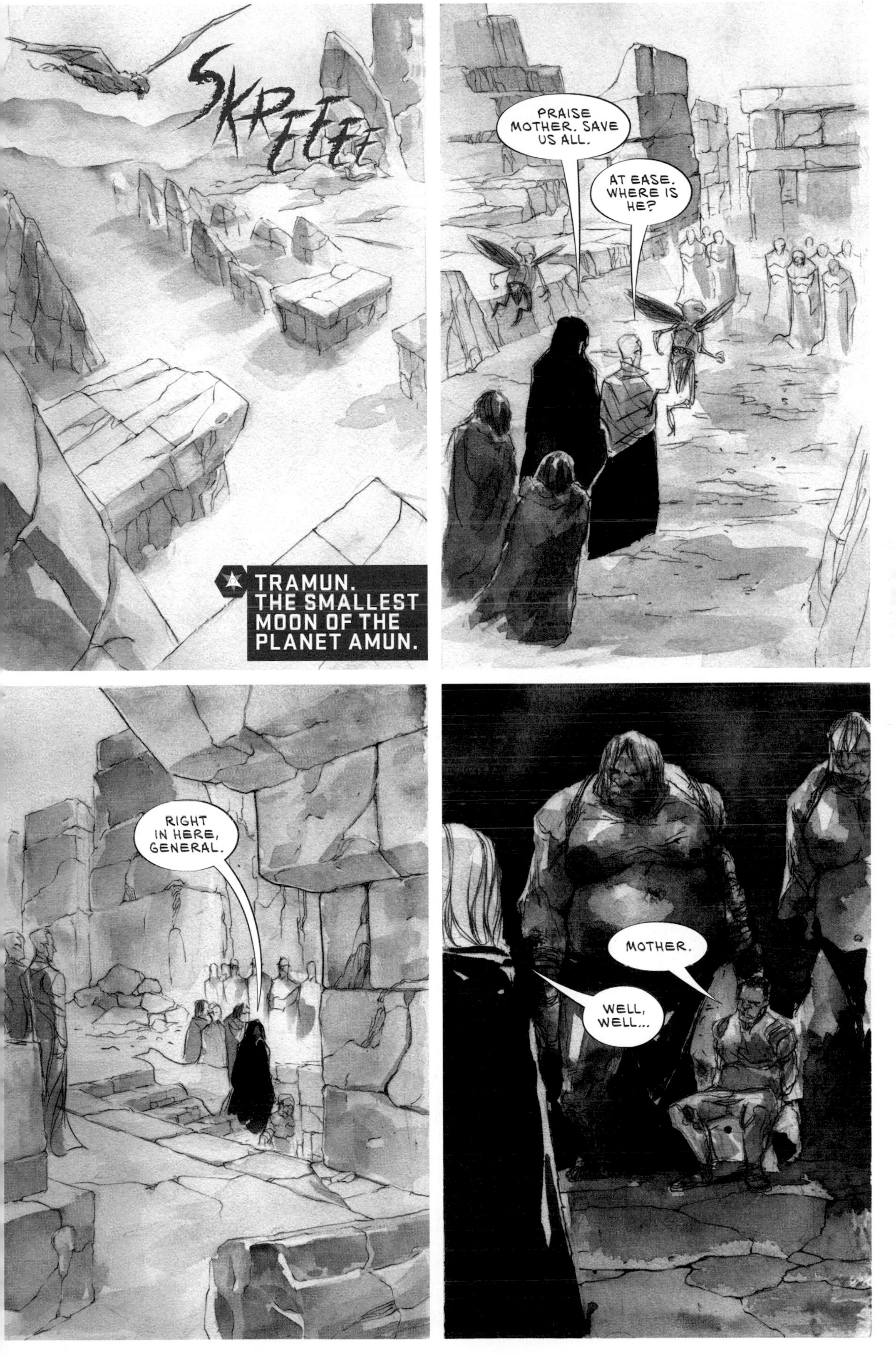

SKREEEE
TRAMUN. THE SMALLEST MOON OF THE PLANET AMUN.
PRAISE MOTHER. SAVE US ALL.
AT EASE. WHERE IS HE?
RIGHT IN HERE, GENERAL.
MOTHER.
WELL, WELL...

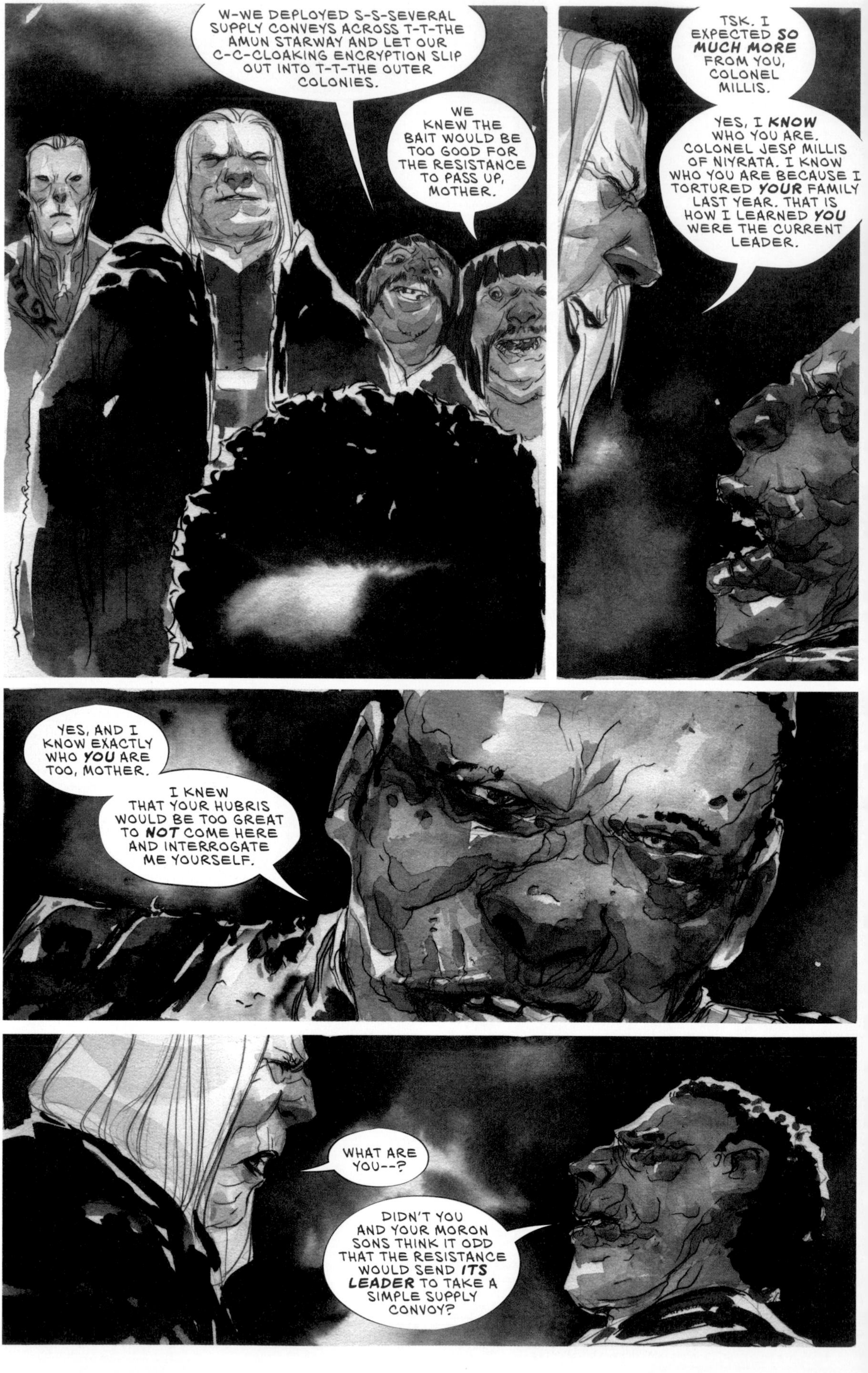
W-WE DEPLOYED S-S-SEVERAL SUPPLY CONVEYS ACROSS T-T-THE AMUN STARWAY AND LET OUR C-C-CLOAKING ENCRYPTION SLIP OUT INTO T-T-THE OUTER COLONIES.
WE KNEW THE BAIT WOULD BE TOO GOOD FOR THE RESISTANCE TO PASS UP, MOTHER.
TSK. I EXPECTED SO MUCH MORE FROM YOU, COLONEL MILLIS.
YES, I KNOW WHO YOU ARE. COLONEL JESP MILLIS OF NIYRATA. I KNOW WHO YOU ARE BECAUSE I TORTURED YOUR FAMILY LAST YEAR. THAT IS HOW I LEARNED YOU WERE THE CURRENT LEADER.
YES, AND I KNOW EXACTLY WHO YOU ARE TOO, MOTHER.
I KNEW THAT YOUR HUBRIS WOULD BE TOO GREAT TO NOT COME HERE AND INTERROGATE ME YOURSELF.
WHAT ARE YOU--?
DIDN'T YOU AND YOUR MORON SONS THINK IT ODD THAT THE RESISTANCE WOULD SEND ITS LEADER TO TAKE A SIMPLE SUPPLY CONVOY?

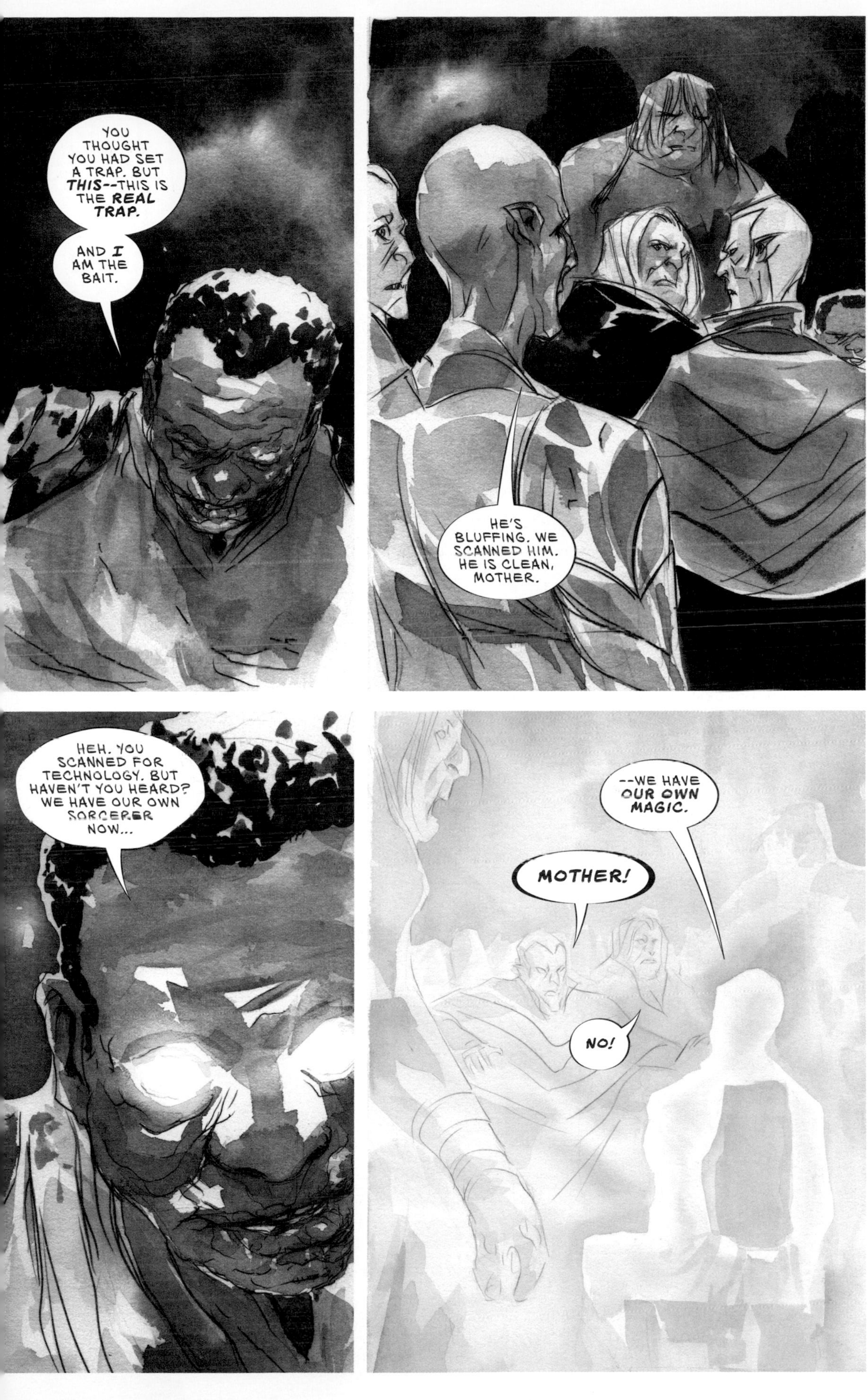
YOU THOUGHT YOU HAD SET A TRAP. BUT THIS--THIS IS THE REAL TRAP.
AND I AM THE BAIT.
HE'S BLUFFING. WE SCANNED HIM. HE IS CLEAN, MOTHER.
HEH. YOU SCANNED FOR TECHNOLOGY. BUT HAVEN'T YOU HEARD? WE HAVE OUR OWN SORCERER NOW...
--WE HAVE OUR OWN MAGIC.
MOTHER!
NO!

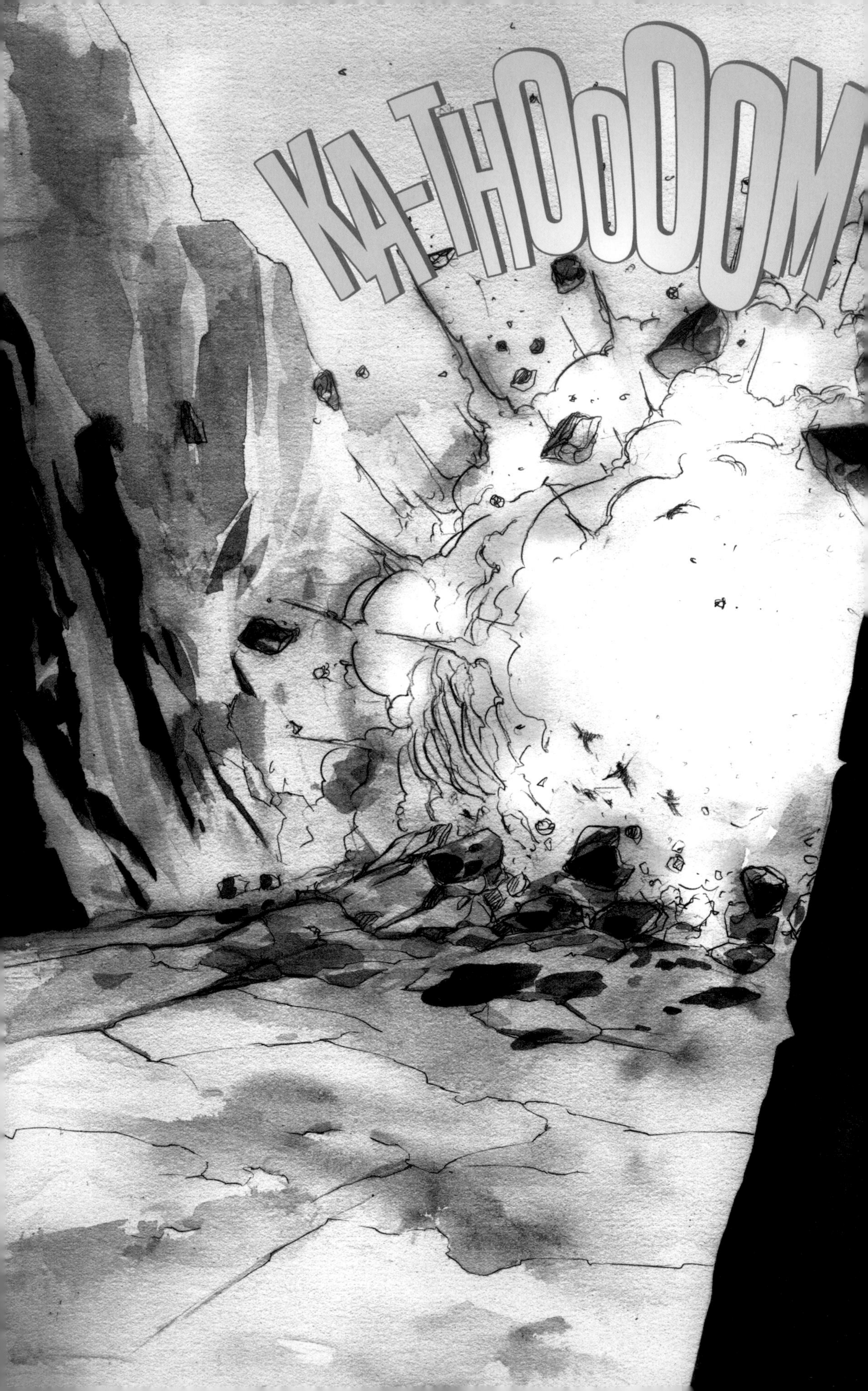
KA-THOOOOOM

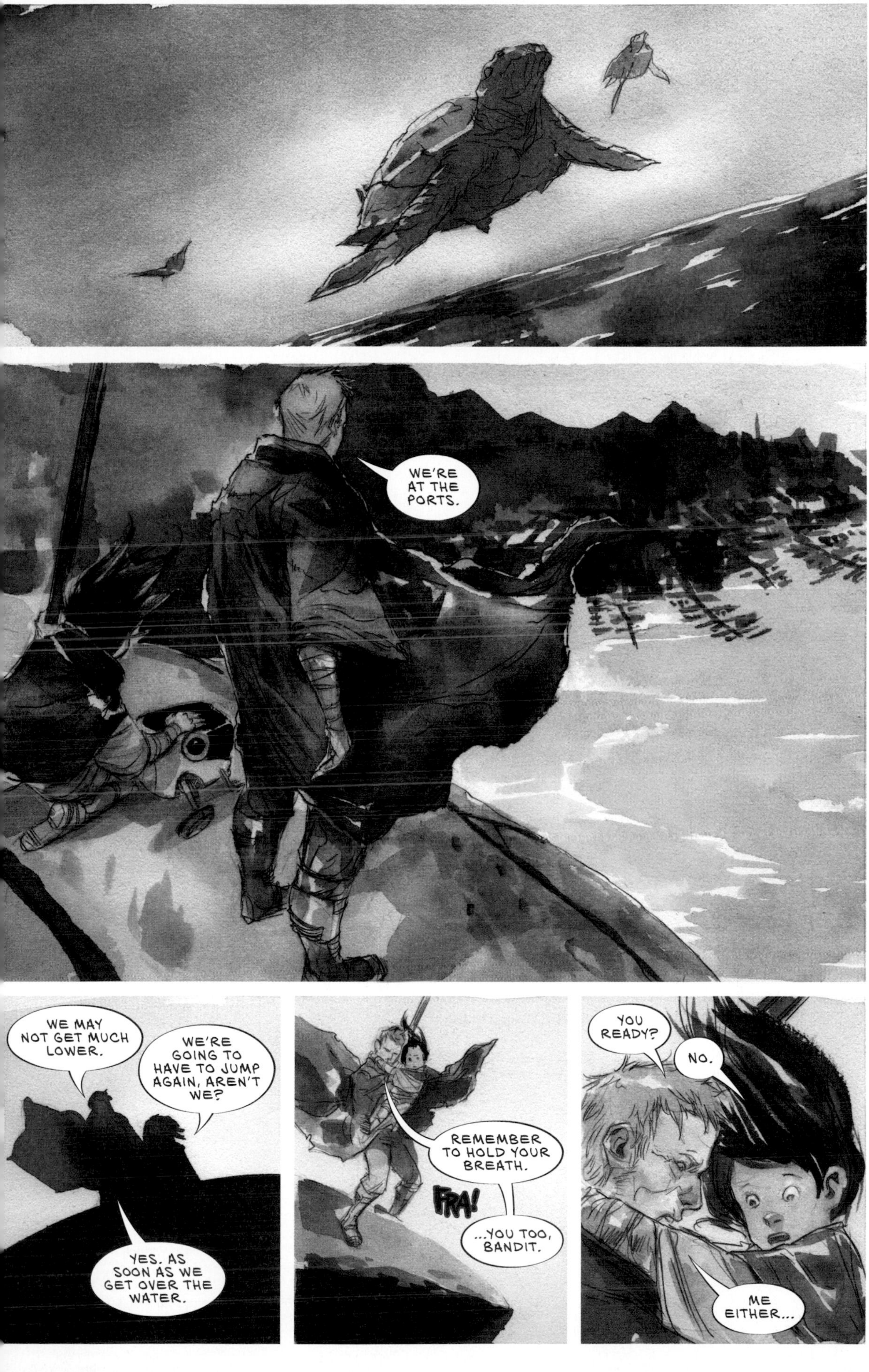
WE'RE AT THE PORTS.
WE MAY NOT GET MUCH LOWER.
WE'RE GOING TO HAVE TO JUMP AGAIN, AREN'T WE?
YES. AS SOON AS WE GET OVER THE WATER.
REMEMBER TO HOLD YOUR BREATH.
FRA!
...YOU TOO, BANDIT.
YOU READY?
NO.
ME EITHER...

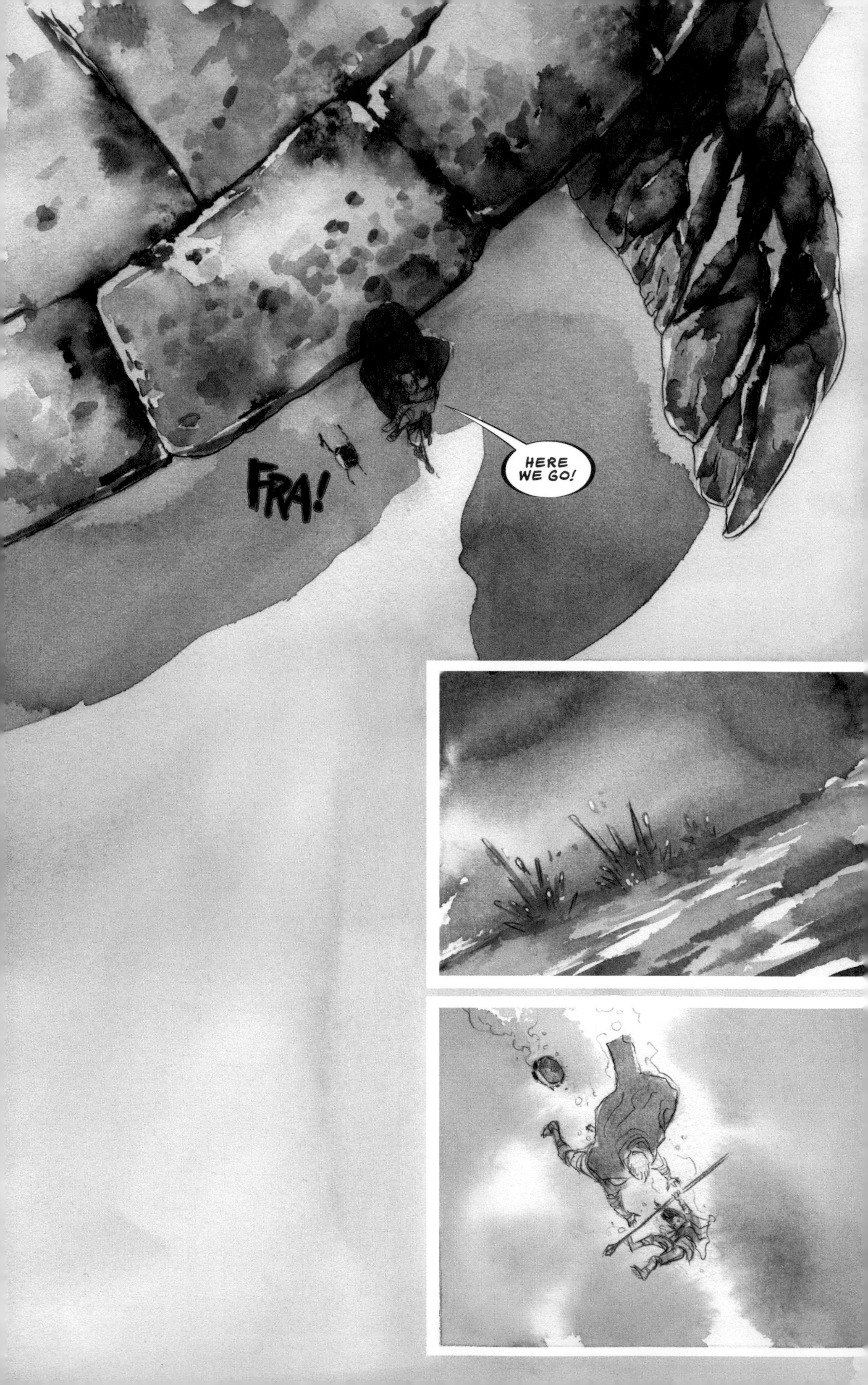
FRA!
HERE WE GO!

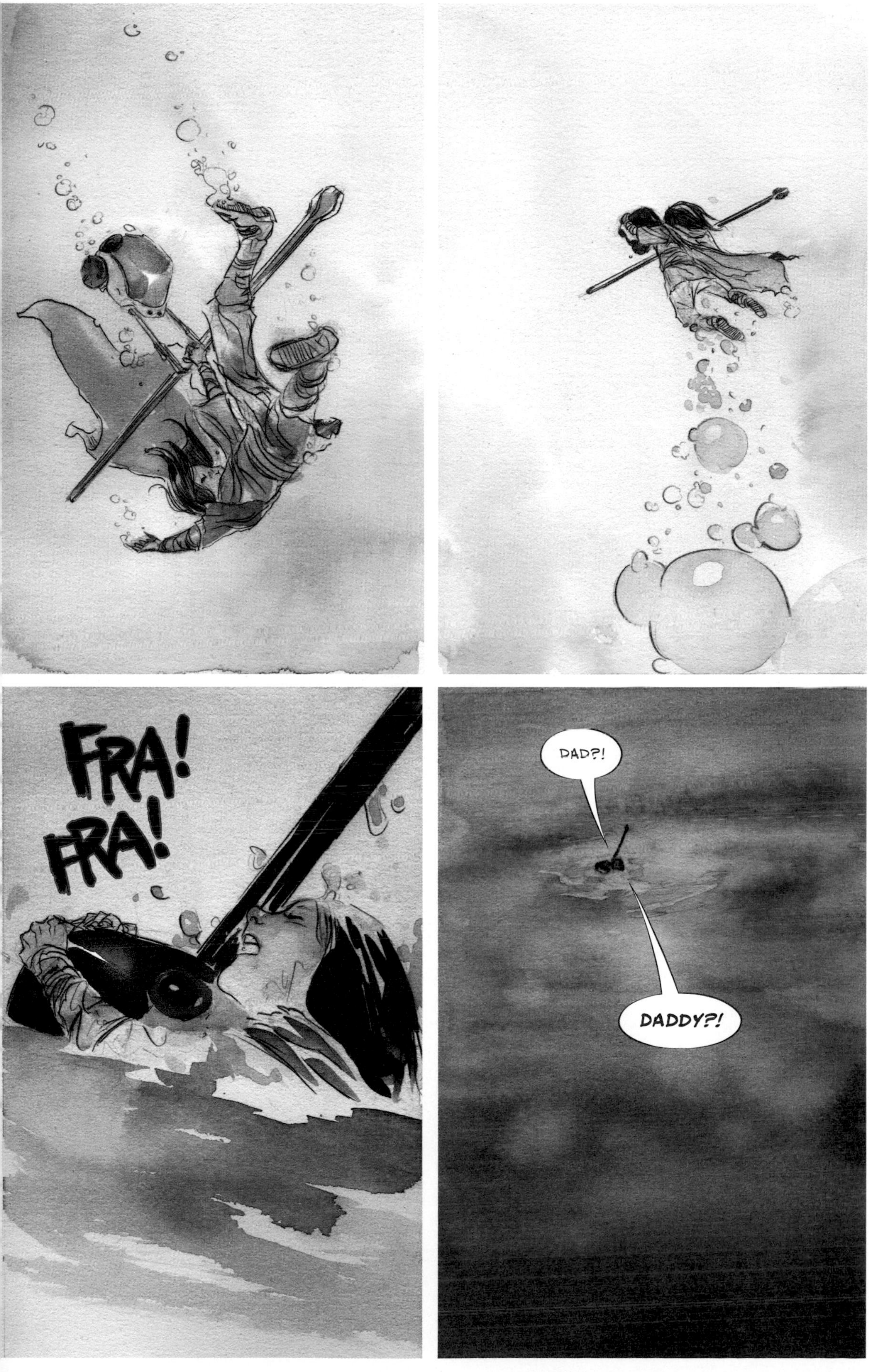
FRA!
FRA!
DAD?!
DADDY?!

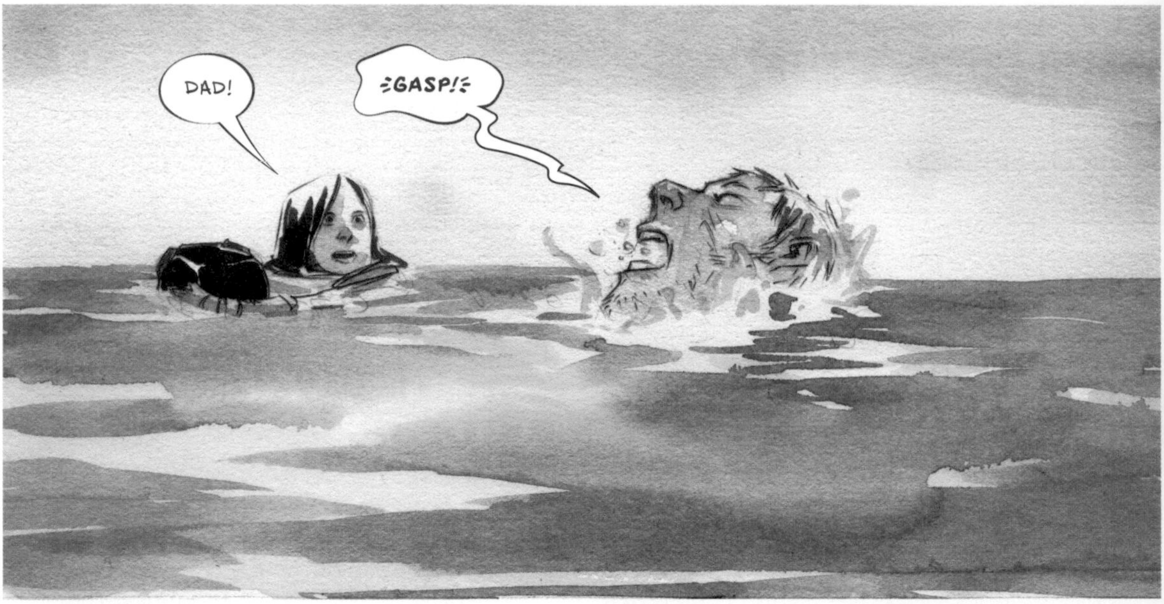
DAD!
GASP!

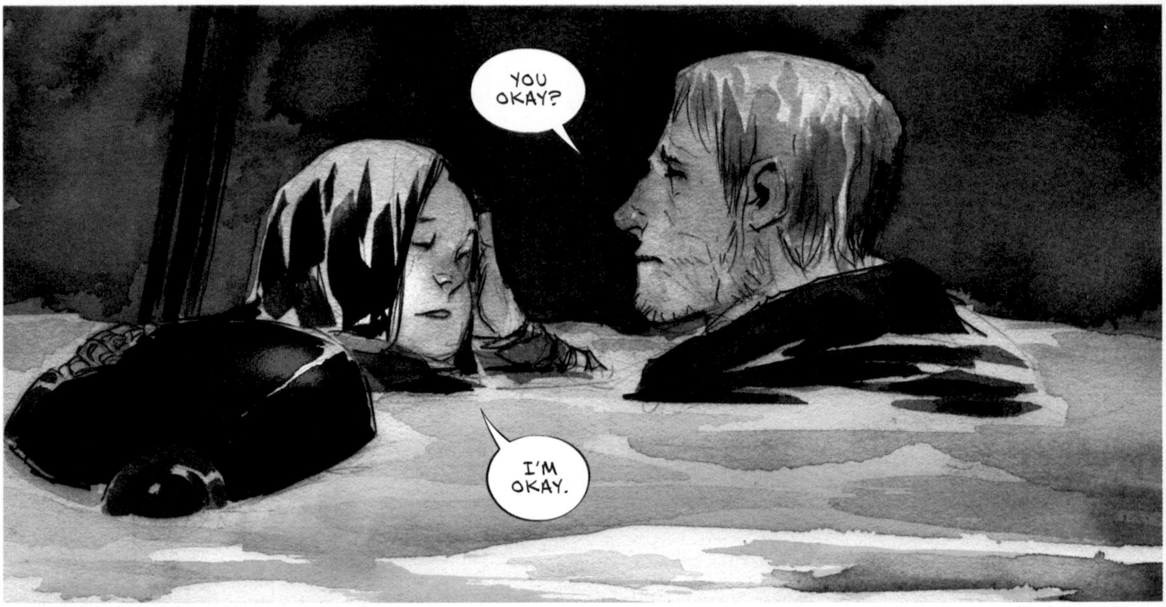
YOU OKAY?
I'M OKAY.

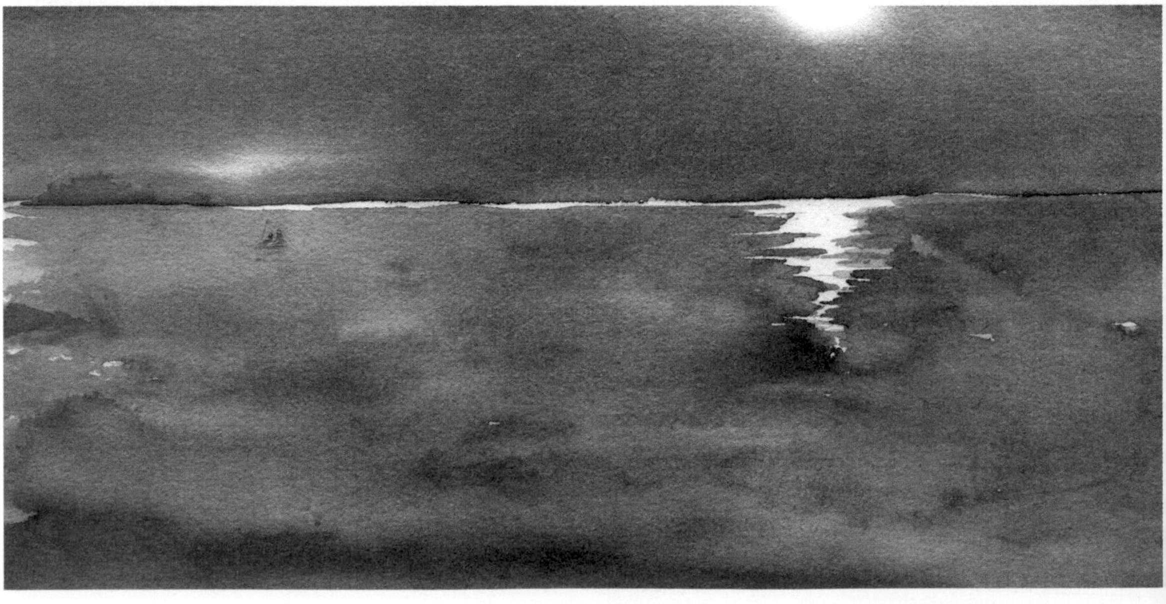

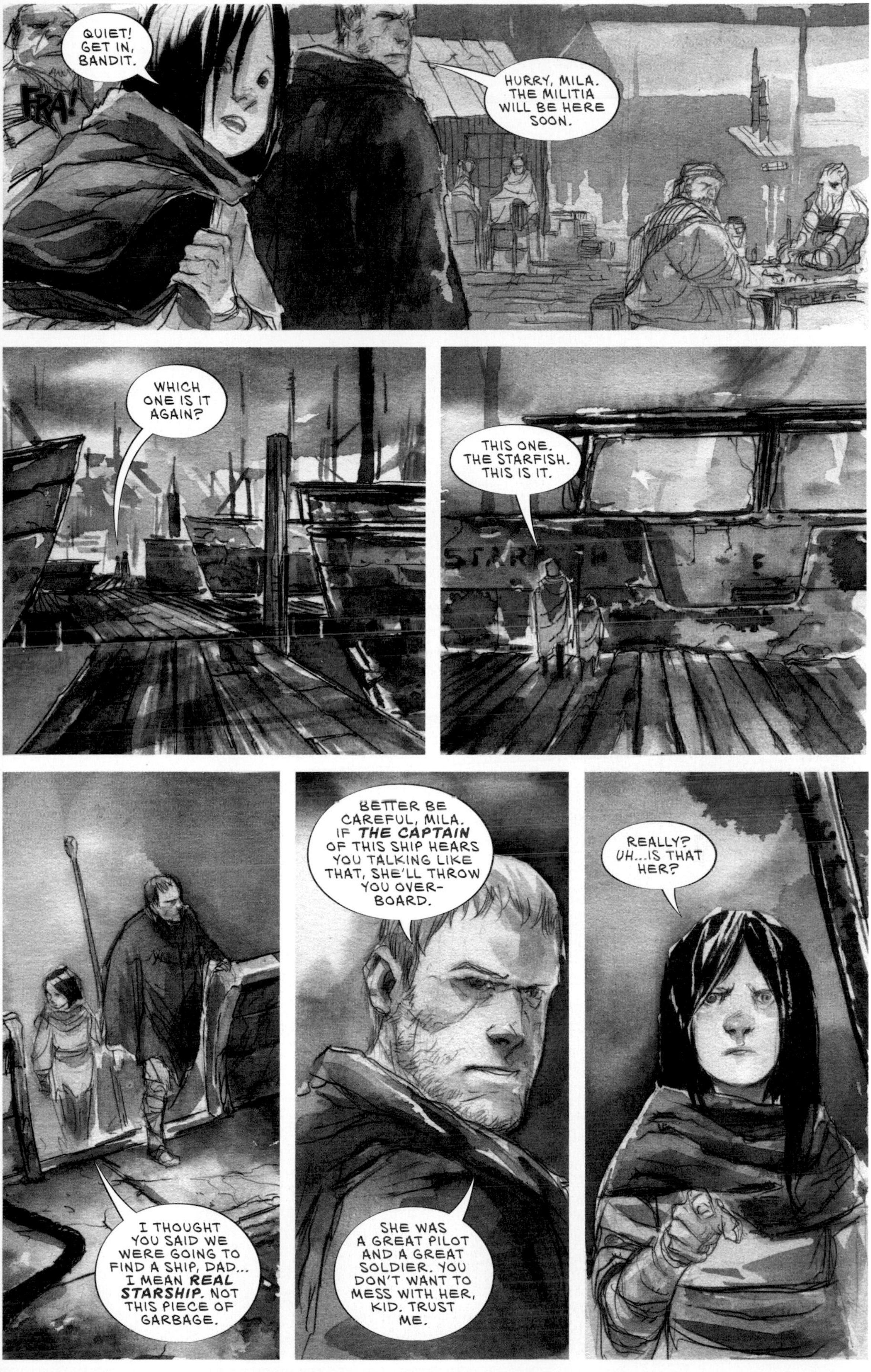
QUIET! GET IN, BANDIT.
FRA!
HURRY, MILA. THE MILITIA WILL BE HERE SOON.
WHICH ONE IS IT AGAIN?
THIS ONE. THE STARFISH. THIS IS IT.
I THOUGHT YOU SAID WE WERE GOING TO FIND A SHIP, DAD... I MEAN REAL STARSHIP. NOT THIS PIECE OF GARBAGE.
BETTER BE CAREFUL, MILA. IF THE CAPTAIN OF THIS SHIP HEARS YOU TALKING LIKE THAT, SHE'LL THROW YOU OVER-BOARD.
SHE WAS A GREAT PILOT AND A GREAT SOLDIER. YOU DON'T WANT TO MESS WITH HER, KID. TRUST ME.
REALLY? UH...IS THAT HER?

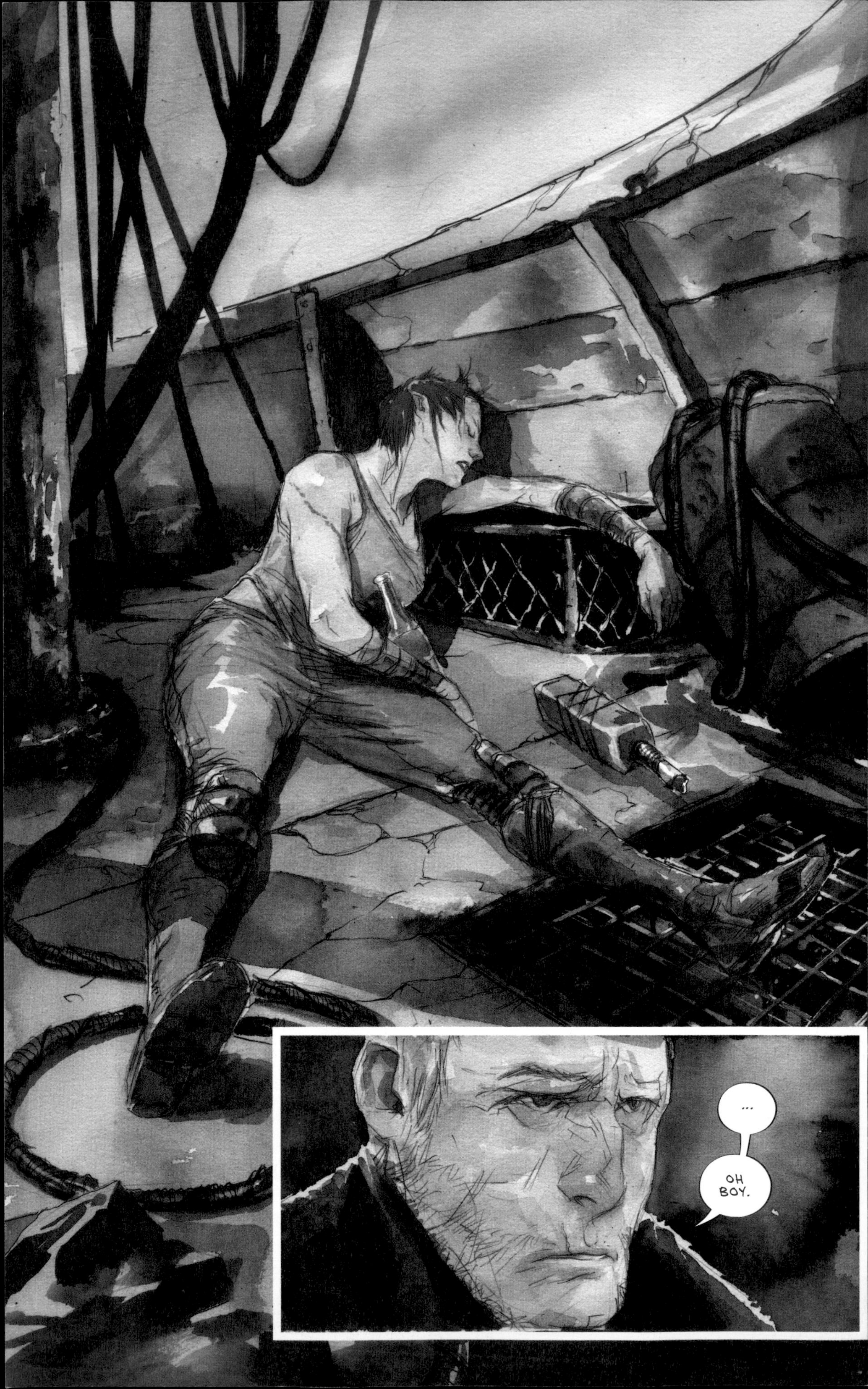
...
OH BOY.

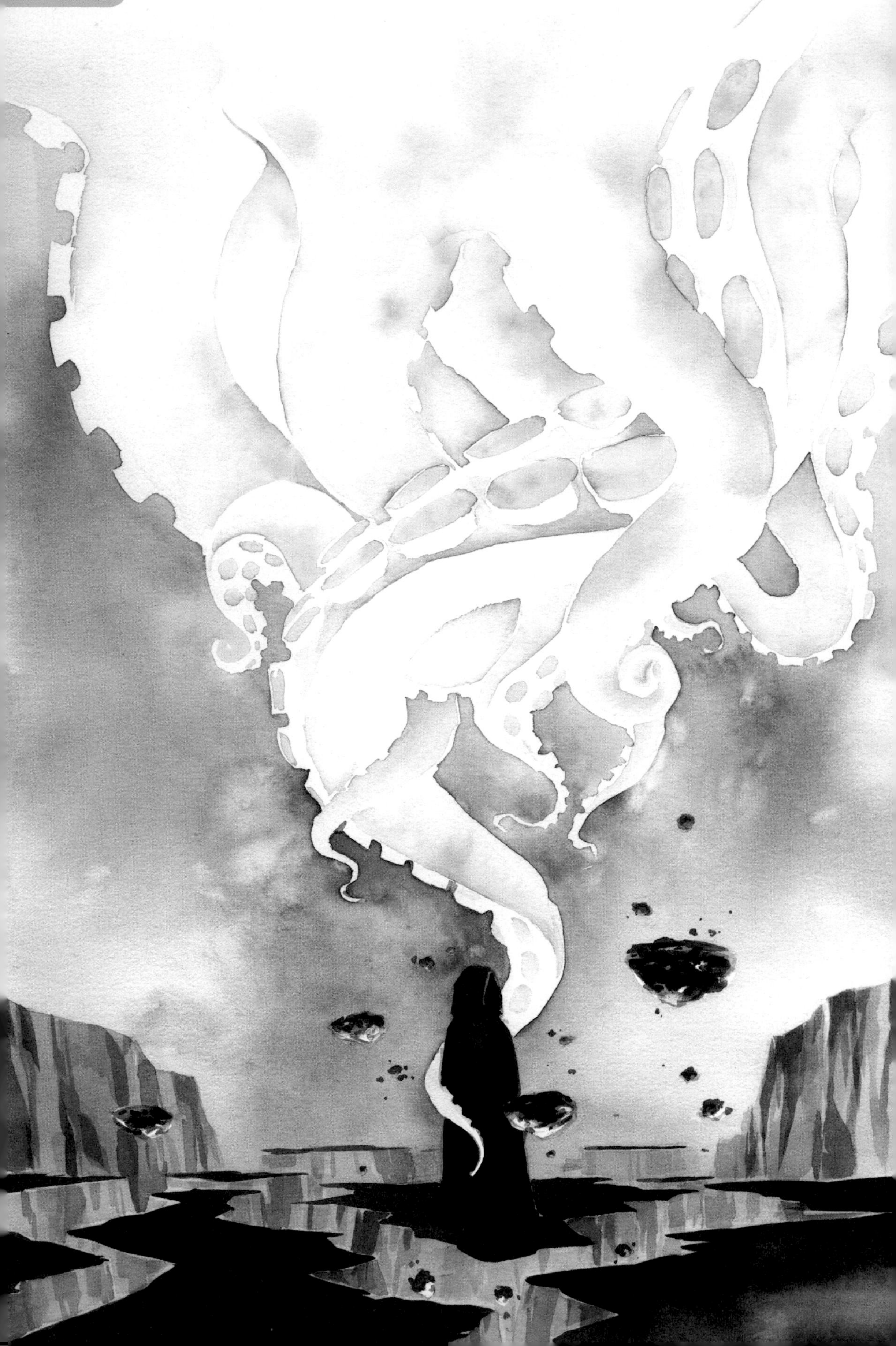

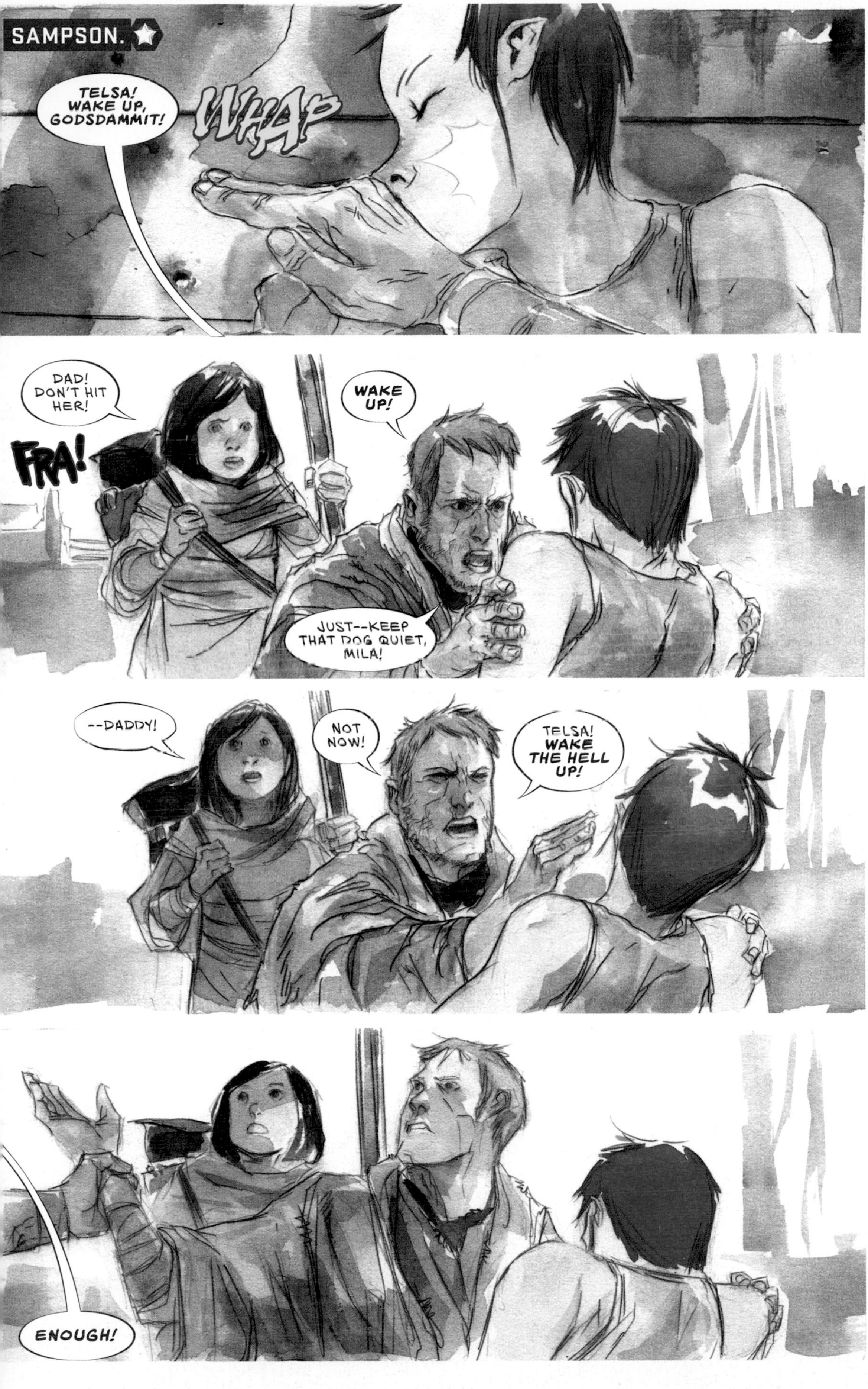
SAMPSON.
TELSA! WAKE UP, GODSDAMMIT!
WHAP
DAD! DON'T HIT HER!
FRA!
WAKE UP!
JUST--KEEP THAT DOG QUIET, MILA!
--DADDY!
NOT NOW!
TELSA! WAKE THE HELL UP!
ENOUGH!

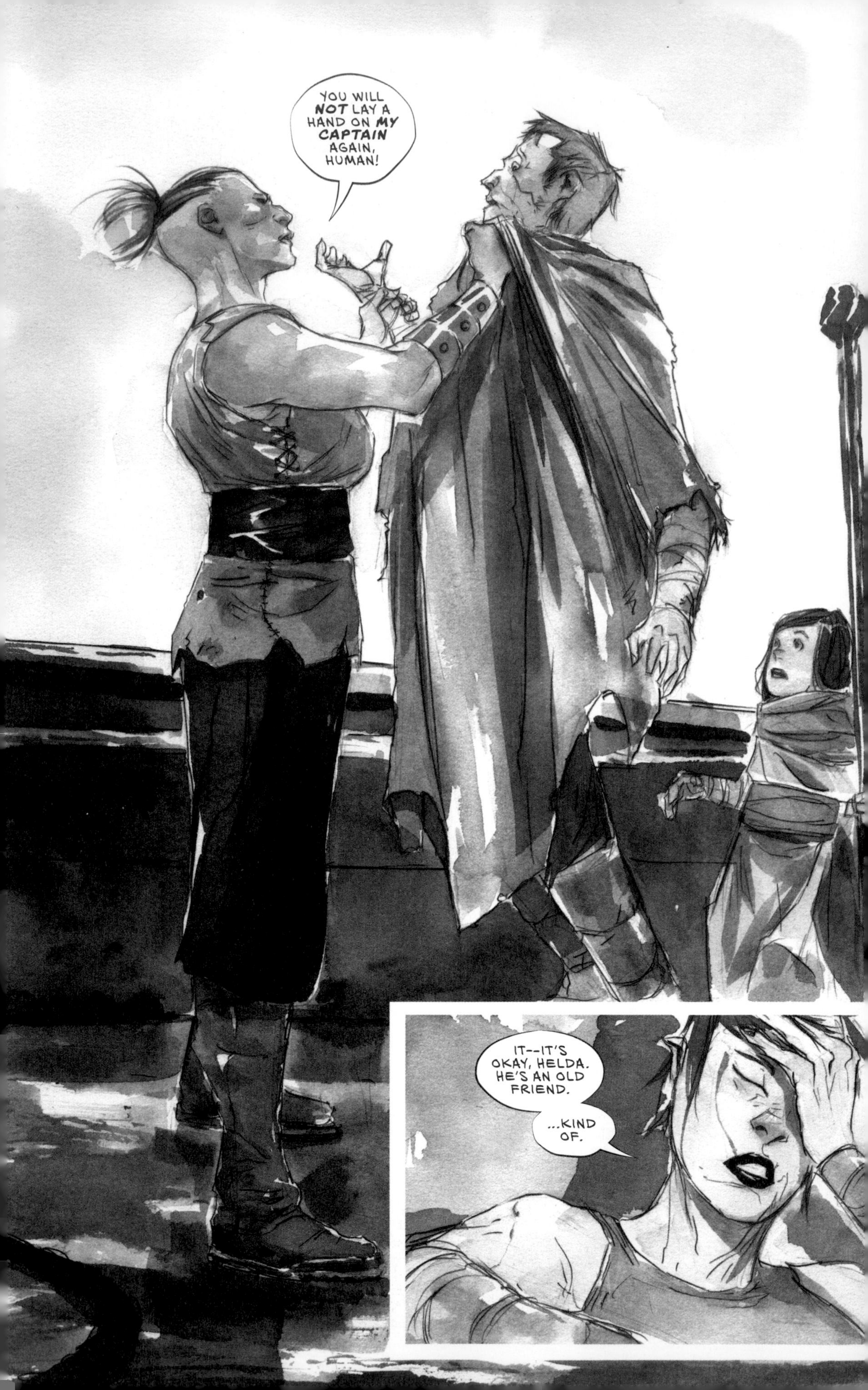
YOU WILL NOT LAY A HAND ON MY CAPTAIN AGAIN, HUMAN!
IT--IT'S OKAY, HELDA. HE'S AN OLD FRIEND.
...KIND OF.

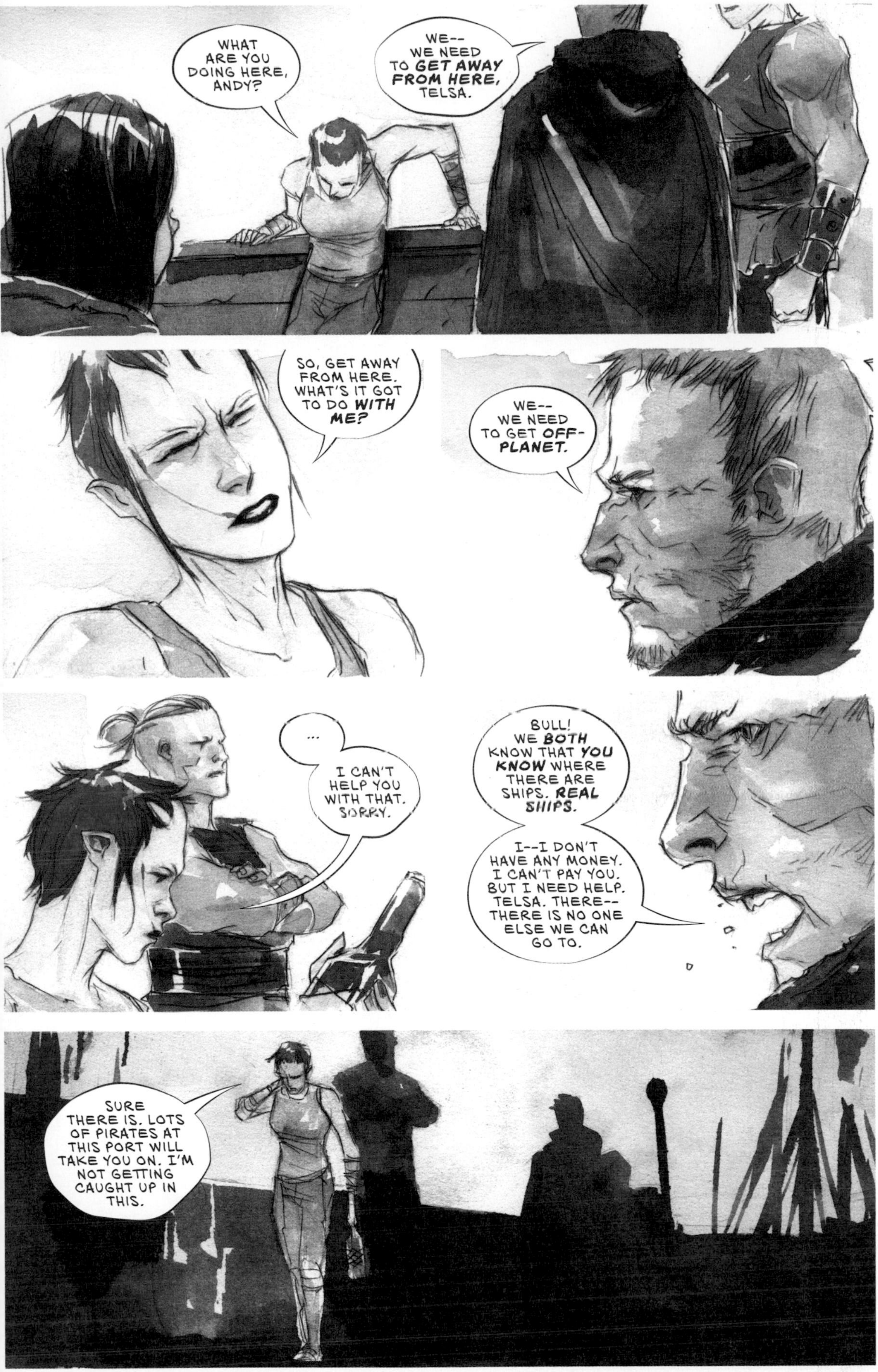
WHAT ARE YOU DOING HERE, ANDY?
WE-- WE NEED TO GET AWAY FROM HERE, TELSA.
SO, GET AWAY FROM HERE. WHAT'S IT GOT TO DO WITH ME?
WE-- WE NEED TO GET OFF-PLANET.
...
I CAN'T HELP YOU WITH THAT. SORRY.
BULL! WE BOTH KNOW THAT YOU KNOW WHERE THERE ARE SHIPS. REAL SHIPS.
I--I DON'T HAVE ANY MONEY. I CAN'T PAY YOU. BUT I NEED HELP. TELSA. THERE-- THERE IS NO ONE ELSE WE CAN GO TO.
SURE THERE IS. LOTS OF PIRATES AT THIS PORT WILL TAKE YOU ON. I'M NOT GETTING CAUGHT UP IN THIS.

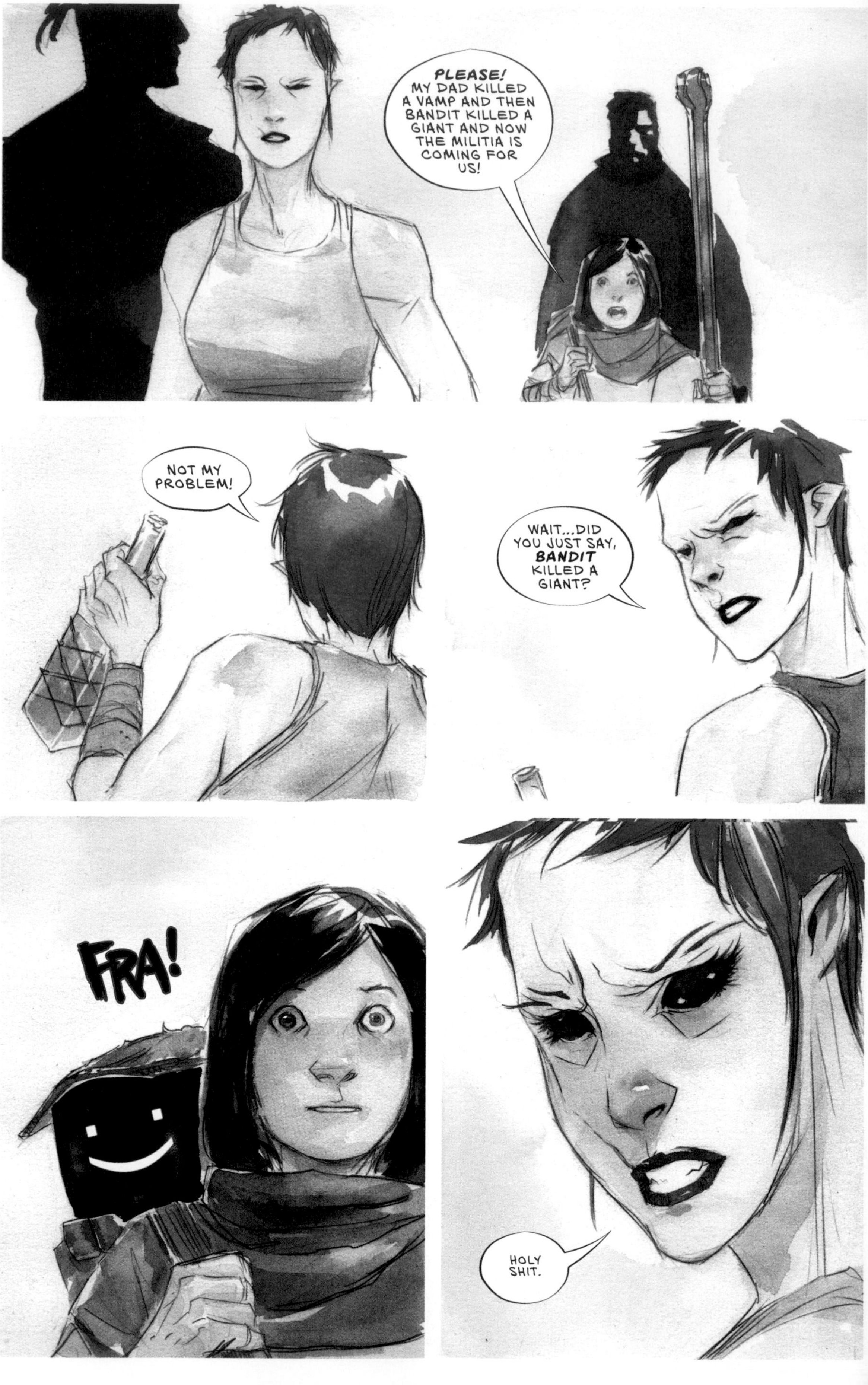
PLEASE! MY DAD KILLED A VAMP AND THEN BANDIT KILLED A GIANT AND NOW THE MILITIA IS COMING FOR US!
NOT MY PROBLEM!
WAIT...DID YOU JUST SAY, BANDIT KILLED A GIANT?
FRA!
HOLY SHIT.

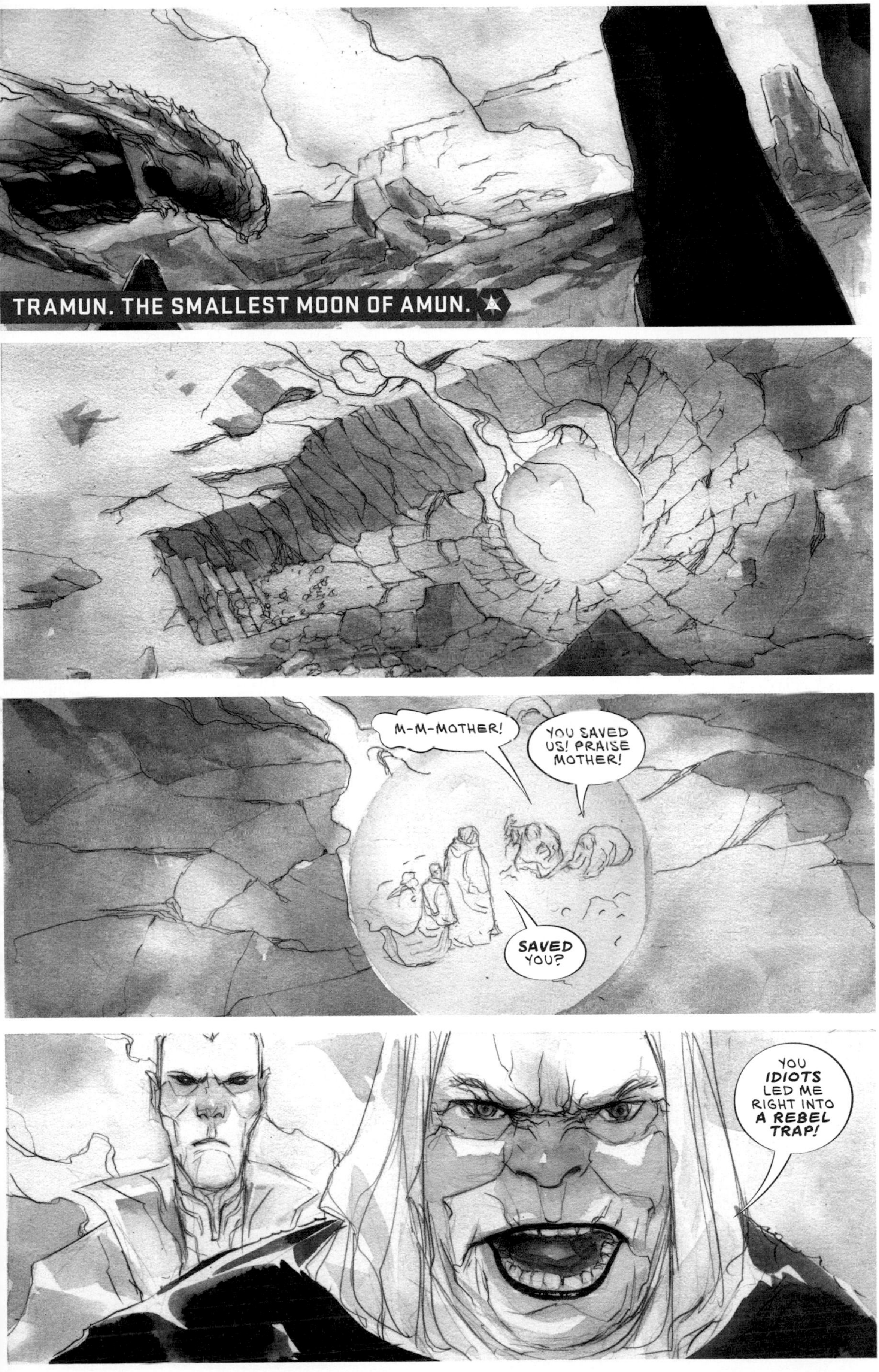
TRAMUN. THE SMALLEST MOON OF AMUN.
M-M-MOTHER!
YOU SAVED US! PRAISE MOTHER!
SAVED YOU?
YOU IDIOTS LED ME RIGHT INTO A REBEL TRAP!

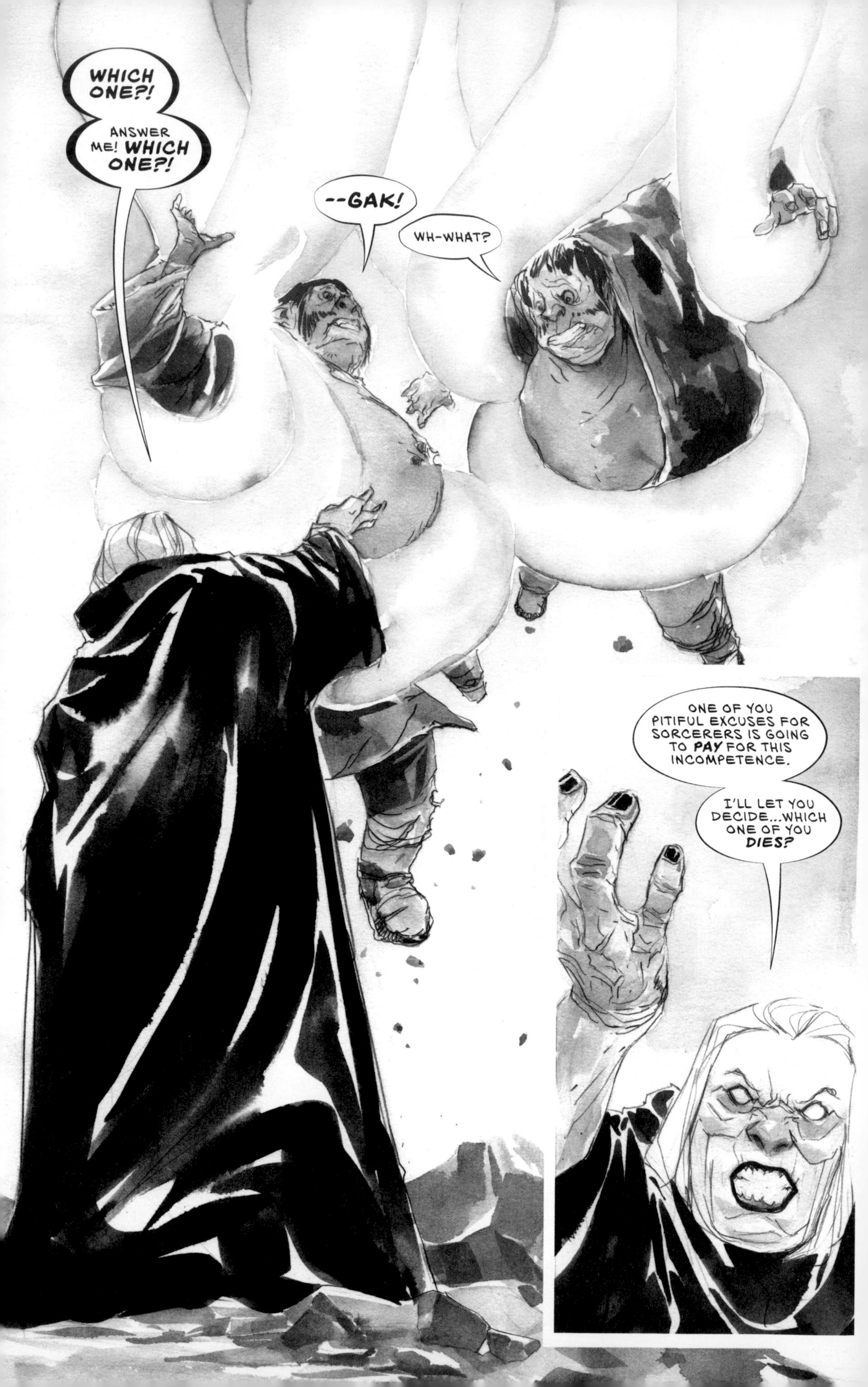
WHICH ONE?!
ANSWER ME! WHICH ONE?!
--GAK!
WH-WHAT?
ONE OF YOU PITIFUL EXCUSES FOR SORCERERS IS GOING TO PAY FOR THIS INCOMPETENCE.
I'LL LET YOU DECIDE...WHICH ONE OF YOU DIES?

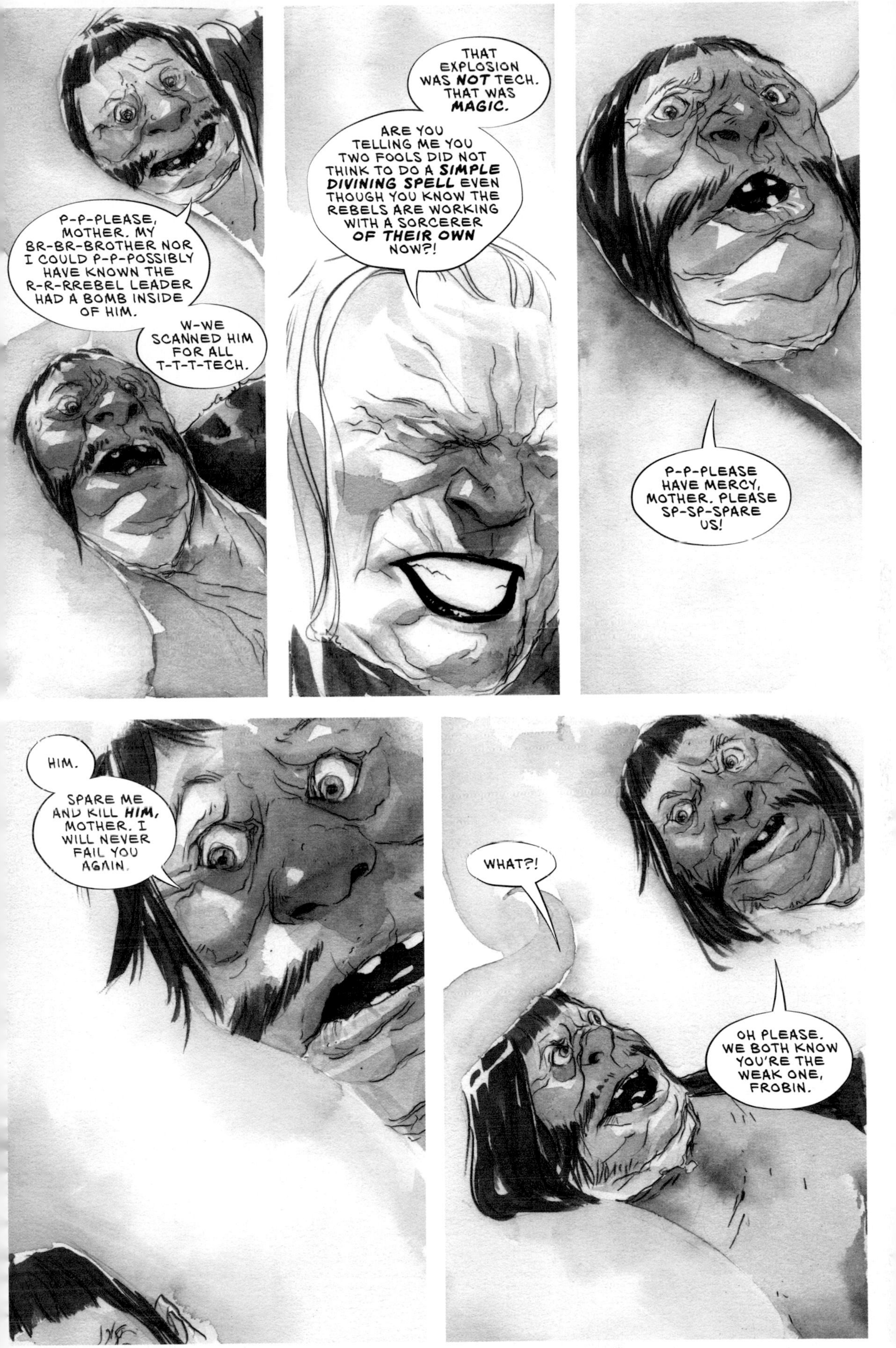
P-P-PLEASE, MOTHER. MY BR-BR-BROTHER NOR I COULD P-P-POSSIBLY HAVE KNOWN THE R-R-RREBEL LEADER HAD A BOMB INSIDE OF HIM.
W-WE SCANNED HIM FOR ALL T-T-T-TECH.
THAT EXPLOSION WAS NOT TECH. THAT WAS MAGIC.
ARE YOU TELLING ME YOU TWO FOOLS DID NOT THINK TO DO A SIMPLE DIVINING SPELL EVEN THOUGH YOU KNOW THE REBELS ARE WORKING WITH A SORCERER OF THEIR OWN NOW?!
P-P-PLEASE HAVE MERCY, MOTHER. PLEASE SP-SP-SPARE US!
HIM.
SPARE ME AND KILL HIM, MOTHER. I WILL NEVER FAIL YOU AGAIN.
WHAT?!
OH PLEASE. WE BOTH KNOW YOU'RE THE WEAK ONE, FROBIN.

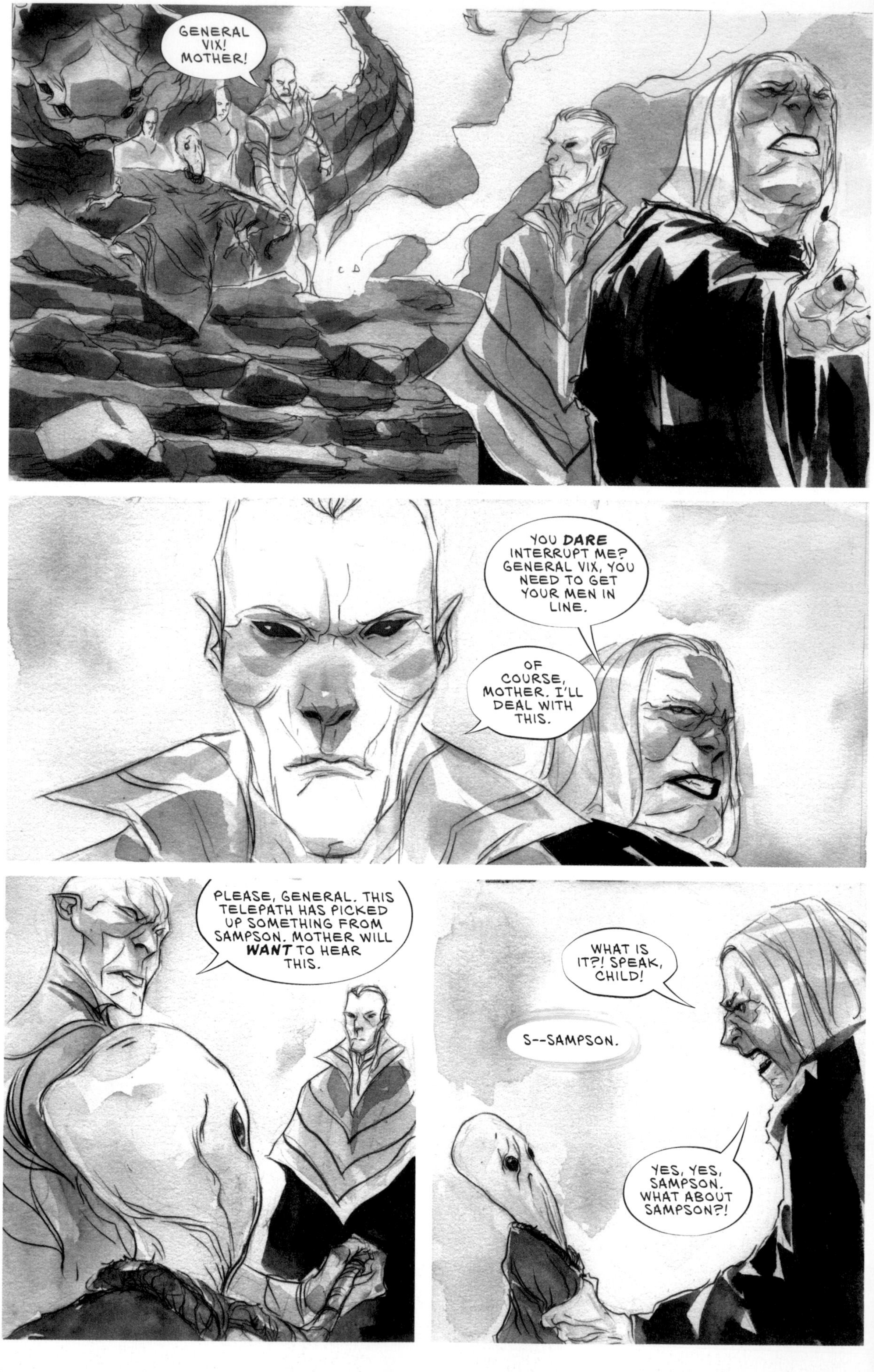
GENERAL VIX! MOTHER!
YOU **DARE** INTERRUPT ME? GENERAL VIX, YOU NEED TO GET YOUR MEN IN LINE.
OF COURSE, MOTHER. I'LL DEAL WITH THIS.
PLEASE, GENERAL. THIS TELEPATH HAS PICKED UP SOMETHING FROM SAMPSON. MOTHER WILL **WANT** TO HEAR THIS.
WHAT IS IT?! SPEAK, CHILD!
S--SAMPSON.
YES, YES, SAMPSON. WHAT ABOUT SAMPSON?!

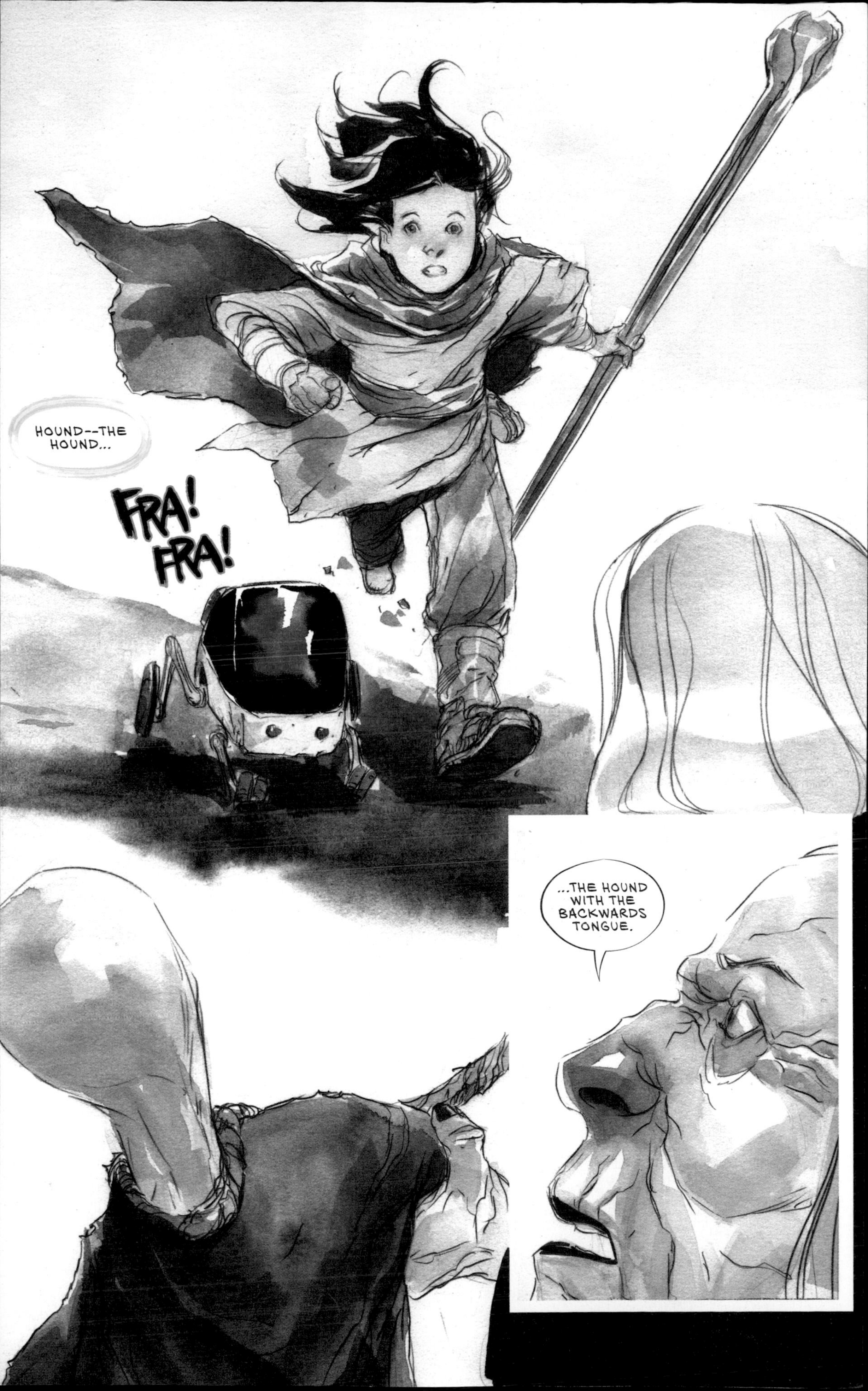
HOUND--THE HOUND...
FRA! FRA!
...THE HOUND WITH THE BACKWARDS TONGUE.

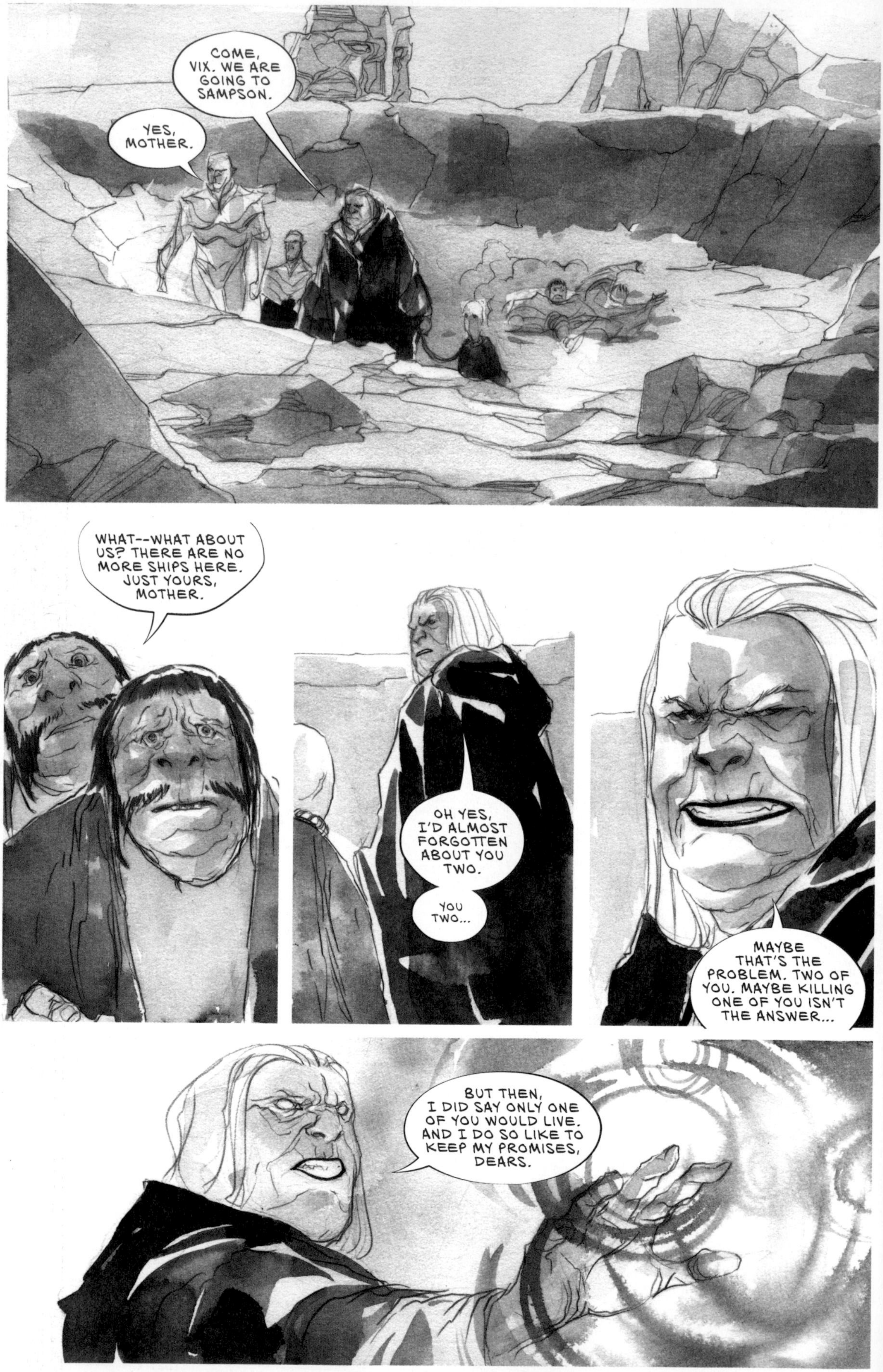
COME, VIX. WE ARE GOING TO SAMPSON.
YES, MOTHER.
WHAT--WHAT ABOUT US? THERE ARE NO MORE SHIPS HERE. JUST YOURS, MOTHER.
OH YES, I'D ALMOST FORGOTTEN ABOUT YOU TWO.
YOU TWO...
MAYBE THAT'S THE PROBLEM. TWO OF YOU. MAYBE KILLING ONE OF YOU ISN'T THE ANSWER...
BUT THEN, I DID SAY ONLY ONE OF YOU WOULD LIVE. AND I DO SO LIKE TO KEEP MY PROMISES, DEARS.

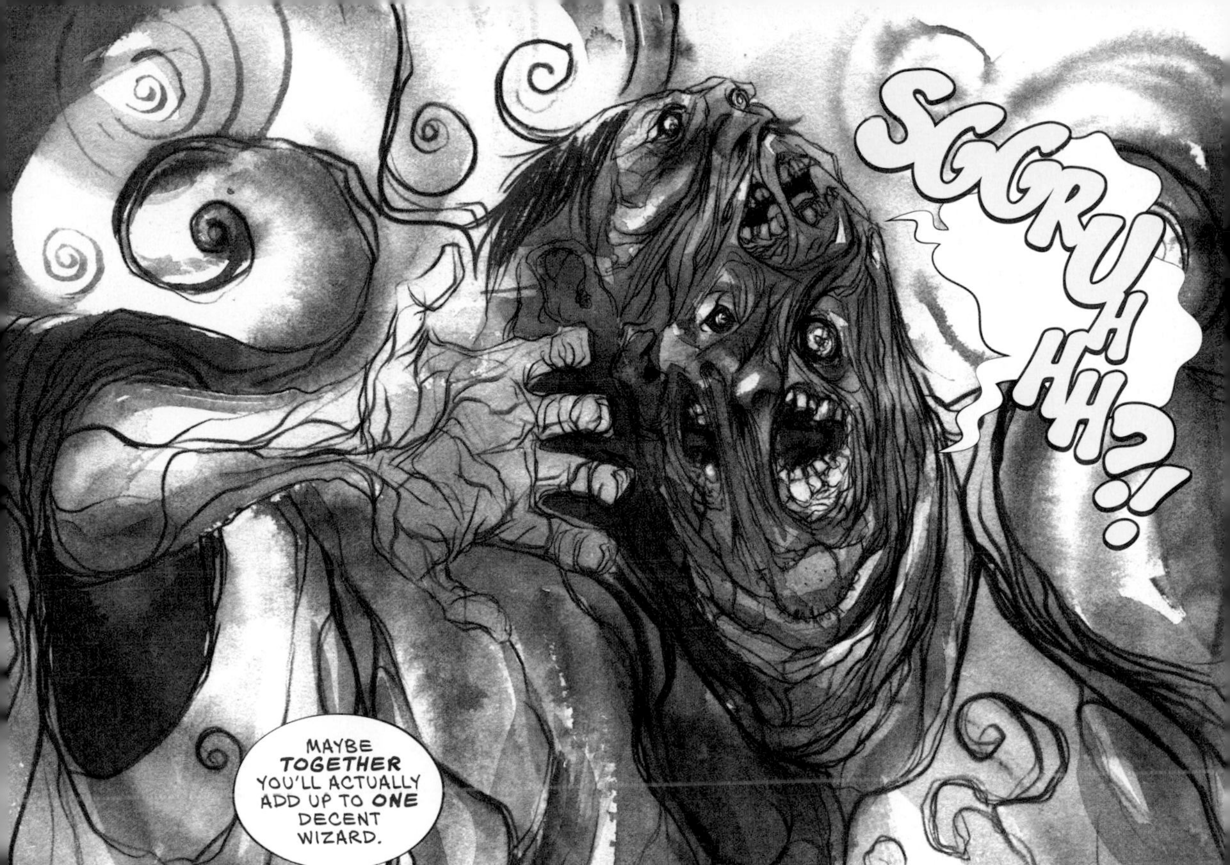
SGGRUHHH?!!
MAYBE TOGETHER YOU'LL ACTUALLY ADD UP TO ONE DECENT WIZARD.

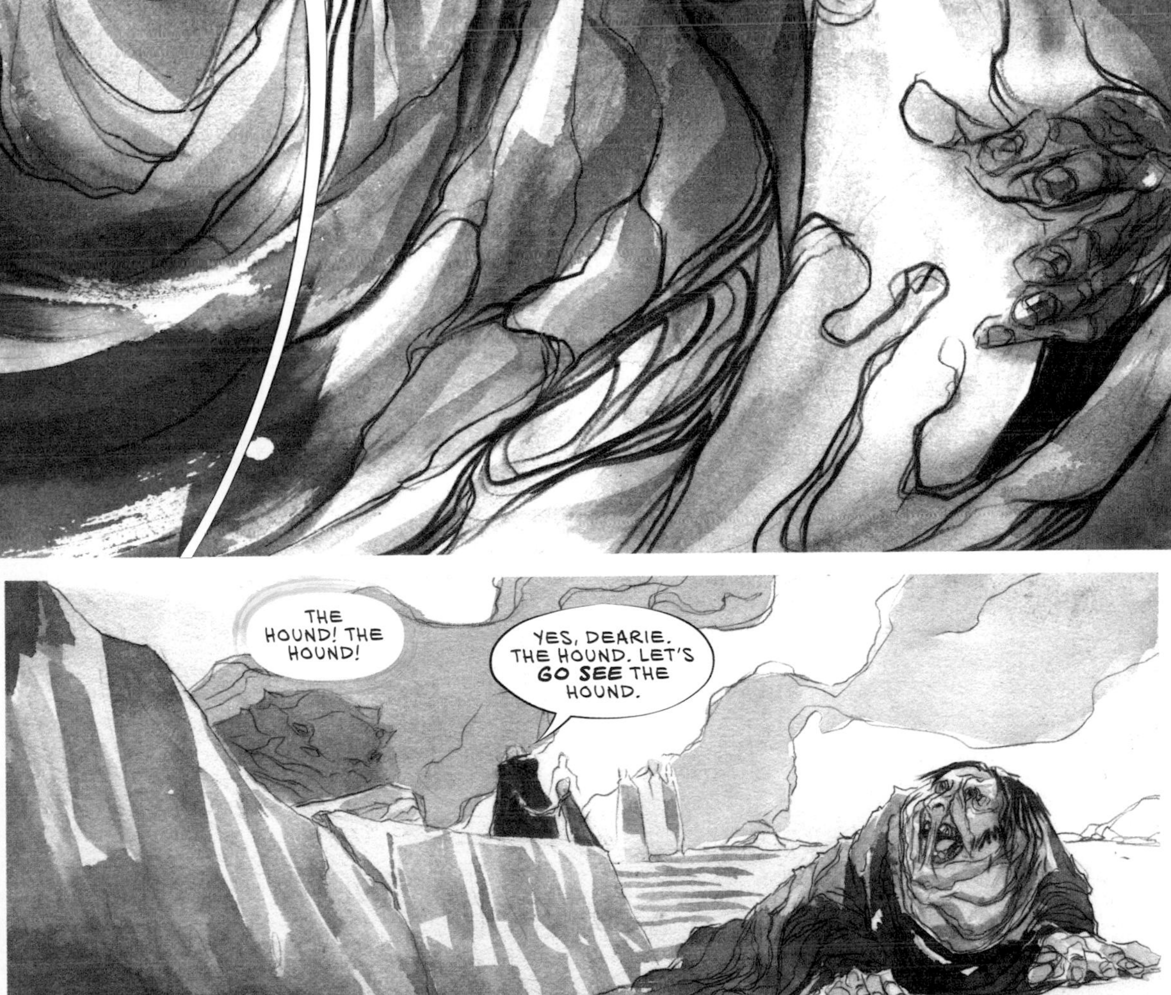
THE HOUND! THE HOUND!
YES, DEARIE. THE HOUND. LET'S GO SEE THE HOUND.

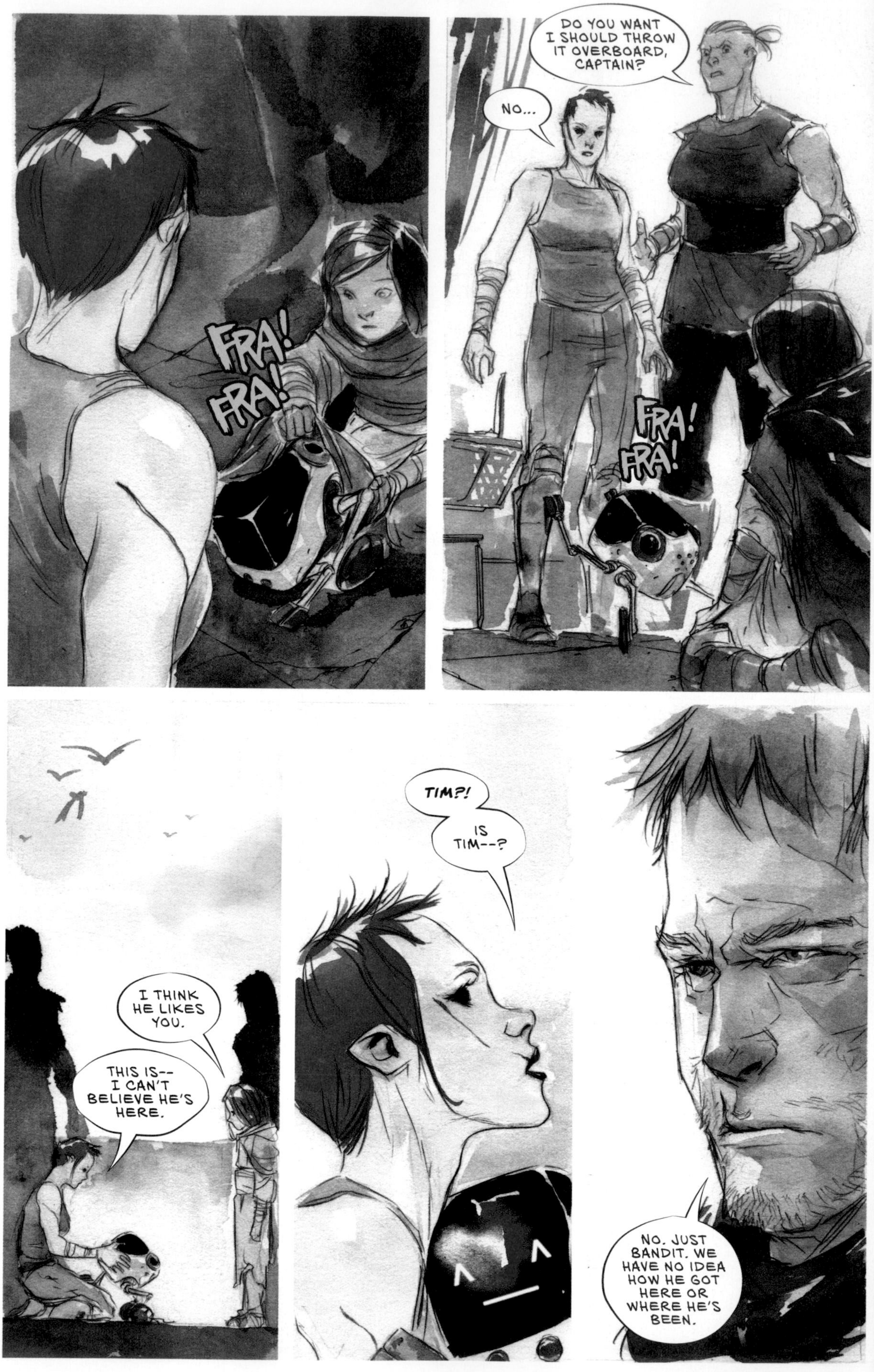
FRA! FRA!
DO YOU WANT I SHOULD THROW IT OVERBOARD, CAPTAIN?
NO...
FRA! FRA!
I THINK HE LIKES YOU.
THIS IS-- I CAN'T BELIEVE HE'S HERE.
TIM?!
IS TIM--?
NO. JUST BANDIT. WE HAVE NO IDEA HOW HE GOT HERE OR WHERE HE'S BEEN.

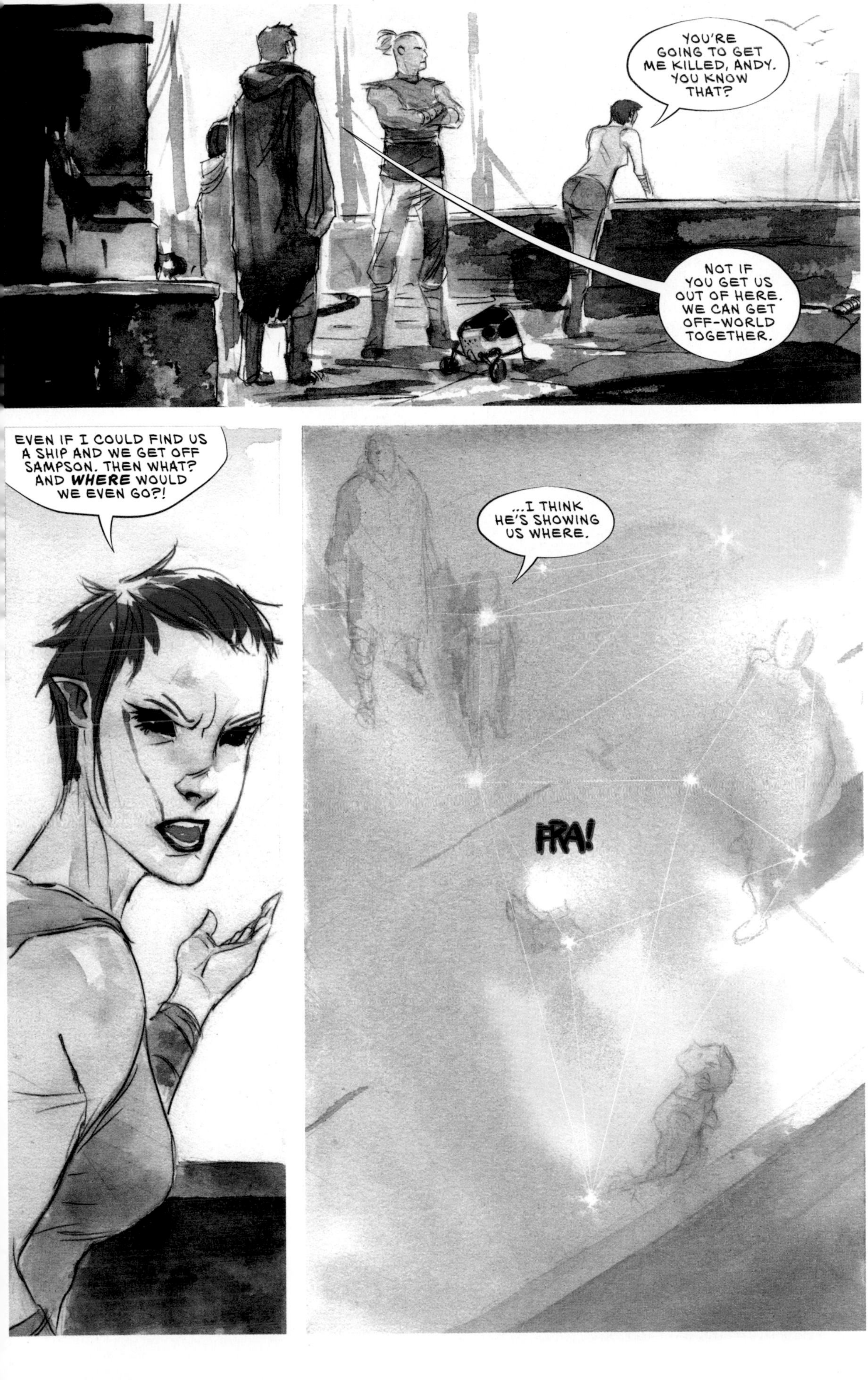
YOU'RE GOING TO GET ME KILLED, ANDY. YOU KNOW THAT?
NOT IF YOU GET US OUT OF HERE. WE CAN GET OFF-WORLD TOGETHER.
EVEN IF I COULD FIND US A SHIP AND WE GET OFF SAMPSON. THEN WHAT? AND **WHERE** WOULD WE EVEN GO?!
...I THINK HE'S SHOWING US WHERE.
FRA!

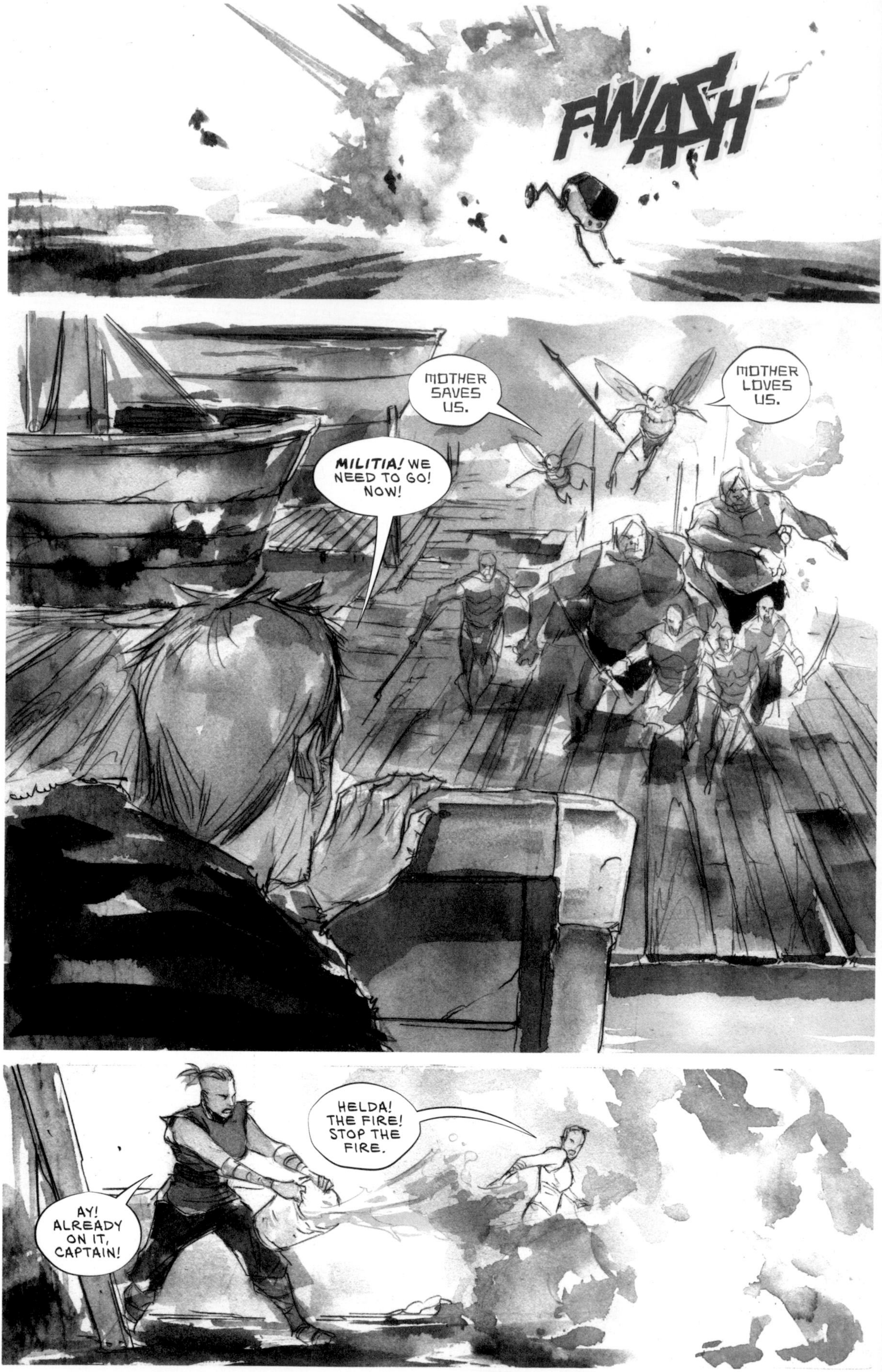
FWASH
MOTHER SAVES US.
MOTHER LOVES US.
MILITIA! WE NEED TO GO! NOW!
HELDA! THE FIRE! STOP THE FIRE.
AY! ALREADY ON IT, CAPTAIN!

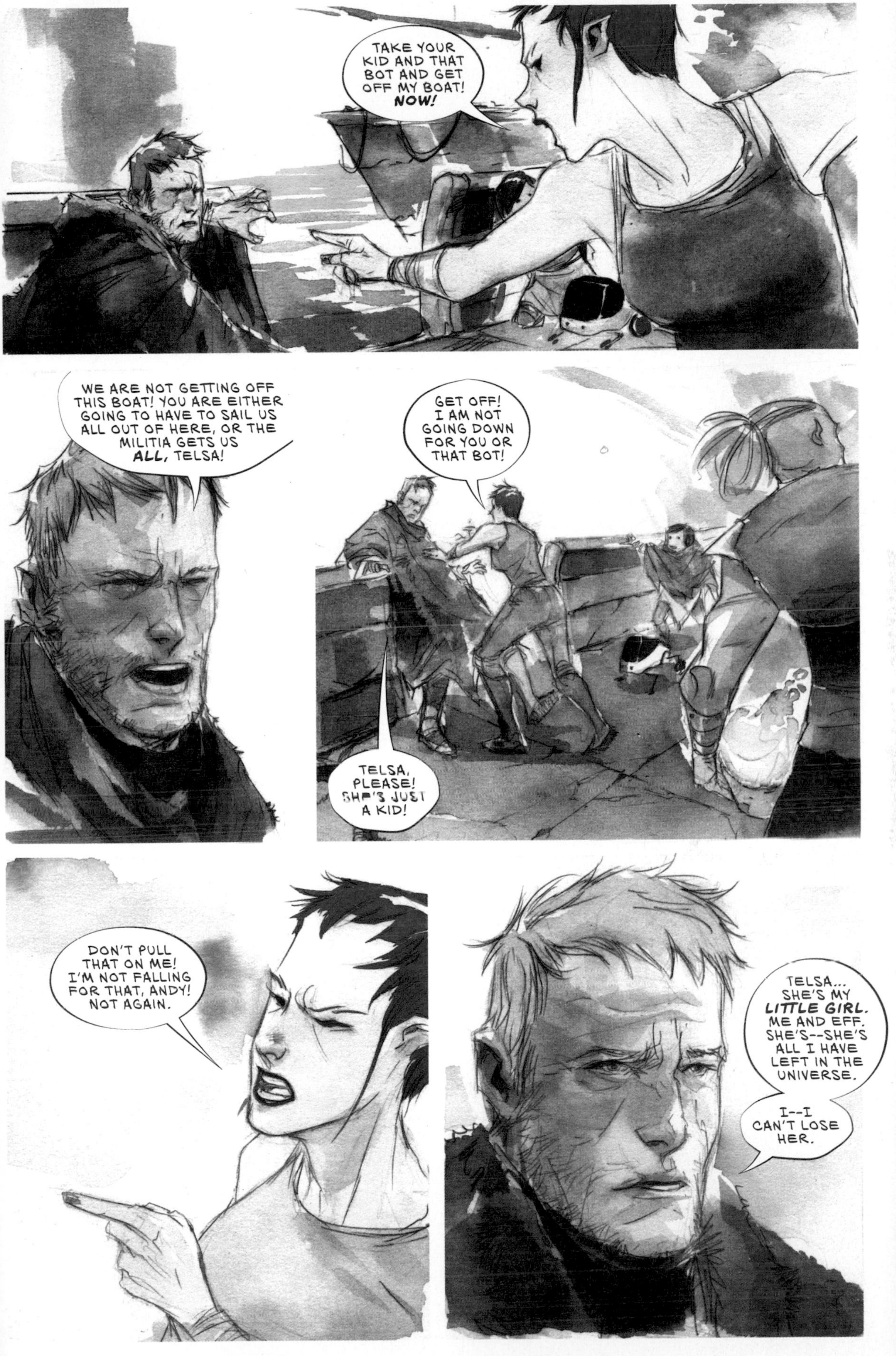
TAKE YOUR KID AND THAT BOT AND GET OFF MY BOAT! NOW!
WE ARE NOT GETTING OFF THIS BOAT! YOU ARE EITHER GOING TO HAVE TO SAIL US ALL OUT OF HERE, OR THE MILITIA GETS US ALL, TELSA!
GET OFF! I AM NOT GOING DOWN FOR YOU OR THAT BOT!
TELSA, PLEASE! SHE'S JUST A KID!
DON'T PULL THAT ON ME! I'M NOT FALLING FOR THAT, ANDY! NOT AGAIN.
TELSA... SHE'S MY LITTLE GIRL. ME AND EFF. SHE'S--SHE'S ALL I HAVE LEFT IN THE UNIVERSE.
I--I CAN'T LOSE HER.

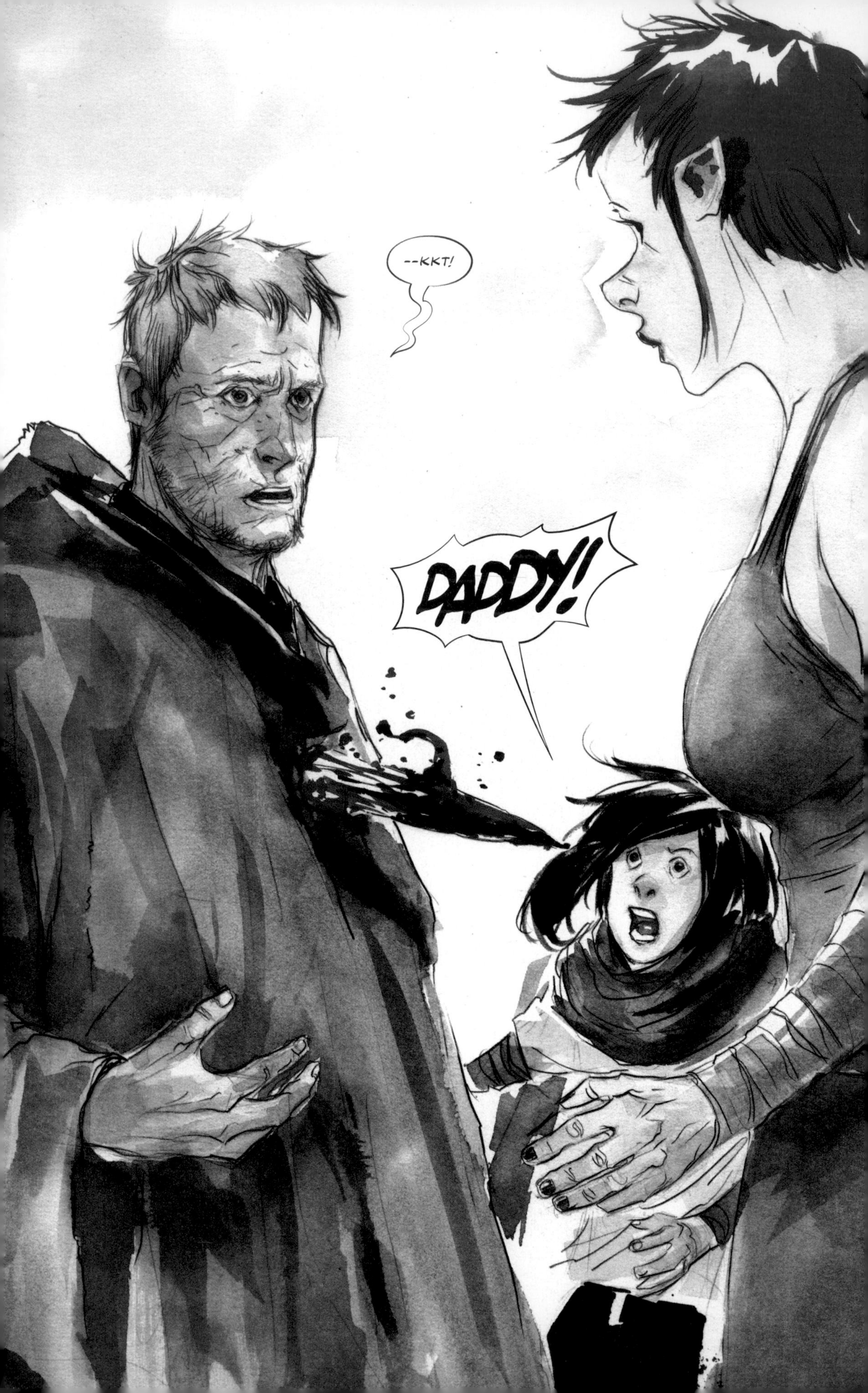
--KKT!
DADDY!

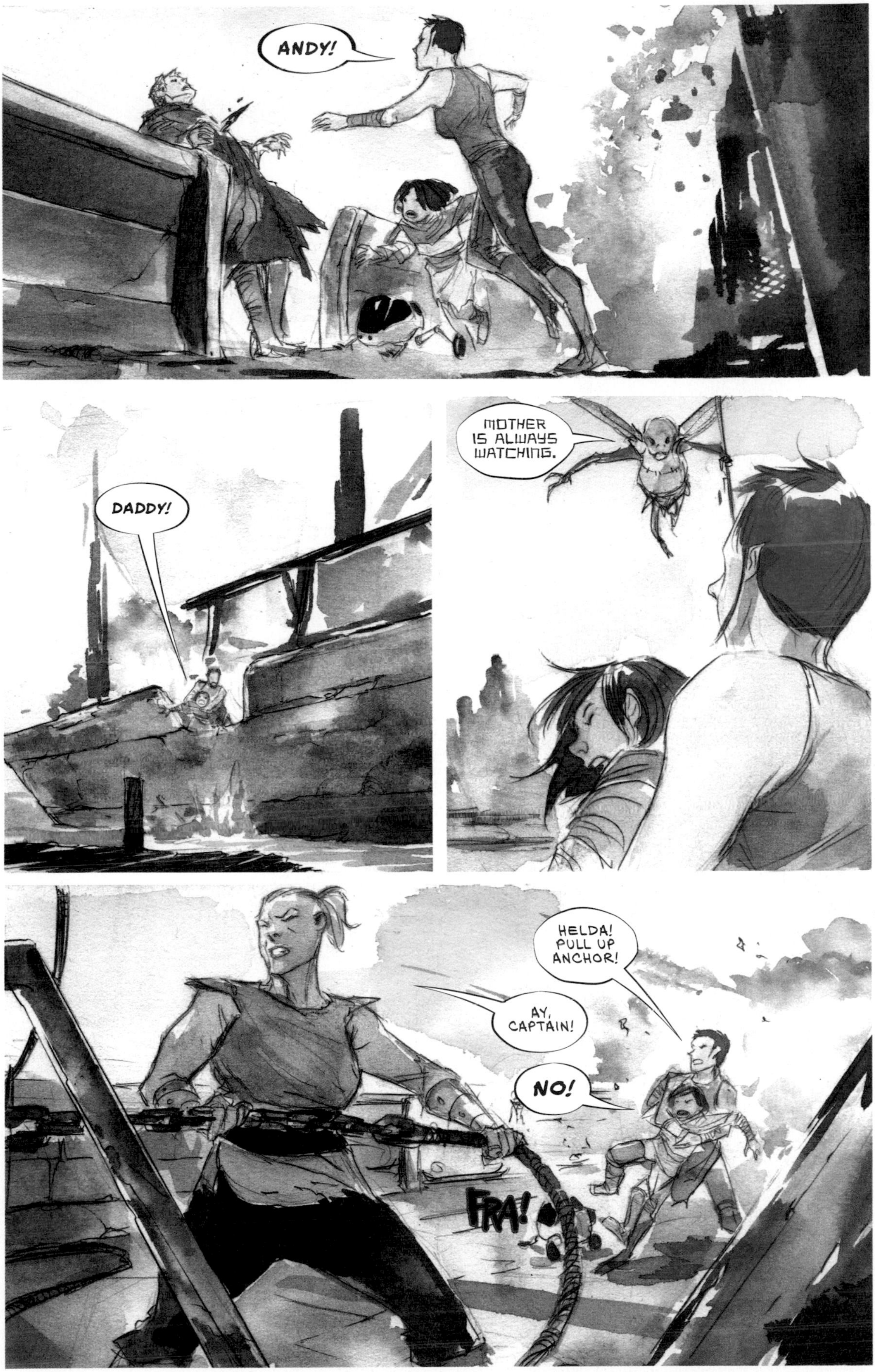
ANDY!
DADDY!
MOTHER IS ALWAYS WATCHING.
HELDA! PULL UP ANCHOR!
AY, CAPTAIN!
NO!
FRA!

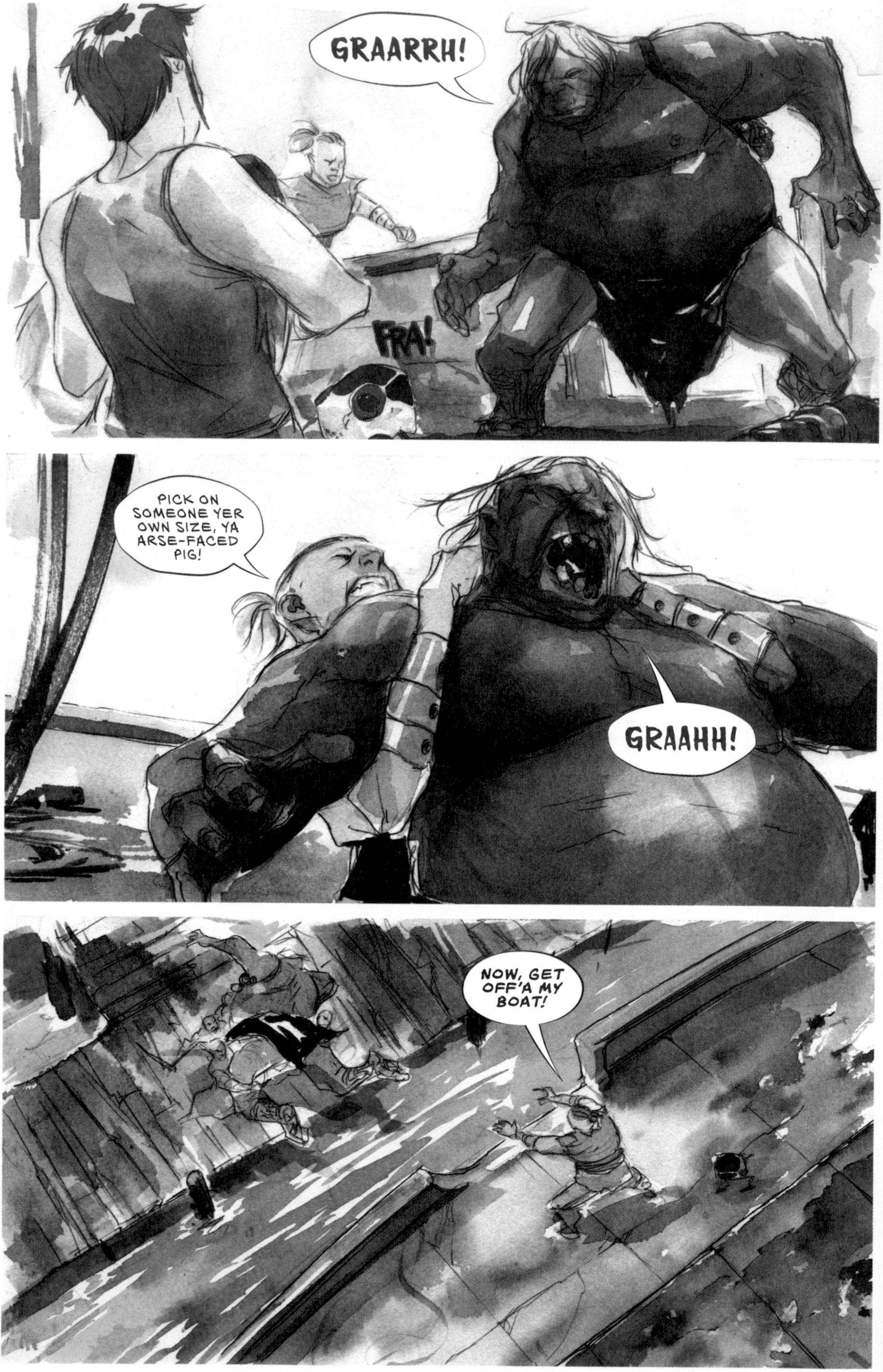
GRAARRH!
FRA!
PICK ON SOMEONE YER OWN SIZE, YA ARSE-FACED PIG!
GRAAHH!
NOW, GET OFF'A MY BOAT!

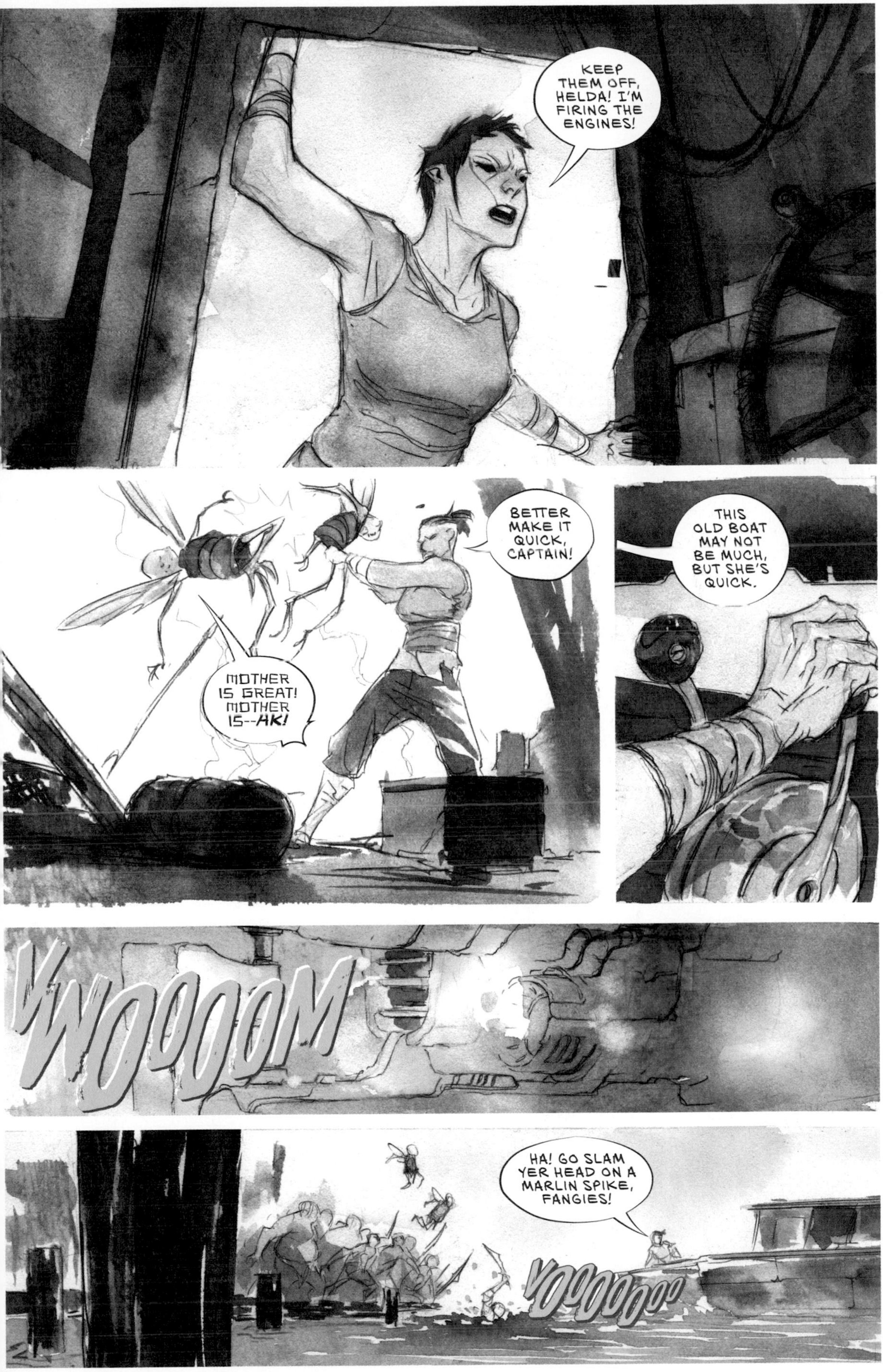
KEEP THEM OFF, HELDA! I'M FIRING THE ENGINES!
MOTHER IS GREAT! MOTHER IS--AK!
BETTER MAKE IT QUICK, CAPTAIN!
THIS OLD BOAT MAY NOT BE MUCH, BUT SHE'S QUICK.
VWOOOOM
HA! GO SLAM YER HEAD ON A MARLIN SPIKE, FANGIES!
VOOOOooo

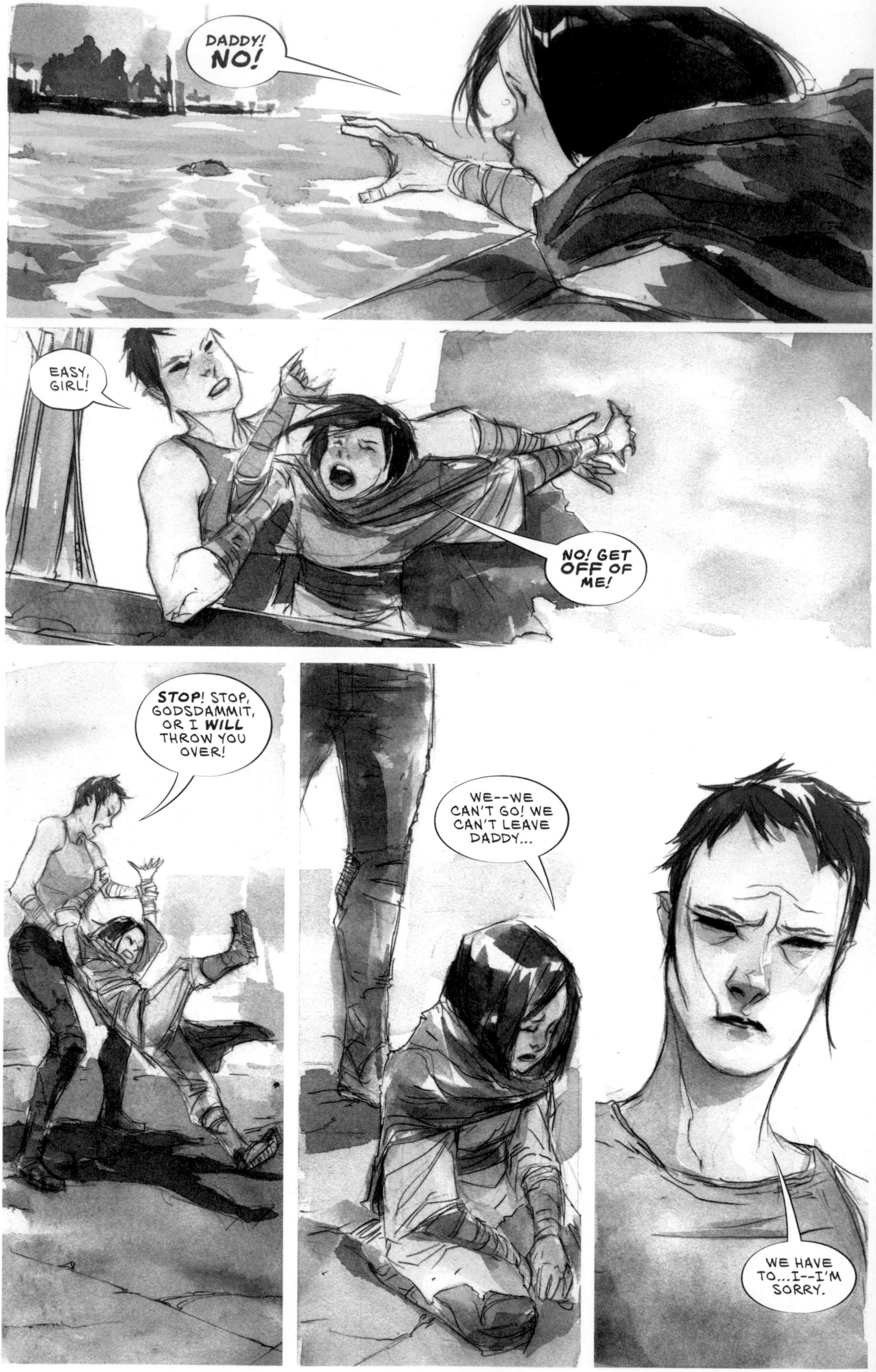
DADDY! NO!
EASY, GIRL!
NO! GET OFF OF ME!
STOP! STOP, GODSDAMMIT, OR I WILL THROW YOU OVER!
WE--WE CAN'T GO! WE CAN'T LEAVE DADDY...
WE HAVE TO...I--I'M SORRY.

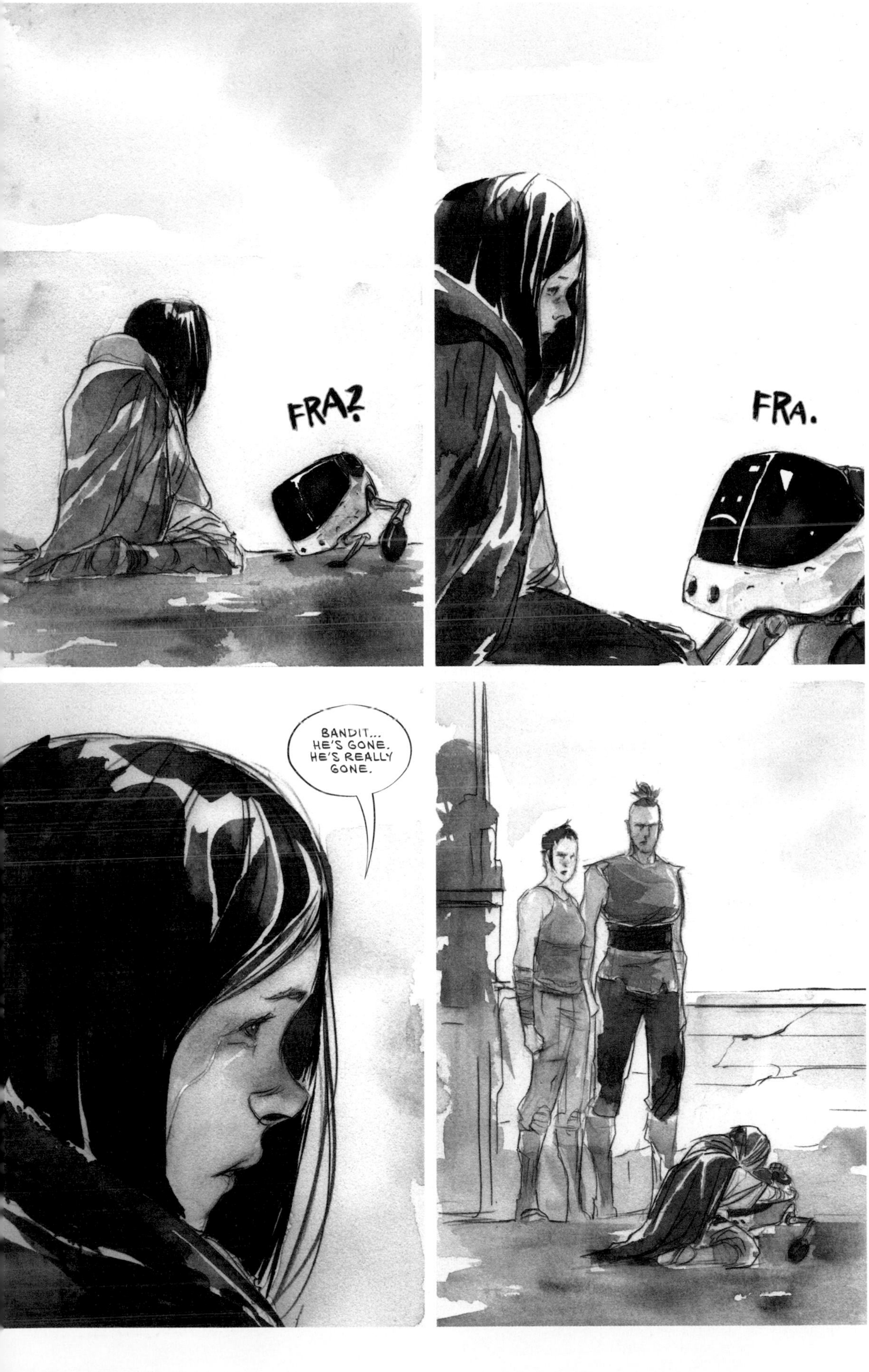
FRA?
FRA.
BANDIT... HE'S GONE. HE'S REALLY GONE.

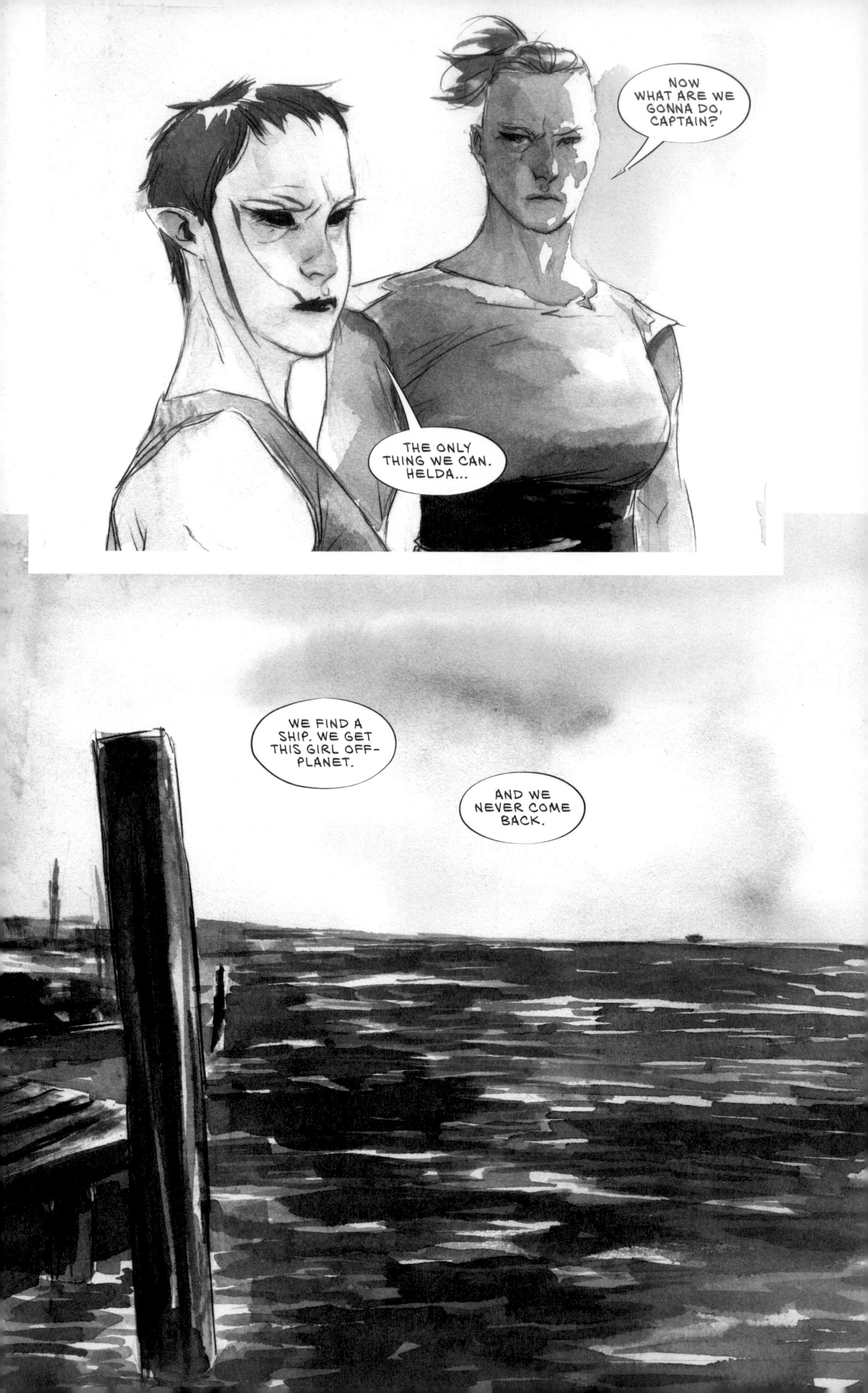
NOW WHAT ARE WE GONNA DO, CAPTAIN?
THE ONLY THING WE CAN. HELDA...
WE FIND A SHIP. WE GET THIS GIRL OFF-PLANET.
AND WE NEVER COME BACK.

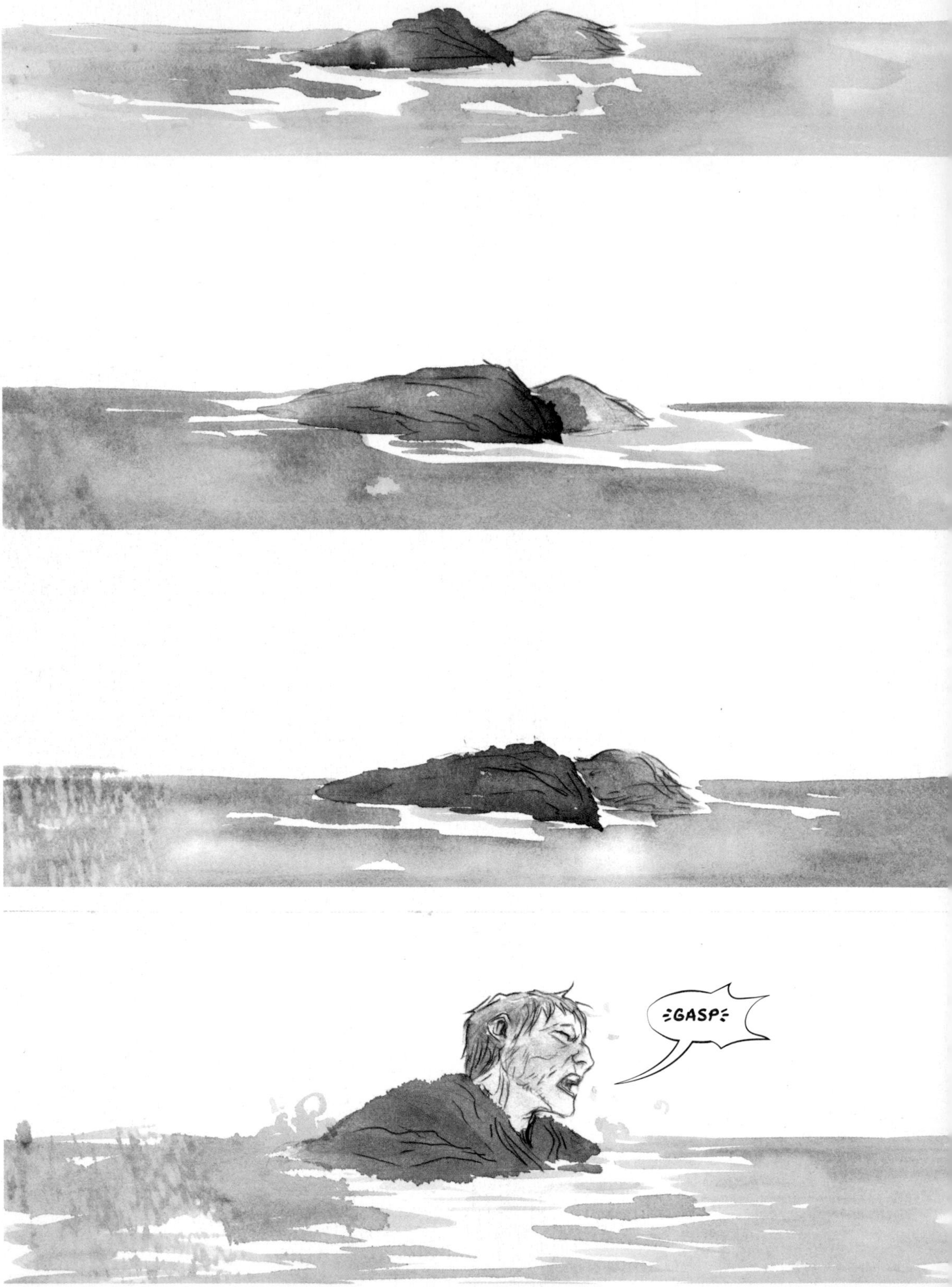
GASP

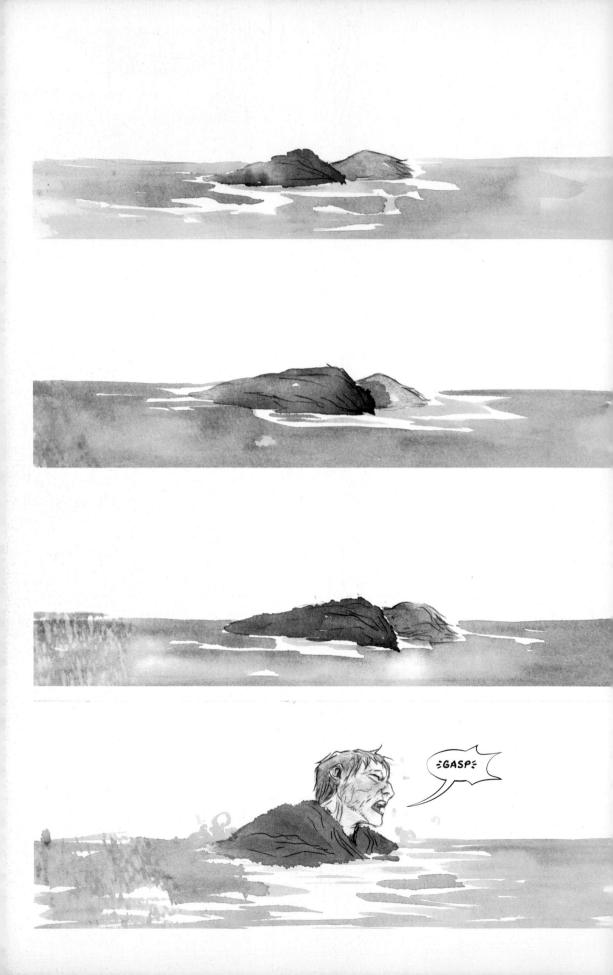

• THE ASCENDER TEAM •

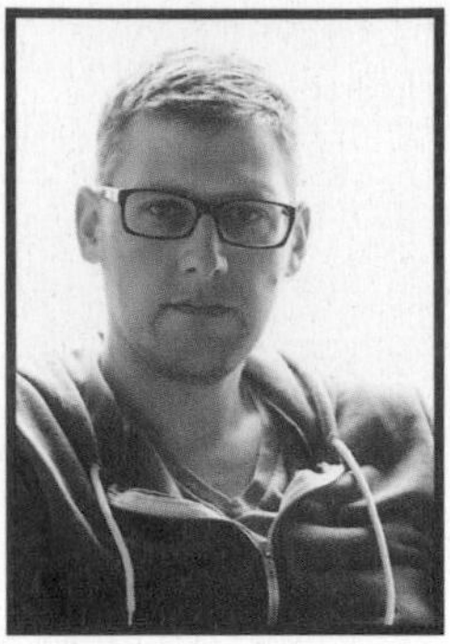

JEFF LEMIRE : Jeff Lemire is the award-winning, *New York Times* bestselling author of such graphic novels as *Essex County*, *Sweet Tooth*, *Underwater Welder*, and *Roughneck*, as well as co-creator of DESCENDER with Dustin Nguyen, *Black Hammer* with Dean Ormston, PLUTONA with Emi Lenox, A.D.: AFTER DEATH with Scott Snyder, and GIDEON FALLS with Andrea Sorrentino.

He also collaborated with celebrated musician Gord Downie on the graphic novel and album *The Secret Path*, which was made into an animated film in 2016. Jeff has won numerous awards including an Eisner Award and a Juno Award in 2017. Jeff has also written extensively for both Marvel and DC Comics.

Many of his books are currently in development for film and television, including both DESCENDER and A.D.: AFTER DEATH at Sony Pictures, *Essex County* at the CBC, and PLUTONA at Waypoint Entertainment, for which Lemire is writing the screenplay.

He lives in Toronto, Canada with his wife, son, and troublesome pug, Lola.

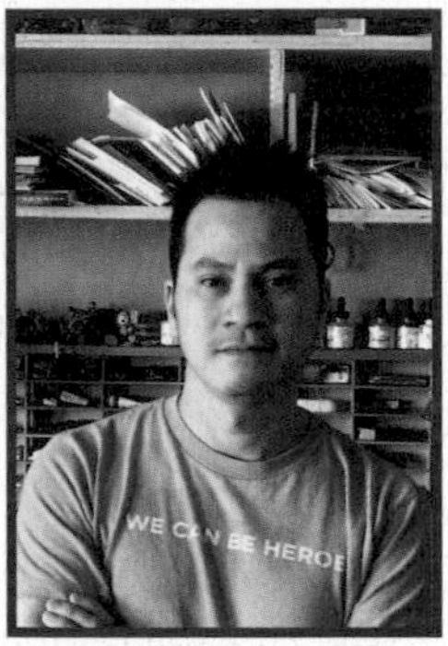
WE CAN BE HEROE

DUSTIN NGUYEN : Dustin Nguyen is a *New York Times* Bestselling and Eisner Award winning American comic creator best known for his work on Image Comics's DESCENDER and ASCENDER, *Batman: Lil Gotham*, *DC's Secret Hero Society*, and many things Gotham related.

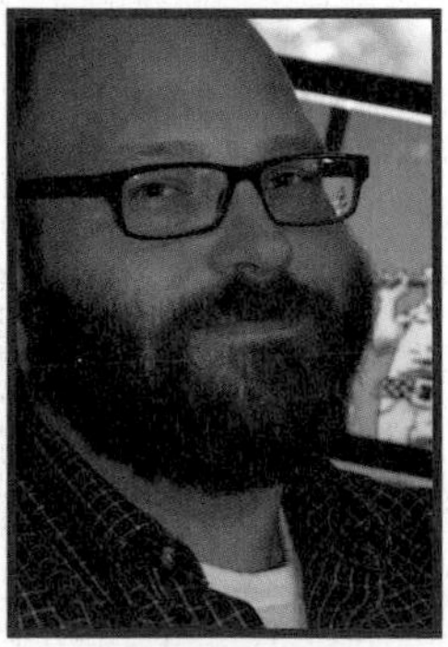

STEVE WANDS : Steve is a Comic Book Letterer, Artist, and Indie author. He works on top titles at DC Comics, Vertigo, Image, and Random House. He's the author of the *Stay Dead* series, co-author of *Trail of Blood*, and is a writer of short stories. When not working he spends time with his wife and sons in New Jersey.

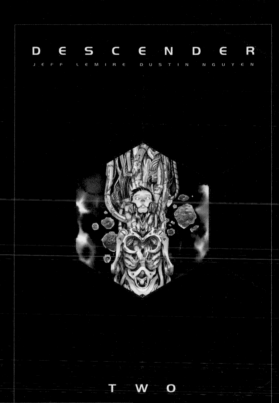

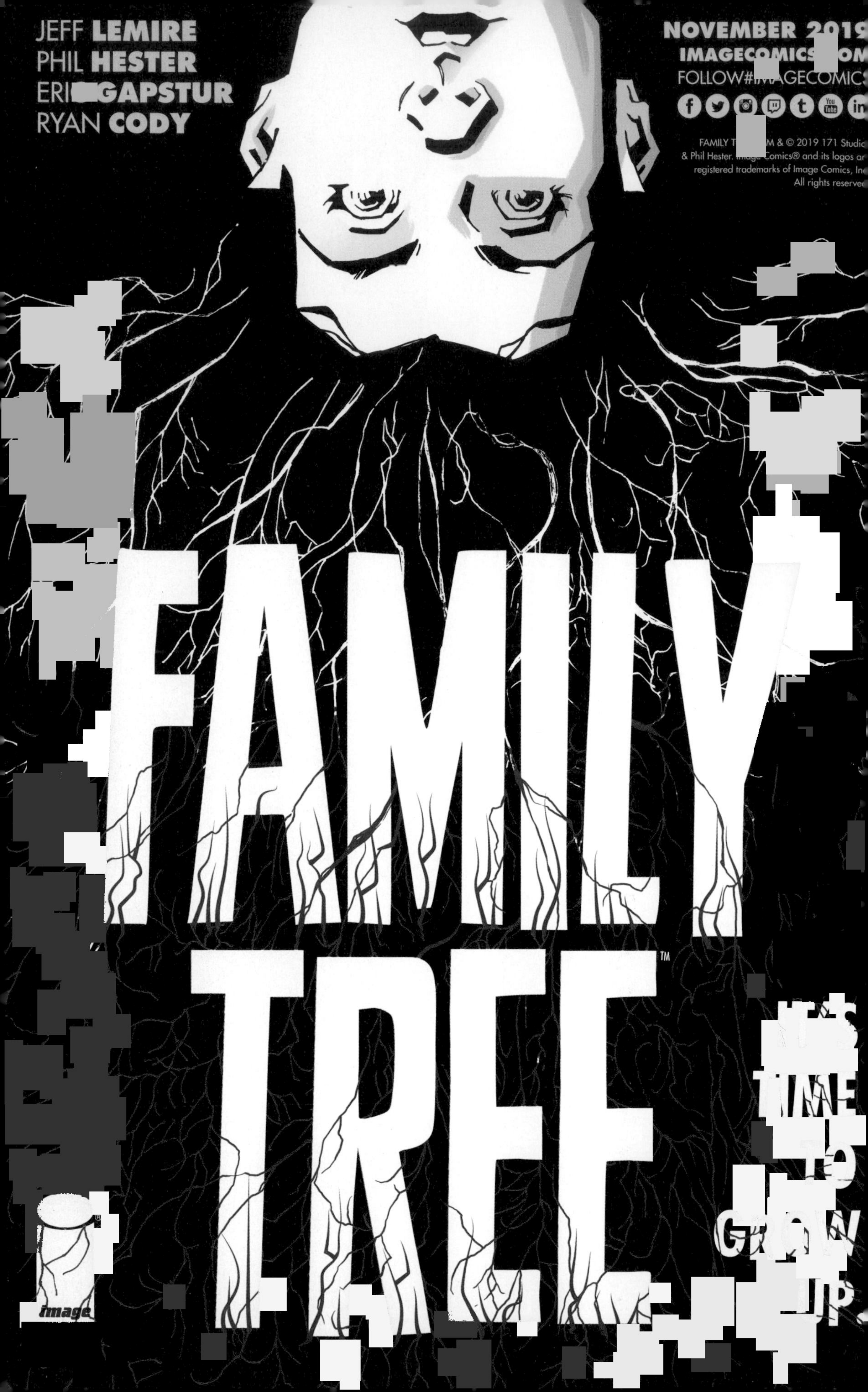

JEFF LEMIRE
PHIL HESTER
ERI GAPSTUR
RYAN CODY
NOVEMBER 201
IMAGECOMICS OM
FOLLOW #IMAGECOMICS
FAMILY T M & © 2019 171 Studio
& Phil Hester. Comics® and its logos ar
registered trademarks of Image Comics, In
All rights reserve
FAMILY
TREE™
TIME
TO
UP.
image